DATING *the* UNDEAD

JULIET LYONS

sourcebooks
casablanca

For Dad, who I miss every day.

Published by Sourcebooks Casablanca, an imprint of Sourcebooks, Inc.
P.O. Box 4410, Naperville, Illinois 60567-4410
(630) 961-3900
Fax: (630) 961-2168
www.sourcebooks.com

Printed and bound in Canada.
MBP 10 9 8 7 6 5 4 3 2 1

Chapter 1

Silver

NEW YEAR'S EVE, ALMOST MIDNIGHT, AND I'M LEAVING the party early.

I say leaving, but actually, "kicked out" is closer to the truth. Anyone would think it was *me* who'd just been caught kissing another girl's date.

"Oh, relax," I say, rolling my eyes at the statuesque blond whose hand is wedged firmly between my shoulder blades. "I'm sure it's not the first time she's had a drink thrown over her."

"It is at one of *my* parties," she retorts snootily.

By now, we've reached the long, narrow hallway leading to the front door. I vaguely remember it from on the way in, though it already feels like a million years ago. Back then, I had a date—one I envisioned kissing at the stroke of midnight and *not* kicking in the balls after catching him sucking face with some Latvian skank.

Life is full of surprises.

I stop dead in my tracks by the coat hooks, enjoying how Blondie stumbles against the back of my heels. "At least let me get my coat," I snap, delving into the dark, lumpy masses on the wall.

As I rifle through them, looking for my gray wool coat, my eye snags on a shiny, cream label that reads "Chanel" in proud, black lettering. Without a second thought, I unhook the slinky beige satin. "Here it is!" I shrill, holding it up in victory.

I deliberately take my time putting the coat on, fastening the buttons all the way down, while Miss Busty Blond taps her foot impatiently on the black-and-white-tiled floor. When I finally meet her cold, blue gaze, I smile sweetly. "Happy New Year," I say in honeyed tones. "And don't worry. I'm sure more people will turn up to next year's party."

With eyes shooting me daggers, she snatches the door open, and I swish past, chin in the air, into the crisp, dark night.

The door slams loudly behind me, instantly muffling the steady thud of music. I get all the way to the end of the narrow path before my smug charade dies a sudden death. I've left my clutch bag behind—money, bank cards, and phone along with it.

My shoulders droop in defeat, and I sigh, shooting a cloud of breath out into the chilly night air. "Shit," I mutter, spinning on my heel toward the house. "Shit, shit, shit."

Now I have a dilemma. I either go back in and face Joshua and his new "friend" or do the dignified thing and leave. Their final memory of me will either be the wine-throwing, ball-kicking incident, or a groveling girl asking for her purse back. Call me vain, but I sort of prefer option number one.

I stare longingly at the black front door. From behind it, distant sounds of merriment drift onto the street, high-pitched voices and laughter swirling amid a blur of white noise.

A voice cuts into the night, a dagger slicing through velvet. "Are you going in?"

I spin around, surprised to see a man has appeared from the darkness. *Funny, I didn't even hear footsteps.*

Pulling myself to full height, I stare directly into his eyes. "Actually, I just left."

When I first moved to London, I took a self-defense class—Dad paid for it; he said it gave him peace of mind—and they told us if a strange man approaches you on a dark street, make direct eye contact. Apparently, it makes you less of a potential victim.

I step aside to let him pass. "It's a crap party," I say, shoving my hands deep into the pockets of the stolen coat. "Unless you enjoy the company of spoiled, overgrown brats living off their trust funds."

Slowly, a smile begins to unfurl from the corner of his mouth. The effect is devastating. His eyes—green and bottomless, framed by a forest of dark lashes—crinkle around the edges. I've been so busy trying to appear *unvictim-like* that I forgot to notice he's something of a hottie. Scrub that—*a lot* of a hottie. I rake my gaze over him, not caring whether or not he realizes I'm checking him out. I mean, if he's going to cruise the streets looking *this* sexy, he should expect a violent eye assault or two.

His hair is dark brown, curling over the tips of his ears and just ever so slightly mussed. *Sex hair*, I think, going a little weak at the knees. His skin is pale and creamy, and when he smiles, a tiny indent appears in each cheek. On some, dimples are cute—on this man, they are dangerous.

He is the antithesis of Joshua—dark where Joshua is light. Joshua is the type of guy who spends a day on a yacht with friends. *This* man looks as though he belongs onstage at a rock concert. If Joshua is a day out on the river, *this* guy is a late night drinking whiskey on a bed of rumpled satin sheets.

"Is that why you're leaving?" he asks, his gorgeous green eyes roaming my body like a secret caress.

His voice has a soothing Irish brogue, like a seductive lullaby, and I shiver, though not from the cold. "Yes. That and I've just made a bit of a scene."

"A scene? What did you do?" He leans back against the gatepost, resting one foot against the red brick, and for some reason, I think of James Dean in that old movie *Rebel Without a Cause*. There's that vibe about him— that he breaks all the rules.

I flip a wavy lock of auburn hair over my shoulder. "I threw a drink over a girl," I say with an unmistakable hint of pride.

He chuckles, cocking his head to one side. "And why exactly did you do that?"

I'm tempted to say, *Because I felt like it*, but I don't. I tell him the truth. "She kissed the guy I came with. Right in front of me."

He half frowns, half smiles. "Who was the guy?"

I shrug. "Just some guy I've been out with a few times."

"What about him? Did he get the same treatment?"

It's my turn to smile. "No, but he got a kick in the nuts for his trouble. He would have got way more if the idiot hostess hadn't pulled me off."

He laughs, and that too is sexy, gravel all wrapped up

in silk. "What's your name?" he asks, looking straight into my eyes.

"Silver," I tell him, staring back unblinkingly. "Silver Harris."

"Well, Silver Harris," he says, my name intimate on his tongue, as though he's said it a thousand times before. "How about I go in, get your bag, and walk you home?"

I scrunch my face up, trying not to show my surprise. "Why do you think I left my bag? I have my phone and wallet right here in my pocket." I tap the side of the empty coat.

He takes his foot off the wall and stands up straight before taking a step closer. Even in my heels, he's a good six inches taller than me. As he leans in, I catch a whiff of his scent—a smoky, masculine blend of leather, aftershave, and soap. "I know," he whispers, "the same way I know that's not the coat you arrived in."

My breath catches and I take a step backward. *How does he know about the coat?* I keep my voice as normal as possible. "Why don't you join the party before I call the police?"

He flashes a smile and then, without warning, completely disappears. There is nothing in front of me but empty air and a slight breeze, the front door of the house flapping open as if caught in a sudden gust of wind. It takes me about three seconds to realize what he is.

A vampire.

A few years back, a famous Hollywood actress, no doubt fed up with being questioned about plastic surgery, publicly announced she was a vampire. Of course, the world's media went nuts with it.

"Vampires Exist!" the headlines screamed. And it didn't end there. Before long, vampires from all over the globe began to emerge from the shadows. They pretty much blew all the old myths out of the water, reassuring humankind that yes, they are real, but no, they don't need blood to survive. Since then, things have remained relatively unchanged and most vampires continue to keep a low profile. I mean, you aren't going to run into one at the village fair buying a lemon meringue pie or walking their Labradoodle in the local park or anything like that. As far as I can tell, they stick mainly to cities or places with a happening night scene. Places like London.

A moment later, the front door slams shut and he's back, holding my small, sequined clutch bag.

I arch a brow, as if superhuman speed is something I see every day. "How did you know it was mine?"

He flashes a cocky grin. "I looked for a girl with a wet face and a bloke holding his crotch in agony. Hey, presto, it was there on the floor."

I take the bag from his outstretched hand, expecting him to hold on to it, but he lets it go easily. "So," I say, pretending to fiddle with the clasp. "You're a vampire?"

"Beauty and intelligence—my two favorite things in a woman."

I look into his chiseled face. Man, he is *hot*. If I'm going to die, there would be worse ways to go. "Just so I know—are you planning to murder me or not?"

He smiles again. Clearly he finds me amusing, which makes a change as, usually, men don't. "Do you really think I'd have fetched you your bag if I were?"

I shrug. "How am I supposed to know? Maybe you like to mess with your victims before you drain their blood."

He shakes his head, still smiling. "I didn't think people believed in that old myth anymore."

"So, what do you want?" I ask, tucking my bag under my arm and gazing at him with narrowed eyes.

"Just to see you home safely," he says. "It's dangerous to walk around London on your own at night."

I give off a little snort of derision and purse my lips, glancing up and down the quiet street. "Fine," I say. "Walk me home." I lean forward in what I hope is a menacing way. "But you should know, I have pepper spray in my purse and I've attended the finest self-defense classes in the greater London area."

He chuckles, shaking his head. "Silver, I have no doubt you're a force to be reckoned with."

I nod, stepping through the wrought-iron gate. "Shall we?" I ask, with a sweep of my arm.

We walk along the street in silence. The night air is chilly, the pavement glittering with frost. Above, the moon is shaped like a sickle, casting an eerie silver glow across the front of the half-brick, half-stucco houses. Each time we pass under the yellow light of a streetlamp, I sneak a look at the vampire, and each time, he catches me, holding my gaze, his brilliant-green eyes piercing mine. In spite of the cold, I burn with desire.

"How old are you?" I ask suddenly. "I mean, how old were you when you turned?"

"Twenty-five," he says. "And before you ask the next question, I'm just a few years shy of my two-hundredth birthday."

I gulp, trying to keep my voice neutral. "Well, you know what they say: life begins at fifty. I guess that works to your advantage."

He laughs. "I suppose. How old are you, Silver?"

"Twenty-four," I tell him, and then, without thinking, "Twenty-four and never been kissed."

"The first bit," he says, "I can believe. As for the other part, I think there's about as much chance of that as there is of you owning the coat you're wearing."

My brows knit together. "What are you trying to say? I couldn't afford a Chanel coat?"

Before he can answer, a rowdy bunch of partygoers appear around the corner ahead. There are four of them—young men, all clearly inebriated—leaning into each other and all talking loudly at the same time.

One of them, a stocky-looking guy in his twenties, leers at me as they pass. "Blimey, she's a bit of all right," he says loudly to his friends, who squawk in agreement, like a bunch of wild monkeys at the zoo. His lazy eyes fall on the vampire next to me. "Be sure to give her a good porking tonight, mate," he says, a sick grin plastered across his puffy, red face.

Another member of the group guffaws loudly, grabbing at his crotch and making thrusting movements. "Yeah! Give her one from us."

One second, the vampire is beside me; the next, he has the two who spoke by their throats and is holding them aloft, one in each hand, several inches from the ground. "I think you owe the lady an apology," he hisses angrily.

I watch, stunned, as the men struggle for freedom, legs thrashing wildly beneath them. When their friends scamper off into the night, he lowers them back to the pavement and lets go. Instantly, they cough and splutter, holding their throats. Their faces are the color of boiled ham in a butcher's window.

"I said, *apologize*," the vampire demands, his low, throaty voice the only sign he's lost his cool.

One of them makes a desperate, wheezy noise that sounds a little like *sorry*, while the other bends double, gasping for air.

"Sorry," he says at last, in ragged breaths.

The vampire takes me gently by the elbow, motioning with a slight jerk of his head to continue walking. At his touch, a tingly sensation shoots from my arm straight to my core. Excitement, rather than horror, unfurls in the pit of my stomach.

As the coughs begin to fade behind us, the vampire looks at me, his jaw clenched tight. "I'm sorry, Silver, but nothing winds me up more than disrespectful men."

If I were the type of girl who swooned, I would, but I'm not, so I flash him a smile instead. "I thought the fat one was going to cry," I say, biting my lip to stifle a giggle.

The vampire smiles back, staring deep into my eyes, and for some reason, I feel suddenly afraid—though not in the way I would expect.

My shoulder brushing his, we turn onto the tree-lined embankment, where hundreds of people are gathered by the river, waiting for the fireworks at midnight. The air hums with voices, and the gray bulk of the Thames is gold and glistening beneath the bright city lights.

I look at my phone—there are just ten minutes until

midnight. "Seeing in the New Year with an undead guy," I say, sliding my phone back into my bag. "I guess that's one I can tick off my bucket list."

He cracks a smile. "Glad I could oblige."

When we reach Oakley Street, just minutes away from my flat in Jubilee Place, I ponder if I should lead him to a fake address. I mean, he's a *vampire*, and although he's behaved like the perfect gentleman, I don't really know him from Adam. Deciding to err on the side of caution, I lead him along a side road a block or so from home.

It's dark and drafty on the street, the breeze blowing up from the Thames swirling between the buildings. I pull the flimsy satin coat tight across my chest and peer ahead, trying to decide which house to pretend is mine. I've just chosen a large, three-story town house when the peals of Big Ben suddenly ring out through the streets. At once, the night is filled with fireworks, their shrieks and bangs ricocheting off the walls around us, the sky as bright as day.

I stop at the gate of the house. "Well, this is me," I say.

He nods, his eyes rounded with some unfathomable emotion. I wonder if he knows I'm lying. "Good night, Silver. Happy New Year."

As he turns to leave, I reach for his arm, my fingers gripping hard muscle through the thin leather sleeve of his jacket. "Don't I get a New Year's kiss?" I ask brazenly.

Some people are cursed with shyness. I am not, nor will I ever be, one of those people.

His brows lift in surprise. I can tell he wasn't

expecting me to say that. Smirking, I take a step closer. My face inches from his, I inhale the leathery freshness radiating from his beautiful body—eau de man...or eau de vampire, depending on how you look at it.

For one awful moment, he remains frozen to the spot, and I wonder if I'm about to be rejected for a second time this evening. But then his arms gently circle my waist, and he lowers his lips to mine.

My life changes forever.

If you must know, I've kissed my fair share of guys in the past, but there has never been anything quite like this. I'm pretty sure if it wasn't New Year's Eve, I'd still be hearing fireworks.

He starts off slow, lips gently parting mine, hands sliding over the contours of my body. I push my breasts against his chest as he begins gently flicking his tongue against mine, and I groan into his mouth.

His hands knot into my hair as the kiss picks up speed, and a lick of heat, as exotic and consuming as a blast of tropical air, roars through me, turning me liquid with desire. If he wasn't holding me up, I'm fairly certain I would be no more than a puddle at his feet.

I mold into him, lost in the sensation of his lips on mine, hard and soft in all the right places, our tongues dancing back and forth in tender rhythm. Wanting to explore, I slide my hands beneath his T-shirt, caressing the taut muscles of his stomach, silky and warm under my fingers.

I now regret leading him to the wrong house. If we were outside my flat, I would waste no time in dragging him inside and having my wicked way with him on the sofa. As it stands, I can hardly admit I've lied.

But there is something else I'm willing to try—something that can be done right here on the street. As his mouth leaves my lips, trailing hot, feverish kisses along my jaw, I lean over, exposing my neck to his mouth.

He pauses, his lips warm on my throat. "Are you sure?" he whispers, voice low, crushed beneath a weight of desire.

"Yes," I say, my voice raspy, running a hand into the waistband of his jeans. "Do it."

There is a faint, exquisite pain as his teeth sink into my flesh, and as my body sags against his, my mind is filled with an unusual feeling of peace. I see a riot of colors—yellows and pinks, like a sunset—and slowly, they flood my senses, pulling me down into a whirlpool of bliss, until all sense of reality is lost.

When I'm finally pulled back into the present, I realize his mouth is no longer at my throat. He's holding me against him, stroking my cheek with the back of his hand.

"Am I dead?" I ask dreamily. "I don't feel the cold."

"No," he murmurs, kissing the top of my head. "But I'm afraid I had to stop."

I pull away a little. "Is kissing a vampire always like that?"

He smiles, a smug glint in his eye. "Without wanting to sound arrogant, it is with me. Or so I've been told."

Smiling, I prod him with an index finger. "Check out the vampire stud."

He chuckles softly and holds open the little gate at the front of the house, standing aside to let me pass. "I have to go now, Silver."

I walk through and turn around, still dazed from the

bite. "Wait," I say, hating the edge of desperation to my voice. "You didn't tell me your name."

Hands in his pockets, shoulders set in arrogance, he grins. "Perhaps I'll tell you some other time."

As quickly as he arrived, he disappears into the night, a mini cyclone of skittering leaves the only evidence of his departure.

I sag against the garden wall, my lips still buzzing from his knee-trembling kiss.

How will I ever go back to human guys after this?

Chapter 2

Logan

BY THE TIME I REACH THE CHIPPED BLACK DOOR ON Broadwick Street, Soho, I'm almost an hour late for my meeting with London's long-reigning vampire overlord, Ronin McDermott. Closing my eyes, I inhale deeply, desperately trying to clear my head. I fail miserably. In spite of the pungent odor of damp and garbage rising up from the London street, the girl's intoxicating flavor lingers, sharp as citrus on my tongue, and her sweet scent— white wine and roses—assaults my nostrils to the point where I imagine she is still in my arms. My cock stiffens as I remember her hands under my T-shirt, her tongue lapping mine, the deep, guttural groan that escaped her throat as I sank my fangs into her creamy skin.

I shiver, opening my eyes. "Jesus, Logan," I tell myself, adjusting the front of my tight black jeans. "Get it together, man."

I dart a glance over each shoulder before stepping closer to the battered door and staring into a tiny camera hidden beside the drainpipe. There is a whirring noise as it swivels toward me, a red dot flashing.

With a sigh, I shove my hands into my pockets and wait. I look around at the empty street—the shop fronts with their metal barriers pulled down, the row of trash bins, garbage bags spilling out like vomit—and wish, for all it's worth, I'd never left the snarky girl in the stolen coat.

Directly opposite is a popular coffee shop, and I wonder, not for the first time, how humans so often miss the obvious. Hundreds if not thousands pound this street every day, but I'd bet money no one notices the crimson splatter of dried blood half pooled beneath the door on the concrete where I stand. Not a single person ever ponders what goes on behind the neglected facade of 66 Broadwick Street.

A few more seconds pass until the door rattles like a snake, a deep clunk resonating through the wood as heavy-duty locks are hauled back. Finally, it opens, and the human doorman, a tall, thin-lipped gentleman with a shock of gray hair, is waiting to usher me inside.

"Evening, Mr. Byrne," he says in a gruff voice. He's dressed in typical nightclub security gear—black suit, white shirt, no tie. There is even a curly communication wire running from ear to collar.

"Evening, Jordan," I say, stepping past him into the long, rabbit-warren-like corridor.

Pleasantries aside, neither of us speaks again. Occasionally, I wonder if Jordan is his first name or last, but by the time I reach the second door, I usually forget all about him. Tonight is no different.

The inner door opens, and at once, the unmistakable aroma of alcohol, smoke, and open veins hits like a tidal wave. I step into the room, looking down from the top of a narrow flight of stairs into the hazy half-light below. Here, in London's most taboo nightspot, vampires and humans coexist in a disturbing tableau of blood and desire.

The New Year's party appears to be in full swing. Right away, I catch sight of a half-naked blond woman spread-eagle across a narrow table. Her arms hang down limply as two vampires, their greedy faces smeared with blood, lap at each wrist. From where I stand, it's hard to tell if her face is contorted with ecstasy or pain— possibly a little of both. I stare, transfixed for a second, before homing my senses in on her pulse.

Normal—for now, at least. Unfortunately, wading into situations like this is how I earn my living. I believe my official title at the club is *enforcer*, a tidy label for spending my evenings plucking humans from the jaws of death, fixing them up, and sending them on their merry way none the wiser. In the beginning, it felt good being able to save a life here and there, but these days it seems so pointless. Most of those I heal are back for more within the week.

Not that I'm one to judge. In my darker days, I also sought solace within the empty embraces of the twisted and depraved. I too was a parasite, sucking meaning- lessly at the open arteries of human beings either too drunk or too desperate to care. Though it's true enough we don't need blood to survive, some crave its sweet taste just as dangerously as if they did. I guess you could say they are the vampire version of alcoholics, and just like alcoholism, such addiction ruins lives. Luckily for myself and the humans around me, my own bloodlust was short-lived.

Apart from this trio, everyone else seems to be behaving themselves. I continue down the steps, glanc- ing around the dark-purple booths lining the walls, where people sit chatting, wispy spirals of smoke lacing the air.

There's a jazz singer in tonight, an eye-catching, buxom redhead with her hair twisted up 1940s style. She is accompanied by a thin black gentleman playing a saxophone. I catch her eye as I pass by the little circular stage and she winks at me. She's human, though her sax player isn't—no heartbeat. She holds my gaze and runs her hands up and down the microphone stand suggestively. On a normal night, I'd smile and wink back, but this evening, I look away. I'm unwilling to dilute the memory of that heated midnight exchange so quickly.

I head for the long, granite bar stretching the width of the club. Paulo, a Hispanic bartender with strangely yellow eyes, spots me and grabs a bottle of spirits to fix me a shot. He's a vampire too, so it's ready and waiting on the bar in an instant.

"Happy New Year, buddy," I say, holding up the tiny glass and throwing the amber liquid down my throat. Although alcohol doesn't work for us in quite the same way it does humans, it makes me feel better somehow. Maybe it's the placebo effect.

"Is he still here?" I ask, wiping my mouth on the back of my hand.

Paulo nods. "Back room." He smirks, looking over my shoulder. "Someone else is here to see you too, by the looks of things."

I groan. Without turning around, I know he means the club's human hostess, Collette. A pair of sun-kissed arms wrap themselves around my chest like tentacles as a soft voice purrs in my ear, "Hey, Logan."

Carefully, I extract myself from her unwelcome embrace, holding one of the manicured hands and turning around. I let go as gently as possible, leaning back against the bar. "Hey, Collette. How've you been?"

She pouts, looking up through thick, spidery lashes. "You haven't been around much lately."

I pause, trying to figure out how to answer without giving false hope. We slept together a couple of months ago and I get the impression she's rather keen on a repeat performance.

Using the gap in conversation to good effect, she pulls herself to full height, pushing out her ample chest. I have to say, outfit-wise, she's pulled out all the stops tonight. She wears a short, black tube dress that leaves nothing to the imagination, a thick coil of honey-colored hair half covering her face. The effect is a shade Jessica Rabbit.

"I've not been available," I say, staring into my empty shot glass.

Collette is a nice girl and all, but even if she wasn't as shallow as a puddle in the Sahara, there's no way I'd be interested in a round two. Human women of a certain age are hardwired to find a mate, something I prefer to avoid at all costs.

She steps toward me, running a red-painted fingernail around the neckline of my T-shirt and toying with the tiny gold medallion at my neck. I lean away, elbows hitting the bar. "You got a new girl or something?" she asks, eyes flashing.

I gulp. Being a vampire does nothing to ease the terror of telling a woman she was just a one-night stand. "Yeah," I say, watching her kohl-lined eyes widen. "I have."

Collette's hand drops from my T-shirt like a dead weight. Her face sours, lips pursed as if sucking lemons. "She won't last."

I brush an imaginary speck of dirt from my shoulder, avoiding her stony gaze. "Maybe. Maybe not."

Stepping away, she places one hand on a jutting hip bone. "No girl can handle a vampire man like I can."

I resist the urge to smile. "Well, as you know, Collette, I'm no ordinary vampire."

She turns, defeated, before walking back across the room with her hips swinging. A dozen pairs of eyes swivel to watch her.

When I turn back to Paulo, he is grinning from ear to ear, his unusual eyes the color of early morning sun. "Is that true?" he asks, polishing an empty glass with a dishrag. "Logan Byrne has finally found love?"

Shaking my head, I motion to my empty glass, putting it on the bar in front of him. "Nah, just needed an excuse."

Paulo grabs a bottle and fills the glass to the top. "What's the deal with you and women anyway?" he asks, sliding my drink across the shiny counter. "I don't think I've ever seen you with the same girl twice. Did someone break your heart or something?"

"You have to give your heart to get it broken," I say, swirling the amber liquid around the rim. "And I'm not in the business of loaning mine out."

Before Paulo can respond, a short, balding man, almost as wide as he is tall, appears through a door next to the bar. "Mr. McDermott is ready for you, Mr.

Byrne," he says, eyes as flat and expressionless as glass. It doesn't take a genius to figure out there's some kind of glamour on him.

I take a deep breath before fixing my mouth into a nonchalant smile and following McDermott's minion into a long, sterile-looking passageway, a door open at one end.

When we reach the threshold, the man stands aside, and I step ahead of him into the room, momentarily blinded by a thick wall of cigar smoke. I see the leggy brunette before I see Ronin—which isn't surprising, considering she's straddling his lap in one of the chairs by the fireplace, lips attached to his face.

His hand leaves her butt long enough to signal I should wait, so I stare around me, ignoring the suckling sounds by feigning interest in the luxurious leather-and-chrome interior of the room. Finally, with a slap on the backside, he dismisses the girl and she climbs off, tugging her short dress down her thighs.

"You're late, Logan," he says in his mellow Scottish accent, gazing after the young woman as she leaves the room.

I step closer, one thumb looped into a pocket of my jeans, trying to create the illusion of confidence. "My apologies. I got waylaid."

McDermott motions to the leather seat opposite him. "Sit down," he says, shoving a fat cigar between his lips. "Excuse the smoke. I always celebrate New Year's with a Black Dragon or two."

I nod, sliding into a tan leather seat. "What was it you wanted to see me about?"

He watches me intently as he pulls a silver lighter from his suit jacket, flipping the lid open and holding the tiny flame to the massive cigar.

Ronin McDermott isn't just the city's overlord; he is also an *ancient*, one of an elite group of vampires who are considered the oldest on earth. With his Celtic looks, I often think Ronin must have been an early Scots warrior—he wouldn't look out of place storming over a hillside, spear in hand. His only weakness appears to be a playboy penchant for beautiful women. Still, as overlords go, there are worse out there. Way worse.

The cigar tip glows as he inhales, his cheeks hollowing out. "There are a couple of reasons I asked you to see me tonight," he says, exhaling a long trail of smoke. "A favor I need and a warning."

One thing I appreciate about Ronin McDermott is he rarely plays games. "Are the two connected?" I ask, leaning back in the chair.

Ronin shakes his head, tapping ash onto the red carpet. "No. The warning is separate. I'll get to that. First the favor." He holds my gaze a moment, a thin line appearing between his thick eyebrows. "Are you familiar with Internet dating, Logan?"

My eyebrows shoot up in surprise. "Internet dating?" Here I was thinking he was about to ask me to hide a body. "Not really. I mean, I've never had any trouble finding women willing to sleep with me."

The overlord laughs, the sound rattling around the office like a roll of thunder. "Of course. Me neither, as you know. But I trust you've heard of the concept?"

I nod. "Sure I have. There's a woman in my building

who uses it, though she complains the men are either married or short."

"Fascinating," Ronin says, puffing vigorously on his cigar. "Did you also know there is now a site which specializes in matching up vampires with humans? V-Date, they call it."

I frown. "That's a new one on me."

"It's thriving, apparently. While our kind remain segregated in most areas of society, it seems romance is the exception."

I cock a smile. "We are a sexy bunch."

McDermott's face remains impassive, as if he hasn't heard me. His blue eyes are as cold as morning frost. "Unfortunately, the whole venture isn't quite as harmless as it may first appear."

"Why is that?" So far, I have no idea what he's driving at.

He flings the cigar into the fireplace and leans forward, forearms balanced on his knees. "Let me get straight to the point. We're being spied on, Logan. Ever since that dumb actress did her big show-and-tell, we've been the focus of government agencies around the world. They know we exist and they want to know everything about us."

Resisting the urge to sigh, I drum my fingers restlessly on the arm of the chair. Politics never gets any more interesting, no matter how many years pass. "What does that have to do with Internet dating?" I ask, biting my lip to stay focused. Now the threat of danger is over, my thoughts keep drifting back to the girl I left in Chelsea.

"I have a man working for me, an inspector at Scotland Yard and a vampire, though his colleagues don't know that. They're using this site, this V-Date, to recruit informants, to gather information—how we work, our hierarchy." He pauses, looking faintly impressed. "It's actually very clever. Imagine how much knowledge the human patrons of this club have gathered over the years. If they could tap into that knowledge…"

"Knowledge is power," I murmur.

"Exactly," he says, leaning back. "A power we need to retain, if we're ever going to maintain the old ways."

Personally, I'm not too concerned about the old ways. They've done little for me over the years. "So where do I come into all this?"

He smiles, revealing teeth as white as freshwater pearls. "I think I've been fair to you over the years, Logan, have I not? I broke your blood tie to Anastasia at the beginning of the last century, given you employment here at the club."

Here it is, the moment I've been waiting for since I began working for him. Ronin McDermott was never going to be the type of man to let a debt go unpaid. I stare into the orange glow of the fire, drumming my fingers on the arms of the chair. "I'll be forever indebted to you for breaking me from *her*, Ronin, you know that."

"Anastasia is a bullying bitch," he says, an uncharacteristic note of bile in his voice. "I'll never regret my decision to free you. You were too good for all her madness, and not only because of your unique gift."

I stare into his ice-blue eyes, trying to read him, but there's not a flicker of emotion. I decide to lay my cards on the table. "I'm not a killer, Ronin. I wasn't for her and I won't be for you. If any part of repaying my debt involves murder, then you might as well end my life right now."

His face is blank for a moment, like a marble statue, and then he throws back his head and laughs, shaking his head. "Logan, no one's going to be killing anyone. These humans, the informants the police are using—I want you to put a glamour on each of them, so when they report back to the police, there's nothing to tell. Better still, you may be able to get to some before the agency approaches them."

"A glamour? That's all?" It almost sounds too good to be true.

Ronin holds out his hands, palms up. "That's all."

"Why me? You have plenty of people working here who would do it in a heartbeat."

He toys with an expensive gold cuff link on his shirt. "I thought you would ask that. The truth is, Logan, unlike most of us, myself included, you've somehow managed to retain your humanity all these years. If I send someone else"—he waves a hand in the air— "Luca, for example, he'll glamour the girl, sure, but he'll also drink from her. My point is I trust you. Also, there's no danger of you falling for any of these girls. You've never been one to make a fool of yourself over human women, have you?"

An image of the girl from tonight pops back into my head. The magnificent gray eyes framed by haughty, slanted brows, the soft, feminine curves—and the real clincher—sass oozing from every pore. Her name, too, resonates in my mind—*Silver*. It suits her. Pure and lustrous but with the potential to be sharp, like a knife's blade.

"No." My voice comes out flat and self-assured, though I'm far from certain. "I don't do long-term relationships. Never have." I look into Ronin's eyes, seeing only the girl's creamy face as I left her. I'd wanted to see her again, ask for her phone number, but she'd lied about her address, and I figure it means vampires are strictly off-limits.

"You're a wise man, Logan," Ronin says. The softness of his voice catches me by surprise, brings me crashing into the present. "I've learned the hard way over the years that human love never works out." He breaks my gaze, a twitch in his chiseled jaw, and stares into the fire. For a split second, his steely arrogance melts away, the mask dropping to reveal profound sadness. He looks older than he ever has. Then, all at once, the grief crystallizes, hardening to indifference. "My contact at the police will have names soon. I'll be in touch."

I'm half out of the seat when his head snaps back around. "I almost forgot. A warning."

With an internal groan, I sink down again. In my haste to leave, I forgot all about that part of the meeting.

"Anastasia is back in town," he says, a note of sympathy in his voice. "She hasn't been here, of course, she wouldn't dare, but she has been seen."

My throat tightens and the room wavers, as if Ronin has just punched me to the floor. "Are you sure?" I ask, my voice as faint as a ghost's.

He nods. "It's been years since you were bloodbound to her, but I felt you needed to know."

My eyes are wide, like a startled deer waiting to be skinned alive. I force myself to nod. "Thanks for letting me know, Ronin."

With a wave of his hand, he dismisses me. "Send Mystery back in on your way out," he says as I get to my feet.

"Mystery?"

"The girl who was in here just now."

I rub my jaw. "Is she really called Mystery?"

Ronin shrugs, cracking a devious smile. "I have no idea. Nor do I particularly care."

I smile back, wondering for the first time if his playboy image is an act to disguise some deep, festering wound. We men are good at blocking emotions.

I duck back out into the corridor where *Mystery* is waiting. On my way past, I check her heavily made-up eyes for signs of a glamour. For her sake, I'm relieved to see none. However, she clearly thinks I'm checking her out. Her red lips curve into a smile, her gaze following me to the door at the other end.

Back in the bar, I salute a farewell to Paulo, cutting across the dance floor to the exit. I keep my eyes straight ahead, unwilling to notice if the woman is still stretched out across the table, a fly in a spider's web.

Jordan releases me, like a caged bird, out into the cold night air, and I sag against the wall outside. My head isn't filled, as it should be, by the arrival of Anastasia or even Ronin McDermott's grand glamour plan.

"Silver," I mutter, enjoying the taste of her name on my tongue.

I chuckle, shaking my head. What was happening to

me? Logan Byrne losing his head over a girl. Peeling myself from the wall, I wonder if her blood is having some strange, hallucinogenic effect—it's been a while since I last drank.

Yes, that must be it—the blood. By tomorrow, I'll feel better. By tomorrow, I'll have forgotten all about her.

Chapter 3

Silver

NEW YEAR'S DAY, I WAKE TO THE SOUND OF MY PHONE buzzing on the pillow. I know who it is without even looking at the screen.

"Just grabbing my keys," I mumble, lifting a corner of my sleep mask. "Give me five minutes."

"Get a move on, woman," Ollie screeches. "The parents won't visit themselves."

I'm so used to waking up the morning after with a hangover that it takes a few seconds to realize I don't feel like something stuck to the bottom of my shoe. Maybe I've been imbued with some unique vampy power.

Remembering the steamy clinch, I dive out of bed, lurching toward the gilt-framed mirror hanging above my dressing table. *No mark.* I turn the other way, pulling my hair back to examine my neck. No mark there either. *What a gent.*

From outside, a car horn blasts, and I roll my eyes, snatching a duffel bag and parka from the back of the bedroom door. I'll have to shower and dress at Dad's today.

Home is a basement flat. After closing the front door, I scramble up the steps to street level. Ollie is leaning against his green, beat-up Mini, one lanky, denim-clad leg crossed in front of the other. His freckled face breaks into a massive smile as I emerge onto the empty street and dash over to hug him.

"Miss me much?" he asks, laughing as I give him the official death squeeze. "Are you really wearing pajamas under that coat?"

I nod, pulling away to get a better look at him. "Your hair got longer. You look more like Ed Sheeran every day."

He smooths floppy, red bangs over his forehead, grinning. "Well, they don't have too many barber shops in the Seychelles."

"Lucky bastard. I can't believe you got to spend Christmas day lying on the beach while I was stuck in Kent with the wicked stepmother."

"How is Sheila? Did she leave you off the Secret Santa list again this year?"

Ollie is referring to the fiasco of last Christmas when Dad and my stepmother, Sheila, decided we should do a secret Santa. A marvelous idea, you might think—but somehow Sheila forgot to add my name to the little bag, so no one got me. I was giftless. I'm pretty sure she planned it.

I laugh. "Ha! They gave me a big check and a box of chocolates to atone for their sins."

He opens the passenger door, and like a contortionist, I squeeze into the tiny front seat, flinging my bag into the back.

"Hope you're ready for round two," he says, folding his tall frame into the car and doing his best evil laugh. "Mwah-ha-ha-ha-haaaa."

I point ahead through the windshield. "Just drive, moron, or I'll force you to stay for dinner and charades."

As we weave our way through early morning Chelsea, past the white, four-story town houses and wrought-iron railings, the leaf-strewn roads are surprisingly empty. An eerie, postapocalyptic stillness fogs the air.

Desperate for some life, I fiddle with the ancient stereo on the dashboard. "You need a new car," I say as the little plastic knob breaks off in my hand.

Even though Ollie works for some top-notch pharmaceutical company and should, by rights, drive a soulless black BMW with a starched, *Mr. Grey will see you now* suit hung in the back, he insists on keeping the battered, snot-green Mini from his student days. It makes me question if these high-flying careers are really worth the effort. They only ever seem to make people nostalgic for the past, when they were penniless but got to do exactly what they liked all day. In Ollie's case, playing bass guitar in a truly terrible indie band named the Cat's Pajamas.

"So, how was the party last night?" he asks as we turn onto Embankment.

Giving up on the radio, I twist in the seat to face him. "Awful. But guess who I met after I was thrown out?"

A wry smile touches the corner of his mouth. "I don't know, Johnny Depp?"

I *tut* with my tongue. "Oh, come on, be realistic. A vampire!"

He almost crashes into a parked car. "You're kidding me."

"Nope," I say gleefully.

"There was a vampire at that posh twat's party?"

"No, outside. Like I said, I got chucked out."

"What about Joshua?"

My lip curls as an image of that rat Joshua attached to a pair of bee-stung lips pops into my mind. "Joshua," I say with undisguised venom, "went off with another girl while I was getting a drink."

Ollie shakes his head. "That guy's an ass. How did you know this other bloke was a vampire?"

"He moved superfast and almost strangled two guys for disrespecting me." I lower my voice slightly. "That, and I let him bite me."

"Silver!"

"What?"

"You can't just go around letting strange vampires bite you. What if he was a psycho?"

I shrug. "No one that hot can be a psycho."

He sputters in disbelief. "Haven't you seen *America's Most Wanted*?"

I dismiss the question with a wave of my hand. "Psychos are nerdy types who torture cats in alleys. Stop being such a killjoy. You're spending way too much time with Krista."

A prickly silence drops over us like a cloak. My dislike for his current girlfriend is a sticky subject, to say the least. I mean, it's not like I hate her or anything—she just bugs the hell out of me. Twenty-five going on eighty, with a soul-sucking job in banking, Krista is a girl who has become old before her time. She has a pension plan, for heaven's sake. I know this because she made Ollie get one too.

"Did he leave bite marks?" he asks, breaking through the wall of quiet.

I quirk a smile, grateful to be past the awkwardness.

"No, it's the strangest thing. There's nothing. And while it was happening, I sort of zoned out. I saw lights and colors. It was amazing, Olls."

"Maybe you had too much to drink."

"Actually, I was pretty close to being sober."

"Pah! Silver, sober at a party on New Year's Eve? I think not."

I chuckle, snatching an ice scraper from the dash and throwing it at him. "Shut it. I'm a vision of sobriety these days."

Krista forgotten, we're us again.

———

The first thing Sheila asks when she opens the front door to find me standing on the doorstep is not *Why are you in pajamas?* but "Where's this Joshua you said you were bringing?"

Here we go.

"He's not coming," I snip frostily. "Things didn't work out." I barge past her into the hallway and shrug off my coat.

Her thin brows shoot skyward, her gaze snagging on my piggy-print nightwear. "Again?"

I take a deep breath, wishing the ground would open and swallow her whole. "Yes, Shelia, again. I'm sorry to disappoint you. I realize at twenty-four, I should be married with dozens of kids by now."

She ignores the sarcasm and tuts sadly, shaking her head. "What happened this time?"

"Turns out he prefers blonds," I say, bending down to pull off my boots.

"Well, it would've been handy if you'd figured that out before I bought extra food."

I'm poised to make a smart-ass comeback when Dad appears through the kitchen door. "There's my girl!" he says warmly, holding out his arms and pulling me into a giant bear hug.

I smile into the comforting warmth of his scratchy wool sweater. "Happy New Year, Dad."

Sheila retreats into the kitchen, clucking her tongue.

"Ignore her, love," Dad whispers. "You know how stressed she gets cooking these big family meals."

I nod into his shoulder. Oh boy, do I.

Dad knows better than to ask about the absence of Joshua. "I'll get you a drink," he says, pulling away. "Diet Coke?"

"Thanks, Dad." I follow him through the immaculate beige kitchen, where Sheila is attacking a yucky-looking yellow mixture with a whisk, and into the large living area at the back of the house—also beige. My three step-siblings are draped across the sofas, and I'm relieved to see Jess is here. She's the only one I find remotely bearable. The other two, Chris and Debra, are of the same ilk as their mother—overbearing, judgmental, and dull.

Jess's face lights up as I walk in. "Yay, you're here!" Grabbing my hand, she drags me onto the sofa beside her. Chris and Debra look up, nonplussed, and mutter greetings before turning their attention back to the TV.

"What's on?" I ask them.

"*Raiders of the Lost Ark*," Chris mumbles in his droll, monotone voice.

Mousy Debra leans forward, grabbing a tube of

Pringles from the coffee table. "I saved you some," she says, throwing it in my direction.

I catch it midair, realizing it's nearly empty. "Thanks."

This will be the extent of our interaction for the duration of the day.

"Tell me about the party," Jess demands, blue eyes lit with excitement. She is almost twenty-one and already planning an escape from the family home. In the meantime, she lives vicariously through me.

I lower my voice so the others don't hear. "It was awful, full of idiots bragging about how much money their families have. Then I'm coming back from getting a drink, and Joshua is full on face-sucking with some Eurotrash skank."

Jess's eyes widen, her mouth dropping open. She lives for this stuff. "Oh. My. God."

I proceed to fill her in about getting thrown out and snatching the coat—she cackles with laughter at that bit. When I mention the vampire, she rockets out of the seat. Snatching my hand, she pulls me up, dragging me through the steam-filled kitchen. "Come outside. I need a cigarette for this."

"Where are you two sneaking off to?" Sheila probes accusingly, her short, gray hair sticking up in clumps. "I'm about to need help with the gravy."

Jess grins. "Sorry, Mum, girl chat."

Outside, we trample through wet grass to Dad's shed, a damp little summerhouse he uses to get away from Sheila. There are tools and wood everywhere, and it smells of sawdust and tobacco.

Jess reaches up and pulls down a rusty, old biscuit tin from a shelf, fishing out a packet of Marlboro Lights. "Smoke?" she offers.

I decline—I gave up years ago. She lights up and happily puffs away as I describe my encounter with the sexy, green-eyed vampire.

"Did you see all the colors when you were kissing or just the biting part?"

"Just the biting part. But don't get me wrong—the kiss is still the best I've ever had."

"I've heard some women only ever date vampires."

I frown. "Really? How do they find them?"

"Duh. Online dating. There's a special dating site for human-vampire relations."

"You're joking. You mean you just go on and start chatting?"

"Yup. Megan's cousin uses it. V-Date, I think it's called. The cost of membership is extortionate, but apparently the men are *panty-dropping* hot."

I narrow my eyes in thought. I wonder if *my* vampire uses the site.

—⁓—

Later, after dinner is over and Ollie has driven us back to London, I walk into my flat and collapse on the sofa in a heap of emotional exhaustion. Spending time with family always sucks the marrow out of me, and not just because I have to go a whole day without saying what I think. Going home to Kent reminds me of how I felt at thirteen when Dad remarried—like Little Orphan Annie, the spare part of the puzzle who didn't ever fit in.

I hold a hand to my throbbing temples, wishing I'd asked Ollie if he wanted to stay and hang out. Having been friends since we were nine years old, he's the only person who understands my childhood.

From inside my coat, my phone vibrates, beeping loudly. It's a message from Jess. Did you look up V-Date yet?

No, I reply. Should I?

The phone beeps again. Yes. Hot men, remember?

Getting off the sofa, I pause in front of the mirror. The skin on my neck is still perfectly unmarked. How is that possible?

Remembering the sexy vampire, a wave of frustration sweeps over me. Even if he wanted to, he can't find me now that I've lied about my address. With a weary sigh, I grab my laptop from the coffee table, carrying it to the long counter that separates the lounge from the kitchen. Hauling myself onto a high stool, I lift the lid and type *V-Date* into the search engine. A few other dating sites pop up but nothing about vampires.

On a mission, I snatch up my mobile and fire off a text to Jess. I searched for it, but there's nothing.

The phone instantly vibrates, skittering across the countertop as if on legs. Type the full address in. It's probably on the deep web.

I enter www.V-Date.com into the address bar and get instantly transferred to a professional-looking website. I'm not precisely sure what I was expecting, but it definitely wasn't normalcy. The site looks like any other dating site—a slick image of an attractive couple plastered across the background. Peering closer at the models, I decide the man *does* look a little pale. Or maybe it's the woman who's a vampire. It's sort of hard to tell—neither are displaying any fangs.

The motto of the site sits neatly beneath the spiky V-Date logo—*Dating with a difference*. "They got that right," I mutter, clicking a button to choose who I am and what I'm looking for. I click *I am a woman searching for a male vampire* and hit Go, waiting while a circle swirls blue dots at the top of the page.

"Damn!" I say as it brings up a payment box. Jess was right about the extortionate charges. Who knew supernatural dating would be such a money-spinner?

I lean back on the stool, drumming my fingers on my knees. Did I really want to do this? I think of Joshua and all the other idiots I've met since moving to London. That one clinch with the vampire had been more satisfying than all those paltry offerings glued together. What's more, human guys and I were proving to be something of a bad fit. Men were either utter douche bags like Joshua, or the settling-down types who try to hold hands in the street. Not my thing. I'm not the relationship kind, nor do I ever plan to be.

I leap off the stool and rummage in the kitchen drawer where I keep my emergencies-only credit card. Feeling a slight flutter in the pit of my stomach, I tap in all the numbers and click Join. I'm relieved to notice, unlike other dating sites, there is no need to complete an exhausting list of likes and hobbies—handy, seeing as my only hobbies are going to parties and shopping.

Once my picture is uploaded—black-and-gold sleeveless dress at work's Christmas party last year—I'm released like an excited puppy into a forum of men's photos. My eyes widen. Jess was right. A sea of male beauty swims before me. My eyes dart from one chiseled jawline to the next. It's like being handed a copy of *GQ* magazine and asked to pick a model to take home for the evening. I grin maniacally and click on a picture of a dark-haired vampire named Christian. He's a poet, apparently. *No thank you*. Poets are notorious hand-holders.

Next, I click on a blue-eyed hottie with perfect light-brown hair swept sideways off his forehead. All it says is *Businessman*. Now this is more like it. Labeling yourself an entrepreneur or businessperson is an unspoken promise of a swanky, all-expenses-paid date. He'll probably own a Porsche. I click on the pink lipstick mark in the corner of his page, which will apparently zap him a link to my details, before returning to the profiles.

I'd gotten so excited by all the square jaws, I almost forgot to check for Mr. Irish himself. I lean closer to the screen, scanning every face for green eyes and deadly dimples. Nothing. I suck in a disappointed breath. Of course he doesn't need Internet dating. All he has to do is hang around the streets looking sexy.

A pinging noise breaks into my thoughts, and when my eyes flicker back to the screen, I see a message waiting from the hot businessman I sent the lips request to.

Hey, it reads. *Thanks for liking my profile. If you're London-based, how about meeting up for a drink?*

I take a photo of the message and send it to Jess. This is going to be fun.

Chapter 4

Logan

SEVERAL WEEKS LATER, RONIN CALLS ME IN FOR A daytime meeting. Not having mentioned the subject of Internet dating since New Year's Day, I'd assumed he changed his mind about using me in his shady scheme. *Clearly not.*

The streets are busy, bustling with lunch-hour shoppers and tourists, taxis and red buses clogging the roads. A light drizzle falls, the sky grayer than the pigeons pecking around the pavement for scraps. A thousand pinched faces blur past, some clutching cardboard cups, others with brightly patterned umbrellas held low over their faces. As usual, no one notices the black, faceless entrance of 66 Broadwick Street.

I lean against the wall until there is a gap in the flow of pedestrians, then look up into the camera.

A crackle from an unseen intercom rips through the air and a familiar Scottish voice erupts. "It's open."

I push the door open and step inside, the buzz and bustle of the street fading as it slams shut behind me.

Down the narrow hall I walk, alone this time, the dim light from the street showing stains and blemishes on the cream-colored walls — dirt, piss, a pinkish mark that betrays old blood. I push open the second door and look down into the empty room. Without the smoke and chatter of nighttime, the room is stripped of its glamour. The black walls are shiny, as if coated in a thin layer of sweat, and the air reeks of stale beer. Beneath it, ever pungent, lingers the unmistakable scent of dried blood.

Ronin is alone, sitting in a purple-upholstered booth next to the bar. He's wearing a white shirt under a rich-blue cashmere sweater, his hair russet beneath the harsh glare of fluorescent lighting. I glance around, expecting to see one of his faithful minions lurking at one of the tables, but it appears we are alone.

He drops me a nod as I slide into the booth opposite him and shake off my denim jacket. It's then I notice a square of white, folded paper on the table between us.

Sliding it across the table, his lips twitch upward into a half smile, half grimace. "Your first assignment," he says.

I reach across to retrieve it, but his index finger lands, swift as an arrow, pinning it to the lacquered wood.

"They were clever with this one," he says, worrying the edge of the paper with his thumb. "But luckily she hasn't been approached yet. That should make your job nice and easy. A simple glamour will do the trick." His usually glacial-blue eyes burn fiercely into mine. "She has no romantic interest in vampires. Never has, never will. Understood?"

I nod. "Why were they clever to choose her?" I ask when he finally removes his finger from the paper.

"Personal motives," he mutters, averting his gaze. For a split second, a shadow of guilt flits across the rugged lines of his face. "Of course, there is every chance she would have refused them anyway, but we can't take the risk."

"Won't they just keep recruiting more and more?" I ask, picking up the white, folded page.

"Then we'll glamour more and more," Ronin says. "But so far, they're keeping the operation small, being selective with who they choose. Which works in our favor."

I slip the paper into my pocket. "Any word from Anastasia?"

Ronin shakes his head. "Nothing. But I'll keep you in the loop."

Taking that as my cue to leave, I slide back out of the booth. "When do you want this done?"

"Tonight," he says. "She's meeting a date in the West End. The details are all there. Shouldn't be hard to figure out who she is, but any trouble, you have her address too."

"Gotcha." I turn to leave, but he halts me, one finger raised.

"A simple glamour, Logan, remember? For her own sake." A worry line dents the space between his brows. In all the years I've known Ronin McDermott, he has never shown the slightest regard for human life. Even the beautiful women he surrounds himself with are treated no better than attractive pets.

Flashing him a grin, I say, "Don't worry. You said yourself the other night—you can trust me."

He sits deathly still for a few seconds, languishing in a frozen daze, and then slowly, his eyes darken. "I hope so, Logan. Because I wouldn't want to be in your shoes if I can't."

Giving him a final nod, my stomach clenching with

a sudden twist of fear, I make my way back up the steps and into the dimly lit passage.

I should wait until I'm back at my apartment to read the details Ronin gave me, but for some reason, out on the overcast street, rain spattering my face, I pull out the paper and unfold it. Maybe it's that I'm searching for a reason behind Ronin's brief look of empathy, or perhaps I knew all along the name I would find staring out from the top of the page.

Silver Harris, 43b Jubilee Place, Chelsea.

—⁓—

Silver

I'm bored. I'm here on a date with possibly the hottest guy I've ever seen—both on and off TV—and I'd rather be at home watching *Friends* reruns in my pajamas.

Stifling a yawn, I glance around the dimly lit, Hawaiian-themed bar. Things are slow for a Thursday night in West London. A group of smartly dressed women sit on rattan sofas by the window, discarded briefcases and trench coats scattered around them in an explosion of tan leather and beige. A couple of men prop up the bar, staring at their phones and sipping from ceramic glasses shaped like tropical fruit. Then there's me and Nathaniel the vampire—conversation all dried up.

"You look bored, Silver," he observes politely.

My eyes snap back to the man opposite. It's definitely not a good thing when you forget your date exists.

He is every bit as handsome as his picture—coiffed light-brown hair, shining, aquamarine eyes. His sharply tailored suit lends him a mature vibe—though he can't have been any older than his late twenties when he turned. Physically, he is exactly my type—anyone's type, really—but there is a lack of energy about him, a sadness I find disconcerting.

Truth is, I thought all vampires would be like Mr. Irish from the other night, sexy and cocky—and did I mention *sexy?* But so far, all my vampire dates have ended in disappointment. And *this* one looks to be going the same way.

Eyebrows raised, he leans back in the chair, toying with the stem of his wineglass. "Be honest. I don't mind."

"I am bored," I begin carefully. "I mean, you're very good-looking, and you've been really nice so far, but…"

He chuckles, eyes crinkling at the edges. "I don't think I've ever met anyone quite like you before."

"I hear that a lot," I say, stirring my drink with its ridiculously oversized cocktail umbrella. "But how so? Please don't tell me I'm the first human you've met whose mind you can't read."

He shakes his head, still smiling. "Vampires can't read minds, Silver. We read body language. If you've lived for as long as we have, you'd be fairly good at it too." He runs a long, tapered finger around the edge of his glass. "Most humans are driven by the same life forces—money, sex, love. Once you work out what drives a person, the rest falls into place." He pauses, brow knitting, head tilted to one side. "I don't get what drives you though. Sadness perhaps?"

I toy with my straw, eyes fixed on his. "Have you dated many humans?"

"Yes, quite a few over the centuries. But unfortunately, there comes a time when they want what I can't give—marriage, children. That's why I use V-Date. The women on there are usually only interested in the short term—which suits me. How about you? What made you want to date vampires?"

"They're hotter than regular men," I say, not missing a beat.

Which is true enough, although not a single date has ended with anything other than a chaste kiss on the cheek. The first, a Russian vampire named Gleb, was so vain, he spent the whole evening checking his hair in the cutlery, and the second didn't look a day over sixteen.

"That's incredibly honest of you to admit," Nathaniel says, clearly amused.

I lean back in the chair. "What's the point in lying?"

We size each other up across the table. Beneath his starched, open-neck shirt, a sharp outline of muscle ripples his chest. Though I'm still not feeling overwhelmed by chemistry, I imagine how his full lips might feel against my throat. Maybe I should give it a chance.

"Nathaniel," I say, pushing my drink to one side and leaning across the distressed wood table. "Would you like to bite me?"

His jaw slackens, azure eyes pulsating. In less than a millisecond, he is out of the seat and tearing the coat from the back of my chair. Ever the gentleman, he holds it aloft while I push my arms inside. Then he grabs my hand, leading me across the bar so quickly, I have to jog in my heels to keep up.

Outside, amid the stench of exhaust fumes, he pulls me through a double line of idling traffic toward a sleek, black Lamborghini parked on the opposite side of the street.

There is a click as he pulls a shiny key fob from his trouser pocket. "This is me," he says, wrenching open the passenger door.

I duck down, folding into a luxurious, cream leather seat, and almost immediately he's beside me, leaning across to fix my seat belt. He smells of expensive after-shave and fresh linen.

"Where are we going?" I ask, peering through the windshield at the cars lining the street.

As he steers the Lamborghini into the melee of traffic, yellow headlights accentuate the exquisitely carved lines of his profile. He really is superhot. To think, just a few moments ago, I actually contemplated ditching him.

"My apartment is near Farringdon," he says, eyes glued to the road ahead.

"I can't stay. I have work tomorrow."

Wrenching the steering wheel to the left, he swerves the car into a dark side street and skids to a halt. His blue eyes shimmer luminously in the low light of the car. "What about here, then?"

"Here works for me," I say, a slight tremor to my voice.

I thought we might kiss for a while first, but his gaze is fixed on my throat as he leans over and brushes ten-drils of wavy hair aside. Cupping the back of my neck, he rubs a thumb in circles across my skin. "It's been a long time," he whispers huskily, as if to himself.

I stare, fascinated, as his mouth drops open. Where earlier his canine teeth appeared completely normal, they now protrude over his lips in sharp points.

Part of me recoils in horror, tells me to run. I am briefly considering listening to that voice when he lunges for me, closing the gap between us and burying his head between my shoulder and jaw.

There is pain, more so than with my first vampire, and unable to stop, I cry out, "Oww!"

He doesn't falter. The fangs sink deeper, the sound of his sucking filling my ears. Then I'm falling, down and down into oblivion, sweet waves of bliss washing over me. This time, instead of colors, I see fields of waving yellow corn. A woman appears. She wears an old-fashioned long skirt and smock, a corset pulling her in at the waist. She is smiling and speaking Italian. I have never seen her before, but gazing at her face, I feel peaceful and loved.

When I come around, I'm still in the car seat. Nathaniel is watching me, a smile tugging the corners of his lips.

"What's the time?" I ask, feeling foggy.

He gently brushes my cheek with the backs of his fingers. "Still early. Don't worry. I'll drive you home."

I sit up straight and put my hand to my neck. A smear of red stains my fingers. I frown, wondering why there's a cut this time, but before I can ask, Nathaniel leans across and takes my hand. He closes his mouth over my fingers, licking the blood from them, and moaning in ecstasy.

"I want to see you again," he murmurs, eyelids heavy with lust.

"Well, of course you do," I say. "You're bound to, after that."

He nods, eager as a puppy.

Suddenly, I want to get as far away from him as possible. "The thing is, Nathaniel, I don't do second dates."

"Huh?"

"I'm still young, and I wouldn't want to get attached—as lovely as it's been meeting you and all."

He looks utterly crestfallen. "Didn't you enjoy it?" he asks. "I mean, you were making all kinds of noises. It sounded like you enjoyed it."

Oh great. He's clingy.

I decide to use the ruse I reserve for men of this nature. "I'm not sure my psychiatrist would approve, Nathaniel. Not after what happened last time."

He looks blank for a few seconds, mouth hanging slightly open, before bursting into laughter. "Silver, I get it. I'll drive you home. You can save your stories for the next poor soul who asks for a second chance." Shaking his head, he turns the key in the ignition, the car purring to life.

Much like New Year's Eve, I have this vampire drop me at a different house. This is London, former home of the Ripper, and you can't be too careful. Although now, of course, I have a five-minute walk back to my apartment through the dark.

Sort of defeats the purpose, really.

The night is chilly and clear, speckled by a blanket of stars. I pull my wool coat around me, holding it tightly at the neck to keep the cold out. Farther ahead, a middle-aged man walking two golden retrievers crosses the road, but apart from him, the street is empty, the only sound the *clickety-clack* of my gold, peep-toe heels as they hit the pavement.

I'm a couple of blocks from home when I realize I'm being followed. There are no footsteps behind me or cars crawling suspiciously along the curbside, but I sense it in that same way you look up to find a stranger staring. An icy prickle creeps up my spine and into my veins.

I keep my pace steady, not wanting whoever it is to know I'm aware of them. To my left, on the other side of the road, is a long row of white stucco townhouses, and to my right, a large, private park, shielded from the public by green wrought-iron fencing. My flat is on the other side of the garden—if I were to cross it, I would be home in less than half the time. Eyes flickering from one side of the street to the other, I weigh up my options. On one hand, it makes no sense to wander into a dark, empty space when I might easily be followed in, but on the other, the element of surprise would work in my favor.

A bench is fast approaching. I could use it to hoist myself over the iron spikes and into the garden. I'm starting to wonder how I'll get back out again when I hear the unmistakable sound of footsteps quicken at my heels. Frenzy grips me, and I spring onto the bench. Using one of the green spikes, I vault over the railings into the undergrowth.

Twigs scrape my face and hands as I elbow my way through the bushes. When I finally break free, I run as fast as I can across the damp, spongy grass. My heart is pumping so loudly it blocks all other sound. With each stride, I expect to feel the weight of the stranger's arms closing around me, dragging me down, but they don't. Somehow, I make it to the opposite side.

The iron fence seems higher from the inside. In the yellow light of a streetlamp, I glance around me, desperately looking for something to stand on.

I luck out. Someone has dumped an empty plastic drum into one of the flower beds. I put one foot on it, and before I slide off, manage to kick my legs high into the air and over onto the street. My coattails catch on a spike as I leap, and for one awful second, I'm trapped. But then a shrill ripping noise cuts through the night as the material tears, and I'm free and stumbling across the street toward home. I dash straight up the steps to the main house, where my elderly landlady lives.

"Vera!" I scream, throwing myself at the solid, black door and hammering with all my might. I pray she isn't having one of her deaf moments.

I keep pounding until a light goes on in the parlor window. But it's too late. A hand closes over my shoulder.

Chapter 5

Silver

I FREEZE IN TERROR. WHAT A WASTE OF DAD'S MONEY those self-defense classes turned out to be.

"Silver, it's just me," a lilting Irish voice says at my ear, the hand dropping from my shoulder.

I turn around to find myself nose to nose with my vampire from New Year's Eve, his bright-green eyes piercing mine.

I'm struck by several conflicting emotions all at once—anger, relief, and in a tiny measure, happiness. Anger wins out. On impulse, I slap him hard across the face, pointing with a white, clenched hand to the garden I've just sprinted across.

"I thought I was about to be murdered, asshole," I hiss through my teeth. "I ripped my coat. My heels are ruined. All because you thought it might be fun to follow me home."

He smirks, nonplussed, sliding his hands into the deep pockets of his navy peacoat. "I wasn't following you," he says, eyes twinkling.

"Oh, that's right," I say, voice dripping with sarcasm. "You were just walking me home again. Except this time from fifty yards behind and without me knowing."

Before he has a chance to reply, the front door flies open and my landlady, Vera, emerges in a long, silky, oriental dressing gown. She is wigless for once, a Pucci scarf twisted into a makeshift turban covering her head. In her right hand, she holds a meat cleaver.

"Step away, you rapist bastard!" she yells, holding the large knife shakily aloft.

I glare at the vampire, expecting him to either throw his hands in the air or take a step backward. Instead, his brows knit together and his mouth drops open. "Etta Marlow?" he asks, staring at her as if she just walked on water.

The meat cleaver lowers a fraction. "What's it to you?" Vera demands, her voice losing some of its previous menace.

I roll my eyes. Of course he remembers her. He's probably seen all her films.

"It is you!" he erupts, wagging a finger in her direction. "You're Etta Marlow! You played Susie De Sousa in *Girl Uptown* with Gregor Lane. I love that movie."

The meat cleaver drops to her side, forgotten, as she pats her turban, eyelashes fluttering. "Fancy you recognizing me," she mutters happily.

"Excuse me, Vera," I interject, "but there's still a potential rapist on your doorstep here."

Vera looks back to the vampire, who shakes his head, smiling. "A misunderstanding, Etta. I was making sure Silver here made it home safely. She got the wrong end of the stick."

Vera, or Etta as she was once known, glances over at me. "Do you know this charming fellow, dear?"

I scowl at them both. "Well, yes, but—"

"Well then, you must come in, dear boy. I could show you my Oscar, if you like?"

The vampire looks as if he's about to pee himself with excitement. "You mean the one you got for *Days Like These* with Vic Stevens?"

She holds out a thin hand toward him, gold bangles jangling on her wrist. "The very one, dear. Come, come in."

I watch, stunned, as he takes her hand, green eyes lit up in excitement.

Before stepping through the door, he hangs back. "Ms. Marlow, I'm afraid it's only courteous to let you know before I enter that I'm not human. I'm a vampire."

Vera's tinkly laugh echoes around the street like a bicycle bell. "Oh, you're so sweet. Didn't you know I've met dozens of vampires? They're two a penny in Hollywood, darling."

Following her across the threshold, he flashes me the cockiest of grins. "Coming, Silver?"

My jaw drops in disgust. I'm tempted to sulk off to my basement flat, but instead, I trail after them and slam the door.

We follow Vera along an elegant, gold-and-cream hallway into her immaculate, monochrome front room. Even though I've been here on numerous occasions, I'm always mesmerized by the sheer extravagance of the place—buttery, white leather sofas, cream fur rugs, one wall is painted black and white to resemble piano keys. It should look tacky, but somehow, it works.

"You two make yourselves at home while I go and make myself presentable," Vera says. "Then I'll dig out that old Oscar of mine."

I know, of course, the Oscar will not have to be dug

out of anywhere. It's always on display in the den, alongside her film stills and other memorabilia.

"I didn't catch your name," she croons to the vampire before she leaves.

He puts a hand on his chest. "Forgive me. I should have introduced myself. Between the meat cleaver threat and getting slapped by Silver here, I seem to have forgotten my manners. I'm Logan. Logan Byrne."

For strange and unfathomable reasons, my stomach flips. *Logan*. It suits him.

"Charming," Vera says. "Don't you go anywhere, Mr. Byrne."

As soon as Vera disappears from the room, Logan collapses into one of the white leather armchairs and puts his crossed feet onto the cut-glass coffee table.

I'm still standing, one brow arched, arms folded across my chest. "So, *Logan*," I hiss, "what the hell is this?"

He grins, dimples putting in their first appearance of the night as he gazes up at me. "Did anyone ever tell you you're particularly beautiful when you're angry?"

"Oh, cut the crap," I say, ignoring the hot flush climbing my neck. "Why did you follow me?"

"Like I told Etta, I wanted to make sure you got home safely, that's all. Though I'm a little confused as to why you have three houses." He holds up fingers to count. "The one I left you at on New Year's, the one Nathaniel dropped you at, and now this—cohabiting with an aged 1940s screen siren."

"It's none of your business," I say, chin in the air. "And anyway, how do you know Nathaniel?"

He shrugs. "I know most of the vampires in London."

I harrumph. "I bet you do."

In the blink of an eye, he is towering over me, face inches from mine. I inhale his clean, masculine scent like a drowning person coming up for air, and as he leans closer, I find myself gravitating toward him—a flower reaching for sunlight.

He pulls the collar of my coat aside and peers into the gap. As his fingers brush my jaw, an uncontrollable shiver zings through me. I disguise it by stepping out of reach and batting his hand away.

"He did a messy job on your neck," he says in a low voice.

"What's it to you?" I snap.

Before I realize what's happening, he closes the gap between us. One hand cupping my cheek, he bends over, lips brushing the place Nathaniel bit me, tongue gently swiping the puncture holes.

"That should stop the bleeding," he says, pulling away. "But you'll still have a bruise in the morning."

I rub my neck and look at my fingers. No blood. "So you can heal wounds? Just another of your unique skills along with beating up drunk men and following young women home for kicks?"

He sinks back into the armchair. "You're a sexy girl, Silver. I'm glad we've met again."

I snort incredulously, trying, without success, to forget the warmth of his hand on my face. "Well, you certainly made sure we did."

"And of course," he continues, pretending to examine a photo on the coffee table, "I'm hugely flattered I've managed to *turn your head* toward my kind."

"You didn't *turn* anything," I say tartly.

He cocks a brow, gaze burning through my clothes like a laser. I feel a sharp twitch between my legs, as though he's controlling my private areas by some invisible string. "Are you sure about that?"

Vera appears in the doorway, carrying a silver-trimmed tray. There are three flutes of champagne balanced precariously on top and, alongside them, her gold Oscar statue. Logan is out of his seat in an instant, taking the tray from her and putting it on the coffee table.

Though still wearing her robe, Vera has managed to pull on a dark, bobbed wig, a string of pearls gathered at her withered neck. "So kind, darling," she purrs.

Logan takes it upon himself to hand out the glasses, winking as he hands me mine.

"To new friendships," he says, holding his drink aloft and waggling his brows.

I raise my own, meeting his eye with a sneer. "And to those poor, sad weirdos who roam the streets of London, desperate for company."

Vera looks between us in confusion before tossing back the yellow bubbles into her puckered mouth.

"You know who you remind me of?" she says to Logan, swirling her empty champagne flute in his direction. "Laurence Olivier." Before he can respond, she dips the glass toward me. "Don't you think Silver here is the spitting image of Vivien Leigh around the eyes? She has her spirit too, but don't let that fool you, dear; she's an utter softie at heart."

"Vera," I mutter. "He doesn't care."

"I do care," Logan says, staring me down. "Tell me more, Etta."

Vera eases herself onto a black chaise longue, arranging her robe over her legs. In spite of her age, there is a timeless elegance about her. She sits back regally, like Cleopatra, Queen of the Nile. "Silver is a lifesaver, my dear. My two sons live abroad. What can I say? I wish I had daughters. They have me rent out the basement for their own peace of mind, so they have someone here to keep an eye on me."

"You *can* be quite a handful, Vera," I say, smirking.

She flicks her hand dismissively. "Oh, you have to be when you get to my age. It's either that or fade into the background. I like to mix things up a fair bit." Staring into the bottom of her empty glass, she giggles. "Remember your first week living here, Silver? The police made that big fuss over me accidentally forgetting to pay for a jar of olives in Harrods. They arrived at the door to arrest me. Can you imagine? Silver gave this marvelous little speech about how London is one of the biggest murder capitals of the world and there they were, arresting a ninety-year-old over a jar of glorified pickles—wonderful girl."

"You don't have to convince me," Logan says.

I make a barf action by pretending to put two fingers down my throat. "Oh, please."

Our eyes lock, and in spite of my irritation, a vicious shiver of want zigzags up my spine. He really is something.

By the time I manage to drag my gaze back to Vera, I notice her head is tipped back, her mouth is open, and she's fast asleep.

"Looks like your time with Hollywood royalty is up, fanboy," I say.

He looks across at the chaise longue. "She was a real beauty in her day, you know? It wasn't all makeup and tricks like it is nowadays. She was the real deal."

I follow his stare to Vera's sleeping face. "I've seen most of her films. She has me up here all the time."

"It's good of you, Silver, to spend time with her like that." His voice sounds different; some of its cockiness has faded away.

I shrug. "There's no kindness to it. She's a hoot. Besides, I don't have too many female friends."

"I wonder why that could be," he murmurs.

A silence descends while we both watch the sleeping Vera. After a bit, I get up and pull a throw from the back of a chair, draping it across her fragile, birdlike frame. Turning back to Logan, I say, "Tell me why you were following me."

His green eyes flick to mine. "I told you why. I was seeing you home safely. Dating vampires—it isn't for you, Silver."

If it's one thing I particularly hate, it's people telling me what I should and shouldn't do. I lift my chin. "What business is it of yours?"

All of a sudden, I'm in his arms and bent over backward, as if we've just finished dancing the tango. I try to straighten up but am powerless. I realize with both joy and horror just how strong he is.

He lowers his mouth to mine, our lips nearly but not quite touching. "You know, if it's vampires you want to date, I'm available."

Heart thudding in my chest, I swallow loudly. I can tell by the smug glint in his eye he knows exactly the effect he's having on me.

I narrow my eyes in defiance. "No thanks. You're not my type."

He laughs, low and throaty, tightening his grip around my waist, and I mold into him like liquid metal. "I was your type a few weeks ago," he says, brushing the tip of his nose over my cheek and shooting a throb of desire straight to my groin. "Don't you remember how badly you wanted me? I could taste the arousal in your blood."

As if to prove a point, he places a soft kiss in the hollow below my ear, and with it, the last of my resolve melts away. I twist my head, lunging for his lips, but a second before they collide, he lets go, depositing me onto a sofa.

"Maybe we should pick this up when you're not still reeking of Nathaniel," he says, a devious smirk at the corner of his mouth.

"Get out," I hiss, getting to my feet. "I don't ever want to see you again."

"Yes, you do," he says, hooking thumbs in the belt loops of his jeans. "You're just afraid of not being in control. Face it, Silver, you want me so bad it *scares* you."

"Ha!" I say, stalking past him and into the hallway. "You're the one who showed up tonight, remember? Personally, I couldn't give a rat's ass whether or not I see you again. That's why I led you to the wrong house New Year's Eve." I pause for dramatic effect. "Because. I. Don't. Care."

He follows me into the hall. "Really?"

"Yes, really," I say, snatching open the front door. "Now, if you don't mind, I have to go home, and I'm not leaving you alone with a vulnerable old lady. Who knows what you might do."

In a blur, he whips past and stands at the bottom of the steps, leaning against the gatepost, one foot on the brick, just like that first night. "If it's all the same with you, I'll see you in safely," he says, watching as I shut the door and flounce down to the street.

He catches my arm as I stomp past, the warmth of his hand burning through my sleeve, as if touching bare skin. "Silver," he says, turning me around. "Stop."

Although I don't usually take orders from anyone, I freeze, my gaze irresistibly drawn to his pulsating, green eyes. They look larger outside, lit up by the silvery light of the moon, and as I stare into them, the pupils dilate like a cat's in darkness. A hazy feeling creeps over me. I couldn't look away if I tried.

"Silver," he says softly, his grip on my arm tightening.

I wait for him to speak, though I have no idea what it is I'm waiting for him to say, but there is only silence.

A frown line appears between his dark eyebrows and he drops my arm, looking over my shoulder into the distance. "Good night, Silver."

The fog in my brain clears and I'm annoyed at him again for dropping me on the sofa. I tut my tongue loudly, cutting him a scathing look before hurrying down the steep flight of steps to my flat. At the bottom, as I rummage in my bag for the key, I glance up to the street, half expecting him to be standing there, looking down at me. But the street is empty. I shove my key into the lock and let myself in, slamming the door as hard as I can behind me, hoping, wherever he is, that he heard it.

———

Logan

I hear the slam of the door from two streets away and smile, thinking how sexy she looks angry—those huge, gray eyes flashing like knives beneath dark, slanted brows, rosy lips twisted up tighter than a bud in spring. I wanted nothing more than to crush my lips to hers, take that sweet tongue in my mouth, and spend all night exploring every delicate fold of her soft, delicious body. I thought my bloodlust was long dead, but now I'm not so sure—I would suck on her like a Popsicle if she'd let me.

Only Nathaniel's scent prevented me from losing control altogether. Despite having lived a long life, the sharp sting of jealousy is a new sensation. Like I told Paulo the other night, I'm not in the habit of giving my heart away, not used to desiring someone so intensely that the idea of them in another person's arms makes me want to lash out like some wild animal.

Smelling another man on her, *a vampire*, took my inner gentleman to some dark, locked-up place. I took a violent, sadistic delight in having her at my mercy and then ditching her on the sofa. Though now, of course, I'm left wanting her more than ever.

I shudder and look up, realizing I'm already outside my apartment in Marylebone. A freight train chugs past on the railway opposite, its wheels squealing along the tracks, slicing into my thoughts like nails on a chalkboard.

Pushing open the front door to the faded hall of my building, the enormity of what I've done—or didn't do—begins to sink in. I was supposed to glamour Silver, leave her disgusted by the idea of vampires, but in that last moment on the street, staring into her beautiful eyes, I couldn't do it.

Disobeying your blood-bonded ancient, in vampire terms, is as good as signing your own death warrant. There will be repercussions. Though Ronin has been good to me, always seemed to *like* me, if he finds out, there isn't a hope in hell of him letting the betrayal slide.

I push my key into my chipped apartment door and step inside the tiny, threadbare space I call home. Unlike other vampires, who have accumulated vast riches over the years, I've never valued material possessions. The flat is small, with peeling wallpaper and carpets that have seen better days. I could afford a swanky penthouse suite overlooking Hyde Park, but I prefer it here. A long time ago, back when I was human and the building was an apothecary, I worked as a chemist's apprentice in the shop downstairs. Though that part of my life was far from happy, I find it's comforting being close to my last living address.

I shrug out of my jacket and toss it carelessly across the room, flopping down onto the long, leather couch I bought specially for watching TV and seducing women.

Now there's only one woman I want to seduce on the sofa, and she's supposed to be strictly off limits.

I slap my hands over my face and release a low growl

of frustration. "I want her," I say to the empty room, and I really do. Not just because I ache to be buried deep inside her—though admittedly, I get hard just thinking about it. No, for once, it goes beyond that. I want to protect her, look after her. I don't want her messed with or harmed in any way. The world needs Silver—just as she is. Without a glamour.

"I'm a fool," I mutter.

And it's exactly like that poet once said: *Love makes fools of us all*.

Chapter 6

Silver

AT WORK THE NEXT DAY, I'M STILL IN A FOUL TEMPER over arrogant ass Logan Byrne and his sofa-dropping ways.

"What the hell is wrong with you?" my colleague Ciara asks as I slam a tray of vintage rings into a display case, rattling the glass like a loose door in a thunderstorm.

"Nothing," I say, removing the white cotton gloves we have to wear and tossing them aside. "Everything's just peachy."

Work, a busy Covent Garden jewelers, is not somewhere I like being at the best of times. But today, I could really do without it. I want to go home, shut the blinds, and lie on the sofa until all Irish-vampire-related thoughts are extinguished from my mind.

"How was your vampire last night?" Ciara asks.

Of course, she is referring to Nathaniel, but that doesn't stop my insides from churning at the thought of teasing green eyes, delicious dimples, and strong arms wrapped tight around my waist.

"Good-looking," I say wearily, glancing around to make sure there isn't a customer in earshot. Luckily, apart from a well-groomed Asian lady admiring an emerald bracelet with our bitch of a boss, Nina, the store is deserted. "But, you know, boring."

Ciara's sculpted brows shoot skyward. Ciara is engaged to her college boyfriend, and to her, boredom is the bricks and mortar of a stable relationship. She once revealed they went six months without sex. *How is that even legal?*

"Well, you know, Silver, like I've told you before, men aren't exciting. You're better off marrying your best friend, like I am."

"No thanks," I say, thinking of Ollie. "I'd rather not marry a guy I've seen pee in the park sandbox, if it's all the same with you."

She holds out a manicured hand, admiring the exquisite half-carat diamond engagement ring on her finger. Sometimes, I think the ring is the love of her life rather than the man who gave it to her. I've seen them together, and she certainly doesn't look at him with the same dreamy, lust-fueled gaze.

As if on cue, the gemstone catches the light in the glass cabinets and twinkles. Ciara lets out a wispy sigh. "There's no future in dating a vampire, Silver."

"I know," I snip. "That's part of the appeal."

"Why don't I set you up with Patrick's friend Neil? He just got promoted at work."

I wince. "Isn't Neil the one who likes to be spanked during sex?"

"No, that's David. Neil is the one with two front teeth missing. He wears a plate though."

I'm about to politely decline her matchmaking offer when the door opens and two gentlemen—one tall, one short—wearing matching beige overcoats stroll in. Ciara's eyes meet mine and we communicate, like all retail staff when customers are around, via telepathy and hand signals.

Not our usual type, her round eyes and pursed lips say.

I shrug and make a heart shape with my fingers, meaning *Men shopping for their wives*.

Sharp-faced Nina looks up from her client, throwing us an accusatory glare, and Ciara cuts quickly across the plush, gray carpet, plastering on a happy smile. "Can I help you?" she asks in her work voice.

"We were hoping to speak with a Miss Silver Harris," the tall one says.

Hearing my name mentioned, I straighten, squaring my shoulders. "I'm Silver Harris."

Their eyes settle on me like owls catching sight of a field mouse in a hedge.

The tall one pulls out a police badge. "I'm Superintendent Linton Burke, and this is Sergeant Lee Davies. We work for the Metropolitan Police, and we're hoping we could chat with you somewhere private."

"Am I under arrest?" I ask, racking my brain to think of anything illegal I've done lately. Cold fear stabs my chest like an icicle—*God, the Chanel coat from the party. Maybe it once belonged to Princess Diana or something.*

"No," the short one says, infusing me with light-headed relief. "You're not in trouble of any kind, Miss Harris."

Nina, who has been watching the situation unfold with scarcely concealed anger, stalks over. "Silver, take these gentlemen through to the back and offer them some tea," she says through clenched teeth. In other words, *Get the cops off the shop floor and stop scaring my customer away*.

I smooth my black work skirt down over my thighs and lead them from the luxurious, spot-lit room to the less glamorous kitchen at the back of the shop. The room is stark white and smells permanently of burned toast. A pile of dirty mugs is stacked up on the drainer—I couldn't make drinks if I wanted to.

They pull out mismatched chairs from around the circular table and plonk themselves down. The short one looks at me hopefully, as if he is expecting me to fulfill Nina's offer of tea.

"No mugs," I point out.

He nods with tight-lipped regret. Still, neither of them speak. "Are either of you going to tell me exactly what all this is about?" I ask frostily.

The pair exchange glances as the tall one, Linton Burke, reaches into his overcoat and produces several folded sheets of paper. He sets them on the table, black print up. "Before we can explain ourselves, Miss Harris," he says in a flat voice, "we must insist you sign the Official Secrets Act."

Sergeant Lee Davies, who looks like he could have been a used car salesman in a former life, rummages in his pocket and pulls out a pen, holding it out toward me.

I snort incredulously, ignoring his chubby, outstretched hand. "Secrets Act? Is this some sort of joke?"

"I can assure you, miss," Davies says, "it's merely a precaution; nothing to concern yourself with."

"You can dream on. I'm not signing anything until

you tell me why you're here." I push my chin defiantly into the air.

The pair exchange clouded looks. "Oh dear," says Burke. "It seems we've been led on a wild-goose chase, Sergeant Davies."

There is a patronizing air about Burke that sets my teeth on edge. I can tell just by looking at him that he's one of those people who always has to be right.

"I never sign anything without my lawyer," I say, eyes flashing.

Burke twitches a condescending smirk. "Very well, Miss Harris. We are sorry to have wasted your time."

They rise from the table in unison.

"Wait," I snap. "What is this about?"

Davies picks up the papers and holds them out. "Trust us, it's something that might be of interest to you." His tone is warmer than his colleague's. I find I don't mind him half as much.

I snatch the papers, and they sit back down. Licking the tip of my finger, I separate the pages slowly, purposely taking my time. I'm too irked to take in much of what's printed there, but I make a *hmm* noise anyway for good effect.

"That all seems to be in order," I say in a snotty voice, shuffling them back together and holding out a hand for the pen.

I sign using a fake signature. *We'll see how well that holds up in a court of law*.

Burke takes the papers, tucking them back into the inside pocket of his overcoat. "Excellent," he says, glancing over at Davies. "I'll start, shall I? Miss Harris, as you are more than aware, it has recently come to light that a certain…subspecies of our kind exist."

The irony of the expression *come to light* amuses me. A smile tugs at the corner of my lips. "You're referring to vampires?"

"I am indeed. These creatures, though they claim not to pose a threat to humans, are nonetheless proving to be somewhat problematic in the greater scheme of things."

"How so?" I challenge. "I mean, if they don't need blood, surely there's no danger?"

"The blood aspect, although indubitably a welcome relief, is not really the driving issue for the powers that be, I'm afraid."

"No?" I ask, sinking into one of the chairs opposite.

"No." Burke sighs and leans across the table, steepling his fingers. "The main concern is their immortality. If they are, as many of them claim to be, centuries old, then they are suddenly of great interest to us."

I frown. "You mean with history? Because they would have lived in eras we've only read about in books?"

"Yes, that's true. They would be of great use to a historian. However, I was referring to their potential value to the Metropolitan Police itself."

"Go on," I urge.

"Historical crimes. We are reexamining unsolved murders, Miss Harris. If these beings are centuries old, it stands to reason they could be held accountable for crimes committed decades ago. Similarly, their strength and speed put a new spin on dozens of unsolved mysteries."

"The Ripper, for example," Davies cuts in. "The princes in the tower. The *Mary Celeste*."

Burke holds up a hand to silence him. "Let's not romanticize this any more than necessary for our young friend, Davies. Those cases are not why we're here today."

"Why are you here?" I ask, eyes narrowed.

Burke looks over at Davies and drops him a nod to speak.

"This leaves the police in a bit of a tight spot, Miss Harris," Davies says. "While, of course, all criminals must be brought to justice, it is easier said than done when dealing with supernatural forces. In short, we have no idea what we're up against. Vampires are a tight-knit community and will not respond favorably to a chat over a brew at Scotland Yard." He pauses, leaning back in his seat. "That's where you come in."

My jaw drops in astonishment. "Me?"

"V-Date," Burke says, eyes flashing. "This dating site people are using, that you're using, provides us with an interesting opportunity."

I lean back in the chair, worrying at the cuff of my white work shirt. I have a creeping suspicion I know where this conversation is headed. "Go on."

"Dating seems to be one of the few places vampires let their guard down, where they allow themselves to mix freely with humans. It's an oversight we'd like to capitalize on." He pauses, throwing Davies a quick glance. "We're hoping you might agree to help us."

I point a finger across the table accusingly. "Wait a second. How do you even know I'm a member of V-Date? Isn't that a violation of my privacy rights?"

Davies smiles, looking smug. "Not for the police, it isn't."

This is exactly why I've always been against playing

by the rules—*double standards*. "Are you asking me to
be your undercover spy?" I ask, looking between them.
The idea is so ridiculous I only half mean it. I'm relieved
when Davies squirms in his seat and Burke breaks out
in a mocking smile.

"No, Miss Harris. We're not asking you to become
an *undercover spy*. We're not MI5. No. More of an
informant."

I almost choke on my own missed breath. "An informant?" I splutter. "Informant of what?"

Davies leans forward, eyes fixed on my face. "It
would be nothing complicated, Miss Harris. At this
stage, we're just gathering information. There may even
be things you already know that are of use—how they
operate, whether or not there is a social pecking order,
that sort of thing. We'd meet periodically—in secret, of
course—for you to deliver your findings."

"You make it sound like writing up restaurant
reviews," I say with a snort of derision. "Why on earth
would I want to put myself to all that trouble?"

Superintendent Burke sits back, examining me with
a lazy expression. "Of all the potential candidates, we
rather believed you might be the best suited."

"Your mother—" Davies cuts in.

My head snaps around to him, every muscle in my
body tensing. "What about my mother? Don't tell me
you finally worked out what happened to her?"

The colleagues exchange glances similar to Ciara
and I when dealing with emotional customers returning
unwanted engagement rings—worried eyes, clenched
jaws.

"We cannot divulge details of specific cases, I'm afraid," Burke says, his tone softer. "But if you help us, you'll be doing her memory a great service."

A wave of nausea sweeps over me. I grip the faded beechwood table like it's a life raft on a choppy sea. "Are you saying vampires had something to do with her"—I pause, the word *death* sticking in my throat—"disappearance?"

Davies's eyes are rounder than two copper pennies as he scans my face. "Nothing is certain. If and when it is, her next of kin will be informed."

"Does my father know about this?" I ask, sharp pain radiating outward from my chest.

"Like Davies said, Miss Harris, nothing is certain. At the moment, there's nothing to tell. Your mother's case remains closed for the time being." Reaching into his pocket, he pulls out a business card. "Here is our contact number. If you do decide to help us, you would use a new account on V-Date, one with a pseudonym. Merely a precaution, you understand?"

I take the card, surprised to see it reads *Andy's Gutters and Window-Cleaning Services*. "Wow, slick," I mutter. "How long did it take Her Majesty's Secret Service to come up with that?"

Davies bites his lip, clearly trying to repress a smile, while Burke ignores the comment completely. "On the back is the account name and password we'd like you to use. We'll monitor your dates through the site, so we'll always know where you are and who you're with. This will in no way compromise your safety."

"If I give you information, will the police reopen my

mother's case?" My heart thuds against my rib cage as my gaze drills into his lined face.

"*If* you give us information, yes, there is a chance it could happen, but we can't make any promises. Also, I should point out that we cannot influence your questioning in any way. Vampires are sharp—if we furnish you with any kind of script, they'll see right through it. We only ask you to probe deeper and report back to us. Who knows where it may lead?"

I twirl the business card like a miniature baton between my fingertips. I'd spent years wondering what happened to my mother. It's only the last few years I've made peace with the fact I'd probably never know.

"I'll do it," I say, the words slipping from my mouth before I even realize they've entered my head.

They nod. Davies even smiles. "Nice to have you on board, Miss Harris."

—◇◇◇—

Logan

For the first time ever, I'm actually rehearsing a conversation with a woman.

"I'm sorry about last night," I mutter under my breath for about the hundredth time today. "It wasn't gentlemanly to drop you like that. Would you like to go out sometime?"

I ball my fists in frustration. As far as apologies go, it sounds perfectly adequate, but the chances of her keeping quiet while I say it are zero. Maybe I should sneak up, cover her mouth with my hand, and whisper it in her ear before she can turn on the sass. I'd probably get another slap in the face, but at least she'd have to hear me out.

"Ahem." A sharp cough cuts into the evening air like a knife.

I leap up from the basement steps, finding myself face-to-face with the woman herself. *Fuck.*

Words escape me as I greedily drink in her daytime look. She is shorter without heels, her hair pinned back in some sort of French-twisty thing, with a few auburn waves breaking loose around the front. I ache to brush them from her face, tuck them behind her ears. *Jesus. I've got it bad.* I open my mouth to deliver the apology, but she beats me to it, just like I knew she would.

"What do you want?" she asks, slicing me in half with a dirty look. "Are you stalking me or something?"

I smile. I can't help it—even though it seems to make her mad. "You say stalking, Silver, but I like to think of it as romantic persistence."

Her beautiful gray eyes narrow as she barges past me down the steps, bag clamped to her side. She pulls out a key and shoves it in the lock with a white-knuckled grip.

"You dropped me on the sofa," she says over her shoulder before opening the door and slamming it behind her.

I leap to the bottom of the concrete stairs in a single bound and yell through the door, "You kissed Nathaniel!" I sound like a spoiled five-year-old whose friend went to a party without him.

The door is wrenched open. She's taken off her long, padded coat and is in her work clothes—a fitted, black pencil skirt that accentuates her curves, with a crisp, white shirt, tight across her breasts. There's a sharp twitch in my pants. I never even knew the sexy-secretary thing did it for me until now.

She crosses her arms, and I notice how the top two buttons on her shirt gape slightly open. I catch a brief flash of white lace on smooth, ivory flesh. *God, to be that bra.*

"For your information," she says in arctic tones, "and not that it's any of your business, I didn't kiss Nathaniel."

I cock an eyebrow. "He bit you," I say, voice low.

She rakes her gaze over me. Even though her jaw is still clenched, her eyes soften, flickering from my eyes to my lips and back again. "Well, yes. But it wasn't—"

"Wasn't what?" My breath catches in my throat.

Sighing, she looks up at the ceiling. "It wasn't the same as that night with you. There, happy now, O vampire love god?"

Chuckling, I lean against the doorframe, resting a wrist on the wood. "You can put it down to my Irish charm. It's a powerful aphrodisiac, Silver, don't beat yourself up over it."

"You really are full of it, aren't you?" she says, gripping the door as if she's about to slam it in my face. "Full of shit."

I straighten up, trying to be serious. "Invite me in," I say, my eyes locking with hers. "I have something I want to ask you."

"I'm not inviting you in," she says, top lip curled in a way that has me yearning to suck on it. "I've seen the movies."

"Silver, I'm not asking in that way. I don't *have* to be

invited." I step into her flat and back out again to prove the point. "I want to come in, that's all."

"Why?"

I pretend to pick a loose flake of paint off the door-frame, suddenly imbued with the dating skills of a sixteen-year-old virgin. "I like you," I say without looking at her. "Does there have to be any other reason?"

I hear a breath stick in her throat. "Fine, but you can't stay. I'm going out tonight and I need to take a shower."

Stepping into the flat, I say, "I don't mind talking in the shower if you want to save time."

She shuts the door after me, shaking her head. "Get on with it, asshat."

Unlike my place, her tiny flat is homey and modern—freshly painted dove-gray walls, cushions scattered on the L-shaped sofa. I cross over to the mantel above the fireplace and look at the row of photos in shiny, chrome frames, picking up one of a pretty, dark-haired woman who looks a lot like Silver.

"That's my mother," Silver says in a voice fragile as eggshells.

I quickly put it down. Something about her tone tells me the subject is taboo. On the other side of the room is a shiny, white kitchenette separated from the lounge by a long breakfast bar. Silver leans against it, watching me with a shadow of suspicion. I wonder whether it's just vampires she doesn't trust or men in general.

"It's a nice place, Silver," I say, taking in the personal touches—a trail of heart-shaped fairy lights around a Van Gogh print, a fruit bowl filled with champagne corks. "What's your bedroom like?"

She arches a brow, eyes flashing. "Comfy. Too bad you'll never get to see it."

Her gaze is haughtiness personified, and just like last night, it stirs some deep, dark animal within me. I cut across the room, placing a hand on either side of her on the breakfast bar, trapping her between my arms.

Hearing the hitch in her breathing, I lean down, lips brushing her hair. She smells like coconut shampoo, freshly cut grass, and beneath that, the sweet scent of arousal. "I could see your bedroom," I whisper, letting my mouth linger for a second on the tip of her ear, "if I wanted."

She gapes up at me, lust and fear swirling like smoke within her dark-gray eyes. I hear her heart hammering beneath her ribs. She swallows heavily, and I move a hand from the wooden counter to rest on her thigh, just below the swell of her bottom. "Ask me," I murmur, my voice rough as sandpaper as I begin to trace a circle into the material of her skirt. "Ask me to bed. I know you've thought about what it would be like."

A little voice in my brain reminds me I'm supposed to be apologizing, but somehow that no longer seems important. My hand moves with a will of its own onto the curve of her backside, and I squeeze, watching as her pupils dilate. It would be so easy to glamour her, fulfill Ronin's orders, but I want her, just as she is. And more than that, I want her to want me too.

She swallows again, though her voice is clear as a bell. "Aren't you supposed to be asking *me* something?"

I smile, my hand still caressing her bottom, erection twitching in my pants like it's on steroids. "There's something about you, Silver," I whisper, pushing against her, pinning her to the breakfast bar, "that makes me lose all sense of reason."

She brings a hand up to my jaw, tracing fingers across my lips, and I catch one in my mouth, sucking on it before she pulls away. Slowly, she lifts her face, and I lean down, capturing her mouth with mine, tongue parting her soft lips. And if I lost all sense of reason before, I lose everything now. I go at her like a starving man at a feast.

Struck by the overwhelming need to *consume*, I knot fingers into her hair, pins popping out onto the countertop as I deepen the kiss, my tongue dancing with hers. Half of me expects her to pull away, maybe even slap me again, but she doesn't. She groans instead, like she did that first night—deep in her throat, the animal noise forming a single word:

"Logan."

Spurred on by the sound of my name, the overpowering taste of arousal, I move my hand back to her bottom, grinding my erection against her.

I find myself moaning her name too. "Silver." Repeating it like a man possessed, and in all honesty, that's exactly what I am—possessed. A thousand Ronins could be out in the world waiting to kill me, and I'd be as powerless against it as I am now.

She pulls away from my lips and we stare into each other's eyes for a few seconds, and everything is laid bare—mutual crazy attraction. Dropping her hand to my waist, she pulls my T-shirt up, toying with the buttons on my jeans.

"Oh God, yes," I say, watching her shaking fingers twist open the fasteners. "Silver, please."

I've never pleaded with a woman to touch me before, never needed to. But now, I feel like if she doesn't do something with the twitching bulge in my pants I'll probably explode.

She releases the last button and slides her hand in, and I watch the look of surprise cross her face as she realizes I'm not wearing underwear.

Her hand brushes my stiffness. "I should probably leave you like this," she whispers, one brow slanted almost vertically, "to pay you back for last night."

I smile. *God, she's a tease.*

"Don't," I say simply, watching as she takes my stiff length in her hand. "I can't take it."

She pauses, and for a second, the briefest look of vulnerability flits across her face, and then she begins moving her hand along my shaft, a devious smirk twisting her rosebud mouth. I take her lips with mine, sucking on her bottom lip as a tide of ecstasy builds within. When I look down and see my swollen manhood thrusting in her exquisite, ivory hand, I lose it completely. Shouting her name as I fall apart, I hold her to me, burying my face in her hair.

"Fuck," I say. "Silver, what are you doing to me?"

"You stained my work clothes," she whispers.

I laugh, drawing back to look at her. "They're about to get worse, I'm afraid," I murmur. "A lot worse."

But as I slide a hand down to part her legs, a mobile phone begins ringing shrilly in the lounge, noisy music shattering the delicate balance of tension between us. We both freeze.

"Do you need to get that?" I ask, hand wedged between her thighs.

She stares at me, wide-eyed, chewing her lip. "Yeah, I should. It's probably Ollie. He's playing a reunion gig tonight."

Ollie. Who is Ollie?

I step back, letting her duck past me across the room. A draft swirls in the space she's vacated. I miss the warmth of her body already.

"Hello," she says, tugging the black skirt down over her shapely legs and then pointing at my groin.

Looking down I realize my fly is still undone. When I meet her eyes, she is smiling.

"Yeah, I'm still coming," she says to the person on the line.

I wink at her. "You will be coming—all over my face."

Her jaw drops. "No, that was the television. No one is here. Okay, see you at seven." She hangs up. "That was my friend."

"Ollie," I say, as if I'm not the least bit threatened.

"Ollie. What, are you jealous?"

I scoff. "Jealous? Me? What could he possibly have that I don't?"

She shrugs. "A heartbeat."

I slap a hand playfully to my chest, as if mortally wounded. "Low blow, Silver. Even for you."

After dropping the phone onto the sofa, she stands swinging her arms beside her. "I should get ready."

It's hard to believe that only moments ago, her hand was in my pants as I unraveled around her. The air has turned fifty shades of awkward.

"I'll let you get showered," I say, straightening my clothes.

A frown line worries the space between her brows, as if she's being torn in two different directions. "Unless..." she says, trailing into silence.

"Unless what?"

"You want to go with me?"

I do.

Chapter 7

Silver

WITH THE ADDRESS OF OLLIE'S GIG TYPED INTO HIS phone, I send the sexy vampire on his way and collapse on the sofa, head in hands.

I must be completely insane. One moment, I agree to become an informant of vampire secrets; the next, I'm pleasuring one against the kitchen counter.

When I arrived home from work to find him sitting and muttering excuses on my doorstep, he was both the last and only person I wanted to see. Still, at that point, I had no intention of asking him indoors, let alone making out with him and shoving a hand in his pants.

I tut, raking hands through my now-disheveled hair. What is it about him that makes me lose all self-control? It can't be the simple reason that he's hot. I've been with good-looking men before—it goes deeper than that, deeper even than his self-proclaimed Irish charm.

"Don't think it," I mutter aloud. "Don't you dare think it."

But it's too late. The words are already swimming around my head like killer sharks at a shipwreck: *I like him*.

———

An hour later, a taxi drops me outside the Fiddler's Tavern, an über-trendy bar in Shoreditch where Ollie and his old bandmates are playing. Several years ago, the place was a complete hole—sticky floors, a permanent stench of stale beer, and their own resident drunk, Sad Sam. These days, however, it's rocking a chic, industrial look—walls stripped back to bare brick, distressed wood floors, high, vaulted steel ceiling. Sad Sam wouldn't be caught dead here anymore.

Pushing open the polished door, I weave my way through a mass of sweaty, Friday-night, post-work drinkers to the little stage at the back.

I told Logan not to bother showing until nine, figuring that would give me enough time to see Ollie play and take off early if the urge took me. Of course, I know that's not really going to happen. Just being in the place where I'll see him again is already giving me heart palpitations.

I've just waved to Ollie, who is setting up sound equipment on stage, when I spot Krista sitting with a few of her banker cronies in a booth. She sees me and waves, getting to her feet and crossing the bar toward me.

Here we go.

"Hi, Silver," she says, leaning in to air-kiss me. "Good of you to come."

"Hey, Krista," I say through gritted teeth. "How are you?"

"Great," she says, patting her perfectly highlighted locks and sliding her gaze over my casual outfit of skinny jeans and biker jacket. "Wow, those are unusual boots. Very *urban*."

Krista is one of those people with the inherent knack for disguising insults with charm—one of the many reasons why I can't stand her.

But two can play this game. "Thanks, I like your outfit too. Did you come straight from work?"

Her smile falters. She tugs at her silky, expensive-looking blouse. "No," she says, the light turning cold in her blue eyes. "I came from Oliver's place."

Another reason for my dislike—she calls Ollie *Oliver*. As if saying his proper name is somehow going to trans-form him into the aristocrat she's hoping to marry.

"Are you here all by yourself?" she asks, sticking out her bottom lip.

The gloves are off. "No," I say. "I'm meeting some-one later."

She tilts her head, as if addressing a five-year-old. "Oh, is it a guy? I was only saying to Oliver last week what a shame it is you haven't managed to meet anyone yet."

Hold me back. I am going to kill her. "Yes, a guy. I've seen him a few times now. I'm surprised Ollie didn't tell you."

Of course, Ollie doesn't have a clue about me seeing Logan again. But the look on her face as I insinuate Ollie keeps things from her is worth its weight in gold.

"No." Her voice wobbles slightly. "Oliver didn't mention it. But then, why would he? It's not like we don't have more important things to discuss. What's he like, this guy?"

"Hot," I say, eyes wide to emphasize my point. "Superhot."

Suddenly, I'm aware of someone standing in the space beside me. A tall someone, whose masculine scent drives a stab of lust shooting straight between my legs.

"Who's superhot?" a seductive Irish voice asks.

Shit. I turn my head to find Logan just a couple of feet away. He's changed clothes from earlier but is no less tantalizing—signature black jeans slung low on slender hips, a gray T-shirt clinging to his lean, muscled body beneath a frayed denim jacket. His dark hair looks mussed, as if he hasn't touched it since I ravished him in my flat. He stands, shoulders set in confidence, mocking green eyes lit up in amusement.

"No one," I stammer, turning back to Krista, who is gawking at Logan, mouth open. "We were having a conversation about Chris Hemsworth's latest movie, that's all."

Logan steps closer and holds a hand out to Krista. "Hey, I'm Logan. Silver's person."

I screw my face up, swinging my head around to look at him. "Person?" I repeat.

Krista doesn't appear to hear. She grasps Logan's outstretched hand and shakes it. "Krista. I'm with the band."

I suppress a violent choke of disbelief. Did Krista, Sloane Square princess, really just say that?

"It's good to meet friends of Silver's," Logan says, flinging an arm around my shoulders. "I've been begging to meet everyone, but you know how shy she is."

My jaw drops. *What the hell is he playing at?*

Krista's brows shoot up. "Really? You must see a different side to her than we do."

Logan reaches down to pinch my cheek. "Sure, *Silvie* here is shy as they come. Probably why I'm crazy about her."

I bat his hand away furiously. "No," I hiss, "you're crazy, full stop."

Krista looks between us, baffled. Before she has a chance to speak, however, a high-pitched whine erupts from the speakers next to the stage and Ollie steps up to the mic.

"Hi, everyone. We're the Cat's Pajamas and we haven't played together for five years. Our first song is called 'Down, Never Out,' and I'd like to dedicate it to Sad Sam, wherever he may be tonight."

The drummer counts in, and at once the chatter is drowned out by Ollie's soulful voice, drifting huskily across the room. Luckily, they're not quite as bad as I remember.

I feel warm lips at my ear. "You're welcome," Logan whispers, as Krista dashes back to her friends.

Even though I long to stay cushioned in the nook of his strong arm, I force myself to step away. "Since when did you become *my person*?" I ask, lips pursed.

"She was making digs about you not having a boy-friend," he says, dimples flashing. "I stepped up."

"I was handling it," I snap. "I don't need you to rescue me, and anyway, you're not supposed to be here until nine."

He hooks his thumbs into the pockets of his jeans, a wicked glint in his eye. "I knew you'd be dying to see me again, so I thought I'd put you out of your misery. Besides," he continues, waggling his brows, "I have an extra spring in my step for some reason. You have the magic touch, Silver."

I roll my eyes, trying to keep a straight face. "Well, don't expect that all the time. I was just checking out the goods. Saves disappointment later on."

He chuckles, leaning closer. "And did you find the goods to your satisfaction, Miss Harris?" he asks in a gravelly tone that has me longing to get down on my knees for another look.

I arch a brow, my gaze dropping like a dead weight to his groin. "Everything seems to be in working order. Though of course, further checks are not out of the question."

His chest brushes against my shoulder, sending a tingly shiver up my spine. "I'm sure, given enough notice, I may be able to organize something. But first, what are you drinking? Whiskey?"

"No thanks," I say, wrinkling my nose. "I'll have a vodka and soda. What will you have? A Bloody Mary?"

He slaps a hand to his chest. "Good with your hands and hilarious—whatever did I do to deserve you, Silver?"

I gesture toward the bar. "Just get the drinks before I regret inviting you."

"I'm going, I'm going," he says, backing away.

I swirl my index finger in circles, mouthing at him to turn around.

I'm enjoying the view, he mouths tilting his head and smirking. *You turn around*.

This man could be the death of me. I flip him the bird and turn back to the stage, pretending to listen to the music for a couple of minutes until he arrives back with our drinks.

"I got you a double," he says, holding out a glass tumbler brimming with ice. "I figured it might make things easier later on if I loosen your inhibitions now."

"Asshole," I say, taking the drink and stifling a smile.

I motion to the dark-brown liquid in his glass. "Do vampires actually need liquids?"

He takes a swig, licking his soft, pink lips. "No. We don't need anything to survive. But it's enjoyable—to eat and drink. Alcohol doesn't affect us the same way it does humans though, just in case you're planning to ply me with booze and drag me off to bed."

I smirk. "I don't think I'd need alcohol for that. I'd say it was there for the taking."

His green eyes latch on to mine, tension crackling between us like static, and for the first time since the night we met, I allow myself the luxury of a full-on stare. I trail a gaze over his body, svelte yet masculine, a sharp outline of muscle straining beneath his T-shirt. Not for the first time, I ache to be naked in his arms. I shiver, turning back to Ollie's singing in an attempt to break the spell. Suddenly, it feels as though it's just the two of us in the whole bar. Even the thumping music is muted by his presence, people around us paling into the shadows like ghosts.

When I turn around, Logan's heavy-lidded eyes are still fixed on my face. This time, I don't look away.

"So, what's the deal with you and the redhead on stage?" he asks suddenly.

"You mean Ollie, my friend?"

He nods. "Are you just friends?"

I frown. Usually, I'd answer cryptically. I'm not above games when it comes to dating, but something about his furrowed brow, the tight set of his jaw, tells me he's serious.

"Just friends," I say. "Since we were nine years old and I rescued him from the school bully."

Logan chuckles. "I can picture it now—Silver the nine-year-old firecracker. I bet you've always had that tiny mark of scorn just above your left eyebrow."

"It did take two lunchtime supervisors to pull me off," I say proudly. "What mark?"

He points to a spot above his brow. "Here. It pops up whenever something pisses you off, which in my company, seems to be all the time."

"You're not pissing me off now," I say, sipping my drink. "You didn't New Year's Eve either. Mind you, that was before you started stalking me."

Smiling, he puts his glass down on the table beside us. "It's only stalking if you don't want to jump the bones of the man following you."

"Have you always been a cocky bastard?" I ask. "Or is it just for my benefit?"

The dimples flash. "Not always."

"What were you like as a kid? I mean, presuming you can remember."

He frowns. "I was the tortured type—dark, brooding, sensitive."

"Christ. What happened?"

Laughing, he shakes his head. "Somewhere around the turn of the twentieth century, I got over it."

"How did you become a vampire?" I ask, instantly wishing I hadn't. The smile drops from his face, sadness passing across his features like a gray cloud blocking the sun.

Just as he opens his mouth to answer, a smattering of applause breaks out around us, signaling the song has ended. All at once, despite the chatter and noise of the bar, the room feels too quiet. His green eyes flash luminously as he takes the empty glass from my hand and puts it carefully on the table beside his.

With the slow grace of a dancer, he extends an arm toward me, saying in a low, gritty voice, "Let's get out of here."

Mesmerized, I take his arm, and he pulls me through crowds of drinkers, out onto the street.

Outside, he fiddles with my jacket, drawing it across my chest and fastening the zipper to keep out the cold. The road is still busy, cars rolling by, headlights strung out like yellow fairy lights. Dozens of workers are heading home, a frantic itch in their hurried strides. He grabs my hands, pulling me into the dark entrance of a closed shop. My breathing is shallow as he leans closer, his clean, soapy scent a balm to the pungent odor of exhaust fumes. My hands move to his chest, tracing the lines of muscle over his flimsy, gray T-shirt.

"Silver," he whispers.

The sound of my name in his mouth wields a strange, illicit power over my body. I feel soft and hard all at once, like molten steel. "Yes?" I say, the word tight in my throat.

We hang, suspended in time. In the oddest way, looking into his eyes is like staring into a mirror. I see desire but with a cloud of darkness stretched out behind it, a shadow in the midday sun. And then the thread holding us apart snaps, and his lips land on mine, my mouth already opening to let him in.

Our tongues collide, softly this time, stroking in a familiar rhythm, as if we've kissed not just twice, but hundreds of times before. His hands move to my face, cupping my jaw, thumbs rubbing circles on my cheek-bones. A wild thought pops into my head: *This is how it must feel to kiss someone you love*. It's as if time has ceased to exist, and all the city sounds—distant sirens, car horns, the heavy drone of double-decker buses as they hurtle along—blur into the background.

I have no idea how long we stay kissing in the shop doorway. It could be seconds or hours, but eventually we break apart, his green eyes dark with indecipher-able emotion.

"You're not bad at kissing, I suppose," I murmur, watching his eyes as they crinkle around the edges.

"High praise, Silver," he whispers back. "For the record, you're not so bad yourself."

We're still smiling and staring when a loud voice cuts in, "Get a room, for Christ's sake."

We look around to see a street sweeper in a high-visibility jacket, standing with his broom, peering into the doorway. "It's bad enough having to deal with the druggies," he says, shaking his head, "without adding love's young dream into the mix."

Logan laughs, grabbing my hand and pulling me away from the shop. "I'm sorry, sir," he says, tipping an imaginary hat in his direction.

"Yeah, yeah, whatever." The man is still grumbling to himself as we laugh, darting into a side street.

"Do you suffer from motion sickness?" Logan asks, arms around my waist, forehead leaning against mine.

I trail hands under his jacket, up over his broad shoul-ders. "No, why?"

"You asked how I became a vampire. I want to show you."

I frown, leaning away. "That sounds ominous."

"Not literally. I want to take you to the place where it happened." He turns around and crouches. "Hop aboard."

"You're kidding me. Piggyback?"

He straightens up. "You'll be ending this evening with your legs wrapped around me one way or another."

My jaw drops, and I swipe him with the back of my hand. "In case you're not familiar with the *consent campaign*, Logan, a kiss isn't a promise of sex."

"What about a hand job in the kitchen?"

"Bend over and stop talking," I say, trying hard to look offended.

He turns his back again. "Be gentle with me, nurse," he teases. "Be sure to use the glove this time."

"Oh, shut up," I say, putting my hands on his shoulders. "You're such an ass, Logan Byrne."

"An ass you can't wait to see naked," he mutters.

As I jump onto his back, he grabs my legs under the knees, and even though *piggyback* has to be the most unsexy joining of two bodies known to mankind, I still feel the burn of his touch through our clothes.

"Ready?" he asks, peering over his shoulder.

I gulp, tightening my arms around his chest and burying my face in his warm neck. Suddenly, I'm not so sure. "Ready as I'll ever be."

"Hang on tight."

I try to say *okay*, but the word is lost in the wind as we take flight, my stomach dropping like a stone into the sea. We move upward, air rushing in my ears, just like

on the roller coasters I used to love as a kid. I open my
eyes a fraction—after realizing they're glued shut—to
see the city lights merged together in colorful, unbroken
streaks. Slowly, the fear of being dropped melts away,
and I twist my head, watching London unfold beneath
us, dark and glittering, like granite.

Logan isn't flying like I thought but leaping, hurtling
across the spaces between tall buildings as if they were no
more than stepping-stones on a stream. I laugh out loud as
we plunge downward, and for the first time in my life, I
feel completely free, awed by the grace and agility of these
creatures who defy every stodgy law of human nature.

Slowly, the air thins out, the taste of salt sharp on my
tongue. The hurricane in my ears settles to a gentle breeze.

We're next to the Thames, frothy waves sloshing
against the bank. In the darkness, the water glistens like
metal, the hulk of skyscrapers reflected perfectly in the
gray water.

Logan loosens his grip and crouches again. "Are you
all right back there?"

"I'm more than all right," I say in a dry voice, wiping
my watery eyes.

I climb off his back and he turns, holding me steady
against a wave of dizziness.

"Ladies and gentlemen," he says, "we have now
reached our destination. Please return your seats to their
upright positions and take any personal belongings with
you from the aircraft."

I poke him in the ribs. "Shut it, loser."

He chuckles, gripping me gently by the shoulders. "It
takes a while to get used to."

Once the giddiness has passed, I lift my head, noticing huge container ships close by, cranes jutting high into the skyline. "Are we at Docklands?"

Finally, he releases me. "We are indeed. The last place I ever lived as a human on earth."

I stare at the vessels and boats. "You mean they turned you in London? I thought it would have been Ireland."

He smiles his devastating smile, draping an arm around my shoulders. "C'mon, I'll show you."

We walk together along a ramp to a wide, concrete path by the side of the river. A fine mist is visible, hanging above the water like smoke, the cloying whiff of algae becoming ever more pungent. We duck beneath a metal barrier with the sign AUTHORIZED PERSONNEL ONLY. Here, there are several large ships docked, all part of a tourist attraction operating out of the museum nearby.

Two of the ships are naval vessels, gray and pointed at the hulls, like gigantic torpedoes, but the last one is older and wooden. It has proper sails, like a pirate ship, but is of a greater height. There are several decks, stacked one on top of the other, recognizable by the small, square windows of their cabins. At first, I can't see a name, but then as we draw closer, I make out the words HMS *Success* painted on the stern in swirly, old-fashioned writing.

Logan has been silent these past few moments. He stops and turns to me, holding out a hand toward the ship. "This was my last home."

I stare up at the impressive hulk. "You were a pirate?"

He laughs. "No. It's not a pirate ship, Silver—it's a prison."

Chapter 8

Logan

SILVER'S SHOULDERS DROOP. "OH," SHE SAYS, STARING out at the stern of the ship. "I'd prefer it if you were a pirate."

I smile, longing to reach out and take her hand, but I daren't. Most women would have freaked out by now. I don't want to push my luck.

She folds her arms across her chest, looking at me without the slightest hint of fear in her steel-gray eyes. "So that brings up the inevitable question—what did you do? Wait, let me guess. Your family was starving to death in the potato famine, so you stole money to send home?"

"Not quite," I say with a smirk. "Though you got the decade right. It was the time of the great famine, but I wasn't imprisoned for theft." I pause, aware my next words may mean the end of whatever it is going on between us. "I was imprisoned for murder."

Her face remains impassive. With a sigh, she kicks a stone into the water, where it lands with a shallow *plop*. "Of course you were. After all, I'm Silver Harris, *bad-boy magnet extraordinaire*."

Okay, she's not running or screaming. This is going well. "But I was innocent."

She continues to jab at loose stones beneath her feet, wavy hair falling across her face like a curtain in a confessional. "Isn't that what they all say?" she asks without meeting my gaze.

I shrug. "Maybe. In my case it's true."

"Why are you telling me all this?" she asks with her familiar snark. "Please don't say I've somehow ended up in the *friend zone*."

I close the distance between us before she even knows I've moved, folding an arm around her waist and pulling her roughly up against me, so that every part of our bodies—from our knees to the tips of our noses—are touching. I stiffen at the feeling of her warm breasts pressed into my chest. She smells like smudged lipstick and clean linen. "You'll never enter my friend zone, Miss Harris," I mutter, twirling a hand into her soft, auburn hair. "But you asked how I became a vampire, and this is it." I loosen my arms, staring up at the prison hulk. "Shall we take a closer look?"

She exhales slowly, as if she was holding her breath the whole time I held her. "Okay."

Tightening my grip again, I clamp her to my side and leap with a single bound onto the upper deck of HMS *Success*. As soon as we land, I regret bringing her here. No matter how many years have passed, how polished the ship looks, the misery I suffered rears up within me like some dark, forgotten beast. I let Silver go, gazing around the vast deck as if I'm staring death itself in the face.

"You know," Silver pipes up, gaping at a thick curtain of rigging hanging from a mast, "when I was a kid, I was obsessed with pirates. I always wanted to climb the rigging."

The sound of her voice dissolves some of my inner darkness. I glance over. She is smiling, without the slanted brow for once, and the effect is very alluring. She looks young and fresh, like a naughty pixie—her eyes match the twinkling stars.

I flash a smile, struck by a sudden, deep compulsion to make her happy, to see her smile like that every day. "Why don't you? Now you have the chance."

She looks between me and the rigging and back again before tossing her bag across the deck at my feet. "I'm doing it," she says, eyes lit up.

I watch her put a foot into a square several inches off the deck and heave herself onto the ropes. About halfway up the rigging is a crow's nest. She looks up at it as she begins to climb. "You better catch me if I fall, Byrne," she yells.

"I will, me hearty," I shout back, my previous unease melting away like snow in the morning sun.

Her hand stills on the rope for a second, and she calls out, "Arrr!"

Chuckling, I cross the deck to stand beneath her. "Your ass looks great in those jeans, by the way," I call out.

"Shut up. I'm concentrating, pervert."

I shake my head, still laughing. When I glance up again, I notice she's no longer moving. The rigging is swinging back and forth, and she's frozen to the ropes, like a fly in ice. "Are you okay up there?"

There is silence for a few seconds before she answers in a wobbly voice, "No."

I'm by her side in a split second, casually hanging from the rope by one hand.

"Stop showing off," she says, scowling. "It's a lot harder than it looks."

Laughing, I scoop her up around the thighs and leap into the crow's nest, letting her drop through my arms onto the uneven, wooden floor.

In silence, we stare out across Canary Wharf and into the distance, the river weaving through brightly lit skyscrapers like a ribbon of spun gold, toward the older part of the city—Big Ben, Tower Bridge, and the ghostly white dome of Saint Paul's.

London is forever changing—governments, buildings, people—but the dark spirit of the Thames remains constant. It feels the same as it did all those years ago when I arrived, fresh off the boat from Ireland.

Fearing Silver is cold, I take off my denim jacket and drape it around her shoulders, lifting her hair out from the back of the collar. She shivers when my hand brushes her neck, and our eyes lock. "So, tell me how it happened," she says. Her voice is as steady as the tide lapping against the hull.

I break her gaze and suck in an empty breath, looking up into the star-spangled, navy-blue sky. I've always related to the stars. Like me, they are dead things that still shine. I sit on the floor of the crow's nest, letting my legs dangle between the wooden rails, patting the space beside me. Silver follows suit, and I fight the urge to place a hand on her thigh. I put my hands either side of my hips instead, nurturing the vague hope she might make the first move this time.

"I don't know where to start," I say, looking into her pretty face.

She puts a hand on the wood, close to mine but not touching. "How long were you in prison for?"

I sigh. It's been years since I spoke of it. "About a year. I was sentenced to transportation to the colonies. But, of course, that never happened. Not in the end."

Silver glances around the ship. "Is it the same as you remember?"

"No." I scoff, remembering grime and grease clinging to every surface, the stench of human excrement that wound its way into your pores like a tapeworm. "It's fine and polished now, but back then, it was a filth pit. Our days as prisoners were spent dredging the Thames. If we didn't work, we didn't get food or water. At night, we were chained to our bunks."

Silver frowns. "I thought people were hanged for murder back then."

"Oh, they were, and under normal circumstances, I would've undoubtedly been one of them, but you see, the prosecution had no real evidence I'd murdered the fellow. They believed I was guilty, of course—I was Irish and a gypsy, an easy scapegoat—but the courts demanded proof, and of that, they had very little. In the end, they offered me a deal. If I would confess to manslaughter, they'd waive the death sentence and transport me instead."

"You were a gypsy?" she asks, eyes narrowed.

I laugh, edging my hand a fraction closer. "Yes. Is that an issue with you? Vampires, fine. Gypsies, no thanks."

She smiles. "No, it's just interesting. How did you even come to be in London?"

I sigh. "Ironically, I wanted a better life. Back in

Ireland, I came from a big family of Romani gypsies. We never stayed anywhere for long. I got tired of it. I wanted to lay down roots and study."

Her brow arches. "Study what? The stalking and seduction of women?"

"No," I say, meeting her teasing gray eyes. "I wanted to learn homeopathic medicine. My mother and my grandmother were healers—some would say witches. They knew a lot about herbal remedies. They taught me everything they knew." I pause, toying with the small gold medallion on the chain around my neck. "I inherited the gift of healing from them. It only gets passed down to one child per generation. I was the one."

She holds up her index finger. "Wait a second. Is that why I didn't bleed when you bit me? Why you healed the marks Nathaniel left?"

"Yep."

"So all other vampires leave bite marks?" she asks, wide-eyed.

I nod, amused by her horrified expression. "Yes. You'll have to stick with me if you want the good stuff. I'm like vintage champagne among a stack of cheap wine."

She looks up at the stars, shaking her head. "Like you needed a reason to be any more arrogant. Did you heal wounds when you were human?"

"No, I could only help with pain. After all, I wasn't the messiah. Cuts were just cuts—until I became a vampire. I'm not exactly sure of the science behind it, but when you turn, your natural gifts are heightened. If you were a fast runner when you were a human, you'd be an even faster vampire. If you had a head for numbers, you'd have the same gift a hundredfold."

"Like superpowers?"

"In a way, I suppose." I pause, lost in a memory of the past—my mother's face as she waved me off at Dublin, green eyes dark with affection, and the only time I saw her after that, when she was on her knees screaming, her eyes dark only with fear.

"Who did they think you murdered?" Silver asks.

A smile plays at the edge of my lips at the word *think*, and I slide my hand across the wood so the lengths of our little fingers touch. Heat ignites at the point of contact, zipping up my arm like lightning. I wonder if she feels it too. "A man named Henry Peppard," I say. "I moved to London in 1841, hoping to find a homeopath willing to train me. I was so naive. No one wanted anything to do with an Irish Romani lad like me. Eventually, I got work in a backstreet apothecary in Marylebone. I think I only managed to get that job because the owner, Mr. Rumbold, was a drunk. His wife had died of typhoid fever a few months before, and he was a total mess. It wasn't long before I was practically running the place. I'd get up around five to open up, and about midday, he'd come down, dispense a few medicines, and be back on the sauce by two in the afternoon. That's how the mix-up happened."

"The mix-up?" Silver asks, her hand still nestled against mine.

I brush my finger slowly across hers. "The mix-up involved a regular customer and his arsenic. Mr. Rumbold dispensed his medicine drunk, gave him too high a dose, and he died. Guess who took the blame?"

She gasps. "Not the drunk owner?"

"No, not the drunk owner. The Irish gypsy boy. I could've understood if he'd merely blamed me for the accident. But he fabricated a great story about how I'd argued with Mr. Peppard the day before over money and threatened him. So I was arrested for murder."

"Inconceivable bastard," Silver hisses. "I hope you went straight over there after you turned and drained him dry."

"No," I say, shaking my head. "I didn't kill him. *She* killed him, but I never asked her to." I briefly close my eyes, trying to blot out the unwelcome image of Mr. Rumbold right before he died—black eyes filled with loathing, rivulets of blood snaking from his neck, and Anastasia's mocking laughter, rattling like loose bones around the chamber walls.

Silver curls her little finger around mine, bringing me back into the present. "Is *she* the one who turned you?"

Opening my eyes, I glance down at our hands, pinky fingers intertwined like tiny bodies. Even though I'd thought it was a mistake to come here, there is suddenly nowhere else I'd rather be. "Yes, it was a woman—if you can call her that." I pause, Ronin's face flashing into my mind like a neon sign of warning, but I go on anyway, the words clamoring inside of me for release. "She was an ancient. There's a group of old vampires who are thought to have roamed the earth since the beginning of time. They're different from the rest of us—some say more like demons. They can turn humans, are stronger and faster. We are all spawned from that one elite group."

Silver shivers. "What was she doing here?"

I break her gaze, glancing toward the end of the ship, where squat, roofed quarters peek out over the deck. It was in one of those tiny cabins I drew my last human breath.

"She was recruiting," I say, worrying at my bottom lip. "Looking for certain types of people to turn into vampires so they might do her bidding. She was going by a fake name back then, Dolores Gericke, a Dutch aristocrat interested in the reform and rehabilitation of prisoners. She had the idea that murderers would make excellent servants, that their ruthless personalities would be ideally suited to her needs."

"Logan," Silver says softly, her voice stripped of its usual sarcasm. "You said turning vampire enhances gifts and talents. Does that mean it works the other way? Can it exaggerate bad traits too?"

"Yes, sometimes. That was her warped logic anyway. She wanted to create a deadly coven of vampires, ones without conscience."

We lapse into silence, listening to the distant sounds of the city, the slosh of water hitting the sides of the boat, the wail of faraway sirens. Not for the first time, I wonder what would've happened if Anastasia never came to visit that day. Would I have died anyway? Licked by the flames of cholera already raging through my veins like wildfire? Or would I have lived? Made a new life for myself in the colonies?

"She thought you were a murderer," Silver says suddenly.

"Yes," I say, rubbing my finger against hers. "The day she came, I was chained to my bed. A wave of cholera had swept through the cabin, and I couldn't dredge that day. The guards believed I was in the early stages of the disease—cold skin, weak pulse, cramps all over my body. She was walking around, giving fake blessings to dying prisoners, like she was the frigging pope or someone, when she stumbled across me in my cell."

"Was she beautiful?" Silver asks.

I narrow my eyes, recalling a silky mane of hair black as obsidian, eyes the color of dried blood. It wasn't a face I liked to remember. "I suppose, but like a statue— inhuman. I wasn't fooled from the beginning. There was a blackness hanging over her, a vacuum, as if she had no soul. Looking into her eyes was like staring into a deep, bottomless pit, one that had never seen the light of day."

"Did she attack you there and then?" There is a whisper of anger in her voice.

"Pretty much. She told the guard to leave us, so she could pray with me. As soon as we were alone, she lifted the blanket, running hands over me like a prize calf on market day. At that point, I thought she was probably a whore and a nutcase. I told her to feck off and leave me in peace. That's when it happened. She reached for the chains on my wrists and yanked them open. The metal broke instantly, disintegrating into dust. I knew I was done for in the worst possible way."

Silver gulps. I hear a sharp intake of breath, and then she covers my hand with hers. I jerk a little at the touch, staring down at the small hand on mine. It feels warm, like a ray of midday sunshine. Our eyes meet, and I lift my fingers, threading them with hers. Slowly, we lean toward each other. I brush her lips lightly with mine.

"Was it terrifying?" she asks, gray eyes soft.

I brush my thumb in circles over her creamy skin. "I didn't really know what was happening. I thought she was having her wicked way with me. She put her head between my thighs and covered my mouth with her hand. Her strength kept me from making the slightest movement. Then she bit the inside of my leg—I suppose she didn't want the guards to see marks—and while she was down there sucking, a strange, green-tinged smoke began to rise from my body."

"What was it?" she asks, brows knitted together.

"Her venom, flooding my system. It was at that point my heart stopped beating, but other than the shock of that, there wasn't much pain. On the contrary, I quickly began to feel better than I had in weeks. My skin turned from gray to cream, my cuts and sores evaporated—my body looked like it had before I was thrown in jail. When she finally lifted her head, I felt invincible. I didn't understand yet exactly what I'd become." I sigh, cradling her hand in my lap. It feels strange to be happy while talking about the very thing that once made me so miserable. "I found out later, of course, when I joined the rest of them."

"How long was it before she found out you never killed anyone?"

"She found out the night she gifted me with Mr. Rumbold. Before that, the other new recruits and I were kept together in a cellar beneath her house on Cherry Garden Street. The first few months of a vampire's life are surprisingly fragile—daylight, crucifixes, *silver* can be lethal. Slowly, you become stronger, and those things can no longer harm you. I was the last of us to make the transition to fully-fledged vampire, and so, for a time, I was all alone. That was when she brought Mr. Rumbold to me. He was drunk, as usual. I think she must have looked into my past—maybe she realized I was different from the others. He was a test of sorts, to see if I was capable of killing. But like I said, she killed him herself in the end. I thought maybe she might release me after that—but she didn't. Not right away. It was two years before that happened. Of course, I should have run away sooner, but I didn't know where else to go. I'm not proud of that part of my life or what came after."

"Did you ever see your family again?" she says, her voice cracking.

On reflex, my hand goes to the pendant around my neck. I stare out at the bright lights of Canary Wharf. "After I left London, I went back to Ireland and tracked them down. They'd heard I'd died, so you can imagine what happened there. Utter mayhem. Romani people weren't as ignorant as some people in those days—they knew exactly what I'd become. My grandmother, a powerful woman, managed to work a spell that rendered me unconscious. When I woke up, they had fled. My mother left her miniature and this necklace, tucked into my shirt pocket. I never saw or heard from them ever again."

Silver's breathing becomes labored, a glistening tear gliding down her cheek. "Don't look at me," she mutters, swiping at her damp face. "It's just—I know what it's like to lose family."

"Your mother?" I guess, dropping her hand and wrapping an arm around her shoulders, pulling her against my chest.

She nods into my T-shirt. "She disappeared when I was nine. They think she was murdered."

Ronin's words pop into my head all of a sudden: *personal motives*. Was her mother the motive? If so, how?

"Her name was Victoria Harris," Silver says, bitterness creeping into her tone.

I reach over, wiping at her salty tears with my thumb. "I'm so sorry, Silver."

She sniffs. "I'm sorry too, about your family deserting you."

We sit in the darkness, feet dangling beneath us, listening to the sounds of the city. In the distance, Big Ben chimes, though I have no idea what time it is.

"Well," Silver says, exhaling sharply, "you certainly know how to show a girl a good time, Logan Byrne."

I chuckle as she begins counting on her fingers.

"Drags me away from my best friend's gig, takes me to a floating prison, and kills my libido by telling me the saddest story known to vampire-kind. Thank you, Logan. It's been a marvelous evening."

Smiling, I reach behind her and push her arms into my jacket sleeves, buttoning up the denim across her chest. "Next time will be better, I promise."

She arches a brow, the haughtiness back in her face. "Who said anything about a next time?"

Taking her hands, I pull her up, stepping forward at the last moment so that her body slams into mine. "There will be a next time," I whisper, trailing a hand over her back to her pert derriere. Her breath is warm on my neck as I hold her close, the scent of tears lingering on her skin. The ache to undress her throbs painfully in my fingertips, but I hold back, stepping away. "I'm taking you home. Will you be okay with piggyback again?"

"Is this a ploy to save on cab fare?" she asks accusingly.

"No, it's faster."

I gather her up and leap down from the ship in a smooth arc, landing on the concrete of the riverbank. "Ready?" I ask, setting her on her feet and crouching beside her.

She jumps on and I grip her under the knees, her arms going around my chest. "I'm ready," she says in my ear.

We take flight again, back to Chelsea and her house, where tonight I will leave her.

Sitting up in that crow's nest, I realized this thing with her was *not* going away—that for the first time in my life, I want more than a one-night stand.

By the time we land in the garden opposite her flat, I feel lighter—hopeful. Ronin will never discover I haven't carried out his orders if Silver is off the dating scene through other means—those means being *me*.

"What are you smirking about?" Silver says as we cross the street toward Etta's three-story Chelsea town house.

I thrust my hands deep inside the pockets of my jeans. Silver is still wearing my jacket, the sleeves covering her hands. Leaning forward, I place a chaste kiss on her rosy cheek. "I'm thinking about my plans to woo you," I say, grinning.

She takes my elbow. "You can think about those indoors. Come on."

I stand firm, watching as her brows knit.

"Aren't you coming in?" she asks incredulously.

"When are you free? For a date?"

Her jaw drops, a look of disgust etched into her pretty face. It's as if I've asked for a threesome with Etta Marlow. "We just had a date of sorts. We don't need another one."

I take a step backward. "Silver, I want to do this properly. Take you out. What about tomorrow night?"

"No," she says, shaking her head. "I'm in retail. I work all weekend."

"Monday night, then?"

"This is a joke, isn't it?" she demands. "You can't just go from molesting a girl in her kitchen to dating. It's just not done." She points to her front door. "Get inside."

I laugh aloud. "Monday night. I'll pick you up at six. I'll pay for a cab." I back farther up the street.

She looks livid. "Get back here, vampire. I felt you up; now you feel me up. That's how it works in the twenty-first century. This isn't Jane Austen. I'm not bloody Elizabeth Bennet."

"Six o'clock, Monday," I say. "Wear that work uniform of yours if you're stuck for outfit ideas." I waggle my eyebrows suggestively. If looks could kill, I would be dead on the pavement. "You're getting that line again," I call, pointing to the space above my eyebrow. "The mark of scorn."

Mouthing a profanity, she flips a middle finger, spinning on her heel toward her flat. And for the second night in a row, the slam of her front door echoes like thunder around the empty street.

I smile all the way home.

Chapter 9

Silver

SUNDAY NIGHT, POST-WORK, FINDS ME WEDGED INTO A corner booth at Nero's Italian Grill opposite the most boring man in all of creation.

Marek from the Czech Republic.

I reach for yet another breadstick, as my date, oblivious to all but the white noise spewing from his mouth, continues to regale me with tales of famous historical figures he's stumbled upon throughout the decades.

"That's when I knew who she was," he says, finishing the unheard sentence and nodding like one of those bobblehead dogs people sometimes have in their cars. He pauses to look across at the other diners, making sure they are listening too. They're not.

Glancing up, I force myself to meet his dead-fish eyes. "Who?"

"Jackie O."

"Oh." I stifle a lazy half laugh at my unintentional pun, fighting the urge to slump forward across the table, chin in hand.

After Logan's refusal to stay over on Friday night, I decided to log on to V-Date and follow through with my plan to turn informant. Marek looked a likely candidate—less handsome than the others and willing to meet at short notice. Of course, I am already in possession of several juicy pieces of vampire information, but no matter how badly Logan winds me up with his ridiculous *here one minute, gone the next* routine, there is no way I would sell him out. I need separate information. From vampires like this one.

"Tell me," I say with forced perkiness, stirring my vodka and soda with its black straw, "are all those vampire myths completely phony?"

He leans forward, the corners of his thin lips twisting into a smile. "You mean do I sleep in a coffin, and will holy water kill me?"

Smiling, I twirl a strand of hair around my finger. Maybe I could flirt information out of him. "Uh-huh."

He grins, revealing yellow-stained teeth that accentuate his paleness—light-blond hair, washed-out blue eyes. I'm not sure why any of the so-called *ancients* Logan mentioned felt him worthy of immortality. Though who knows? Maybe he was a regular bite gone awry. "No and not anymore," he says.

I raise my brows, feigning mild surprise. Obviously I know this already from Logan, but if Marek repeats it, I can pass it on guilt-free. "Not anymore?"

His voice drops to a hush. "At first, when you turn, certain elements can kill you—holy water, wooden stakes, silver."

I blanch hearing my real name mentioned. Even out of context, it leaves me feeling exposed. "Then they just stop having an effect?"

"Yes, after a few months, once the transformation is fully complete."

"So, after that, nothing can harm you?"

Marek shakes his head. "Not really, no."

"Not really?" I repeat, leaning across the table in intrigue.

"Well, the definition of *immortality* is 'one who cannot die.'"

"So, no vampire has ever died?"

He squirms on his seat, looking uncomfortable. "It's not something I'd wish to discuss with a lady."

I snort, brushing an imaginary speck of lint from the tablecloth. "Haven't you been around twenty-first-century girls before? Anything goes for us these days."

Taking a sip of his white wine, he says grimly, "Decapitation."

I lean back in my seat. At last we're getting somewhere. "That's the only way?"

He fiddles with his knife. "As far as I know, yes."

"What happens to the vampire body afterward?" I ask, eyes narrowed.

"Can't help you there. Never seen it."

I slump forward, disappointed. "Oh."

"I can tell you who I did see die though."

Here we go. "Who?"

"Frederick J. Rosenhead," he announces proudly. Without further encouragement, he launches into the story.

The next day, I wake up with a tummy churning like the spin cycle on a washing machine and a head that feels stuffed with cotton wool. It takes a few seconds to work out it's because tonight is my date with Logan. I haul myself into a sitting position and lean across to the nightstand, picking up the note I'd found shoved under my door last night.

Don't forget, 6 p.m. tomorrow.

Your romantic stalker,
Logan

At the bottom is a little smiley face drawn with two vertical lines at the corners of its mouth for fangs. I grin like a buffoon. Tonight, I will pull out all the stops. There is no way I'm leaving that man outside on the street again. One way or another, we will finish that moment against the kitchen counter.

Seven hours later, all stops are officially pulled. I stand in front of my full-length mirror chewing nervously at my painted-red bottom lip and wondering if I went too far. Though I'm confident enough to know I'm attractive, I've always considered myself sexy in that disheveled, rock-chick way—tousled hair, jeans, leather jackets, girly dresses teamed with biker boots. Tonight I'm feminine.

I wear a tight-fitting, dark-green dress I bought in last year's sales, with high, black suede heels. The dress's sleeves are long and the neckline high, but the back dips low, exposing inches of bare skin. I've left my hair straight instead of its usual waves, silky smooth and falling just past my shoulders. I gulp, tugging the stretchy material of my dress farther down my thighs. I never usually get nervous or self-conscious before dates, but tonight, I'm both.

A clutch of fear grips me as I meet my smoky-eyed gaze in the mirror. *What if he doesn't show up?*

Taking a deep breath, I decide I'm in desperate need of one of Vera's famous pep talks. I grab a coat and dash upstairs to her polished front door. On the street, the sky is darkening, a light, misty drizzle starting to fall. I thump the silver knocker hard, hoping she'll hear over the faint strains of Sinatra drifting from the house. She does. The front door swings inward.

"Darling!" Vera says, arms already open as if she's been expecting me. She is wearing her trademark black—a long-sleeved jumpsuit that somehow, in spite of her age, she manages to pull off. There are oversize, gold hoops in her ears, and in one hand, she holds a long, black cigarette holder. She could be Holly Golightly in her golden years.

I step into her smoky, Chanel-perfumed embrace, taking care not to brush against her shiny wig for fear of knocking it askew. "Hi, Vera."

She takes my hand, standing back to look at me. "My goodness, you're a knockout. Who's the lucky fella? That vampire I met?" She takes a drag on the end of her cigarette, thick, kohl-lined lashes fluttering. "I haven't seen a man that handsome in a long time."

Closing the door behind me, a hot flush creeps up my neck. "Yes, *him*."

"Come through to the kitchen, darling, and I'll fix you a drink. I'm expecting Stan over, but he's running late as usual. Some tedious charity gala with *her*."

Stan is Vera's *gentleman friend*. They've been embroiled in a love affair since the fifties, despite him being married to someone else their entire relationship. Once, I asked why she's put up with being a mistress all these years. She said simply she is powerless to stop it, a notion I find unfathomable. I mean, surely you just delete their number?

In her spacious black-and-chrome kitchen, she opens a cupboard and pulls out a crystal decanter of scotch. Even if there isn't so much as a scrap of cheese in Vera's gigantic refrigerator, she always keeps enough liquor to stock a downtown bar.

"A small hit of this," she mumbles, cigarette holder hanging precariously from the corner of her mouth, "and you'll feel like Greta Garbo."

I slip onto one of the high stools around the kitchen island, as she glugs a dose of brown liquid into a crystal tumbler before sliding it across the counter like a barman in the Wild West. "Bottom's up," she says, easing herself onto the stool beside me.

Taking a gulp, I almost choke. It burns like fire all the way down my throat.

"Good stuff, isn't it? Vintage, of course." She pulls on the end of her cigarette holder, blowing a cloud of smoke from the side of her withered mouth. "Now, the man situation. Whatever you do, don't sleep with him tonight."

"Why not?" I ask, still clutching my throat. "If that's all I want from him anyway."

Vera arches a perfectly sculpted brow. "That isn't all you want from him," she asserts, tapping ash into her hand. "Or you wouldn't be wearing that dress, *and* you wouldn't have blushed redder than a bonfire when I asked about him."

"But…" *Damn*. Why are old people always right?

"With men like *Logan*," she continues, "you have to play the game—lead the chase. They have to feel you're the ultimate prize. You can't give it all away before the starting pistol goes off."

I put the glass down on the tiled surface with a clink. "Vera, I'm not Mother Teresa. There's only so long I can hold out." I daren't tell her I'd have bedded him three days ago given half a chance—or that first night if only I hadn't lied about my address.

"All I'm saying is make him wait. The longer he waits, the harder he'll work. Look at Stan. I made him wait five years before I even let him kiss me."

"He was married."

She shrugs, taking a drag on her cigarette. "True."

"Plus, Logan is a vampire. I might as well enjoy it while it lasts. God knows how many other women he has on the side." Though my voice is steady, my insides recoil in horror at the possibility of him seeing some-body else.

"They are all bastards," Vera mutters, staring into space. "Especially the good-looking ones."

I nod in agreement, almost reaching for the scotch again, but the doorbell rings.

"That will be my bastard," Vera says with a coy smile, sliding off the stool.

"I better go anyway," I say, standing up.

I follow her back into the hallway, where she opens the door to Stan. Back in the day, Stan was a hotshot Hollywood director and supposedly quite the looker. Now he is shriveled and stooped, with gray hair and liver spots, an oversized pair of black-rimmed glasses perched on the end of his beaklike nose.

"Silver, sweetheart," he says in his New York accent. "Ain't you a sight for sore eyes." Vera clears her throat, placing a hand on her hip. "You too, of course, doll," he murmurs quickly, leaning over to kiss her white-powdered cheek.

"Silver has a date with a vampire," Vera tells him.

Stan nods politely. "Well, I'd say knock 'em dead, kiddo, but in this case, he's dead already."

"Oh, ha-ha," I mutter, as they both bend over, clutching each other and giggling like teenagers.

Vera straightens up. "Remember what I said about tonight." She holds up her index and middle fingers in a pistol gesture.

"I'll remember," I say, though really, who am I kidding? I didn't wear matching lingerie for nothing.

"He really is so handsome," Vera says wistfully, gazing out into the night.

"Hey, you got prime beef steak right here, doll," Stan teases, puffing out his chest.

Vera shoves him. "Stan, your best-before date expired decades ago."

I give a wave as I leave them, retreating back downstairs.

At six o'clock on the dot, there is a knock at the door. Stomach in knots, I reach for the latch with a sweaty hand and snatch it open. My breath catches—I feel dangerously like I might pass out. Logan stands in the doorway, wearing his usual black, faded jeans, but this time with a tight-fitting shirt that hugs his muscled body like a second skin. There is a thin, black strip of a tie hanging from the collar and his hair is swept back off his forehead with some kind of wax. I have never seen anyone sexier.

There is silence. I watch the cockiness leak from his face as his wide, green eyes drift over my dress. At one point, he attempts to speak, but the words stall in his throat.

As if waking from a trance, I suddenly realize he is holding something out in front of him—a small bunch of wilted-looking snowdrops, tied at the middle with twine.

"Are those for me?" I ask in a croaky voice.

He blinks several times and extends the bouquet toward me, running a nervous hand through his dark hair. "I didn't know your favorite flowers, so I brought you mine."

"Snowdrops," I say, nodding. "Why, thank you, Mr. Byrne."

A slow smile unfurls from one corner of his mouth. "I did promise *wooing*, Miss Harris."

I reach for the flowers, my fingers brushing his. "You did, and so far, all expectations have been surpassed— though considering there were none to begin with, I wouldn't take that as too much of a compliment."

As I close the door behind him, his eyes drop to the hem of my dress.

"Stop it," I say, unable to stop smiling.

"Stop what?"

"Doing that bug-eyed, staring thing. You either really hate my dress or you just came in your pants."

He laughs, shaking his head. "I love your dress. I'm

just not sure I can last an evening without finishing what we started the other night." He crosses to the counter, patting the wood with his hand and arching a brow. "Maybe we should stay in after all."

I wag a finger, propping the flowers on the mantel and grabbing my coat from the sofa. "No way. You promised a night of stalkery romance and Jane Austen chivalry, and you'd better deliver."

"You bought that dress solely to torture me, didn't you?" he teases, stepping away from the counter and taking the coat from me.

"Even if I did," I say, allowing him to help me into my jacket, "it's no more than you deserve."

I push my arms into the sleeves, and he pulls my hair from the collar, fingers skimming my neck. I feel him close behind me, his chest pressing into my back. A hand moves to my hip, burning through my clothes like a red-hot poker.

"I could get used to you torturing me like this." His tone is rough, like jagged glass, and the words send an electrifying shiver down my spine. My nipples harden beneath my dress as I lean back against him, eyes half-closed. His hand squeezes my hip.

"Don't start what you can't finish, Byrne," I whisper breathlessly.

He releases me, breaking the spell. "You're right," he says, with heavy-lidded eyes. "We should go before the lure of the kitchen counter becomes too much. Besides, our taxi is waiting."

I narrow my gaze. "It's not something weird like a pony and trap, is it?"

He smiles, showing dimples. "Just because I was born into a gypsy family doesn't mean I pick up dates with a horse and cart, Silver. Next you'll be after a crystal ball reading." He offers me the crook of his elbow. "Shall we?"

I nod, grabbing my keys and looping my arm through his, trying to act nonchalant despite the tingly feelings that zip through me at the point of contact.

Outside, I slam the door shut behind us.

"I think this is the first time you've slammed the door with us both on the same side," Logan muses, a mischievous glint in his eye.

"Yeah, well, don't get used to it. I'm sure it won't be long before I'm slamming it in your face again."

There is a black cab pulled up at the curb, engine idling. Logan pulls open the door and bows. "Miss Harris," he says, waving a hand toward the backseat.

The driver peers over his shoulder at us and shakes his head, clearly unimpressed by all the time wasting. "You get in first," I say, not moving. "I don't want you ogling my rear end."

Logan chuckles, climbing in and offering me his hand, and I step in after him, shutting the door. The driver, impatient to be off, slams into first gear, lurching away from the pavement. Not yet sitting, I stumble, landing on Logan in an undignified heap.

He catches me, one arm gripping me around the waist, the other across my thighs. "You couldn't wait, could you?" he murmurs, inching tapered fingers up my leg and stroking my inner thigh. "You just had to find a way to sit in my lap."

"You wish," I whisper, turning to meet his burning gaze. Unable to stop, I lean slowly toward him, drowning in his clean, freshly shaven scent.

But before my lips can hit their target, he scoops me up and deposits me neatly into the seat opposite. "Put your belt on, Miss Harris," he says, grinning. "You're in for a bumpy ride."

Chapter 10

Silver

I'M UNABLE TO HIDE MY SURPRISE AS THE TAXI STOPS outside the glitzy, chrome facade of the Savoy.

Logan raises his brows. "Will this do?"

"You booked us a hotel room?" I ask, outwardly wearing a look of disgust while internally jumping for joy.

He grins. "No, I'm not that presumptuous. We're only here for the culinary experience. I've never been. Have you?"

"No," I say with a little snort. "I know I live in Chelsea, but that's a pure fluke. I'm poor."

"Not tonight," he says, reaching past me to pay the driver. "Tonight, we dine like kings."

He flings open the taxi door and hops out onto the street, offering me his hand. I know I joked about Elizabeth Bennet, but I do feel ladylike as I put my hand in his and step out from the cab.

The taxi reverses, leaving us standing on the street, grinning at each other like two clowns on acid. I feel so light-headed and, well, *happy* that I don't even realize he's still holding my hand. On reflex, I snatch it away, pretending to smooth my hair, which is starting to frizz in the misty rain. I see a brief look of disappointment flash in his green eyes.

"Come on," he says, walking backward toward the

bustle of people buzzing around the brightly lit entrance. "Our table will be ready."

Inside, we are led through a white-and-gold lobby to a low-lit room with dark-red, lacquered walls. Our table is next to a mirrored pillar and as I sink into the soft, gray chair, I catch a glimpse of an almost unrecognizable me—flushed and wide-eyed. *Hopeful.*

Logan's eyes are glued to mine as the waiter fusses with napkins and menus, rattling off a long list of specials that I don't even try to hear. *I'll have him*, I want to say, *for my main, on the side, and slathered in whipped cream for dessert.* In the midst of an X-rated fantasy involving me, Logan, and a blindfold, I realize the waiter is asking me what I'd like to drink.

"Er—"

"Champagne," Logan cuts in. "If that's okay with you, Silver?"

I nod. Champagne is more than okay with me.

The waiter finally leaves, and I lean back in the seat, trying to relax. I exhale sharply and Logan flashes a dimpled smile. "Are you okay?"

"I'm fine," I say, fiddling with the shiny cutlery. "How about you?"

"Really fine."

Arching a brow, I ask, "Is this your modus operandi? Champagne, fine dining?"

"No," he says, studying me carefully. "Not by any stretch of the imagination. I'm not really into material things."

I remember Nathaniel and his Lamborghini. "Are most vampires wealthy?"

"Some," he says, resting his forearms on the table. "Most of us are comfortable anyway. That's one bonus of living for centuries." He narrows his eyes playfully. "Are you asking me if I'm rich, Miss Harris?"

"Just curious. Also, this Miss Harris thing—it's like I'm fifteen again, getting frog-marched to the headmaster's office."

He cocks a brow. "I can frog-march you to my office if you like."

"Do you have an office?" I ask, my tone accusing.

"I have a bed."

I swallow, running eyes over his broad shoulders, the ripple of muscle beneath his shirt, long, artistic hands on the starched tablecloth. Chewing my lip, I imagine them under my dress—between my legs. Somehow, I tear my gaze away. "What do you do anyway? For a job?"

He fiddles with the cuffs on his shirt. "I've worked at a club in Soho for the last year or so. Before that I was in Peru, working as a homeopathic doctor."

"You realized your dream after all."

"Yes, kind of."

"What do you mean, kind of? Don't tell me you forged the medical certificates."

"Silver," he says, chuckling. "You have so little faith in me. I took all the exams and passed, set up my own clinic in a poor area just outside Lima."

"So what happened?"

"When vampires went public, the townspeople caught on to what I was. They aren't quite so forgiving as Londoners."

I frown. "What did they do?"

"Burned down my clinic," he says matter-of-factly.

The knife I'd been toying with clatters onto a plate, my jaw dropping in disgust. "You're kidding?"

He smiles sadly. "No. That's why I moved back. I even got my old flat back in the place where Rumbold's apothecary used to be."

"Isn't it weird? Living in that place after what happened?"

"It should be. But I find it oddly comforting. When I walk through the door I remember."

"Remember what? The good ole days?"

"Being human."

Fiddling with the tiny gold medallion at his neck, he seems suddenly forlorn. On impulse, I lean forward, reaching across the stiff linen cloth to cover his hand with mine.

The waiter arrives with our champagne, making a big show of popping the cork, but we ignore him. My eyes flicker from our clasped hands on the table to his chiseled face and back again, butterflies tearing at my insides, cheeks burning hotter than the flaming sambucas at the next table. Suddenly, I'm aware the waiter is still standing beside us, tapping a polished shoe impatiently and holding his digital notebook aloft.

"I'll have the chicken," I say without looking up.

Logan passes our menus back, eyes the color of a stormy, green sea. There are tiny flecks of gold at the center I hadn't noticed before. "The steak. Rare."

"Maybe," I mutter, as the waiter turns away, "you should change that to *still living*."

He moves his hand farther up my arm, to my wrist, thumb on my pulse. "I know what I'd rather be eating."

I cross my legs, attempting to stem the throbbing ache building at my core. "Do you mean that in the blood sense or the bodily sense?"

"Both," he says quickly. "All of it. There are so many ways I want to take you I don't know where to start."

"I should go to the bathroom," I whimper. But I don't. I stay, basking in the promise of sex with a man I'm crazy about.

Dinner passes in a blur. We don't speak about the past again. We don't really speak about anything. The chicken is perfect, tender and juicy, but I might as well be eating cardboard for all the attention I give it. Logan too picks at his steak. Even the champagne sits barely touched. All I can think about is his body and his mouth and all the places he might put them.

When I come back from the ladies' room, Logan looks tense, clenched jaw, eyes blazing.

I slide back into my seat. "What's up? Was the bill massive?"

He shakes his head. "What would you say if I booked us a room here? For the night. Would you slap me in the face again?"

His eyes are wide, as if he's half expecting me to lean over and smack him. I reach forward for my champagne glass, insides churning with excitement. "Hypothetically, I would remind you that wooing doesn't usually involve shagging on a first date." I pause, exploiting the power of the moment by taking a slow sip of bubbles. "In reality, I'd probably race you to the elevator."

The worry melts from his face. He picks up a white plastic card from under his napkin. "I got this while you were in the ladies' room."

I slam down my glass, feigning a look of offense. "Oh, so you did bring me here for sex?"

"No," he says, holding his hands up. "I swear, it was meant to be for food only, but I thought..." He trails off when he realizes I'm grinning from ear to ear, and stands up, snatching the champagne bucket off the table and extending a hand toward me. "Let's go to bed, Silver Harris."

With those six words, I am officially undone. The restaurant and the other diners fade into the background as I grab my coat from the back of the chair and place my hand in his. Like coconspirators, we hurry from the room, scanning the lobby for the lifts. A bellboy rushes forward to help us, and for a horrifying second, I think he intends to lead us all the way upstairs. But he merely presses a button and backs out into the foyer, leaving us alone in a cloud of swirling tension.

As soon as the doors close, we turn to each other. In spite of our bravado, I feel strangely nervous.

Logan squeezes my hand, forcing me to look up into his hazy eyes. "What are you thinking?" he asks.

I twitch a smile. "Thank God I'm wearing matching underwear."

He chuckles, low and dangerous, holding my chin gently between his thumb and forefinger. "I've been hard for you all night."

My nerves evaporate, swallowed by a blistering wave of desire. Heat blooms between my legs, nipples hardening to bullets. My heart pounds in my ears as he brings his warm lips down on mine.

The string of tension snapping is intensified by the crash of the champagne bucket as Logan drops it, frothy liquid chugging out onto the plush, gold carpet. Hands matted into my hair, he forces me back against the marbled wall, his mouth opening mine, our tongues fiercely lashing together. He tastes like warm champagne and fresh mint gum.

I feel his hand between my thighs, working upward to my panties, leaving a trail of fire in its wake. "Touch me," I plead into his mouth. "Just touch me."

He groans, toying with the damp strip of lace between my legs. Moving the material aside, his callused fingertips find their way into my slick folds, and I sag against him.

"Logan," I whimper, head tipped back as he strokes me, thumb rubbing circles into my aching nub. He brings his other hand to my breast, massaging a hard tip through the thin material of my dress, until a white-hot wave of pleasure threatens to spill. "Logan," I cry out, forgetting I'm in an elevator with doors that could pop open at any second.

There is a loud *ping* and we jump apart as if shot with Tasers. I hastily pull my dress down as the doors slide open. No one is there.

"Our floor," Logan says, bending down to retrieve the champagne bucket, which has been rolling all over the place during our clinch. He grabs my hand, pulling me into the corridor.

Inside our luxurious room, I barely notice the plush,

chintz furnishings. I cross straight to the bed, perching on the end and tossing my coat onto the floor. The door slams, and in a split second, Logan is on me.

Picking up where we left off, he rucks my dress up around my waist, spreading my legs wide. His eyes are pulsing, dark with need, a line etched between his brows. I reach up to his now-mussed hair, grabbing handfuls of the thick, silky strands and tugging on the ends as he kneels on the floor between my thighs and slips soaked panties down past my hips.

"God, you're beautiful," he says, the end of the sentence muffled as he buries his face into my wet heat.

I throw my head back as his tongue glides through my folds. Gripping my knees, he laps furiously, grazing my swollen clit with the rough skin on his jaw. My breathing comes in short, sharp bursts, pleasure building to an unbearable crescendo. I drop backward, balling fists into the shiny, floral bedspread as he inserts a finger into my soaking core, pumping in and out, faster and faster, his mouth clamping around my aching nub. Just when I think it can't feel any better, he sucks hard, flicking with the tip of his tongue, and I lift up from the bed, exploding around him, warm juices trickling onto my thighs. The scream that erupts from my throat is feral—in the back of my mind, I pity the people in the adjoining room. I drop, semiconscious, onto the covers.

It takes a good minute to float back to my body. My chest is heaving, my eyes screwed shut. Logan crawls next to me.

"Well," he says in his soothing Irish lilt, "I guess we're even."

"We'll never be even," I say, panting like I've run a marathon. "Now kindly remove your clothing."

He laughs, working at the knot in his tie. "Gladly."

"God, Logan," I say, the back of my hand on my face. "I can't feel my legs."

Unleashing his tie, he hovers over me, kisses my swollen lips. "It's not over," he whispers. "Not by a long shot."

I sit up, wrapping my legs around his hips. "I'm a mess. Look what you've done to me."

He rakes hands through my tangled hair, leaning his cool forehead against my sweaty one. "I've never seen anyone more beautiful."

I gently brush his lips with mine, tugging his shirt from the waistband of his jeans, and he reaches down to the hem of my dress, yanking it up over my head.

"Jesus," he mutters, staring at my barely there, black, lacy bra, and tracing a finger along the line where the material meets my skin.

"Take it off," I urge, sucking at his bottom lip as I go to work on his shirt buttons.

He reaches around my back, expertly flicking open the clasp and slipping the delicate material down my arms. My nipples stand up, puckered and hard, and he rubs his thumbs over the tips, pinching them between his rough fingers. I moan, my core clenching almost painfully.

"Suck them," I demand, abandoning his shirt buttons. I lean back to give him better exposure, grinding myself into the hard bulge at the front of his jeans. I watch through heavy-lidded eyes as he leans toward my chest, a sexy smirk playing at the edge of his mouth, soft hair falling forward, tickling my breasts. There is the faint rasp of stubble, bristly against the sensitive, pink skin of my nipples, before one disappears between his lips.

A tingly ripple of pleasure shoots through my nerve endings as he sucks—slowly at first and then with increased vigor. I rock faster against him, feeling the delicious snag of his sharp fangs.

"Shit, yes," I mumble, feeling another wave start to build.

Suddenly, he stops, fangs retracting. "I need to be inside you," he says, eyes feverishly dark.

I lean forward, panting, nodding mutely as I tear at his shirt. When we've managed between us to get the top half-open, he pulls the rest over his head. It lands in a puddle of material on top of my dress. I suppress a gasp at the sight of his bare upper body, running hands over his sculpted chest and down the tight ridges of his abdomen. Never in my life have I seen such a perfect specimen of man.

"Work out much?" I murmur, ghosting a touch along the planes of muscle, velvety soft and rock hard beneath my fingertips. My eyes drop to the trail of dark hair disappearing into the waistband of his jeans. I remember how his erection looked in my kitchen—a rod of silk erupting from a pool of dark, wiry hair—how it felt—stiff and unyielding as I pumped it in my fist.

He releases a low moan as I fumble with the buttons on his jeans, helping me to push the denim down over his hips. I climb off him, leaving room for his erection to spring out.

"No underwear again, I see," I say with a gulp, staring at the thick, hard pole protruding between his legs.

"No," he says, flashing a smile and following my gaze to his stiffness. "I never can find them large enough."

We meet each other's eyes, smiling.

"It's beautiful," I murmur, placing a flat palm on the satin shaft and rubbing a thumb over its glistening tip.

A low growl erupts from his throat. "*You're* beautiful." His hand closes over my wrist. "But this time, I need to be inside you when I come."

He wriggles away from me, off the end of the bed, stepping out of his jeans. A breath catches in my throat as I savor him fully naked for the first time—slim thighs, lean, muscled legs. I gape openmouthed, unable to believe my luck. He is my own personal Adonis.

I push farther up the shiny bedcover to the pillows, patting the space beside me, suddenly aware of being completely and utterly *buck naked*. He drops to the bed on his knees, crawling on all fours until he has me beneath him. But instead of spreading my legs and plunging into me, he falls onto his elbows, chest pressed into mine, and gently tucks a sweaty strand of hair behind my ear. He gazes into my eyes, as if searching for an answer to some unspoken question, a shadow of fear flickering behind his dark-green eyes. "Silver," he whispers, tracing the line of my jaw with his fingers, "what is this with us?"

I put my arms around him, trailing fingers along the arch of his back, my hands resting on steely buttocks. "I don't know," I say quietly, and in all honesty, I don't. "But I like it."

He smiles, eyes drowsy with lust. "I like it too."

I reach into the gap between our bodies, tenderly

stroking his satiny erection and parting my legs, whimpering as he positions its head at the entrance of my slick heat. He slides into me slowly, my name escaping his lips, and I tangle my fingers in his hair, our eyes locking.

"Logan," I murmur, barely recognizing the desperate, vulnerable voice as mine.

"Silver," he says into my mouth, our noses touching as he pushes deep inside me.

I close my eyes, arching my back to meet his urgent thrusts as we begin to move together in a frantic rhythm. He lays his hands flat on the bed on either side of me, using the traction to plunge deeper. Warmth spreads like a wildfire around my loins, waves of pleasure building and coiling inside me. I yelp like a wild animal, my release inching closer with every euphoric thrust. I dig my nails into his shoulders, and he scrapes his fangs on my neck, sharp, delicious pain pushing me closer to the brink.

"Bite me," I plead, as he circles his hips, grinding against my sensitive nub. "Please, Logan."

He sinks his fangs into my neck, thrusting deeper than ever as I fall apart, rocked by wave upon wave of bliss rushing up over me like high tide on a beach. Right before I sink down into oblivion, he shudders between my thighs, and the last thing I hear before I succumb to the power of his bite is my name as he shouts it loudly into the room.

Chapter 11

Logan

EVEN IF VAMPIRES SLEPT THE WAY HUMANS DO, I wouldn't catch a wink with Silver's creamy, postcoital body nestled snugly against mine. I lay a hand on the curve of her hip and nuzzle the back of her neck, listening to her slow, rhythmic breathing, and inhaling the smell of her shampoo—a fruity scent now laced with the sweet aroma of dried sweat and sex. Every time she stirs and her body brushes mine, I'm hard again. Despite making love half the night, I'm not sure I'll ever get enough.

I allow my hand to drop from her hip to her stomach, tracing a circle around her belly button.

She inhales, writhing beneath the covers and emitting a long sigh. "Sleep, pervert," she murmurs, grinding her ass into my groin and sending my hardness into overdrive.

"Just so I know I'm acting in full accordance with the consent campaign," I whisper, my fingers curling into the soft, downy hair between her legs, "could you confirm you're fully awake?"

She chuckles, sliding backward into a spooning position. "Affirmative."

"Good," I say, sucking the tip of her ear as I push two fingers into the warmth between her legs.

A low groan erupts and she shivers, rocking her hips

into the pressure of my hand. "I don't want to make you any more arrogant than you already are, Logan Byrne, but you are exceptionally talented with those fingers of yours."

I grin into her hair, circling her clit with my fingers. "Why, thank you. I've attended some of the finest sex schools in Europe. It's good to know the tuition money wasn't for nothing."

"Shh," she says, snickering. "Don't spoil it with your nonsense talk."

"I'm not spoiling anything," I murmur, trailing kisses along the nape of her neck and rubbing my hard-on into the soft skin at her back. "You're begging for it."

"Seriously," she whispers, her breathing shallow, "just shut up and keep going."

I moan, continuing to stroke her slick folds, wedging my knee between her legs and positioning my erection between her thighs.

"Yes," she hisses as I push the tip against her damp opening. "Do it. Please, Logan."

"How many times have we done it now?" I tease, circling her entrance. "You can't get enough, can you?"

The truth is I'm the one who can't get enough. I feel pushed to the brink of madness by her. Like I would do anything and everything in my power to never leave this bed.

"No," she says, "and neither can you, so quit teasing."

"Fair point." As I sink deep inside her, she shudders, gasping with pleasure, her body melting around me like hot lava. I move my hand to her breast, pinching a silky tip between my fingers and eliciting a quiet sob of gratification.

"Silver," I whisper. The euphoria of saying her name while I'm inside her is overwhelming—like a drug. I pull out halfway before plunging deep again, repeating the motion, listening to her short, sharp breaths as they grow more ragged with each thrust. When her breathlessness turns to vixen-like shrieks, I run a flat palm over her firm tummy and down between her legs, rubbing at her soft, wet bud. I've always considered myself a good lover, but to this woman, I'm a slave. I would do anything to give her pleasure. If there were a choice between her climax and mine for the rest of eternity, I would choose hers in a heartbeat. When her cries reach fever pitch, I pinch her bud between my fingertips, giving one final thrust into her tight sheath as she spasms around me. Only then do I pour into her, a powerful orgasm rocking my body, my sweat mingling with hers.

We lie quivering, bodies wrapped tightly together, the sound of panting filling the air.

"I could spend the rest of my days hearing you come," I say, brushing auburn hair from the ivory column of her neck.

She reaches behind and pats my shoulder. "Keep doing it like that and I might let you."

I pull out, turning her toward me, needing to see her face. A yellow glow from the street casts a sheet of light onto the bed, and I gaze, mesmerized at her flushed-pink cheeks, eyes softened to the color of rain clouds. Her mouth is red from kissing, a pink rosebud in spring. I trace my fingers over her soft lips and along her jaw, hearing a hitch in her breathing as I lean forward to take her mouth with mine.

She tastes even more intoxicating after sex—sweet and winey, like the nectar I lapped from her core. My arms tighten around her as the kiss becomes more urgent, my hands combing through her hair. I'm hard again in an instant.

"Will you bite me?" she asks in a small voice.

I smile at her unswerving desire. "Are you sure? I already drank a fair bit of blood."

"Yes," she murmurs, tipping her head back. "I love how it feels—like sin itself."

Chuckling, I cup her face in my hands. "You are a wanton, Silver Harris." I pause, dropping a hand onto her perky nipple. "If it's sin you're after, I could bite you here." I rub the supple underside of her breast. "And then, if that's to your satisfaction, how about we try here?" I place a hand between her legs, gently pinching her inner thigh.

"Yes," she hisses, draping a bare leg across my hips. "Do all of it."

Tipping her onto her back, I hover over her. "Silver Harris, where have you been all my life?"

———

When the amber rays of streetlights turn to the dull gray of morning, I finally drift off into a semiconscious daze of happiness. It isn't until a few hours later, when I hear running water, that I open my eyes to the now-bright room. I sit up and reach across the bed, finding only warm, rumpled sheets. The door to the bathroom opens and Silver steps out. Her hair is wet, hanging in damp waves around her face, and she's wearing my shirt. It hangs loosely off her small frame, skimming past her hips, only just covering her ass.

"Jesus," I mutter, as the sheet covering me from the waist down tents upward with my stiffness.

Silver averts her gaze, a sexy flush in her cheeks as if she is some innocent and not the woman I've just spent the whole night fucking to within an inch of her life.

"I borrowed your shirt," she says, tugging at the hem. She points with her thumb over her shoulder toward the bathroom. "They have Jo Malone shower gel in there. I might smuggle some out in my coat."

I chuckle, running my gaze from her blushing face to her naked thighs and back again. "Do it. I've got your back."

She nods, smiling. This bashful act of hers is doing nothing for my hard-on. She stays standing, making no attempt to rejoin me in bed. No matter how many years pass, how liberated human sexuality becomes, the power of the morning after is infinite.

"What time's checkout?" she asks, looking around the room. Seeing a welcome pack on the marble-topped chest of drawers, she reaches over for it. The shirt lifts, revealing the black, lacy knickers I discarded in a frenzy last night. My cock twitches beneath the sheet. If she doesn't come back to bed now, I'm going to end up touching myself.

"Do you regret last night?" I ask, watching her flip through the cardboard booklet.

Her gray eyes meet mine and she arches a brow, tossing the pack back where she found it. "Are you mad? I had about fifty million orgasms."

I grin like a Boy Scout being awarded a badge of honor. "You'll want a second date, then?"

She narrows her beautiful eyes. "Are you getting needy, Logan Byrne?"

My dick is getting *needy*; I know that much. "No. But I would hate to deny you a further *fifty million orgasms*. Also, don't kid yourself by trying to pretend I'm not the finest ride you'll ever have."

Her jaw drops and she folds her arms across her chest. The movement pushes her breasts together—a line of cleavage just visible above the neckline of the shirt. I fight the urge to groan. "Maybe it's like that with all vampires."

"It's not."

She lets her arms drop, pointing to the obvious bulge beneath the covers. "Do you need some help with that?" There is a wicked sparkle behind her gray eyes.

Suddenly, I can't think of a single smart-ass comment. I nod like a mute and pull the sheet aside, enjoying the flash of lust that lights up her face.

"My God," she murmurs, climbing onto the bed. "It's really hard."

The way she says *hard* in her sweet voice unleashes the beast in me. As soon as she's close enough, I pull her down on top of me, shoving my hands under the shirt and palming her full breasts. "Hard because of you," I say throatily, as she arches her back, rubbing herself on my stomach muscles. The friction of wet lace panties on my skin sends me out of my mind with lust. I grip her pert buttocks, and as she straddles me, I know beyond a shadow of a doubt that the sight of her wearing my shirt and writhing around like a harlot will be forever etched onto my brain.

She leans down, flicking her tongue over my nipples, reaching behind her to stroke my twitching length. I drop back against the pillows, watching her trail kisses over my chest and down toward my waist. By the time I feel the tickle of hair on my groin, it's me who is begging for it.

"Silver, please," I beg.

"Pretty please," she says, brushing her lips over my wet tip.

I ball my fists into her hair. "Pretty please with a fucking cherry on top."

Laughing, she gazes up at me, her eyes meeting mine, one brow slanted almost vertically as she positions her wet, pink mouth at the top of my raging hard-on. "As you wish," she says, before sliding her lips down the length of my shaft and taking me wholly in her mouth.

We don't leave the room until well after midday, when the frantic hammering of the maid on the door signals checkout is long overdue. Silver is back in her tight, green dress and heels. She takes a look in the gilt mirror hanging near the door. "Oh, bloody hell. Look at the state of me."

I smirk. To me, she looks perfect. She has that satisfied, rosy glow women get after a decent bout of lovemaking—a faint smudge of mascara beneath her lashes makes her eyes look sensuous and smoky, and her lips are red and full from kissing, like ripe strawberries. I reach across, smoothing down her wavy hair and tucking it behind her ear. "You're a vision, Miss Harris."

She shoves at my shoulder. "You have to say that."

We both stand, staring at each other like fools, until another flurry of knocking forces us into action.

"Will we take a taxi or the *vampire express*?" she asks, snatching her purse from a velvet chair as I wait for her to lead the way out.

"As it happens," I say, opening the door to the hall and flashing a grin at the scowling maid, "the *vampire express* only works at night."

Silver wrinkles her nose, stepping past me. "Why?"

"Daylight weakens our speed," I explain as we trail slowly toward the lifts. "It's the only negative impact of the sun."

"So all that sex we had this morning was solely because—"

"Because I'm a naturally magnificent lover."

She rolls her eyes, jabbing at the metal elevator button. "Good thing I didn't have breakfast or I might throw up. You realize you only get away with the supreme cockiness because of the Irish accent, don't you?"

I chuckle as the mirrored doors slide open. "Don't forget the good looks. Those help too."

Outside on the street, it's as if a year has passed. Although the overcast sky is the same as yesterday—gray and white like marble—and people are still scurrying past like ants, something somewhere in the universe has shifted. Silver and I stop by a row of black cabs. She turns to face me, and I gaze deeply into her eyes, at the amber flecks among gray, flickering like sunlight through clouds.

"I guess we'll get separate cabs," she says, "if you're heading back to Marylebone." I glance down at her hands, fists clenching beneath the sleeves of her coat. On impulse, I reach across to hold one. She swings her arm in the opposite direction. "I'm not much of a day-time hand-holder," she says, frowning.

I cock a smile. "How do you know I was going for your hand?"

She laughs, pricking the bubble of tension.

"Let me get this straight," I continue. "You won't hold my hand in public, but biting on a street corner is perfectly acceptable? Then there are all the things we did last night." I close the gap between us, my lips brushing the silky tendrils around her ear. The warmth from her body hits like a current of hot air, drawing me in. "All that sucking and licking and bodily fluids spilling. All that nakedness…"

Her eyelids flutter closed for a brief second. "I see your point."

"As for the taxi, I'd like to see you home safely." I hold my hands up. "No touching."

She worries at her bottom lip, and it occurs to me that apart from our obvious sexual connection, I have no idea what's going on in her head.

"Okay." Her voice is filled with trepidation.

I motion to a black cab waiting by the curb. "Will we take this fine carriage, good woman?"

Shaking her head, she steps toward the taxi and opens the door. "You get in first, remember? In case of ass ogling."

"Ass ogling?" I repeat, wiggling my brows. "I've no

reason to ogle anymore, Silver. I've seen everything and then some."

Before I step past her, I lean in, placing a swift kiss at the corner of her mouth. She clambers in behind me, her cheeks a shade redder than they were outside.

"I love how you do that," I whisper, as she settles on the seat opposite.

"Where to, mate?" the cabbie calls over his shoulder.

"Jubilee Place, Chelsea," I say, before flicking my eyes back to her.

"Do what?"

"Blush over something as innocent as a peck on the cheek when you spent all night riding me with wild abandon in a hotel room."

Silver's eyes go wide. She jabs a thumb over her shoulder at the driver. "Shut up," she hisses.

I flash a grin. "He doesn't care. In fact, I might lean out the window and shout it loud for all to hear." I jerk toward the sliding panel of dirty glass to my left, and Silver jumps up in horror, grabbing my arm.

"You are absolutely mental, aren't you?" she says. In spite of the mark of scorn above her brow, her lips curve into a smile.

"You might have to sit next to me and hold my hand if you don't want your wanton secret out of the bag," I tease, drumming my fingers on the glass.

"I don't do blackmail, Logan Byrne. Besides, I have no shame."

Her flashing eyes are like a red flag to my inner bull. I wrench the grimy pane open as we squeak to a halt on the main road. "Silver Harris of Chelsea gives fantastic head!" I yell, startling a group of gray-haired tourists who are standing around a woman with a green umbrella.

Her palm covers my mouth, as she fights to close the window one-handed. "Okay, I have shame." She collapses onto the seat next to me, laughing as I offer her my hand.

"You're such a weirdo," she mutters, slapping her small, ivory palm into mine. "Why can't I meet a nice, normal vampire?"

I close my fingers around hers. "Because they're boring."

She nods, sighing in resignation.

When the cab clears the glut of traffic around Trafalgar Square, my mind drifts to our imminent parting. I glance down at our intertwined fingers, deciding it's now or never.

"So, you didn't answer my question about a second date back at the hotel," I say, trying to keep my voice neutral.

She sucks in a breath, pushing the hair away from her face. "What did you have in mind?"

Deep down, I'm hoping she'll invite me in when the taxi stops. Invite me in and never ask me to leave. But something in her brooding demeanor tells me that won't be happening. I decide to tread carefully. "Dinner. I'll come over and cook for you."

Her brows shoot up. "You cook?" she asks in disbelief.

I lean back into the seat, spreading my legs a bit so my thighs touch hers, a flame licking the space where our legs meet. "Yes. I cook. Can't everyone over the age of twenty?"

"No. I live on ramen noodles and takeout."

"All the more reason for me to cook for you. What time do you finish work tomorrow?"

"I'll be home by half past six."

"In that case, I'll be on your doorstep at six thirty-five."

The taxi turns onto Jubilee Place, and Silver shouts out the number to the driver. A little farther up, we squeak to a halt. I grab the red handle and push the door open, jumping into the street.

Silver steps out after me, rummaging in her purse for keys. "Thanks for the ride," she says innocently.

I burst out laughing as her face goes slack, the unintended double entendre hitting home. "Well, you know," she says with slanted brow, "thanks for both types of ride."

I grin. "Thank *you* for being a worthy passenger."

She flicks at my shoulder with the back of her hand. "See you tomorrow, Logan." She exaggerates the first vowel in my name, oozing sarcasm, and I push my hands deeper into my pockets to refrain from slamming my mouth to hers.

"See you tomorrow, Silver."

When she's at the bottom of the steps, she turns back, looking up to the street with a mischievous smirk. She pushes her key into the door and lets herself in. The door, for the first time in my presence, clicks softly shut behind her.

Chapter 12

Silver

AT WORK THE NEXT DAY, I CAN'T STOP SMILING. CIARA even catches me humming a tune as I polish the cabinets.

"What's got into you today?" she asks, hand on hip, as I rub the yellow duster over the glass in vigorous circles.

"Nothing," I say, leaning forward to breathe on a particularly stubborn fingerprint. "Why do you ask?"

"You told Nina you liked her earrings. You never compliment Nina. You say she's Hitler with hair extensions. Plus, you're skipping around with that cloth like Mary Poppins at Disneyland." She pauses, narrowing her eyes. "You got laid, didn't you?"

I lightly flick the duster toward her. "Yes," I say loudly enough to draw a look of disapproval from Nina on the other side of the shop. "A whole bunch of times."

Ciara looks disgruntled. I've noticed people in sexless relationships don't take kindly to news of others' bedroom shenanigans. They prefer to think of single people as odd types who play with train sets in their attics.

"Are you seeing him again?" she asks a shade aggressively.

"Tonight," I say and, unable to refrain from gloating, "He's cooking me dinner."

She purses her lips. "I'm sure he has more than dinner on his mind."

I grin so manically, my face strains from the pressure. "Let's hope so."

Logan's bedroom technique was a gratifying surprise to say the least. Though the chemistry between us always promised an explosive encounter, I did wonder if he'd turn out to be one of those good-looking, selfish-in-bed types. How wrong I was. As well as a generous lover, he was tender, thoughtful. Sex in the past has sometimes made me feel lonely, the means to someone else's end, but with Logan, it was as if our bodies thrummed to the same tune. He was *aware* of me in a way I've never experienced before.

Ciara pulls a face. "Enjoy it while it lasts," she says in a tight voice. "The hot ones are notoriously difficult to keep on the porch."

Ugh. First Vera and her starting-pistol metaphor and now this. "As long as he stays long enough to give me a decent go on the swing, I'm not bothered," I snap, turning my back on her. To think, I had to congratulate *her* on tying herself for life to Mr. No Sex. Is it too much to ask for a simple high five of congratulations?

At lunchtime, I'm pleased when I find out it's my turn to pick up the sandwiches. I take my time, ambling slowly through the cobbled streets of Covent Garden, past the theaters and market stalls, a whiff of roasted horse chestnuts permeating the stale city air. Even before I landed my job at the jewelers, I always loved it here. On good days, when there are fewer people, I can imagine London as it used to be, before cars and Starbucks and pricey boutiques, all sandstone arches and timber-framed inns.

I pick my way carefully through the dawdling shoppers, zipping up my thick, padded coat. Though the sun is
out for once, the chilly air prickles my skin like needles.
Still, it's good to feel sunlight on my face. I can't imagine
how it must have been for Logan in the beginning—shut
away from daylight for all those months on his own.

I'm so absorbed in Logan-related thoughts I almost
don't notice the stocky, bald man in a black bomber
jacket walking beside me. Feeling his eyes on my face
and suspecting he's a pickpocket of some kind, I speed
up, but he keeps pace, bobbing along six inches or so
behind me like an irritating wasp. I walk straight ahead
as fast as I can without breaking into a run and, at the
last second, duck into the golden warmth of the supermarket, hoping to give him the slip. Grabbing a basket,
I head straight to the sandwiches.

I'm reaching for Nina's hoisin duck wrap when a
voice at my shoulder says, "Jenna Gold?"

I whirl around to find stocky pickpocket man from
the street standing behind me. Face-to-face, I recognize
him instantly. Rounded cheeks, wide, car-salesman-
esque grin—it's Sergeant Davies in casual clothes.

My eyes dart sideways, wondering if Burke is going
to pop out too. "I thought you were a thief."

Davies shakes his head, clutching his side. "I'm
undercover. Blimey, girl, you walk fast. I've given
myself a stitch."

"You could have made yourself known," I say, dropping the wrap into my basket.

He glances around before gently steering me toward
a stand of greetings cards at the back of the store. "We

have to be discreet. Probably should have warned you our meetings will be like this."

"Our meetings?"

Davies leans in, speaking like a ventriloquist, from a corner of his mouth. "We noticed through your V-Date account, *Miss Gold*, that you went on a date Sunday evening with a vampire named Marek. I'm here to collect the information."

"Just like that?" I ask. "In Tesco's?"

He nods. "One of our many mottos at the Met Police is 'trust no one.'"

"Intriguing," I mutter sarcastically. I tuck hair behind my ear, breaking his eager-eyed gaze. "The thing is, I didn't really find out much."

"No?"

"Well…" I fidget with the basket, hooking it over an arm, frantically trying to separate my sources of information. "They can only die by decapitation."

Davies's eyes narrow. "What else?"

I suck in a breath, all set to ask them to remove me from the investigation, but then I remember why I was asked in the first place—Mum—and my mouth clamps shut again. At last, I say, "They are susceptible to daylight, holy water, and crucifixes in the first few months of their transition."

His eyes widen and he nods, urging me to continue.

"They can't move fast in daylight. It weakens them." *Shit, that was one of Logan's*.

"Anything else?"

I shake my head, stomach clenching with nausea, feeling like a traitor.

"Well, we look forward to your next date, *Miss Gold*." He smiles, pointing at the sandwiches. "The chicken Caesar salad is excellent on whole wheat."

I barely hear him. I'm filled with self-loathing as I watch his stocky shape retreat down the aisle toward the automatic doors. Logan may be cocksure, but he doesn't deserve me spilling his secrets. I remember the way he looked that night on the ship—lost and vulnerable, green eyes filled with sadness. There was something about the way he spoke, a rawness, which made me certain he didn't usually talk about his past. I sigh, my good mood obliterated by guilt, as I angrily throw the rest of our sandwiches into the basket.

<center>~~~</center>

Hours later, when I arrive home, I notice a thin halo of light around the edge of the front door. I push my key into the lock, assuming it's Vera. Often when she's feeling lonely, she lets herself into the flat and curls up on the sofa. It's one of the many Vera-related reasons my rent is so cheap. I grit my teeth and push open the door, wondering how I'll manage to get rid of her before Logan arrives.

I hear his voice through a haze of steam. "Don't freak out, Silver. Etta let me in."

Logan is standing in my kitchenette, holding a wooden spoon over a bubbling saucepan. He wears a white T-shirt that clings to his muscles and a pair of tight blue jeans. His dark hair is all over the place, messy strands curling over the tips of his ears. If it wasn't for the Kiss the Chef apron tied around his middle, he could have dropped straight out of a rock video.

I fling my bag onto the sofa and slam the door behind me. "Breaking and entering now as well as stalking?" I ask, folding my arms.

His eyes crinkle around the edges as he chuckles, dimples showing. "Etta found me sitting outside with shopping bags and took pity on me. She loaned me a casserole dish."

I eyeball his outfit, flicking a finger at the garish red-and-black apron. "That isn't mine."

Logan pulls at the material. "Etta thought it would make you laugh."

Rather than laugh or shout, I'm suddenly possessed by the all-consuming urge to indeed *kiss the chef*. I cut the short distance between us and fling myself into his arms, crashing my lips to his warm mouth. The wooden spoon clatters back into the saucepan as he lifts me into him, sliding his tongue over mine and knotting his hands roughly into my hair. He tastes of whatever it is we're having for dinner—something with spices and black pepper—and crisp night air. As he carries me backward to the kitchen counter, I run hands over his tensed biceps, savoring tight muscles beneath silky skin. Though we are still kissing, he seems to be trying to mumble something into my mouth. I pull back, out of breath.

"I missed you," he says, eyes as calm as a flat, green sea.

My own eyes widen to the size of moon craters, guilt nibbling the edges of my conscience. I open my mouth, wanting to say it too—because I have missed him, really, truly—but instead of speaking, I kiss him again, stroking his stubbly jaw with my fingers.

When we finally break apart, he lets me slide through his arms to the floor, leaning down to kiss the top of my head. "Is this how you usually greet your burglars?"

Smiling, I step back to unzip my coat. "Always. I find it helps with rehabilitation."

But he doesn't hear me. His gaze is glued to my body as I shrug out of my jacket.

"Oh sweet Jesus, it's the work uniform," he mumbles, biting at his lower lip.

I toss the coat with dramatic flair onto a high stool, placing a hand on my hip. "What about my work uniform?" I ask, sticking my chest out.

His jaw is slack, his gaze running the length of my body like a soft caress. "It gives me impure thoughts," he murmurs, leaning against the opposite counter. "And I have to turn the meatballs in five minutes."

I snicker. "What about *your* meatballs? Don't they get any attention?"

He folds his arms and smiles, a dimple appearing, looking up at me through thick dark lashes. "*Those* meatballs will have to wait."

Holding his gaze, I move my hand to the top button on my white blouse. "That's a shame. I was going to ask for help getting changed." I pop open the button. "This shirt is beginning to feel...*tight*."

"Are you goading me, Silver?" he asks, staring at my fingers as they linger on another button. "Because I'll have you know, I've a ton of willpower at my disposal."

"Really?" I say, brow furrowed. "Willpower."

He nods, jaw clenched. "Go on, undo another. In fact, rip the whole thing off. When it comes to cooking, I

let nothing come between myself and the culinary arts."
Eyes fixed on my face, he reaches over the pan and
begins stirring one-handed.

As I slowly twist open the button over my bra, he
flinches, the bulge at the front of his jeans swelling with
arousal. "You like to tease, don't you?" he asks, his
voice deep and throaty.

"I'm not teasing," I say, although that's exactly what
I'm doing. Up until now, I've had no intention of actually taking my clothes off. But watching his eyelids
grow heavy with lust, knowing what's waiting for me
the other side of that denim-clad crotch, it's suddenly
all I can think about. I begin to feel an ache deep in my
groin, my nipples hard as pellets beneath my lace bra. I
continue on to the next button, and then the next, until
the front of my shirt flaps open. Now I've come this far,
I figure I might as well go all the way. I shrug the material from my shoulders, noticing how his hand stills on
the wooden spoon, and fling it in his face, watching as it
tumbles to a heap on the floor.

Just then, the little pig-shaped timer next to the
cooker rings. "Your balls need turning," I say, smirking.

For a split second, I think my vision is blurring. The
oven door opens and closes ridiculously fast and in the
blink of an eye, he is gone from the kitchen. A breeze
stirs the air. I spin around on the spot. The lounge is
empty, but in my bedroom doorway, lying abandoned
in a heap, are his jeans and T-shirt.

I dash around the counter to my room, hitting the
light switch on the way in, to find him sitting up in bed,
my cream floral duvet pulled up to his neck.

"What about dinner?" I ask, enjoying the way he looks in my bed, dark-brown hair splayed against the pillows, green eyes smoldering with desire.

"I turned them," he says, pulling back the duvet.

I laugh, clapping a hand to my mouth at the sight of the tacky Kiss the Chef apron covering his otherwise naked body. "You're going to have to wash that thing before you give it back to Vera."

He twitches a smile, cupping his groin. "It's already a bit *sticky*."

"If you weren't so hot, you'd be gross, do you know that? No woman would ever want to sleep with you."

"Good looks are a blessing as well as a curse." Fixing his eyes on my bra, he pats the space next to him. "Are you coming in? Or do I have to drag you?"

Needing no further encouragement, I dive onto the bed, and he loops an arm around my middle, drawing me into the hard, satiny contours of his body. We lie for a while without moving, gazing silently into each other's eyes.

Reaching up, he brushes a strand of hair from my face, delicately, as if I'm made of glass. "Silver," he breathes, trailing the backs of his fingers softly down my arm. "Why is this all I can think about?"

I gulp, heart hammering as I push aside the scratchy apron and place a hand over his heart. "Logan," I whisper, my breathing labored, as if all the oxygen has been sucked from the room. "I think I like you."

His eyes widen, golden flecks flickering like dapples on a river. "I think I like you too."

There is silence for a few moments, and then I say, "This all just got very after-school special."

He laughs, pulling the apron over his head and tossing it aside. "They don't screw each other's brains out in after-school specials, and correct me if I'm wrong, but that's exactly what we're about to do."

I poke him playfully. "Being naked in a woman's bed doesn't guarantee she wants to sleep with you."

"What is a guarantee?" he asks, eyes burning.

"This," I murmur, capturing his half-open mouth in mine and melting like wax in a flame around him.

Groaning, he holds me tight until we're pressed together from our knees to our chests. I drown in his warm scent—aftershave mixed with bodywash—running my hands over his strong back before dipping between our bodies to caress the silky erection prodding my stomach.

He emits a soft growl deep in his throat. "Silver," he whispers as I stroke the sides of his pulsating hard-on. "You're ruining me."

All of a sudden, I'm aware of being half-dressed. I feel too covered, too restricted. I let go, fighting to find the zipper on the back of my skirt. His hands brush mine aside as he yanks it down, sliding the black material off my hips.

"Oh shit," he says, hands on my thighs, fingers burning me like fire as they rub circles into my skin. "Did they have to be stockings?"

I grin. "Sometimes I wear them instead of tights."

He toys with the black lace at the top, fingers skimming dangerously close to the pulsing, wet spot between my legs. A shiver tingles up my spine. "I'll never have a moment's peace again, knowing you're out in the world wearing these."

"Good," I say. "Now take them off with your fangs."

His eyes flash and he flips me onto my back. For a moment, he remains suspended above me—hair in his face, erection quivering, muscles tensed like a Greek god in a painting. I'm struck by the realization that life will probably never get any better. I mean, how could it?

"You're a very demanding woman, Silver Harris," he teases, the tips of his fangs visible at the corners of his lips.

I smile lazily, hooking a foot around the warm skin of his hip. "Just do it."

Arching a brow, he ducks between my legs, the delicious sensation of his stubble grazing my thighs, making me tremble all over. I inhale sharply, barely remembering to breathe as I feel the rasp of fangs, rough against my skin. When he arches backward into a sitting position, there is a black strip of nylon between his teeth.

"You've done this before, haven't you?" I ask suspiciously, resisting the overwhelming urge to reach up and force his head down again.

"Never on a second date," he says, removing the stocking from his mouth and coiling it between his hands like a magician's silk. "Now, put your hands above your head."

My jaw drops, a thrill zipping through me like an electrical current. "Am I under arrest?"

He chuckles, low and throaty. "Yes. House arrest. Or don't you want to be tied up and fucked?"

Part of me wants to tell him where he can shove his light bondage—I've never understood the fascination with all that *yes, master, no, master* business. The other ninety-nine percent of me, including the part which controls the erogenous zones, can't think of anything better. It feels like my loins are having a Christmas party and all my nerve endings are invited. I nod mutely, my hands smacking together like magnets. He smiles, holding my wrists in one hand and gently wrapping the stocking around them with the other.

"You could have warned me you're a kinky bastard," I say.

His smile widens. "Shh, or who knows where the other one might end up."

We snicker like naughty children as he lifts my hands over my head, knotting the loose ends of the stockings around the rails. I say a silent prayer of thanks I chose this bed and not the leather one without slats.

Leaning over me, bare thighs straddling mine, I realize for the first time that I am completely and utterly at his mercy—and not because of the restraints. He stares at me, eyes blazing, and I wonder if he's thinking the same thing, if he feels as out of control as I do.

"You're not going to spank me, are you?" I whisper.

Chuckling, he kisses me softly on the mouth. "Only if you're really bad."

Why does that sound so appealing? "Put your hands on me," I say in a deep voice I barely recognize.

He places a kiss just below my jawline. "All tied up and still bossing me around."

I writhe about, attempting to rub my aching core against him, until finally, he runs a flat palm over my breasts and down between my legs.

"You're soaking wet," he says against my neck.

But I barely hear him. I've already checked into Hotel Pleasureville as I close my eyes, surrendering to the delicious sensation of his fingers pushing aside my panties, dipping inside my wet folds.

"Yes," I hiss, grinding into his hand as the pad of his thumb circles my nub. "Keep going."

But then he stops, a draft of icy air swirling between my legs as he pulls away. I open my eyes, wondering what the hell he's playing at. Leaning back on his haunches, he slides my lacy knickers off, pausing to rub them on his stiffness before flinging them aside. Then he grasps my ankles and hooks my legs over his shoulders.

"I've decided to go deep," he says, his voice like barbed wire wrapped in silk.

I can only nod as he pushes the tip of his erection around my drenched opening, moving it along my slit in a torturously slow rhythm.

A wave of ecstasy coils in the pit of my stomach, my legs trembling on his broad, muscular shoulders.

"Silver," he pants, dragging his nails along my remaining stocking and raining hot kisses over my thighs.

"Logan, please."

No sooner have I made my plea than he plunges into me. I gasp, the angle of our bodies taking him deeper than he's ever been. Our eyes are locked as he circles his hips, sliding in and out again and again. I arch off the bed, desperate to be filled by him.

On one of his thrusts, he reaches forward, pulling the flimsy ties from my wrists, and I waste no time tangling my hands into his silky hair. "Harder," I urge, watching a flash of lust light up his green eyes as I utter the word.

Pinpricks of hot pleasure rip through my body, my breath coming in labored spurts. But even as I sense release building to a raging inferno within me, I know I will never get enough of this man.

"Oh God yes!" I cry, feeling the snag of his fangs against my inner thigh.

"Silver," he cries, pumping faster, the friction of his teeth on my skin increasing with every push. Right before I explode, he bites me—sweet, exotic pain mingling with blissful waves of euphoria as crimson rivulets zigzag down my pale leg. I scream loudly, hips bucking from the bed. This time, I don't lose consciousness, the sunset colors swirling behind my closed lids like a kaleidoscope. Another rush of pleasure follows as Logan spasms hotly inside me.

I open my eyes.

Panting, Logan gently lays my legs down, placing a hand on my heaving chest. He sweeps his tongue across the spot where he bit me, leaving the skin smooth and unblemished. Flopping down on top of me, he buries his face in my hair.

"That was—" he starts.

"Incredible," I finish, a trickle of sweat sliding between my breasts.

Logan lifts his head and rolls onto his side, following it with his finger before sliding a hand inside my bra and beading a nipple between his thumb and forefinger. "How is your bra still on?"

I laugh, moaning as he increases the pressure on my aching tip. "One stocking too."

He reaches around me, releasing the clasp of my bra and dragging the straps over my arms.

"Logan?" I say, shaking off the lacy material.

"Yes?"

"What is that when you bite me? The colors and semiconsciousness? Is it some kind of venom?"

"Not venom," he says, stroking around the delicate skin of my breasts. "It's more of a vision, an exchange."

I turn to the side, propping myself up on an elbow to allow him better access. "An exchange?"

"I don't know the official explanation, but I believe when a vampire bites a human, an exchange takes place. We have your blood and you get a glimpse of our life essence. There's always a balance in life, give and take."

"Your life essence?" I repeat.

"Our life essence comes from our soul—the one moment, or memory, that makes us who we truly are."

"And yours is a load of nice colors?"

He nods, flashing a cocky grin. "So the ladies tell me."

"When Nathaniel bit me, I saw an Italian peasant woman."

Frowning, his hand briefly stills on my breast, and a twisted thrill passes through me that he's jealous. "That, at a guess, would be a woman he truly loved. She's probably long dead by now."

I meet his steady gaze, thankful to the stars there's no other woman polluting his life essence. "Will you stay the night?" I ask suddenly, the words spilling from my mouth before I've even thought of them.

He smiles, looking happier than I've ever seen him. "I have no intention of going anywhere."

Chapter 13

Logan

FOR THE NEXT WEEK, WHEN I'M NOT WORKING MY SHIFTS at the club, I spend every night with Silver. Each morning, after we've made love and dressed, I walk her to her job in Covent Garden, where we linger outside the shop like teenagers, kissing and making plans for the evening. On her day off, we don't even bother to leave the flat.

For the first time since turning, I forget what I am. I feel like any ordinary twenty-five-year-old fella who's met a woman he's completely and utterly besotted with. Ronin McDermott and the dark dealings of the vampire world fade into the back of my consciousness like a bad dream.

By Thursday, I'm starting to think Silver and I need a frank discussion about how things stand between us. I want to make it clear, without scaring her off, she's the only woman I intend to date for the foreseeable future. As terrifying as it is for someone who has never trusted another with their heart, I need her to know I am completely and utterly hers.

Trailing through the old market square of Covent Garden, I decide I'll bring it up tonight before sex. That way, she can't blame the conversation on pheromones.

"Are you even listening?" she asks, breaking into my thoughts.

I glance down at her bright-eyed pixie face and shake my head, resting a palm lightly on the small of her back.

"I said Ollie is coming over tonight, just to see if I'm still alive after not hearing from me all week."

Ollie. The friend-zoned lad. "Shall I not pick you up, then?" I ask, a strain of disappointment creeping into my voice.

She averts her gray eyes, looking at a trader as he hauls a metal rack of cheap-looking key rings across the cobbles. "I thought maybe you'd want to meet him," she mumbles, barely moving her lips.

I lean down to hear her better, my hair brushing hers. "Say it again."

She stops dead in her tracks and looks up at me—shorter in her flat work shoes than the heels she sometimes wears. "It's no big deal, but if you're there and he's there, then you might as well meet. It's no big deal," she says again.

"Is this the Silver Harris equivalent of meeting the parents?" I tease, unable to help myself. There is nothing sexier than seeing her all cross and flustered.

Her cheeks flush a shade pinker, and I feel a familiar twitch of arousal in my jeans. "No. Because he's coming around anyway, and—" She breaks off to take a playful swipe at my shoulder. "Look, will you still come or not?"

I grin. "I'll be there."

She smiles, and I feel a sharp twinge in my long-dead heart. Not for the first time, it hits me how crazy I am about her. I look up and see we're almost at the shiny glass door of the shop.

"Pick you up at six?" I ask, stepping closer and locking my arms around her waist.

"Yes," she says, lifting her face so I can kiss her good-bye.

We stand for a while, mouths pressed together, eyes closed. The taste of her lips, the feel of her warm body against mine is as close to heaven as I'm ever likely to get.

"I'll pick up pizza," I say, releasing her and walking backward.

She pushes the door open. "Okay. Remember the garlic bread—you know, if it doesn't kill you."

I lay a hand on my chest. "Still hilarious even at eight in the morning."

Smirking, she mouths, *I know*.

I wait until the door swings closed behind her before strolling back through the covered market and out into the open.

Like the other mornings, I walk home, a confident swagger in my step. The sun hangs low in the crisp, blue sky, drilling bright rays through gaps in the buildings. A sparkling frost glitters on the pavement, white and pure against the backdrop of exhaust fumes. Though it's still early morning, London overflows with life.

Back in Marylebone, an endless stream of commuters hurry in and out of the redbrick railway station. The air smells like ground coffee and smoke, the hiss and rush of trains mingling with sirens and car horns on the street. Usually, I'm not keen on rush hour, but today all feels right with the world.

Outside my building, I am about to open the door

when I see the latch is broken. I frown, pushing against it, noticing a round hole in the wood where the lock is missing. For the life of me, I can't remember if it was like that yesterday. I've been in such a lust-induced stupor all week, it could well have been busted for days. Inside the faded hall, I scan the walls for any maintenance notices before dashing upstairs.

Halfway up, I freeze, a familiar scent hitting me—the coppery smell of blood mingled with lilies. I shake myself, continuing up the narrow stairwell, fists clenching at my sides. Some bizarre region of my psyche must be trying to pollute my happiness, remind me of past misery. When I reach the top and notice the door to my flat is open an inch, a dreadful, icy chill creeps up my spine as Ronin's words come tumbling back: *Anastasia is back in town… She has been seen.*

No. No. No.

I push open the door and stand on the threshold. Nothing is out of place. It all looks exactly as I left it yesterday afternoon—coffee cups on the drainer, a few discarded clothes on the couch, curtains closed. But the scent from the stairs is stronger than ever, the whiff of blood, both dried and fresh, as pungent and vivid as murder itself.

If my heart still beat, it would be leaping out of my chest. I follow the metallic smell to my bedroom, wincing as I place a flat palm against the wood.

The sound of her honeyed voice seizes me like a hand around the throat. "Hello, Logan."

Anastasia sits in the chair beside the window, long legs crossed at the knee. Having not seen her for so many years, I'm struck by how different she looks in modern clothing—how normal. She wears spiky, high-heeled boots with an expensive-looking cream trouser suit, her loose hair, as black as onyx, cascading over her shoulders. Like I told Silver that night on the prison hulk, her beauty is a thing of stone—a mirage of perfect features set around cold, empty eyes.

"Anastasia," I say, trying to make it sound as though her appearing in my bedroom is the most normal thing in the world. "What are you doing here?"

She unravels her legs like a spider and pushes up from the chair, holding her arms out toward me. "What?" she asks, voice oozing nastiness. "No hug for your old foster mommy?"

I ignore her outstretched arms by shrugging out of my denim jacket and tossing it onto the bed. "What do you want?" I ask, forcing myself to meet her piercing, red-brown eyes.

Her arms drop to her sides. She steps toward the chest of drawers in the corner, running a red-painted finger along the edge of the wood. "Why should I have to want anything?"

Anger rises like bile within me, replacing my fear. "I've nothing to do with you anymore, remember? Ronin and I blood-bonded over a century ago. He'll not be happy you're back in London."

She whips her head around and laughs, an unhinged crone's cackle. You can tell a lot about a person from their laugh. "Do you really think I'm worried about Ronin McDermott? Tell me, is he still shoving his dick into any female that moves?"

I ignore the question. "What do you want, Anastasia?" I ask again.

"The name's actually Maria Bryant now," she says, grabbing a book and turning it over with long, bony fingers. "I'm a wealthy widow from Bulgaria, the patron of several large orphanages across Africa. Isn't that hilarious, Logan? Me in the same sentence as children. It's amazing how blind money makes people."

Unable to prevent it, a shudder rips through me. She drops the book and fixes me with an evil glare, a slow smile unfurling from one corner of her wide mouth. "There's something different about you, Logan. I can't quite put my finger on it. Maybe it has something to do with that female scent you're drenched in." Her smile widens as she strolls toward me, and I try not to flinch as she leans in, the stench of new and old blood crawling up my nostrils like lice. "Not the only time you've been with her, is it?" she asks, a look of triumph flashing in her eyes.

"You're wrong," I growl. "Yes, I've been with a woman. What healthy, red-blooded vampire doesn't enjoy a night of meaningless sex?"

Her eyes narrow. "You're in love." The words are like a weapon, deadly as a mace. She emits a short, wispy sigh. "I'm guessing she's human. I blame that Stephenie Meyer woman for all these ridiculous human-vampire love stories that are playing out all over the world."

"You're wrong," I repeat, the words sticking in my throat.

"No," she gloats. "I'm not. You've always been a terrible liar." She pouts, pulling a sad face. "Poor Logan, the honest gypsy boy forever in the wrong place at the wrong time. Always the victim. To think, I once believed I could change you into something better."

"You wanted to change me into a murderer," I hiss, rage simmering, "like all those other sadistic puppets you turned."

"Of course," she continues, as if she didn't hear me. "I should have ended your pathetic life when I found out the truth about your wrongful imprisonment. But then I discovered your gift." She pauses, eyes flashing. "I'll never forget your desperation that night down in the cellar, trying to save the man who betrayed you. A regular Pollyanna, aren't you?"

"It's called decency," I sneer, "and forgiveness. You wouldn't know the first thing about either."

She turns on her heel, crossing back to the window and looking down onto the street. "I don't recall you being all that decent when you fed on the blood of whores night after night."

"I never killed anyone," I whisper, balling fists at my sides. "I wasn't in my right mind back then, but I never took a life."

"Save it for the pearly gates, Logan," she mutters. "If they'll have you." Turning to face me, she smiles, her lips a perfect, red crescent. "I do hope you and your little human will be very happy together. Does Ronin know you've found love?"

I clench my fists tighter. "There is no love, Anastasia. It's all in your head."

Her eyes widen. "Oh, he doesn't know. Is that why you're so afraid? I mean, it's not like *I* could ever harm her, or you for that matter. We ancients have our code of conduct to abide by—*thou shalt not harm another's servant* or something like that. I get them muddled with the Ten Commandments at times. I hope you realize though, if you ever *upset* Ronin, if you betray him, you lose that protection. If he doesn't kill you himself, you become fair game to the rest of us—fair game to *me*."

There is a roaring in my ears. In my mind's eye, I see Silver as I left her this morning, rosebud mouth upturned to meet mine, her smile as she made her joke about garlic bread. Already, she feels far away, out of reach. "Get out," I growl, throwing the bedroom door wide open. "Don't ever come to my apartment again."

She stands with a knowing smirk on her crimson lips. "As long as we understand each other. I would ask you to pass on my regards to Ronin, but I'm sure I'll see him myself before long."

I blanch at her thinly veiled warning, remembering his words right after I assured him he could trust me—*I wouldn't want to be in your shoes if I can't.*

An image of the first time I met Ronin flashes into my mind—a raucous bar in Dublin, chatter, smoke, and the clink of tankards swirling in the stale air. I sat in a shadowy corner, weighted down by the unconscious woman in my lap, a barmaid, the inside of her collar scarlet with blood. Unbeknownst to me, Ronin had been there, watching as I knitted up the ragged gash in her neck with my tongue. That chance encounter was the beginning of the end to my darkest days.

Anastasia breezes past, the scent of dried blood cutting through the air like a knife's blade, her eyes dark and gloating. I watch her blur toward the front door where she stops, turning to face me. "Good-bye for now, Logan."

In a sudden fit of rage, I grab a knife from the block on the kitchen counter and hurl it at her smug face. The door slams, the knife neatly embedded in the wood. A bloodcurdling laugh drifts up from the stairs below as the door to the building bangs shut behind her.

Head in hands, I slide down the doorpost and onto the floor in a heap. How could I be so stupid? Ancients can read body language like an open book. I should have kept a better check on myself. Now she'll go squealing to Ronin, and he'll find out I've been seeing the same woman he sent me to glamour—the girl who was supposed to be disgusted by all vampires by now, not screwing one night after night. Not very possibly even falling in love.

I could come clean to Ronin, beg for a reprieve. But at best, he would force me to glamour Silver. Either that or he'd have another vampire do it instead. The worst-case scenario is he kills me and glamours her anyway. I can't allow either to happen.

I take out my phone and pull up her number, staring transfixed at the screen. I'm sorely tempted to call her right now and tell her everything. But even if she forgives me and wants to be with me, what then? It won't be long before Ronin finds out, either through Anastasia or one of her cronies. I'd be dragging her into a world of danger and lies. Besides, gut instinct tells me she would never speak to me again if she found out about Ronin, the club, and the grand plan she was a part of.

The only other alternative is to lie low and hope Anastasia leaves London. My chest tightens. Just the thought of not seeing Silver tonight is enough to fling me headfirst into a pit of despair, but the notion I'd have to leave her alone for weeks or months on end is inconceivable. Yet it's my only hope if I am to both keep her safe *and* have a chance at a future with her.

Taking a deep breath, I tap out a text with trembling fingers, every character a needle in my heart. By the time I hit Send, I can no longer make out the words. They are fragmented and blurry, hot tears distorting them into a black mess.

Can't make tonight.

Why did I think for one second this could ever last? I get off the floor and cross to the window, where golden sunlight pools into the room. After pulling the curtains closed, I slide down the wall and sink into the shadows, melting into the darkness, where I belong.

Chapter 14

Silver

I'M SURPRISED BUT NOT OVERLY CONCERNED WHEN I see Logan's text about not being able to meet. We have been spending crazy amounts of time together lately. Maybe he has to do his laundry or something.

When Ollie comes over that evening, I tell him all about Logan—though obviously not the sex part. That's just tacky. I'll save all that for Vera.

"Are you mental?" he asks, looking at me as though I've just announced I'm seeing a serial killer. "You're dating a vampire?"

"What's with the face?" I say, mimicking his scrunched-up expression. "Vampires are people too, you know. When did you become such a *vampist*?"

"A *vampist*? Is that a thing?"

"It's going to be if we let narrow-minded types like you loose in the universe." I push my plate of ramen noodles away from me. Usually I enjoy nothing more than Chinese chicken flavor, but since having regular exposure to home-cooked meals, I realize they actually taste a lot like plastic worms.

Ollie twists his fork around the plate like he's eating spaghetti. "What about the future? You'll age and he'll still be young. Have you thought about that?"

My shoulders slump. He's Ciara all over again. "It's

called living for the moment, Ollie. Just because you and Krista have baby names all picked out doesn't mean the rest of us have to follow suit."

He breaks my gaze, muttering something unintelligible under his breath and jabbing his fork into his noodles.

"What was that?"

"We broke up. You were right about us. She was trying to change me into something I'm not." He sighs, shoveling food into his mouth.

I reach across to lay a hand on his. "Ollie, I'm sorry," I say with genuine sympathy—though obviously I'm relieved I'll never have to make conversation with the stuck-up bitch again.

A smile plays at the corner of his mouth. "Nah, you're not. I know you hated her."

"Hate is a strong word. But yeah, pretty much detested her from the word go."

We both chuckle.

"You know what really ended it for me?" he says, staring off wistfully into space.

"The way she still referred to her parents as *Mummy* and *Daddy*?" I ask, brows raised.

His grin widens. "No. Though, yeah, that was annoying, now you mention it. But no, it was the other weekend when I took her to Brighton. I wanted to go to the amusement park on the pier, and she kept saying there was no point because we don't have kids. And then when I eventually got her there, she wouldn't ride the ghost train. Not because she was scared—that would have been cute—but because she thought it was childish."

"Evil bitch," I cut in.

"I can't spend my life with someone who won't ride the ghost train."

"A life without ghost trains is no life at all," I agree.

"But seriously. There's no point if you can't have fun with the person you're with, is there?"

"No." I think of Logan and our zany conversations, that time he stuck his head out the cab window and yelled at a bunch of tourists. I unsuccessfully try to smother a goofy grin.

When my eyes flicker back to Ollie, he's deep in thought and looking at me, head tilted to one side. "You're happy, aren't you, Silv?" he asks, brow furrowed.

My heart clenches. "Aren't I always?"

His frown deepens as he shakes his head slowly. "I mean, you're never miserable or anything—a little spiky at times maybe. I don't know, you seem *softer*."

"That'll be the sex," I say, instantly regretting it as he squirms uncomfortably on his seat. I'm not sure how it works with other boy/girl best friends, but Ollie and I don't really do below-the-waist talk.

"If he makes you happy," Ollie continues, ignoring my comment, "then I'm happy."

I look across the table at his freckled face, red bangs falling in his blue eyes, the tiny chip on his front tooth he got from riding his BMX down a slide at the park. For some odd reason, tears prick the corners of my eyes. "He does make me happy, Ollie. I mean, sometimes I want to kill him, but—" I break off, shrugging. "I really like him," I say simply.

He puts his fork down. "You were never going to fall for someone normal, were you?" he says, not unkindly.

I shake my head and smile. "Where's the fun in that?"

—∿∿—

Later on, after Ollie leaves, I text Logan to say good night—he doesn't reply.

All night, sleep comes in fits and starts. At one point, I dream someone is knocking on the front door and I wake up, in a tangle of sheets, straining my ears in hope that it's Logan, and checking my phone for the thousandth time since sending the text. Nothing.

By the time I get to work the next morning, I feel as if I haven't slept for a month. I spent the whole bus journey with my phone in my fist, staring at the screen. I've become the girl I never wanted to be.

"No good-bye kiss at the door this morning?" Ciara asks as I tear off my coat in the cluttered staff room.

"Nope," I say bluntly, avoiding her eye.

She frowns. "Did you guys fight or something?"

"Nope," I say again. The last thing I need is another lecture from her *boring men are the best* repertoire of relationship advice.

"Maybe it fizzled out," she says.

I have to mentally count to ten to keep from hitting her in the face with my handbag.

At around ten, I decide if I don't hear by this evening, I'll call him. It's enough to see me through the rest of the day without strangling Ciara and her pitying looks with a vintage pearl choker.

I turn onto my street later on, heart pounding in my chest, half believing I'm going to find Logan outside my flat. Even when I reach the steps and find them empty, hope infuses me with an image of him standing in the kitchen, cooking. It's so powerful I can practically see him smiling, hear him make a lewd comment about my work uniform as I take off my coat.

But the flat is as dark and empty as I left it this morning.

I flick the light on and slam the door shut behind me, rifling through my bag for my phone as if my life depends on it. Tissues, bus tickets, and hair ties fall to the carpet like ticker tape. My heart pounds in my chest so loudly it almost drowns out the dial tone. After about five rings, it connects to the network voice mail. I hang up without leaving a message.

What the hell is his problem? He didn't seem any different yesterday morning. It began like all the others—waking up wrapped in his arms, a thick hard-on pressed into my back. We'd made love, showered, made out for so long the toast burned, and then left in a cozy bubble of hazy, postcoital happiness.

I'm no stranger to breakups. I've been breaking up with men since I was fifteen years old. A girl gets good at reading the signs—distant behavior, little or no eye contact, and the general sixth sense they're about to run for the hills. There was none of that with Logan. If anything, he was too keen. He'd promised pizza, for heaven's sake. The only reason I can think of is that the idea of officially meeting Ollie scared him off.

Not fancying an evening of phone watching, I grab my keys and stomp upstairs to Vera's. Even an *I told you so* is preferable to a cold, lonely flat.

When she opens the door, I have to bite my lip to

keep from bursting into tears on her doorstep. What is happening to me? Next thing I'll be eating ice cream straight from the carton and watching *Beaches*.

"Silver?" Vera says in a voice so laden with sympathy that a rogue tear squeezes out of my eye and escapes down my cheek. "Has someone died?"

I let out a throaty laugh that sounds disturbingly sob-like. "Not yet. But never say never."

She steps onto the doorstep in her slinky black robe and drapes a thin, birdlike arm around my shoulders, drawing me into the house. "If it's not death, it's man trouble," she says, ushering me past the front room and into her cozy, retro furnished den further up the hallway. "Let me guess—the hottie vampire?"

Nodding, I drop into a squishy, red armchair. "Why are men assholes, Vera?"

Vera crosses to the fifties minibar shaped like a ship's stern and picks up a half-full bottle of gin. "Some say it's inherent. Personally, I think it's because they know they can get away with it."

I look up, watching as she scoops ice into a tumbler with tongs shaped like pineapples. "But it doesn't make any sense. Yesterday he was all over me, and today he's ignoring my calls."

"Men are like stray dogs. If there's a better cut of meat on offer elsewhere, they're off faster than a greyhound from a trap." She skillfully pours gin into the glass without taking her dark, hooded eyes from my face. "I don't want to have to say it, darling, but I warned you about going to bed with him too soon."

I take the drink from her liver-spotted hand and sigh.

JULIET LYONS

"I know you did. But this didn't feel like *just* sex. I've never had someone look at me the way he did. He made me feel adored." I take a swig of the drink, enjoying the tingly warmth as it slides down my throat and remembering the way he murmured my name during the heat of climax, the kisses that felt like love.

"I'm sure he adored you at the time. But in the cold light of reality, it's a different story."

"Bastard," I mutter, swigging more of my gin. Deep down though, I don't believe it. There was never the slightest doubt we were anything other than two people growing more and more crazy about each other. Surely he wasn't that good an actor.

When Stan arrives half an hour later, I plod miserably back downstairs. My phone is still where I left it on the sofa. I pick it up, hope filling me like helium in a balloon, praying I'll find a message. There's nothing. Flopping down against the cushions, I ignore my growling stomach and comb through my memory of yesterday morning for any look or strange comment I might have missed.

In what has become my knee-jerk reaction to any form of rejection, I wind up thinking about Mum. A psychologist would say it's because I never properly dealt with the trauma of her disappearance when I was a kid. Who knows? Maybe I didn't. But it wasn't like we didn't try. Dad didn't go into a depression or drink himself unconscious—he was there for me. We dealt with it together. The only part I still can't deal with is the not knowing. It's like trying to heal a wound you can't quite reach or solve a puzzle with half the pieces missing.

For a couple of years, I tried convincing myself she wasn't dead. I pretended she'd run away with a rich millionaire and was living out on the ocean in a yacht somewhere. I'd pick away at the scab with sordid pleasure, hating her, blaming her, telling myself she was a selfish bitch who never loved us in the first place. It seemed far easier to hate someone than to grieve them.

Putting the phone to my ear, I decide to give Dad a call.

Sheila answers, sounding crotchety as usual. "Hello?"

"Hi, it's Silver."

There is a short intake of breath. "Silver, how nice to hear from you. I'll just pass you over to your dad, if that's okay. *Grey's Anatomy* is on and Meredith just went into labor in the middle of a blackout."

"Oh. Sounds serious," I say in a droll tone.

"The phone lines are down," she explains.

"What about her mobile?" I ask quickly.

"It fell into a water-filled ditch."

"Ah. Then she really is screwed." Nice to know I wasn't the only one down on my luck.

"Anyway, here's your dad. Bye."

There is a mutter of low voices and clunking as the phone switches hands. Then Dad's voice booms down the line, "Silver! How are you?"

I flinch, holding the phone away. Dad always speaks twice as loudly on the phone. As if he feels the need to compensate for us being miles apart. "Hi, Dad, I'm fine," I say, lying through my teeth. Unless Logan walks in that door right now, it's going to be a long time before I feel remotely fine again.

Neither of us speaks for a few seconds. I get the feeling he still has one eye on the TV.

"Dad, I wanted to ask something about Mum."

That gets his attention. "Oh," he says, his voice dropping several decibels. "What is it you want to ask?"

I screw my eyes shut. I hadn't planned on ever talking to him about this, but since I'm depressed as hell anyway, I figure why not go whole hog and throw some mother issues into the mix?

"Was there any mention of vampires involved in her disappearance?"

For a moment I wonder if he's still there. Finally, he says, "No. The police never mentioned anything like that."

I frown into the phone. Dad is the most honest person I know. When I was seven years old, he blurted out that Santa Claus wasn't real because he couldn't bear the deception. But for some reason, maybe it's the frailty in his voice, I get the impression there's something he's not telling me.

"I see," I say, staring across the room to her photo on the mantel.

"Why do you ask?" he says next.

"Just curious," I lie. "It just occurred to me that, back then, they didn't realize vampires existed. I thought maybe it might make a difference."

There is another long pause. I hear his shallow breathing down the line. "Did she ever say anything to you about this? Maybe something when you were little that you're only just remembering?"

This was getting weirder by the second. "No. Why would she?"

He sighs. "It doesn't mean anything, I'm sure."

"What doesn't?" I ask in confusion.

"Hang on." I hear shuffling and a door creaking shut, a soft thud of footsteps. "I couldn't talk with your stepmother in the room," he says when he comes back on the line. "I'm upstairs now."

Patience isn't my forte. "Oh, for God's sake, Dad. What is it?"

He tuts loudly. "There's no need to snap."

I roll my eyes like I used to at age fourteen. "Sorry."

"Silver, I met your mother when she was twenty and I was twenty-seven."

"I know," I mutter irritably. I still have no idea where he's going with all this.

"Before me, she was involved with another man. He treated her badly—physically and mentally. She'd met him when she was quite young, around fifteen. It was a few years into our relationship before she trusted me enough to tell me."

My heart stills in my chest. "Who was he?"

"A fella named Stephen Clegg. When she told me about him, I thought she was having me on."

"Dad?" I say. I'm suddenly finding it hard to breathe. "He wasn't—"

"A vampire, yes. It took a lot for her to open up about it. I was the only one she ever told."

White dots swim around my vision, and my palms sweat so badly the phone almost slips from my grasp. "But why didn't you mention it to the police?"

"I did, but they thought I was having an episode of some kind, that her disappearance had made me unstable.

There were questions about my ability to raise a child, talk of social services. I couldn't have that, Silver, so I shut up. I figured they knew what they were doing."

"But they didn't. Not really." Without realizing it, hot tears begin to slide down my cheeks.

"I guess not," he says, sighing. "But anyway, that's why I was so surprised when you brought it up, why I thought you might have somehow overheard us talking when you were little."

"No," I mumble. "Like I said, it just suddenly occurred to me, that's all."

"I'm sure if it was relevant, they would have connected the dots."

I think of Burke and Davies. While they definitely know of the link, they didn't say whether it was because of what Dad once said or not.

"Nothing will bring her back," Dad says in a voice that sounds as brittle as cracked glass. "She's gone."

I suck in a lungful of air. My head feels light and my stomach growls again. "Dad, I better go. I need to make myself some dinner."

"Are you okay? I can drive up if you need me."

"No, I'm fine. Just hungry. Thanks for talking to me about it."

"Anytime. You know where I am. Why don't you come home next week? We'd love to see you."

"I'll try," I say noncommittally.

"Please do. Bye, sweetheart."

"Bye, Dad."

We hang up, and even though I've just learned some earth-shattering news about Mum, the first thing I do is check to see if any messages have come in while I was talking. Such is the nature of my desperation. When I see there's none, I sink back into the sofa, thinking about what Dad said, the irony that my own mother once dated a vampire herself.

If Logan were still around, I'd ask about Stephen Clegg. After all, he did say he knows all the vampires in London. I could kick myself for not being brave enough to ask Dad about it sooner. I could have been focusing on him instead of random questions about holy water and coffins.

Toying with my phone, I hit Logan's number again, my breathing ragged as I wait for the dial tone. Only this time there isn't one. It switches straight to voice mail, meaning he's either somewhere with no phone signal or it's switched off. I let out a scream of frustration. How could I let my guard down like this? All the years I've spent carefully not holding hands with guys, refusing second dates, only to wind up driven half-crazy anyway.

To stop me replaying the last morning again in my head, I pick my laptop off the coffee table and flip it open, quickly typing in the V-Date website address. If Logan has disappeared, maybe I should go on another date and, this time, ask about Stephen Clegg. A voice in my head tells me to stop, to put down the computer, that no good will come of it. But the way I feel inside, like an animal caught in a snare—hopeless and bleeding— propels me on. I need the complete distraction of fool-ishness. And besides, since when have I ever listened to my sensible voice?

Chapter 15

Logan

FOR THE NEXT FOUR DAYS, I DON'T LEAVE THE FLAT. I don't trust myself not to walk along Silver's street, materialize in Covent Garden when I know she's coming out of work.

Like a ghost, she haunts me. I see her gray eyes in the soft light of the moon, hear her sighs of pleasure in the rush of the trains outside my window. During the empty nights, I begin to wonder if memories are not just pieces of ourselves we leave behind in other people. If we don't have to somehow break apart, leave a shard of our soul in another person's heart. Maybe that's why my life essence has always remained pure—no face, no moment I've ever wanted to remember. Until now.

After Silver's text and call, I crush my phone to pieces in my fist. The temptation to answer is too great. I think back, trying to recall if I told her my address. A massive part of me hopes I did. The urge to see her is all-consuming. I burn with the insatiable delirium of a drug addict needing a fix.

On the fourth day of madness, a neighbor slips my post under the door. Among the junk mail is a simple note without an envelope, written in swirly black ink on thick, ivory paper.

I need you at the club. Ronin

I turn the page over, but those are the only words. I feel light-headed, clutching at the kitchen counter for support. Would Anastasia have told him already? Is he suspicious that the report of my happiness with a human has coincided with my mission? Or is it just a social call to see why I haven't shown up to work these past few days? Either way, there's no avoiding him.

It's around seven by the time I make my way to Soho. The moon is full tonight, a glowing smudge behind silvery wisps of cloud. The streets are emptying out—the smartly dressed hurrying home from work, tourists chattering about their day as they head back to the safety and warmth of their hotels.

Outside the black door, I don't give a moment's pause to gather my thoughts. Whatever fate awaits, I want it over with as quickly as possible. I stare into the camera and wait for the dreaded clunk of locks as they rattle like old bones in the door.

The doorman isn't Jordan tonight, but a new gentleman I've never seen before—thin and wiry, with rusty-brown eyes and hair slicked back with so much gel that it's impossible to tell what color it is. I ponder if this subtle change is an omen, if this will be the last time I ever cross this threshold.

Surprisingly, he doesn't ask for my name, but merely stands back against the grubby wall to let me pass.

I slip by like a ghost, moving briskly along the dark tunnel toward the main bar. Emerging into the sultry, low-lit room, the first thing I notice is that Ronin isn't alone. A cold stab of fear pierces my heart when I see him sitting in a purple booth flanked by two other vampires. One is Luca and the other is Vincent, a vampire I haven't seen in decades. Though all three of us are tied to Ronin, we're not expected to live in his pockets. Much like myself when I lived in Peru, some vampires go years without seeing their blood-bonded ancient. Vincent has long lived a separate life. It's odd, therefore, to find him here. Maybe he is the plant at the Metropolitan Police that Ronin mentioned. I seem to recall hearing he works in law enforcement. Odd though, as I always remember Vincent as honest and straightforward. Ronin must've laid it on thick to convince him to spy on his employers.

"Logan," Ronin calls. The calmness in his mellow Scottish accent melts the fear in my chest. He doesn't sound like a vampire about to commit murder. "Come and join me. Luca and Vincent were just leaving."

The pair—dark-skinned Luca, dressed casually in jeans and deep-blue cashmere sweater, and Vincent, in a sharply tailored charcoal suit—rise from their seats.

"It's been years, Logan," Vincent says, offering a hand. He always did have impeccable manners. French aristocracy, if I remember rightly.

I grasp his long, smooth fingers in mine, returning his smile. "It has," I agree. "I didn't even know you were in London."

Vincent's blue eyes flash, flicking to Ronin and back again. He runs a hand through his golden hair, breaking my gaze. "I've been back a while now."

"I'll be in touch, Vincent," Ronin says, cutting him off. "Luca, I'll see you tomorrow night."

Vincent drops a nod to Ronin, the dull light of the room accentuating dark circles beneath his eyes, before following Luca up the narrow flight of stairs. I watch them leave, my eyes on Vincent's tightly set broad shoulders. I would put money down he's the inspector working for Ronin. The thinly veiled look of worry is a perfect match for my own.

Once the door closes behind them, Ronin waves a hand toward a seat. "Please. Sit."

I slide in the opposite side, shoulders back, spreading my thighs. I can't afford to give off any nervous vibes. As it turns out, I needn't have worried about creating the right impression. Ronin is distracted by a whip-thin, flame-haired vampire stepping out from the door by the long, granite bar. It's actually pretty difficult not to be distracted, considering she is hardly wearing any clothes save for a low-cut bustier and matching black satin thong. Jesus, doesn't this guy have other hobbies?

"Mr. McDermott," she purrs, in an Eastern European accent. "What about *our* meeting?"

Ronin twitches a smile. "I'll be there in a minute, Valentina."

Valentina slinks like a cat to a booth in the corner.

"Ronin," I pipe up, unable to help myself, "did you ever consider taking up golf?"

The overlord explodes into laughter, the hard lines of his Celtic features softening. I see a glimpse of how he must've looked as a young man—a real young man, not just trapped in the body of one—handsome and strong, with blue eyes the color of a warm summer sky.

"Logan," he says, shaking his head, "if I ever do, I want you to join me."

I return his smile, refusing the offer of a drink as he gestures to an empty glass on the table.

"Down to business," he says, the warmth snuffed out like a candle in a draft. "Did it all go to plan the other night?"

I nod, making sure not to break eye contact. "Yes, it did."

"Excellent. I have another girl for you."

My heart sinks. "Oh?"

"I did warn you there will be several, Logan."

I blink. "Yes. You did."

He reaches into his trouser pocket and pulls out a square of folded paper, flicking it across the lacquered table toward me. "I don't know too much about this girl," he says as I catch it in one hand. "It's tomorrow night though. The details are all there—a simple glamour just like the last one. I don't have a home address, so you'll have to be creative. The restaurant name is on the paper."

I slip the details into my jeans pocket. "No worries."

"Has Anastasia caught up with you yet?" he asks suddenly, gaze drilling into me.

"Yes. She showed up unannounced a few days ago, acted her usual charming self." I pause, picking at the table edge with my thumb. "She said I'd be fair game to her if I ever lost your protection."

Ronin chuckles, shaking his head. "Anastasia will be hit the hardest by the changes we face. She loses power by the day. It's the only good thing to come out of our exposure."

"How so?" I ask, frowning.

"The past has a way of catching up, Logan. There's only so far we can run. I wouldn't worry too much about Anastasia if I were you. Soon, she'll have bigger fish to fry than losing you all those years ago. Besides, why would you lose my protection?"

I pretend not to hear the question. "Didn't you say the old ways must be maintained?"

He grins. "Where Anastasia is concerned, they can crumble around her ears like a stick house in an earthquake for all I care."

Not for the first time, I ponder the root of Ronin's fierce loathing of Anastasia. Although few ancients can claim to be friends, there is often respect between them—a bit like a dysfunctional family. Still, his words provide me with a tiny sliver of hope. With Anastasia gone, I can be with Silver. I'd still have to avoid Ronin's detection, but there are ways around that.

"I haven't seen Vincent for a while," I say in an effort to change the subject.

Ronin's blue eyes narrow. "Vincent owed me a favor. As you know, I always call them in."

The chill is his gaze instantly crushes the flicker of hope in my heart. He leans back against the crushed velvet purple seat. "Valentina. I'm ready for you now."

—⁂—

Later at home, I'm still deliberating over Ronin's words when there's a knock at the door. I freeze, my hand stilling over the coffee press, my thoughts going to Silver. Has she come to bawl me out? Slap me across the face again? God, I hope so. I yearn to see her so badly that in the time it takes me to cross from the kitchen to the hall, all the reasons I'm supposed to be keeping my distance have paled into insignificance.

I fling the door open to find a woman in a long beige coat standing outside. Only it's not Silver; it's Collette from the club. Disappointment hits like a punch to the throat.

"Collette," I say weakly. "What are you doing here?"

Instead of speaking, she reaches up to where her blond hair is piled on top of her head, releasing it from its clasp. She shakes it loose, golden strands spilling over her shoulders like sunshine. I could be dead from the waist down for all the effect it has on me.

"Ronin sent me," she says, running her tongue over bright-red lips. "But I think even if he hadn't, I would have come anyway."

"Oh?" I say, deliberately ignoring the second part of the sentence. "What does he want now?"

Without speaking, she begins working at the knot on her belt. She twists a button open, shaking the coat from her bare shoulders. Although there is a beautiful woman undressing in front of me, all I can think is that the coat is very much like the one Silver stole from the party that night. All I see is Silver's pointy face in the darkness when she asked if I would murder her.

Collette smirks as the material pools around her ankles. "The question probably should be what do *I* want now?"

I step back inside the flat, poised to slam the door.

"Wait," she says with a sigh, picking her coat up from

the floor and shaking it out. "Ronin said to tell you he expects you to make up the hours you missed this week."

Damn. I thought I got away with it. "Okay."

Wrapping her coat around her naked body, she sighs again before retreating down the hall.

I close the door and lean against it, listening to the soft thump of her footsteps as she trudges down the stairs.

In the face of my complete indifference, I finally say out loud the words that have been crushing me for weeks.

"I'm in love with Silver."

―—⁓―—

Silver

On some level, I think I've always known that really, really liking someone would push me to the brink of madness. Maybe my previous lack of emotion was nature's way of protecting humanity from the insane, stalkery beast I've become.

I stare down at my mobile phone, Google Maps open, and check the street name against the one in front of the half-stucco house I'm staring at: *Boston Place.*

Using an ancestry website, I managed to nail the location of the old apothecary Logan said he worked for and now lived at. I'm like a scheming hybrid of Miss Marple and Alex Forrest from *Fatal Attraction.*

I sigh, my breath puffing like smoke into the chilly night air as I gaze up the narrow street. One side is flanked by a high, redbrick wall separating the road from the railway tracks of Marylebone Station; the other, lined by flat-fronted houses with Georgian windows. Though the moon is as flat and glassy as a mirror, its silvery light can't quite reach between the houses; the edges of the mottled path are blurry with shadows.

As I walk, I realize I've entered the street from the wrong end—the numbers here start at ninety. At the opposite end, jutting into the skyline, is the dark silhouette of a taller brick building. My stomach twists. I'm certain that must be it. All the other houses look too small to be flats.

Breathing shallow, I begin to wonder what I'll say when I see him. Of course, physical violence is not out of the question. I had been doing well until now, focusing on my vampire date tomorrow night and trying not to call his switched-off phone more than twice a day. Then I remembered the talk of him living at his old address. Before I knew it, I was fiendishly searching online, and now here I am, as emotionally needy and deranged as the next person.

Eyes locked on the dark shape of the building, my pace quickens. I glance down at my phone—the apothecary used to be at number twenty-two. The squat house next to the four story building is number twenty. This has to be it. I stop, standing in the yellow glow from a streetlamp and staring at the chipped, wooden door. I'd been dreading a buzzer system. I mean, if he can't answer his phone, what are the chances of him picking up that? But on closer inspection, I notice the lock is broken.

"Flaky," I mutter. *A flaky door for a flaky guy.*

It swings open easily beneath my sweaty palm and I step inside, an automatic light flashing to life above my head. I look around the hallway, searching for any clues as to who lives in which flat. One wall is covered by rows of red metal postboxes, each with a number printed on the front. A number but no name. I exhale sharply, glancing around me at the faded, floral wallpaper. Someone has left a muddy bike propped up next to the wooden staircase. It's the only sign of life whatsoever. I debate whether to start knocking on doors.

Just then, footsteps from above begin to echo down the stairs. I freeze, my heart thudding hammer-like in my chest.

At the top of the stairs, a pair of black high heels appear and I watch, mesmerized, as a blond woman wearing a beige overcoat comes into view. She barely flicks me a glance as she struts past.

I decide it's now or never. "Excuse me?"

She stops, whirling around to face me. "Yes?" she asks coolly.

Now I'm seeing her straight on, I notice her face is caked in heavy makeup. It's difficult to tell if she's actually pretty or not.

"I'm looking for Logan Byrne," I say, my voice shaky.

The woman does a double take as she slides her gaze over me, penciled-in brows knitting together.

"What do you want him for?" she asks, gazing at me through clumpy, black lashes.

For the life of me, I can't think of a good reason. I really should have thought this through. I open my mouth, and before I can stop myself, I say, "I'm his person."

A wry smile twitches the corners of her red-painted lips. "His *person*?" she asks, clearly amused.

I draw myself to full height. "Yes. Do you know which flat is his?"

She emits a short, hollow laugh. "Top flat. I just left."

My jaw slackens, a cold hand seizing my heart. "What?" Her features blur before me, dots dancing across my vision.

"I said, I just left." Her tone is suddenly cruel, like a wet slap in the face. "I was once his *person* too, before he tired of me. That's what he does, you know. Sleeps with you and then tosses you aside. Don't waste your time on him."

My mouth opens and closes like a fish caught in a net. I shake my head frantically from side to side.

"Sorry to be the one to break it to you," she says, and with a final sweeping glance, she turns on her spiky heels and disappears onto the street.

I don't breathe. After a few seconds, I follow her from the building and sag against the wall outside. In the distance, the clip of her heels rings out like gunshots against the concrete.

Before I can stop myself, hot tears cascade in rivulets down my face, dripping off my chin. My breath chokes in my throat, chest heaving as if I've just run a race.

"Asshole," I mutter. "That fucking asshole."

In all my deliberations these past few days, I never for one minute believed this would be the reason he disappeared, that all those nights, all those tender moments of laughter and happiness we shared, were fake—that he was never anything more than a player.

Scraping myself from the wall, I stare at the door. I could go up there, shout at him, show him how badly he's hurt me, or I could lope off with my last shred of dignity intact.

I swipe salty moisture from my cheeks. No wonder I've always avoided these situations. They really do only bring pain—trauma and tears on dark street corners—just as I always suspected they would. I turn away from the building, echoing the blond woman's steps back up the street, my heart crushed to pulp, raw and bleeding.

A memory surfaces at the back of my mind, of a long time ago when I was around twelve. Dad had yelled at me for staying out after dark and I'd screamed he was as bad a parent as Mum. I can still see Dad's face as it creased with lines of confusion, his mouth agape with incredulity. It was back during the time I liked to pretend she had run away with a millionaire. *But she's dead*, he said and the simple truth of the words floored me in the same way I'm floored now. That's all love is—leaving yourself open to a truth you're better off not knowing.

The old Silver was right all along.

Chapter 16

Silver

A LUMINOUS YELLOW MOON HANGS LOW IN THE SKY AS I emerge from the Overground station at Chiswick.

Usually, a full moon gives me tingles—the good kind—but tonight I can't seem to shake the feeling that somehow it's a bad omen.

Gerhard, the vampire I'm meeting, said he will pick me up, that I'm to look for a silver Porsche Boxster. The only cars I see, however, are moving—dozens of them, all edging through almost stationary traffic like slow-marching ants.

I pull out a tiny, star-shaped mirror from my purse to check my eye makeup. After spending most of last night bawling, I had my work cut out trying to cover up the puffy lids and red-rimmed eyes. Still, I'm not here to impress the guy. Just ask about Stephen Clegg and leave.

I sigh, sliding the mirror back into my bag and smoothing my navy satin pencil skirt over my thighs. It's not my usual look, and neither is the cream-colored, strappy top I've matched it with. The only part that's *me* is the pointy boots I've added to balance out all the *boobiness*. If Logan were here, he'd have an aneurysm. I close my eyes against a wave of sadness, trying to blot out the image of his sea-green eyes and dimples.

I'm quick to remind myself of yesterday's anguish, the words of the blond girl in the trench coat: *That's what he does, you know. Sleeps with you and then tosses you aside.*

"Bastard," I mutter.

Last night, in between crying and swearing, I called and left a message for Burke and Davies, and earlier today, Davies materialized outside the corner shop while I was buying milk. He'd been particularly interested in the information about the female ancient and the fake name Logan said she went by, Dolores Gericke. I didn't mention what Dad had said about Mum being involved with a vampire. I figure that can wait until after tonight, when hopefully I'll have more to tell.

The loud blast of a horn crashes into my thoughts, and I look up to see a silver Porsche pulling up on the double yellow lines at the side of the road. An arm emerges, a flash of gold cuff links on a pin-striped shirtsleeve, as the passenger door is pushed open.

I hurry over and sink into the low vehicle, slamming the door shut behind me and turning in the seat to greet Gerhard.

Right off, I don't like him. His face is harder than it looked in his pictures on V-Date—*older*. He must've been in his mid to late thirties when he turned. The photos portrayed a much younger, softer character. This man is large-boned, with a wide, fleshy face and mousy, thick hair that looks like it needs cutting. That and the way he touches my knee as I sit down instantly set alarm bells ringing. It isn't a fatherly *There you are* sort of pat, but a primal *You're an object* squeeze. If the traffic hadn't suddenly lurched forward, I would have got right back out.

"So, Gerhard, where are you taking me?" I ask, trying to push aside the negative thoughts. After all, I have a whole evening to get through.

He flicks me a bored gaze. "La Trompette," he says without much enthusiasm. There is a nasal twang to his accent—South African mixed with something else. "I hope you like French food."

"French is fine with me." Every time the Porsche brakes, I fight the urge to swing open the door and make a dash for it through the melee of cars.

When we stop at the traffic lights, he turns to face me, his pale-blue eyes flat as glass as they slide over the contours of my body. "My goodness, you're a beautiful young woman," he murmurs, a sly smile twisting the corners of his fleshy mouth.

I now know exactly how Grandma must've felt right before the wolf ate her. My hand, with a will of its own, falls on the shiny chrome door handle. He doesn't miss a trick, his pale eyes following my every movement.

I pass off the gesture by tugging my skirt down. "So, what do you do for a living?" I ask him. "It wasn't clear from your profile."

The traffic lurches forward and he turns away. "I own nightclubs, one in Johannesburg and the other in Zurich."

"For humans?" I ask.

He laughs, though I'm not sure why—it's a perfectly reasonable question. I get the impression he's the sort of guy who exists purely to mock others. "Yes, for humans.

Mostly. Do you enjoy clubbing? You certainly look like a party girl. I can usually spot a woman who knows how to have a good time."

The words, though innocent enough, are saturated in double meaning. If the evening continues in this vein, it won't be long before I'll need a sick bag.

"Not really. I'm the bookish type," I lie, hoping to steer the conversation to more neutral ground.

Another slimy grin spreads across his face. I could probably tell him I'm a librarian who knits bed socks for cats in her spare time and he'd find a way to make it dirty.

"Shy types are often the naughtiest."

"Not this one," I murmur, avoiding his penetrating stare by pretending to watch a woman walking a black Labrador along the pavement.

A short while later, we arrive at the restaurant. He pulls into a disabled spot and turns off the engine.

"I don't think you're allowed to park here. It's for blue badge holders," I say in a tight voice.

He roars with laughter, shaking his head. "They know me here. Don't worry. The owner and I have an understanding."

Pushing the car door open, I scramble out before he has a chance to make it around to help me.

"You modern girls," he mutters, reaching the passenger side to find me already standing on the pavement. He offers me the crook of his elbow and I take it reluctantly, my fingers brushing the shiny material of his suit jacket as lightly as possible.

Inside, amid the buzz of talk and clink of cutlery, the

restaurant is a trendy mix of beige and cream with plain, sanded wood floors and leather, high-back chairs. The walls are bare except for a few modern paintings, the wood tables covered with simple, white linen cloth. An aroma of freshly cooked fish and red wine laces the air. Despite the company, my tummy rumbles in anticipation.

A maître d' walks toward us, holding out a hand to Gerhard. "Mr. Johnson," he says warmly, grasping his hand. "I've reserved your usual table. This way, please."

The sweet relief at being released from the arm holding is short-lived. He stands back, allowing me to walk ahead, and as the waiter ushers us through, I feel his large hand between my shoulder blades. Immediately, my thoughts go to Logan and the gentle fingers at the back of my waist, his green eyes wide with a look that seemed to ask *Is this okay?*

I swallow my melancholy like a bitter pill as we are led to a secluded area at the back of the dining room. There is a folding screen to one side of the arch that can be closed for privacy, and for one terrible moment, I think the waiter means to pull it across. I hold my breath while he fusses with a bottle of champagne and hands us two supersized menus. It's only when he leaves, making no attempt to close the concertina-like folds, that I allow myself the luxury of exhaling.

The vampire pours golden bubbles into tall flutes, holding one out for me to take. I remember the last time I drank champagne. The contrast between then and now is so jarring that a wave of horror rises up inside me, dark and impenetrable, like a wall. *I may never feel that way again.*

I snatch the glass from his outstretched hand and tip back my head. Gerhard is left, arm poised in midair, while I throw the entire contents down my throat in one gulp.

"I hope I don't make you nervous," he purrs, eyes lit up with amusement. To my absolute horror, I feel a hand brush against my knee. In reflex, I jerk it upward, hitting the table and making the cutlery and glasses rattle.

I'm all out of good manners. "Don't touch my leg again and we'll get along fine," I snap.

Rather than act offended, he grins. "I like my women with a bit of spirit." With a fleshy finger, he gestures to the menu in front of me. "I highly recommend the crab."

I hold the menu in front of my face, using the brief respite from his ogling to give myself a mental pep talk. *Get it together, Silver. Ask about Clegg and get out of here.*

"I'll have the crab then," I say, shrugging out of my cropped jacket. His heavy-lidded eyes land directly on the line of my cleavage and I lean back in the chair, putting as large a gap as possible between us. Ignoring the leer, I force a smile onto my face. "Tell me about your nightclubs."

Like most people, he seizes the opportunity to hop on board the me train. "Well, I'm not sure they would be appreciated by bookish types like yourself, actually. They're both gentlemen's clubs, you see?"

Lap dancing. Could this guy get any sleazier? If it wasn't for the fact the police are funding my account these days, I would seriously consider asking V-Date for a refund. "Is there much of a market for those places in Zurich and Johannesburg?"

He smirks, fish eyes trailing across my body like a

grope in the dark. "Isn't there always a market for beautiful girls, Jenna?"

It is the first time he's used my fake name all evening. Too bad both myself and my alter ego are out of patience. "For men like you, I suppose there is."

His eyes narrow, a flash of anger sparking to life in their cold, blue depths. "And what kind of man is it you think I am?"

Reaching forward, I grab the champagne bottle and top up my empty glass. "Confident and wealthy. Used to having his own way."

"Well, you got that right," he says, eyes flashing. "I *always* get my own way."

Just then, the waiter returns with his little electronic tablet, stylus poised. "For mademoiselle?" he asks.

Quick as lightning, Gerhard snatches our menus up and thrusts them unceremoniously into the waiter's chest. His gaze remains fixed on my face. "She'll have the crab and so will I. Bring another bottle of champagne along with it."

My mouth drops open. Dad always says you can tell everything you need to know about a person by the way they treat waitstaff in restaurants.

"Do you date much?" I ask him, brow slanted in what Logan once referred to as my *mark of scorn*.

He unravels a thick napkin with his plump fingers. "Yes. Can't you tell?"

"Do you always have to answer a question with a question?" I ask, irritation leaking into my voice.

"Why?" he replies, tucking the white cloth into his collar bib-style. "Does it bother you?"

The mask slips. I can no longer disguise the rage simmering within me. "Will you excuse me?" I say icily, slipping my jacket on and grabbing my clutch bag. "I need to use the bathroom."

He doesn't stand the way dates have in the past when I've gotten up to go to the ladies'. He leers instead, puffy eyes fixed on my rear end as I follow the restroom signs to a door in the corner of the restaurant.

As soon as it swings shut behind me, I sag against the wall and breathe a massive sigh of relief. There is no way I'm going back out there. My limit has been reached. I push open the door to the ladies', praying there's a sizable window to make my getaway.

No such luck. Apart from a tiny air vent high up on the stone-tiled wall, the place is sans exit. For my troubles, I snatch the shiny bottle of Molton Brown hand soap next to the sink and shove it in my bag.

Old habits die hard.

Stepping back into the corridor, I decide to try my luck in the men's. The room, however, is an exact mirror image of the female bathroom. It even has the same air vent above the hand driers. I consider going through the restaurant and blatantly ditching him, but something tells me that might be a bad idea. If he did follow me out onto the street, I don't stand a hope of outrunning him. Then where would I be? Sneaking out is by far my best option.

The only other door is the cleaning cupboard. I know this because there is a yellow-and-black warning sign stuck on at eye level, reading CLEANING MATERIALS ONLY. Closing my eyes in silent prayer, I pull at the handle. When I open them, I find myself looking into a dark room with a small window. The milky-blue glow of the moon shines through the frosted glass like a mirror.

"Thank you, Jesus," I mutter, pulling on a white cord by the door and blinking against the bright, yellow light that floods the room.

Letting the door swing closed behind me, I clamber over bottles of bleach and toilet paper, desperate to put this whole sorry evening behind me. There's a dreadful moment when I reach the window and think it's not going to open. It's a couple of feet in height, half that in width, with a metal rod running horizontally across the center. I flip the rod up and push. Nothing happens. Then I realize it opens from the middle. I force the glass until it pivots back on itself, cutting the space into two halves. My relief at it not being stuck is short-lived by the realization I only have a square foot to wriggle through. Not quite the exit I hoped for, but then, none of this evening has exactly gone as planned.

Tilting the window so it's fully horizontal, I toss my bag out and step onto one of the white boxes piled up next to the wall. I poke my head through the gap, inhaling a delicious lungful of nighttime air. Despite the cooking smells wafting out of the kitchen a little farther down, freedom tastes pretty sweet.

The only problem now is that my shoulders won't fit between the panes. I pull back out, pushing my arms ahead of me, Superman style. As the cardboard boxes start to give way beneath my feet, I dive forward, biting my lip against a wave of pain as my tummy grazes the edge of the window. Once my head and torso are through, my hips are the next inconvenience. They jar against the frame, leaving my body hanging half-in, half-out.

I try not to imagine what I must look like.

Using the outside wall to push against, I thrash violently, twisting my body from side to side like a giant cork stuck in a bottle. Thankfully, the satin material of my skirt works in my favor. After a few moments, gravity takes over, popping me out onto the ground in an undignified heap.

I scramble to my feet and dust myself off. My hands are grazed and my tummy hurts from where it struck the windowpane, but all in all, it could be worse—I could still be sitting indoors with Mr. Euro Creep. Snatching up my purse, I look around the shadowy backyard for a gap in the redbrick wall.

It's at this point I realize I'm not alone. Gerhard the vampire is standing just a few meters away, hands thrust into his trouser pockets, a brow quirked in smug amusement.

My eyes widen as he smiles, moonlight reflecting off long, pointed canines, eyes flashing like cold, dead stars. "To think," he says, taking a step across the cracked concrete, "that I was going to have to wait until the end of the evening to get you alone."

A cold trickle of panic drips down my spine, my heart freezing to ice in my chest. I taste fear, as sharp as a copper coin on my tongue. Remembering my self-defense classes, I force my chin into the air. "I lost an earring," I say. My voice belies my fear, sounding wobblier than the knees knocking together beneath my pencil skirt.

He takes another step across the deserted backyard. "You weren't wearing any earrings," he says in a deep, guttural voice that sounds distinctly less human than it did earlier.

I clear my throat. "Well, I think we should get back inside, don't you? They'll be serving up those crabs of ours by now." Trying to be discreet, I dart glances around the gloomy yard, frantically searching for another exit. But the only gap in the wall is filled by Gerhard's beefy frame. It's only now he's standing in front of me, blocking my escape route, that I notice just how large he is.

"There's no way out," he goads, inching ever closer, a cat stalking its prey. "You know something? You've been incredibly rude this evening. I've brought you to a Michelin-starred restaurant, provided you with champagne, indulged your idle chitchat, and you've humiliated me by crawling out of a bathroom window."

"Cleaning cupboard, actually," I mutter under my breath. I never did know when to shut my mouth.

His eyes flash with barely concealed rage. "I rather think you'd better start making it up to me. Don't you?"

Meeting his glacial stare, I decide I have two options—run or scream.

In the end, I do both.

Beyond the window I crawled through is a set of double doors that must lead to the restaurant kitchens. A thin halo of light glows around the edges of the doors, a faint rumble of voices coming from inside. Spinning as fast as I can and screaming my head off the whole time, I pelt across the concrete toward them. I'm pulling back my fists to hammer on the plain black doors when rough hands grab the back of my jacket, lifting me from my feet.

For a second, I'm suspended midair, dangling like a terrified puppet in a useless bundle of limbs. Then with a grunt, the vampire spins around, hurling me across the yard into the wall on the other side.

My back hits the wall full on, the wind knocked from my lungs as I slide down the brick like a melting snow-ball. At first, the struggle for breath consumes me, the pain burning through my body muted by shock. It isn't long, however, before my brain catches up. Gray dots dance across my vision as a dizzying throb of agony explodes at the base of my spine. From the building, a security light flickers to life, and within its white glare, a shadow falls across me. I look up, gasping for breath and almost blinded by pain, into the gloating face of Gerhard. Oddly enough, it hasn't occurred to me until this moment that I might die here, murdered by a vam-pire. I feel detached, as if I'm watching myself in a dream. I wonder if this is how everyone feels before they die.

A fleshy hand closes around my throat, dragging me to my feet and pinning me to the wall, his eyes shim-mering like broken glass. As he leans toward me, I smell aftershave on him and, now that he's closer, the metallic tang of blood. "No," he says menacingly. "I'm afraid I'm not quite done with you yet."

A lizard-like tongue emerges from pulpy lips, slid-ing across the jagged points of his canines, and I stare, transfixed with terror, eyes bulging, as he moves closer. Perhaps it's the sight of his fangs about to sink into my

flesh or the shock wearing off at last, but suddenly, I
jolt to life. I struggle against him, my hands thumping
against his chest, thrashing my head from side to side.
I try, unsuccessfully, to bring a knee into his groin, but
he only laughs, tightening his grip and shaking his head,
as if I'm a toddler throwing a tantrum in a supermarket.
I try to scream but find I can't, his hand tight as a noose
around my throat.

I'm so consumed by my escape efforts that I don't
notice another dark shadow fall across us. I hear the
noise first—a swishing, like a bird in flight cutting
through the air, followed by the sound of flesh tearing from bone, and for a split second, I think it's me,
that I've been killed and my senses haven't caught up.
Next comes a hissing sound, like steam from a kettle
whistling at my ear. The grip on my neck loosens, drops
away completely. I try to focus on the vampire, only to
find he isn't there. I slide down the wall, my legs giving
out under me, and it's only now I see it—his body, fizz-
ing and shrinking on the ground—*headless*.

There is a surprised cry in a familiar Irish brogue.
"Silver?"

I notice a figure above me—flashing eyes; thick, dark
hair; dimples.

I gasp. "Logan!"

Chapter 17

Logan

THE LAST TIME I SAW GERHARD JOHNSON WAS OVER 150 years ago, at Anastasia's house on Cherry Garden Street. I remember the night she brought him back, leading him like a show pony across the shiny, black-and-white-tiled hallway of her lavish home. Even though he was filthy—hair and skin color indiscernible beneath a thick layer of grime—and smelling badly of excrement, she beamed like she'd hit the jackpot.

"Sentenced to hang for murder in the morning," she said, her voice ringing like a golden bell around the room. "What an excellent find."

His sly, pale eyes glowed, hollow with greed. Like most of her other *finds*, I disliked him instantly.

I sit on the opposite side of the room, nestled discreetly into a corner of the bar with a glass of malt whiskey. I didn't want malt whiskey, or anything for that matter. But the barman insisted if I'm going to loiter, I should at least buy a drink. So here I am, overpriced spirits in hand, watching a murderer sitting alone at a table across the room. Despite the modern suit, he looks just like he did all those years ago—a toad-like head disappearing into his neck like a cut of boiled ham, heavy-lidded eyes that are growing darker and angrier with each passing moment.

When I arrived, I assumed he'd been stood up. But then I noticed the half-empty champagne glass on the table opposite, the chair pushed back as if someone left in a hurry, and the way he keeps darting glances toward the toilets in the back corner of the restaurant. Clearly the standing-up part is unraveling before my eyes. It's nice to see he hasn't lost his touch with women. Jenna Gold must be an excellent judge of character.

Like Ronin said, I need to be creative with this date. It won't simply be a case of waiting near her house like it was that night with Silver. I will have to follow her— though if she's given him the slip already, there isn't a lot I can do.

The guy behind the bar pushes a small glass bowl of peanuts under my nose. "Face it, mate. You've been stood up."

Tearing my gaze away, I look up at the grinning barman. "I think you might be right."

When I eventually flick my eyes back to Gerhard's table, I freeze. He's no longer there. The door to the restaurant is closing, a gust of wind blowing in and ruffling the hair of the patrons. If it were any other vampire, I would think he made a swift exit to save face, but he is one of Anastasia's minions, and suddenly, I'm very worried for Jenna Gold.

At the other end of the bar is an open hatch for diners to watch the chef at work in the kitchen. When I first arrived, a man in starched chef's whites was standing, slicing venison with an oversized carving knife and fork. The knife is still there, wedged into a pinky-brown splatter of remains. As soon as the barman turns to serve another customer, I leap off the stool. Speeding to the hatch, I seize the knife and blur out into the night before anyone can so much as blink.

I dart through the narrow, cobblestone alleyway running adjacent to the restaurant, following the smell of stale food and spices, hoping to find the backyard empty.

It's not. Just as I suspected, Gerhard has his prey pinned to the brick wall, her face obscured by the thick ham of his neck, greasy hair curling over the back of his collar. There is no mistaking his intentions. I edge closer, the knife gripped tightly in my hand, moonlight flashing off its silver blade, as the girl begins to struggle.

If he wasn't cawing with laughter, he would hear my approach. But he doesn't, intent as he is on the girl thrashing for freedom within his iron grip.

I swing the crescent of metal wide, putting all my strength into the tip of the blade, and bury it in Gerhard's dough-like neck. It sears through flesh, his decapitated head instantly disintegrating to dust and bone as it flies through the air. The rest of his body begins to fizz and hiss as the years claim him. His corpse drops to the concrete, twisting like a snake, shrinking to nothing more than a pile of clothes filled with dust and bone.

Only then do I look into the face of the woman collapsed in a terrified huddle at the bottom of the wall.

My stomach clenches. I wonder if I'm going mad. "Silver?"

Her wide, gray eyes meet mine, terror melting to relief. "Logan!"

She propels herself upward and I catch her in my arms, holding her shaking body tightly against mine.

"What the hell is going on?" I ask into the top of her head, stroking her hair. "Jesus, Silver, he was about to murder you."

I feel wet tears against my T-shirt, her hands clutching fistfuls of my denim jacket. "Logan, I think I've broken something—my back." She looks down at the remains of Gerhard, and at the dusty carving knife lying on the ground beside him. "Since when did you turn into Buffy the Vampire Slayer?"

I shake my head. "Since when did you start dating psychos?"

Her eyes flick back to me, narrowing to slits. Hands on my chest, she shoves me away. "How did you know where to find me? Are you following me again?"

As the last word leaves her lips, she sways, stumbling back into my arms. "I hate you," she mumbles. "This isn't hugging. It's a matter of necessity. If I thought I could raise my arm without fainting, I'd slap your face."

In spite of the situation, I smile into her hair. "We need to get out of here. Can you climb onto my back?"

"I need the hospital, Logan," she says, hanging limp as a rag doll in my arms.

I hold her steady. "I can fix you better than a hospital can. I'm going to lift you fireman style, just hang over my back. Leave the rest to me."

Stooping down, I grab her around the knees and toss her over my shoulder, holding her in place by the thighs.

"I think I'm going to be sick," she mutters. "Wait! I need my handbag."

I turn on the spot, scanning the ground. "Where is it?"

"I can't remember exactly. I was too busy getting murdered, remember?"

"Jeez, Silver. Do you ever stop with the sass?"

A short distance away, beneath an open, frosted-glass window is a dark lump on the concrete. I leap across and snatch it up. "Got it."

"Don't drop it. I'm on contract with the mobile."

I let out a snort of derision. "Are you ready?"

Without waiting for an answer, I take flight, leaping onto the roof of the restaurant and heading toward Chelsea. Despite the situation and the fact that Silver is groaning with pain and nausea, a quiet part of me rejoices at having her close again. Her fresh, lemony scent eases the ache that's been building in my heart since that morning last week when I left her. I try not to think about the fact that I've just killed one of Anastasia's wayward servants, or that very shortly, I am going to have to tell Silver exactly what I was doing at the restaurant.

Outside her basement flat, a light, misty drizzle has started to fall. I rummage in Silver's bag for her keys. "Are you okay back there?" I ask, patting her thigh with one hand and twisting the key in the lock with the other.

"Fan-fucking-tastic," she says. Her voice, though croaky, drips with sarcasm. "How do you think I am?"

I kick open the door with my toe. "Home sweet home," I say, dropping her bag on the sofa and flicking on the light.

"Fuck you," she mutters.

"Let's not get ahead of ourselves, Silver. We have to get you patched up before we can start any of those shenanigans."

There is a small grunt of disgust in reply.

In the bedroom, I lower her carefully onto the foot of her bed. "Can you sit?"

She gasps in pain, shaking her head. "No, it hurts to sit down."

I flip her onto her side. "Is that better?"

"Yes," she says, eyes screwed shut, face half-buried in a fold of the cream-colored duvet. "It hurts at the base of my spine."

I stroke her cheek, damp with spent tears and rain, and tuck a strand of silky, auburn hair behind her ear. "I'm going to need to take off your clothes to fix it."

Her lids flip open, gray eyes flashing with angry fire. "Are you taking the piss?"

I hold up my hands. "I swear, it's for medicinal purposes. It only works skin on skin. Naked." My eyebrows, which often have a will of their own, waggle suggestively on the last word.

She continues to glower at me, top lip curled. "If you're doing this to take advantage—"

"I'm not," I cut in. "Besides, it's not like I haven't seen it all before. There isn't a square inch of your body I haven't kissed, licked, or stroked. Or did I miss a spot?"

For a second, her eyes soften, a breath catching in her throat, then the steely glare returns, water freezing to ice. "Fine," she barks. "Strip me."

I try unsuccessfully to stifle a smile and she catches me, a brow slanting almost vertically into her forehead. To my shame, my trousers tighten, the thought of kissing her smudged, angry mouth sending a flame of desire pulsating through my body.

"Stop looking at me like that," she snaps.

"Like what?" I ask, eyes wide with innocence.

"Like you're not the same man who's been ignoring my calls for the past week."

I frown, tenderly grasping her under the arms and turning her over. "I'll take your jacket off first."

She buries her face in the duvet, gasping in pain as I remove the torn blazer. Beneath it, her skin is red raw, whorls of scarlet bruises trailing across her back like miniature crop circles. Her white, spaghetti-strap top sticks to the places where she's bled in dark-red splotches.

"Bastard," I whisper, clenching my fists in anger. "He's lucky he's already dead."

"Is it really bad?" Silver asks, her voice muffled by the duvet.

"There's some bleeding. This bit may hurt," I say, unzipping her strappy top.

"Which bit might hur—*ow!*"

I peel off the fabric like a Band-Aid, exposing the cuts where the rough-brick wall punctured her skin. To get a better angle, I straddle her, one knee on either side of her hips. Then I lean down, running my tongue over the scrapes, the skin instantly puckering, knitting back together. Her blood tastes sweet, familiar, and I'm ashamed by the violent twitch of arousal in my jeans.

Silver moans loudly. "God," she says, lifting her head. "That feels better already."

Straightening up, I unzip her tight pencil skirt and roll it off her hips. I suppress a groan at the sight of her pert bottom encased in a pair of plain black knickers. They're different from the ones she usually wears, which probably means she never intended for them to be seen. *Thank God*. I rub my hands together and place them on her shoulder blades, trying to ignore the growing bulge between my legs as I run flat palms down her back. When I reach the base of her spine, there is a click in her tailbone.

"The pain's gone," she says with surprise.

I trail my hands farther south, resting them on the soft, warm flesh of her buttocks. "It was your coccyx. Fractured, probably. It's fixed."

Pushing up on her elbows, she glares over her shoulder at me. "Your hands are lingering on my ass rather a long time. Is that broken too?"

For a minute, I forget Gerhard, forget that I'm going to have to tell her the truth. Our eyes lock. Mesmerized, I stare into her gray eyes, a flutter of dark lashes on pink cheeks. I squeeze her peachy butt, the erection in my pants at full mast, desperate to be buried in those perfect, creamy thighs. "It could be," I say, my voice a low growl. "I think a full-body examination might be in order."

Her mouth opens, a bead of moisture clinging to the cleft of her upper lip. We stare, held together by an invisible string of tension, and I lean forward, pushing her hair to one side, my mouth irresistibly drawn to the pulse battering like a jackhammer in the side of her neck.

"Silver," I murmur.

But before my lips can connect, she twists, flipping over and shoving me away. "Stop," she says. "Don't you dare touch me."

I sit back, hands dropping to my sides. "Let me explain."

"There's nothing to explain," she hisses, holding her unzipped top over her breasts.

The gesture breaks my heart. On one of her days off, we spent the whole day naked. I know from memory every line of her curves, every secret fold of her body. There is no need for modesty—she covers up because I've hurt her. I see it in her eyes, gray and stormy as a wind-whipped sea, and the only comfort I have is that to feel so betrayed, she must have felt as deeply as I do.

"I had to back away, Silver," I begin. "For both our sakes."

"Why? So I didn't get too attached? So when you move on to your next woman, you don't have yet another girl showing up at your flat in a trench coat and spoiling things?"

I frown. "What?"

She breaks my gaze, swinging her legs over the side of the bed and standing up. A pulse throbs in her tightly clenched jaw. "Last night. I went to your flat." Instead of making eye contact, she stares at a corner of the ceiling. "I had an interesting conversation with a blond in a beige overcoat. She said this is your modus operandi. You sleep with women and then chuck them away when you're bored. Like you did to *her*."

"Collette," I say miserably.

Her gray eyes cut back to mine. "Oh, *it* has a name."

"I slept with her last year, before I met you. She was just a one-night stand. I never even really *liked* her. Silver, you don't really think I've not answered your calls because I'm bored?"

Shivering, she folds her arms over her chest, pinning

the falling top in place. She looks vulnerable, more so than I've ever seen her, worrying at her bottom lip. I imagine this is how she looked as a child, as she still looks on the inside, beneath the sarcasm and the anger. I'm struck by the urge to protect her, heal her—inside and out.

"You disappeared," she says in a broken voice— the same voice I heard once before, when I'd picked up the photo of her mother in the lounge. "I became a desperado stalking the streets of London with Google Maps. I signed up to an ancestry website just so I could find the apothecary you said you worked at."

I bound across the room, but she holds a hand up. "Don't." Her eyes finally meet mine. "It's over. Even if this Collette person does have you all wrong."

Drawing back like a wounded puppy, I sink down onto the edge of the bed. "I have to tell you the truth, Silver, and then you can say it's over."

She shivers again, rubbing the sides of her arms, and I pull my jacket off, standing up to wrap it around her.

Snatching it, she holds it over her chest. "What truth? What other grubby little secrets are knocking around your closet?"

"You're cold. Put a robe on."

She spins around, grabbing a T-shirt from a chair next to her bed. "First time you've ever asked me to put clothes *on*," she mutters, tugging it over her head. As the crumpled top slips to the floor, my eyes snag on the brief flash of her full breasts before the material covers them. "Stop staring at my boobs."

"I wasn't," I lie. "It's my T-shirt, that's all. I was wondering where I left it."

"Well, you can take it with you when you leave in a few moments, can't you?"

I motion to the bed. "Will you sit?"

Glaring at me, she climbs onto the bed, leaning back against the pillows. "Spit it out. I'd like to take a shower."

I sink back into the folds of the crumpled duvet, trying not to let my thoughts drift to the showers we took together in her cramped bathroom—our bodies slick with soapy water as I slid inside her, slender legs wrapped tight around my hips.

"There's a reason I was at the restaurant tonight," I begin. "A reason I showed up here that night you ran across the garden and slapped me outside Etta Marlow's front door." I sigh, toying with a button on the bottom of the quilt. "You remember I told you about Anastasia? About how much I hated her?"

Her tone softens. "Yes, of course I remember."

I look up, filled with wild hope, but her eyes are still as hard and unforgiving as steel blades.

"Even after I went back to Ireland, I was still tied to her. A vampire remains linked to their ancient for the rest of their lives afterward. There are laws, and if you break them, it's punishable by death."

"Laws?" she asks, frowning.

"A code of conduct. It's supposed to stop chaos from breaking out among vampires, but some, like Anastasia, use it to manipulate and control. She loves toying with people."

She sighs loudly. "What does this have to do with me?"

I smile grimly. "I'm getting to it, I promise. Even

after she let me go, she continued to toy with me—threatening me, goading me. If my family wasn't gypsies, they would've been in grave danger. But thankfully they were good at slipping into the shadows, and like I said, I never knew where they went after that night I showed up like a ghost by the campfire. It was during this time I had the bloodlust pretty badly. I don't remember much. It's sort of like asking an alcoholic to recall his past debauchery, but I know I never killed anyone."

Silver doesn't speak. She continues to watch and wait with slanted brow. My fingers itch to touch her. Sitting here with no physical contact feels unnatural. Even when we were arguing, I always managed to find a way to hold her. Now, I don't dare. Not until I've said what needs to be said.

"One night, I was drinking, for want of a better word. The *donor* was a barmaid. I healed her, just like I did all of them. But I was being watched. Another ancient, Ronin McDermott, was at the tavern. He saw everything—my gift, what a mess I was. He offered to break my bond with Anastasia."

"How did he do that?"

"The sharing of blood. A simple ritual. We did it palm to palm, the way you sometimes see kids do it, though it can be done from any part of the body. An ancient's blood, or venom if they bite you, overpowers the vessel it enters, even when the person is already a vampire. It's like a rebirth."

"This guy Ronin—was he good?"

"Compared to Anastasia he's a saint. He's still around," I say, seeing her frown deepen.

"So now you're linked to him?"

"Yes, but more than that—I owe him. It's not a matter of honor either; it's life and death. He may be a better person than Anastasia, but he's still an ancient—a demon. If I were to betray him in any way, he will snuff me out. I've seen it happen before."

Silver gulps, a crease forming between her brows. "Carry on."

"When I lost the clinic in Peru, I came back to London. To work for him. He runs a club where he conducts most of his business. Like I said, I owe him. I could hardly refuse."

"What kind of work do you do?" she asks suspiciously.

I take a deep breath. "The club is a place where humans go to meet vampires. It's been around for years. Long before the whole world knew about us. My job is to make sure no one gets hurt. If they do, I heal them. That's why Ronin was so keen to acquire me all those years ago. Like I told you before, there aren't many vampires who can do what I do." I break her gaze, focusing instead on the selection of beads and belts hanging off the end of the white metal bedstead. "Then New Year's Eve, he gave me something a little different. I was heading out to see him the night we met—that's why I left you at your fake house. When I got to the club, he told me about V-Date, that the authorities are using it to spy on vampires."

She flinches, the color draining from her face. Until now, I've ignored the fact she was on a date this evening under a false name. But now there's no denying it—her pale features freeze in horror. I know beyond a shadow of a doubt that I've failed—both to glamour her and to win her over enough to stop her getting involved with the police.

I close my eyes before taking the final plunge into the abyss of truth. "There's a trick we vampires use. It's called a glamour. We can hypnotize humans into certain actions. Ronin sent me to you. To glamour you into not dating vampires. That's how I found you. That's why I showed up here after your date with Nathaniel and that's why I was at the restaurant tonight."

Chapter 18

Silver

A DEATHLY SILENCE SHROUDS THE ROOM. I HEAR THE
tick of my bedside clock, the hum of a car engine running on the street outside. Hard to believe I'd been
growing anxious about explaining Jenna Gold. I gape at
him. The soft-green eyes and their forest of dark lashes
look the same as they always have. The tenderness is
there too, which is why I hadn't believed that he played
me until I showed up at his flat. Yet everything is shift-
ing, the whole of our history rearranging itself in my
head. The moments we shared, the things we said, all
switching angles and unraveling, becoming tarnished
with murky doubt.

"Are you kidding me?" I say at last.

He shakes his head, looking as sad as he did that night
on the ship when he told me about his family. "I wish I
were. Silver—"

"So, those times you showed up here, that was to
glamour me?"

He holds up his hands. "No. I mean, yes, but I never
would have gone through with it. I wanted to see you
again. I hadn't stopped thinking about you."

A memory surfaces of him grabbing my arm as I
stormed past him that night after we were at Vera's. The
way his eyes changed like a cat's and I couldn't look away.

I leap off the bed. "You bastard. I bet you were going to glamour me all along, just thought you'd get a bit of sex out of it first."

"No," he says, standing up, running fingers frantically through his thick, dark hair. "It wasn't like that. Silver, I'm crazy about you. I've never felt this way before, not about anyone. These past few days—"

"Yes," I interrupt, my heart pounding. "Let's not forget these past few days." My nostrils flare, anger coursing through my veins like fire. "If you're so crazy about me, where have you been?"

He takes a step closer, his green eyes rounded, tiny flecks at the centers shimmering like gold. "The morning after I left you, I went home to find Anastasia in my flat. She could tell I'd been with a woman. I tried to lie, to say it was a one-night stand, but she didn't believe me. She knew I was in love."

The fire in my veins freezes, my heart clenching at the words. *What did he just say?*

"She also figured out Ronin didn't know about it. Ancients are even more sensitive to body language than ordinary vampires. She made the point that if I ever lost his protection, she would be free to kill me. I panicked. I was worried she would trace me back to you, report it to Ronin. I figured if I left you alone for a while, she would think she'd made a mistake."

"So you switched your phone off and made out like you were dead," I say, making a mini round of applause. "Great choice. How about calling? Or telling me you were going out of town? At least I wouldn't have been left wondering."

"I almost rang you. I wanted to tell you everything, but I was afraid I'd lead her right to you. I didn't want to drag you into all this. Of course, you managed to do that anyway. All by yourself."

My mouth drops open so wide it feels like my jaw is dislocated. "Excuse me?"

"Oh, come on, *Jenna Gold*, why bother to deny it? You're working for the police. How much have you told them? It's funny. I never had you pegged for a snitch."

I cross the carpet and slap him across the face as hard as I can, my hand stinging as it catches on the bristly skin of his jaw. "I'm no snitch, asshole. I'm doing it becau—"

But before I finish the sentence, he's on me, his mouth crashing down on mine, rough hands raking through my hair, gripping the back of my head as he slides his tongue between my lips.

The kiss is violent, bruising, and yet I respond instantly—anger and tension leaking away, my body boneless in his arms as he assaults my mouth with his. I snatch handfuls of thick hair in my fists, our tongues thrusting in frenzied rhythm, animal groans of pleasure escaping my throat.

Although seconds ago we were fighting, the reasons seem suddenly muted, dulled. Women in trench coats, evil vampires, even the thought of *my mother* isn't enough to dampen the lust raging through me like an insatiable inferno.

"I want you," I say, panting, attempting the impossible feat of removing his shirt without taking my tongue out of his mouth.

He moans, shoving a hand under the oversized T-shirt I'm wearing and cupping a breast, circling his thumb around a puckered nipple. I fumble with his belt with shaking hands as he pinches the hard tips, abandoning the effort when sharp shocks of arousal zip straight to the throbbing spot between my legs.

"Please," I say. "Logan, please."

He stops, chest heaving, a bead of sweat clinging to his top lip as his hand drifts down to rest on my ass. "Aren't we supposed to be fighting?" His voice is so crackly with lust he could be at the other end of a bad phone line.

"Yes, we are," I say between ragged breaths. "This doesn't mean anything. I still hate your guts. Now for fuck's sake, fuck me."

His green eyes flash, and then I feel his fingers at the edge of my T-shirt. He yanks it up, over my head, before tearing off his own.

"Take those off," I say, pointing with a trembling hand at his jeans.

He smiles, unbuttoning them slowly, as if he's enjoying making me wait. "Have you always been this demanding?"

"Shut up," I snap. "I don't want to hear your stupid Irish voice."

His brows shoot skyward as his jeans pool around his ankles, and my gaze jumps straight to the thick hard-on springing from his jeans.

He looks down at the twitching length and smirks, dimples flashing, staring up at me through spidery lashes. "I think someone's missed you."

I push my knickers over my hips, kicking them off my ankles. "I said, *shut up*."

Like magnets, we collide midair, kissing and tearing at each other like it's been years since we had sex. I claw at his back with my nails, digging into satiny, muscled shoulders as he pushes me backward against the wall, his fingers probing the wet heat between my legs, rubbing at my swollen nub, and turning my legs to mush. I open my eyes to see him staring at me—hair, damp with rain, falling across his face, green eyes blazing, lips curled into a half smile. Whatever he's done in the past, whoever he works for, I know I'll never have it like this with anyone else. *Ever*.

My breathing is labored as a crest of pleasure builds. Our gazes still locked, he pushes a finger inside me, swirling it around my slick walls until my legs almost give out. I wonder why he isn't saying something dirty to go with it like he usually does, but of course, I told him to shut up. I'm my own worst enemy a lot of the time.

Leaning forward, he takes my bottom lip between his teeth, biting gently, scraping his stubble on my chin. The delicious pain combined with the finger pumping in and out of my slippery core is too much. My whole body shudders, my breath sticking in my throat as I give out around him.

Before I can stop it, I'm shouting his name. "Logan!"

He smiles, staring into my eyes and bringing soaked fingers to his lips, licking them and moaning. It's quite possibly the sexiest thing I've ever seen.

"Turn around," he growls, reaching down and grabbing my wrists.

I do as I'm told for once. I don't think I'll ever see my pink-and-gray floral wallpaper in quite the same way again. He pins my hands flat to the wall, his voice gravelly. "Leave them there. Don't move them."

I feel his erection pressing into my back, a hand slide up over my tummy, brushing lightly over nipples so hard they threaten to bore holes through the plaster. His lips travel slowly across a shoulder blade, hair tickling the nape of my neck as he parts my thighs, positioning his stiff, velvety erection at my slick entrance before thrusting into me.

I cry out, my hands balling into fists as he moves deeper, his shaft swelling, hitting my sensitive spot, my body liquefying as I rise and fall around him.

Time stands still. My only thoughts are of the throaty grunts of pleasure next to my ear, the delicious rub of stomach muscles on my back as he thrusts into me over and over again.

He wedges his head between my shoulder and jaw, stubble scraping my neck. "Silver," he whispers. "Oh God, Silver, I'm yours."

Hearing those words, feeling the rasp of his jaw on my skin tips me over the edge. My hands drop from the wall, and he catches them, his length jerking inside me, our bodies shuddering as wave after wave of ecstasy rolls over us.

He hasn't bitten me, and yet I feel detached, as if I'm floating on the ceiling. My eyes are closed, my trembling thighs still parted around him. His sweaty forehead rests on my shoulder as if he's collapsed.

Finally, he says, "Does this mean I'm forgiven?"

When my breathing slows and the feeling in my legs returns, I push him away and turn around, covering my breasts. "No," I say, still panting. "Far from it." I cross quickly to the cupboard in the corner of the room and drag out a fleece throw, wrapping it mummy style around my body, tucking the edges in under my arms.

"Well, that should keep me out," he murmurs, as my bare skin disappears.

"Stop it," I say, glaring at him, trying to keep my eyes firmly on his face. Despite my efforts, I can't help but gape at his beautiful naked body—planes of silken muscles rippling his chest and arms, slender hips, the semierect manhood bobbing between an explosion of dark, wiry hair. *How can anyone stay mad at a man who looks like this?* I narrow my eyes. "You may physically induce a primal reaction in me, Logan, but you still disgust me."

I shuffle back to the bed penguin style, the tight blanket restricting my movements. Despite the drama and sex, the moment is a shade comical. Our eyes meet and a smile touches the corner of his mouth.

"Don't you dare smile," I threaten, glowering at him.

He tilts his head to one side, watching me as if I'm a puzzle he can't solve. "I think I love you."

The words knock me off-kilter. My heart batters my rib cage. "Oh please," I mumble as I climb back onto the bed.

Once again, my anger dissolves, fear scrambling to take its place. Because *what if he means it?* Even crazier—*what if I feel the same way?* A hot, red flush rises up my neck.

"I'm helping the police because of my mother." The words pour out like water from a hose. "I didn't know for sure until I spoke to my dad the other night, but she was apparently involved with a vampire once."

Logan blinks as if waking from a dream. He dips down to retrieve his jeans from the carpet. "I had no idea, Silver. I'm sorry."

"The police said if I helped them, it might lead to them reopening the case. I was only going to give them details from other vampires, but then last night after I saw that blond at your apartment…"

"You told them? The things I told you?"

I nod, not meeting his eye. "I was angry."

Sighing, he sits beside me. "I should have been honest with you from the start."

Oddly enough, I feel far more bothered by this Collette person than his revelation about a vampire overlord. "How do I know you're telling the truth about that girl leaving your building?" I ask in a fragile voice.

He looks me directly in the eye. "You know how I feel about you, Silver," he murmurs.

My heart flutters and I look away. "I guess it doesn't matter now anyway." I feel his gaze drilling into me. Holding my breath, I ask, "Do you know a vampire named Stephen Clegg?"

I turn back to see a cloud of confusion set in his features. "How do you know that name?"

"He was the vampire my mother knew when she was young."

His face slackens. Dad's words vibrate through my

head: *He treated her badly—physically and mentally. She'd met him when she was quite young, about fifteen.*

"Stephen Clegg was turned with me."

"Wait, you mean he was one of the convicts?"

He nods. "I never found out *why*. He was too slick to reveal much about himself."

"What was he like?" I ask, my throat tight, palms beginning to sweat and shake under the blanket. After all these years, I'm finally about to get some answers.

"He was the most charming guy you'll ever meet." He pauses. "Are you sure you want to hear this?"

"Yes," I say. "I need to know."

He sighs. "Most of us in the house at that time were from poor backgrounds, but Clegg was well-educated. He used to boast his father was an earl, that he was the bastard offspring of a dalliance with a parlor maid. The earl apparently footed the bill for private schooling, provided him a small income. If it was true, it didn't do much good. Stephen was into every vice going. Superficially, he had all the markings of a gentleman, but that's where it ended. His real nature was far from gentlemanly."

"Go on," I urge, soaking up every word.

"He was sharp—witty but also manipulative. Women loved him. He had that way of making them feel special. He was instinctive when it came to females, always targeting the weak and vulnerable. I think he got a sick pleasure from having a woman completely at his mercy. Of course, he must've been that way before he turned, but like I told you before, becoming a vampire can heighten a personality trait. Sometimes, I even fancied

Anastasia was under his spell. He was a favorite of hers, of course. She had him in her bed most nights. I guess that's also why I never liked him."

"Did you ever sleep with Anastasia?" I ask suddenly, only half wanting an answer.

His green eyes flash. "Don't ask me that, Silver."

"Did you?"

He sighs, fiddling with the duvet cover. "On a couple of occasions. Most of the other vampires were begging for it, but to me, she was repugnant—the most repulsive creature on earth. Needless to say, she enjoyed toying with me. I hadn't had a lot of experience with women at that point. I was a challenge to her."

"Were you a virgin?"

"Not a virgin, no, but I didn't like to use women in that way unless I was serious about them. I lost my virginity in Ireland, to a woman named Bertha Watson."

Jealousy kicks me hard in the stomach. "So this Bertha was your girlfriend?"

A brief smirk flits across his face. "Why? Are you jealous? No, I wouldn't call her a girlfriend. She was a lot older than me. But she was kind and we were fond of each other for a while. I'm grateful to her for showing me that side of sex. There was none of that when Anastasia finally got her claws into me."

I feel a twinge of empathy, the same as I did that night when we sat up in the crow's nest on the prison hulk. Except this time, I don't hold his hand. "Tell me about Clegg, about how he was with women."

"Clegg had women everywhere. Some of them even knew what he was. He fed on them regularly, but his real delight was glamouring them. For men like him, it's always about control."

"Do you think that's what happened to my mother?"

He places a tentative hand on my ankle, his fingers rubbing circles into my skin. I pretend not to notice, waiting as I am with bated breath for his answer.

"Possibly, though that most likely came later, after he'd worked his charms on her."

The knots in my stomach tighten as I imagine her— young and afraid. "You said he liked having them at his mercy. How?"

"Rich widows were a favorite with Stephen, those or comfortably off spinsters. He charmed his way into their beds and hearts, and afterward, he would humiliate them, take their money, taunt them." There's a pause. "I'm not sure this will be easy for you to hear, but he used to beat them. He got a kick out of it. If you want me to get all Freudian, I don't think he ever forgave his mother for his illegitimate start in life."

I'm speechless, a lump the size of a boulder forming in my throat. A tear escapes, trickling over my cheek, and Logan is beside me, brushing it aside with his thumb.

"Where is he now?" I ask in a small voice.

Logan holds my gaze. "Dead."

"How?" I ask, wide-eyed. "When?"

"I don't know the details—who, when, *why*. It happened well over a decade ago."

We lapse into quiet.

"Will you tell the police?" Logan asks.

I shrug. "If he's dead, there isn't much point." Nausea twists my gut as I remember the other dead vampire—Gerhard's headless, dusty corpse lying at my feet.

"What will happen now? With Gerhard and the police? They'll find his body surely, and if it gets back to your boss, he'll know who he was on a date with. He'll know it's you."

I've seen Logan look sad before, nervous, but the flash of fear behind his eyes is entirely new. He swallows, the Adam's apple in his throat bobbing. "I don't know, Silver," he says as if speaking from far away. "I just don't know." He squeezes my hand through the blanket. "Would it be crazy if I said I don't regret any of it?"

"Killing Gerhard?"

"Meeting you."

I inhale sharply. "What would you have done if we'd never met New Year's Eve? If you'd just showed up that night after my date with Nathaniel to glamour me?"

He reaches over, tucking hair behind my ear in what has become a familiar gesture. The fight has left me. I let him do it, rubbing my cheek against his long, tapered fingers like a cat.

"It didn't matter when we met, Silver. I fell for you. I mean, how could I not?"

A smile twitches at the corner of my mouth. "I suppose I am sort of irresistible. Wait a second, how do I know you haven't already glamoured me? Maybe you've forced me to find you sexy."

He quirks a brow, a devious spark in his eye. "Please, with this body, there's no need. You saw the effect I had on Collette."

I smack his shoulder. "Too soon for jokes, and by the way, her shoes are tacky."

"I don't recall paying too much attention to her foot-wear the night we—" He stops when he feels my death glare boring through him like a laser and smirks. "I've said it before and I'll say it again—you're incredibly beautiful when you're angry."

I roll my eyes. "Ugh."

He places a flat palm on my thigh, the heat of his hand burning through the blanket. "Angry and flushed from sex is my favorite look on you."

Even though I want to curl into him, ditch the blanket by the side of the bed, and let him wrap his naked body around mine, I shove him away. "I need to take a shower. Alone."

"What about your back? Someone needs to scrub your back, Silver. There's still blood on it."

I clamber off the bed. "I have a loofah with a long handle, so thanks, but no thanks."

His voice drops dangerously low. "I have a long handle too."

We both chuckle, dispelling some of the tension between us. For a moment, it feels like the way it was a couple of weeks ago—lighthearted banter and innu-endo. I drag open a drawer and take out a clean bra and knickers. "Yes, I know all about your *long handle*, Logan Byrne, and I must concur, it does hit those hard-to-reach places."

His grin widens, cutting into his dimples, and my heart sinks. *Why can't anything in life be simple?*

"I'll make you something to eat, then," he says,

standing up. "I could probably hear your stomach rumble from a mile away. Unless…"

"Unless what?"

"You want me to leave?" He gives me a look like a puppy who's about to get chased off the porch.

"Do what you like," I say, chin in the air. "You always do anyway." I shuffle in the blanket toward the bathroom door, and even though I don't see it, I know he's smiling.

Chapter 19

Silver

IN THE BATHROOM, I BRUSH MY TEETH AND STARE INTO
the round porthole mirror above the sink. My reflection
sums up the events of this evening perfectly—knotty
hair standing on end, makeup smeared around my eyes,
and despite Logan's healing, a splotchy neck from
where Gerhard pinned me to the wall. My bright pupils
tell the other side of the story, however. They sparkle
with satisfaction, and I glower, trying to get the angry
feelings back, thinking of this whole glamouring malar-
key and how he deceived me. Try as I might, I can't
seem to isolate the bad from the good—Logan striking
down Gerhard, the sex, saying he's in love with me,
the sex...

"You're a total pushover," I mutter under my breath.

I turn away and take a towel from the heated rail,
violently twisting the lock on the door so that Logan
hears it click. I yank open the sliding glass shower door
to turn on the water, but before I climb in, I twist the
lock back round again. *What is wrong with me?*

The pummel of hot water on my skin feels heav-
enly. I stand under the jets for ages, watching the
water go from pink to clear, the horror of my bad
date disappearing down the drain. Tomorrow, first
thing, I will call Burke and Davies and tell them my

foray into vampire dating is finished. I don't see how they can find out anything new about Mum now the man who most likely held all the answers is dead. I'm still not sure whether to inform them their whole operation has been infiltrated. That depends on what I do about my other problem—the sexy vampire in my kitchen.

Squeezing shower gel onto my palm, Logan's bombshell goes off in my head.

I think I love you.

My stomach clenches. In the past, if a man said those words, I changed phone numbers. Once I even faked an immigration to Australia. Logan saying it scares me for a whole different reason. That reason being that I'm pretty certain I could end up saying it back. Even more terrifying—I'd mean it.

When I'm done scrubbing my face and body, I lather my hair, all the while expecting the steamed-up glass to slide across and for a naked Logan to climb in. I'm disappointed when I finish rinsing my hair and turn the water back off, no vampire in sight.

I pat my hair dry with a towel and put the clean underwear on, wandering back into the now-empty bedroom. From the kitchen comes the sound of crashing pots and pans. A whiff of cooking hits my nostrils, making my stomach growl like a ravenous beast. I wrench open my wardrobe doors and pull out a pale-yellow T-shirt dress, quickly tugging it over my wet hair.

In the kitchenette, Logan is the picture of domesticity. He is back in black jeans, naked from the waist up, and holding a large mixing bowl in the crook of his arm.

His dark hair is a mess, some bits sticking up, others falling in his eyes. The tiny gold disc around his neck catches the light, his green eyes glittering like sunlight on a river. He has never looked sexier.

"What are we having?" I ask, folding my arms.

I catch the once-over he gives me, gaze lingering on the hem of my dress. The whisk he's holding stills in the batter as our eyes lock.

"Pancakes. You look beautiful," he murmurs.

I pluck a wet strand of hair away from my face. "You've seen me look like this before," I say, blushing.

He begins stirring again, his muscles tensing as he works the whisk. *Sweet Jesus, how can one man make mixing batter look like sex on the beach?*

"I was actually just thinking about that day we spent naked. Remember?"

My blush deepens. "Are you kidding? It's burned onto my brain."

He grins like a naughty schoolboy. "Mine too."

I push myself up onto a high stool. "Too bad that will *never* happen again."

"I'm not sure your version of never is the same as most people's, Silver," he says, smirking. "Didn't you say earlier, *Oh, Logan, you'll never touch me again*; then, minutes later, we're going at it against your bedroom wall." He stops whisking to gesture at his body. "I think it's fair to say you're powerless against the lure of *this*."

I grab an oven mitt from the kitchen counter and fling it at his head. "In your dreams."

"Oh, I do dream. A lot." He starts whisking again,

making silly sex faces at me as he pounds the batter, and I can't help but dissolve into laughter.

He steps closer and stops mixing, cupping the side of my neck. "The marks are fading."

"Yeah," I say, barely breathing as his thumb brushes my skin. "Thanks to your magical healing powers."

Smiling, he begins whisking again, but he stays standing close, his groin pressed against my knees. I reach up and place a flat palm on his chest, my heart starting to pulse faster, as if it's beating for both of us. I trail a hand up to his throat, taking the gold chain between my fingers and examining the tiny medallion. "Did you ever find out what happened to your family?"

Logan shakes his head. "It was harder to find people in those days—no *Facebook*. Also, chances are my grandmother put a protection spell over them. She was a skilled witch." He pauses. "I do wonder though. Especially about my sister, Mary Beth."

"You had a sister? I thought it was only brothers?"

"Four brothers, one younger sister."

"What was she like?"

He frowns. "She was like an angel, though at the time people said she was simple. I got into a lot of fistfights over that."

I smile, toying with the gold. "I bet you were a good older brother."

"Mary Beth needed protecting. She had the gift of sight."

"Sight?"

"She could see into the future. We all got something from our mother. Mary Beth read palms and had visions."

My eyes widen. "Did she ever see what would happen to you?"

He chuckles. "She did say once I would live a long life, though I don't think she quite meant it this way."

I let the circle drop back into the hollow of his throat. "I wonder why they never tried to contact you."

"The way they saw it, I was no longer me. 'Touched by demons' is what my grandmother said."

A glimmer of sadness flickers across his face and I reach up, touching his hair lightly, ghosting a caress along his jaw. He half closes his eyes. "Do you forgive me, Silver? For not being honest?"

"I think so," I murmur. "Though you'll never be completely off the hook."

"I can live with that," he says, a smile forming at the corner of his mouth. "I like having you mad at me. It turns me on."

"I've noticed. Lucky for you, I'm the type of girl who's always angry about something."

He laughs, twirling the whisk. "Just one of the reasons I'm utterly mad for you."

My tummy flutters and I break his gaze, worrying at my bottom lip. He puts the bowl down on the counter and reaches for me, his hands cupping my face as he leans down to kiss me.

The kiss is tender, questioning, his lips gentle and soft against mine. This time there is no urgency, no rampant need. I keep my eyes half-open and so does he. It feels a lot like that first time we kissed on the street, as if the world has stopped turning.

Then he says it, breathily, in between kisses. "I'm in love with you."

I flinch, afraid, though not of being hurt or rejected. I'm scared because suddenly, there seems to be so much to lose. I don't breathe for a few seconds. "I'm in love with you too."

We stare at each other, locked into the moment, love and fear swirling around us like fog.

"I feel happy and sad all at once," he whispers.

"I know," I whisper back. "It's terrifying."

My stomach growls loudly, breaking the spell. We chuckle.

"I must feed you, love of mine," he says, stepping toward the stove.

"Let's get one thing straight, shall we, Logan? No pet names. No 'babe,' 'hon,' 'sweetheart,' and especially no 'love of mine.' Okay?"

He unscrews a bottle of oil, pouring some into a frying pan. "How about 'darling'?"

I shake my head vigorously. "Not if you want to keep your balls on the outside of your body."

"'Baby'?" he asks, grinning.

"Silver. Just Silver. Say it with me, Logan: *Sil-ver*."

"How about Silvie? I like Silvie. It's cute."

"No way. Silvie is an old lady name. Silvie pulls one of those bags on wheels along the street and can't get her panty hose to stay up."

Logan whips a sly glance over his shoulder. "From what I've seen, you're not great at keeping *your* panty hose up either."

I gasp as his broad shoulders shake with mirth.

"Cheeky bastard. They'd stay up just fine if it wasn't for you peeling them off and tying me up with them."

He pours a perfectly round circle of batter into the pan. "Don't pretend you don't love every second."

I lapse into silence, my cheeks burning. He has a point, of course—I do love every second. I watch him twist the pan, filling in the edges of the pancake with creamy liquid, enjoying the delicate play of muscles beneath the smooth skin on his back. *My boyfriend*. In spite of the heat in my face, I shiver. It's true what he said—happiness and sadness go hand in hand. Because really? Where can this go?

"Do you want anything on them?" he asks, flipping the pancake.

I jump off the stool and cross to the cupboard next to him, reaching up to grab a bottle of chocolate syrup, and he drapes an arm around my waist, squeezing me through the thin material of my dress.

"Don't," I say quickly.

"Don't what?"

"Make a joke about the sauce. I'd like to eat my food without your smutty comments."

"Silver, would I do that? What you do with chocolate sauce is your own business." He raises his brows. "Good to know where it's kept though. You know, for future *pancake making*."

I shove his arm, letting my fingers linger on the taut skin as he flips the pancake again. "Pervert."

He bends down to plant a kiss on my cheek before shimmying the thick pancake onto a plate. "You can eat that while I start the next one. Try not to get sauce all over your face."

"See?" I say, carrying the plate to the counter. "Here we go with the smut."

He grins, shaking his head. "That's not smut. It's your horny mind twisting my words."

Squeezing out the syrup, I notice him watching me over his shoulder, a smirk on his lips. "I like my food *moist* too," he mutters.

"I knew you couldn't resist." I set the bottle down on the counter and pick up my fork, carving into the fluffy pancake and shoving a piece into my mouth. My stomach groans in gratitude. These past few days, what with all the drama, I haven't really been eating. By the time Logan turns around, my plate is clear. He pushes another from the frying pan onto the plate, smiling as I wait to pounce, fork poised.

"Promise me," I say between mouthfuls, "when the sexual attraction fades and we hate each other's guts, you'll send food parcels to me."

He chuckles, setting down a large glass of orange juice next to me. "Is that what you think this is? Overwrought sexual tension messing with our brains?"

"I don't know. What do you think?"

"I think," he says, twisting the pan, "that I've lived for over 190 years and never felt the way I do now."

The lump of pancake in my mouth slides down my throat half-chewed. I swallow loudly, lost for words.

"I should let you finish your food before I start openly exploring my feelings." His smile is coy, dimples softening his rugged features.

For a second, I catch a glimpse of him as a child, full of wonder, a boy who wanted to travel, change his life for the better. There is so much of him I will never know, not just the past but in the future. All the years that haven't been lived yet—years I won't be around to see. It's the first time I've considered the stark difference in our life spans—eternity versus old age. A pang of deep-rooted regret grips me in a cold fist. I finish the pancake in silence, avoiding his dark, round-eyed gaze.

He flips the last one on my plate and puts the pan in the sink, leaning back against the countertop, arms folded. "I've freaked you out, haven't I?"

I shake my head. "No, it's just…"

"Just?"

"What happens when I start to age? When I start to go gray and hit menopause and you're still looking as hot as Ryan Gosling?"

He cocks a grin. "I like to think your bone structure will see you well into your sixties."

I narrow my eyes. "I'm serious."

"So am I. Listen, I don't know what will happen. All I know is this thing between us, whatever it is, doesn't happen every day. Now we've found it, we have to seize it—even if it only lasts for ten years, even if it only lasts for ten minutes. Otherwise, what's the point of living?"

"Is that one of Oprah's speeches?"

"No, it's a Logan Byrne original. Have you finished with that?" He gestures to my now-empty plate.

"What will we do?" I say, handing it to him. "About what happened tonight and your boss and the crazy lady who turned you?"

Sighing, he says, "I'm going to suggest something now

and you're going to ridicule it. You're going to think I've gone all Romeo and Juliet, star-crossed lovers on you."

"Kill ourselves?"

He clunks the plate onto the counter. "Run away together."

My brow knots. "Define 'run away.'"

Cutting the short distance between us, he holds me gently by the shoulders, the contact searing through the thin material of my dress like fire. "We could go somewhere abroad. Somewhere with no ancients or vampires, and just live our lives. Together."

I lay my palms on the corded muscles in his broad shoulders, his skin soft, like velvet over iron. "Do you really think they'll be onto you after tonight? Will your boss care? You could say you rescued Jenna Gold—you wouldn't be lying."

His green eyes flicker with worry, his jaw set. "*He* might not care about Gerhard Johnson, but Anastasia will. If either of them connects the dots… Would you give up your life here if we had a chance somewhere else?"

For a few seconds I don't say anything. I look into his face, dimples in repose, just two faint lines in the hollows of his cheeks. A muscle in the corner of his chiseled jaw twitches, and I brush a thumb over it absentmindedly. I've so rarely trusted anyone in my life that the words falling from my lips almost sound as though they're coming from another person. "Yes. I think I would."

His whole face lights up, eyes crinkling at the edges, the green of his irises softening to the color of a faded summer lawn. "There will be a lot of hand-holding involved."

I squeeze his shoulders. "Just hand-holding?"

"Biting too."

"Now we're talking."

"How long would you need? To get things sorted here?"

"Well, let's see. I hate my job most of the time, I live in a different city from my dad, and my best female friend is a ninety-year-old alcoholic. That leaves Ollie... A day?"

He laughs, ducking his head to fasten his lips to mine, drawing my tongue slowly into his mouth, hands curling into my damp hair. I slide off the stool, winding my arms around his neck and molding myself to his body.

A hand breaks free from my wet, tangled hair and drifts down my back, pausing to stroke the bare skin around my neckline, fingers leaving a trail of tingly warmth in their wake. He cups my bottom, squeezing me through my dress, holding me to the stiffening length in his jeans.

"I want to show you something," he murmurs, his lips leaving my mouth, traveling in aching slowness along my jawline.

"I've already seen it," I tease. "It's become something of the third wheel in our relationship."

He chuckles. "Not that. Something else. On the sofa." He wraps my legs around his hips and carries me to the settee under the window, laying me down on the cushions.

My eyes narrow, though my tone is hopeful. "Is this something kinky?"

Straddling me, he smiles, hands flat on either side of

my head as he hovers over me. Without another word, he presses his lips to mine, the cool metal of the gold medallion swinging against my throat. I hook my feet around his thighs, trying to force him closer, but he remains suspended above me, elbows digging into the sofa, silky strands of hair tickling my face and jaw as he grazes his fangs along my throat.

I tense in anticipation of his bite, a bolt of desire shooting through me, coiling in the pit of my abdomen like a snake waiting to strike.

"Silver," he whispers into my neck, lips vibrating against my skin.

"Yes," I say. To him and his bite, the answer is always yes. I stroke the ridges of his stomach, my hand moving to the trail of downy hair that leads into the waistband of his jeans.

His fangs snag the skin on my throat, coming to rest in the juncture between neck and shoulder. I hiss as they slide into me, at the odd mixture of pleasure and pain—two sides of the same coin. I arch my back, my life essence ebbing into his mouth like warm wine from an uncorked bottle. If I had to choose a way to die, this would be it. No sharp severing of mind and body, only a blissfully slow sense of submitting to a greater power—like that strange window between waking and sleeping, when nothing makes sense and everything is possible.

I swirl around a vortex of unconsciousness, my pulse fluttering mothlike in my ears, before I'm sucked into the kaleidoscope of peaceful sunset colors.

But something has changed.

In the midst of the hazy yellows, a navy-blue sky appears, dotted with stars, and I see a woman—young, with wavy, auburn hair and wide, gray eyes—her face is filled with empathy as her hand covers mine. The scene fades and the same girl is beneath me, our bare skin fused together, passion, longing, and regret binding us as one.

It's a few seconds before I realize the girl is me.

My eyes snap open. I'm back on the sofa, still wearing my yellow T-shirt dress. Logan is curled beside me, resting a cheek on his hand.

"It's changed," he says, not a question but a statement, as he lays a flat palm on my stomach. I put a hand to my neck, feeling for puncture wounds, but there is only a faint smudge of crimson on my fingertips. Logan takes my hand, licking off the blood. "Hasn't it?"

"How did you know?"

He bunches the material of my dress. "I just know. It's the Silver Harris effect."

"I suppose I'll *have to* run away with you now," I say, smiling.

He cocks a brow. "You know, our vampire laws say the person who changes your life essence has to provide blow jobs at least twice daily."

I smack him on the arm. "You always have to kill the romance."

Laughing, he rolls on top of me. "Maybe I'll let you off with once a day."

"Keep pissing me off and you'll be lucky to get one a month."

He smiles, shaking his head.

"What?" I ask, smoothing the hair from his face.

"Us. This. All that's happened tonight and we still manage to behave like horny teenagers."

My conversation with Ollie from last week pops into my head.

"Logan," I begin, "if we went to an amusement park, would you ride the ghost train with me?"

At first he frowns, but then slowly, a crooked grin unfurls at the side of his mouth, his green eyes twinkling. "Always."

Chapter 20

Logan

LATER, WHEN SILVER FINALLY FALLS ASLEEP, COCOONED in a tight tangle of limbs, I begin to worry, fear crawling up my spine like creepers up a wall. Should I have gone back to the restaurant and disposed of Gerhard's dusty remains? How long will it be before Ronin hears the vampire on a date with Jenna Gold is now dead?

But it isn't just Gerhard's demise troubling me. Knowing Silver feels the same as I do is both exhilarating and terrifying all at once, like being presented with a dagger of pure gold and then learning it will someday kill me. I try to push the negative thoughts to the back of my mind, tightening arms around her warm body and inhaling the clean, peachy scent at the nape of her neck. In sleep, she looks peaceful and pure. With her rosebud mouth, the sweep of dark lashes against ivory skin, she could be Snow White in the glass coffin. I'm struck by the nagging doubt that soon she'll come to her senses, want nothing more to do with me.

All too soon, a weak light filters in through the blinds, filling the room with lumpy, gray shadows. I find my thoughts drifting to my sister, Mary Beth, her whimsical fairy voice the day I left her at the quayside in Dublin. I lied to Silver when I said Mary Beth never predicted what would happen to me—she had, though as usual, it was shrouded in mystery, woven into riddles created by her innocent mind trying to make sense of the things she couldn't understand.

There's going to be a lot of blood, Logan, she said, a small, white hand tugging gently on the sleeve of my coat. Her mahogany eyes were wide and swirling, like silt kicked up in a stream. *It will begin and end with the demon, but you will walk in the light again.*

At the time I brushed it off. Mary Beth rarely made sense. Then, after Anastasia turned me, I wondered about it occasionally. Now, having everything to lose, her words lodge themselves like icy splinters in my brain.

Silver's breathing becomes labored, and she stirs, squeezing my wrist. "What time is it?"

"Early," I whisper, kissing the hollow below her ear. "Go back to sleep."

She reaches behind her, twisting strands of my hair between her fingertips. "Did it all really happen?"

"Yes," I say, rubbing my bristly jaw into the soft skin on her shoulder. "Good and bad."

She turns over, creases crisscrossing one side of her face where her cheek rested on my arm. "You're worrying, aren't you? Usually we're having sex by now."

I laugh. "I'm not a total sex pest, Silver. I do have some self-restraint."

"Not much."

"True," I agree, "not where you're concerned."

"Have you thought of a plan?" She yawns, stretching like a cat, as if the situation is no more serious than planning our evening meal. I'm relieved by this blasé attitude—I'd half thought she might wake up and regret everything.

"The only thing I need to do is go back to my flat for my passport, pack a few clothes. I can be in and out within half an hour." I frown, realizing how small a mark I'll leave on the city I've spent the last few years of my life living in. "How about you?"

"I need to call work and the police, then tell Ollie, Vera, and my dad. I have to say, I'm disappointed not to be handing my notice in to bitch Nina in person. I've been planning the speech ever since my first day."

"What were you going to say?" I ask, smiling.

"Oh, something along the lines of 'You're a stuck-up, power-crazy bitch whose bitterness will eventually lead to body parts freezing up and dropping off,' that kind of thing."

I laugh. "You could always write her an email."

Her eyes light up, glowing like silver stars in the dull light of the room. "That's a good idea. I can send it from wherever we end up. You can take a picture of me sipping a cocktail on a beach with a blazing-orange sunset in the background."

I swipe thumbs across her cheekbones, leaning in to kiss her forehead. "I'm sure that can be arranged. Do you think maybe we should aim to leave London by tonight? We could head toward your father's and stay near there for a few days while we plan where to go."

A smirk twitches her lips, her gaze faraway and dreamy.

"You look like you're up to some kind of mental mischief, Miss Harris."

"I was just thinking about what my stepmother will say when I introduce you. It's possible you might have to glamour her."

"Please. Older ladies love me. Mrs. Biggins from the ground floor leaves a casserole outside my door every Sunday. She says I remind her of her late husband."

"Maybe Mrs. Biggins fancies you."

"Probably. Doesn't everyone?"

"No," she says, swatting me like a fly with the back of her hand. "But anyway, I think that's a good idea about staying near Dad's. Though God knows what I'm going to tell him."

"Tell him the truth: you've met the best sex you've ever had and you're off to sunnier climes to ride the life out of him."

She bursts out laughing, the tinkly sound echoing around the dim room like a ray of sunshine. The sound melts some of my inner turmoil. We grin at each other against the pillows, and my manhood stirs, as if it's only just noticed there's a naked woman lying in my arms.

"Looks like our third wheel just woke up," Silver says, rosebud lips parting as she reaches down to stroke me.

With a growl, I grab her by the shoulders and flip her over, capturing her mouth with mine. Her legs part, her hand guiding my now-twitching erection to her hot warmth. Groaning, I bury myself in her heat, her cry of ecstasy mingling with mine as I grab soft, warm buttocks, sliding in and out of her in a slow rhythm. She comes quickly, back arched, head flung back, the supple, ivory column of her neck quivering as she shouts my name. I continue to pump, her animal yelps and trickling warmth consuming me like a powerful drug, and it isn't long before I explode inside her, waves of pleasure washing over me like a vicious high tide against the shore.

After, we lie motionless in a knot of limbs and spent passion, my head snug against her warm breast, her fingers anchored in my hair. All these years and no one has ever really mattered to me. I've always been running, always afraid to let someone trust me, scared of letting them down. Secretly, I think I was glad when my family rejected me. It left me with nothing to lose, no one Anastasia could hurt. But I can't run forever.

I curl against her milky body, her hand tightly clasped in mine, Mary Beth's words reverberating in my head.

It will begin and end with the demon, but you will walk in the light again.

And even though she rarely was, I pray this time she's wrong.

Silver insists on coming with me to get my things.

"I'm not letting you disappear again," she says as we weave through the hubbub of commuters outside Marylebone Station. "No way."

I smile, trying unsuccessfully to ignore the feeling of nausea in my gut. "Fine," I say, one arm draped around her waist. "But at least wait in the station for me."

She frowns with all the naïveté of one who has never come face-to-face with an ancient monster, and peers inside the doors at the large digital clock on the information board. "I'll give you until quarter past, and then I'm coming in."

I take a deep breath and turn her around. It's as if we've gone back in time to last week, that morning I kissed her good-bye in Covent Garden. I clasp my hands behind her waist, and she looks up at me, her eyes a perfect match for the marbled-gray sky.

"Don't say good-bye," she says. "I'm going to be waiting in that little café. There's nothing that can happen in half an hour."

There is though. Lots can happen in half an hour, but I don't want to scare her. I lean down and brush my lips against hers in a whisper of a kiss. "I'll be as quick as I can."

We step apart, a draft instantly swirling in the space between us. I freeze, struck by the urge to tell her I love her.

As if she knows what I'm thinking, she holds out her hand and our fingertips touch. "If Collette's there, tell her I'm going to kick her ass."

The tension lightens and I smile, putting on a deep Arnie voice. "I'll be back."

I turn away, into the glare of the sun, the silhouette of her bright-eyed features burned like a photo negative into the back of my eyelids as I trudge toward Boston Place.

Outside, the door is still broken, though someone has pinned a notice onto the wall inside:

Repairman called for door.

I check my mailbox, relieved to find it filled only with pizza flyers and taxi cards. Though I'm not sure what I was expecting—a poison-pen letter written in the blood of virgins? Surprisingly, that's not Anastasia's usual style.

I climb the stairs slowly, my nostrils trying to pick out any unfamiliar scent. But the building smells the same as always, of stale cooking and damp pavements. I shove my key into the lock, turning until the latch clicks. Pushing open the door, I pause on the threshold to listen. But the only noise is the hiss of trains from outside the window, the tick of the clock on the wall. I breathe a massive sigh of relief, chucking my keys onto the counter and stepping into my bedroom that, unlike the last time, is blissfully empty.

Moving fast, I haul the holdall from the top of the wardrobe, feeling in the front pocket to make sure my passport is where I left it. Until a few years ago, all vampires used forged documents to travel around the world—it's difficult to apply for legal identification when your date of birth is two centuries ago. These days, society having finally accepted us, we can travel with relative ease.

I chuck in spare shoes, a pile of T-shirts, and jeans and grab my personal papers from the drawer in my bedside table. I'm done within ten minutes. Back in the kitchen, I take the key from its chain, leaving it in the fruit bowl next to the microwave. I'll call the building manager later and let him know I've left. He can do what he likes with the rest of my things.

Sighing, I run my hands through my hair, threading fingers around the back of my neck. It's strange to think this is the last time I will ever stand in the building that was once Rumbold's apothecary. A feeling of hope races through me, like a chink of sunlight at the end of a long, dark tunnel. Everything can be different now that I've stopped running from love. I pick up my holdall and sling it over my shoulder as knocking reverberates through the flat. I shake my head, grinning and looking at the clock on the wall.

"It's only been fifteen minutes," I shout, bounding across the room. "Can't keep away, can—"

The words stick in my throat as I swing the door open, my heart dying for a second time. Ronin McDermott stands on the threshold, his blue eyes dark and unearthly in the weak light of the hallway.

"Is this a bad time, Logan?" He could be a neighbor asking for a cup of sugar he's so casual, his Scottish accent as calm as a lullaby.

I freeze like a deer in headlights, unable to hide my horror. "I was just on my way out," I say, the words sticking in my throat like tar.

He looks past me into the room. "Mind if I come in to chat for a few minutes? Unless someone's waiting for you, of course."

The mention of a "someone" sends a new wave of fear through me. Does he know?

I do my best to plaster a casual smile on my face. It's then I remember I still have the holdall flung over my shoulder.

I drop it on the carpet. "I was on my way to the gym."

Ronin stares at the bulky bag. "I never had you pegged for the fitness type, Logan."

"I go occasionally," I say, stepping back into the apartment.

Ronin walks in behind me, casting his gaze around the room. It's hard to tell from his stony expression what he's thinking.

"Would you like anything to drink?" I ask, voice wavering.

The overlord waves off the offer with a flick of his hand before turning to face me, his eyes that shade of blue the sky turns right before dawn.

"I'm surprised you haven't been in contact today," he says, tearing his eyes from a pile of sports magazines on the oval coffee table and penetrating me with an unflinching stare.

I don't say anything. I clench my fists at my sides instead, flicking a glance to the clock on the wall. There are still fifteen minutes before I'm due back to meet Silver.

"Because," he continues, pushing his hands into his trouser pockets, "we had a bit of a situation at a restaurant in Chiswick last night. You must know it. It was the same one I gave you the details of a couple of days ago."

"Gerhard Johnson," I say.

"Yes. One of the chefs found his remains. He had nipped out back for a cigarette. Personally, I think that's exceptionally bad hygiene, don't you, Logan? A chef smoking and then preparing food for paying customers?"

An icy trickle of fear drips down my spine as I realize he's toying with me, batting me between his paws like a cat with a mouse. Still, I say nothing.

Ronin's eyes remain fixed to my face as he begins tipping backward and forward on the balls of his feet, as if he were waiting in line at the grocery store.

"Luckily, the manager of the restaurant is a regular at the club. He contacted me and I arranged to have Gerhard's body removed before the police got involved. The girl he came with was nowhere to be seen and neither was the other vampire my manager friend saw that evening. The one with dark hair and an Irish accent loitering at the bar."

I close my eyes for a brief second. "He was about to murder her."

"Really?" he asks. "How can you be so sure? Would he really have been so careless? The whole restaurant saw them arrive together. If she'd been found dead or disappeared, it wouldn't have taken long for the police to figure out who the killer was."

"Forgive me," I say in a low voice, hit by an uncontrollable surge of anger, "but when a guy has a woman pinned to the wall by her throat, fangs bared, it's easy to imagine he's about to kill her."

"Are you sure you didn't let your emotions get in the way? We all know Gerhard was one of Anastasia's."

"Exactly," I hiss, unable to keep the fury from my voice. "One of her killers. So I apologize if I got the wrong impression."

"It's strange," he continues, ignoring my rage. "Anastasia came to see me yesterday."

My stomach flips. "Oh?"

"She was under the impression you've fallen in love. She said when she saw you recently, you reeked of a human and that you got very defensive. I put her straight, of course, told her you don't usually have relationships, vampire or human—not in all the years I've known you.

Then I threw her out." He sucks air through his teeth, eyes narrowed. "I hate that woman."

I swallow. "That makes two of us."

"Seeing you now though, looking like some lovesick Romeo about to fall on his own dagger, I'm wondering if she might have a point."

"She doesn't," I lie.

Ronin stares pointedly at the bulky holdall on the carpet and sighs. "You know what I'm going to say, don't you, Logan? It's why you're already packed."

My chest tightens. I wish he'd get it over with, stop twisting the knife. I dart another glance at the clock. There are just ten minutes until Silver shows up. I'm still nurturing the hope he doesn't have a clue about the depth of my betrayal. If I can just get him out of here, we may still have a chance. "Tell me," I say.

A crease dents the space between his brows. "You've killed one of Anastasia's kin, which means you lose my protection and she is free to avenge herself however she sees fit."

I feel the blood drain from my face. "That's not a law. I've never heard of it."

He frowns. "If you've never heard of it, why are you running?"

I open my mouth to deny it, but at the last moment, change my mind. "I don't want to work for you anymore, Ronin. I'm done."

He takes his hands out of his pockets. "Resignation accepted. When Anastasia finds out it was you who killed Gerhard, I'll say our blood bond is broken and that I have no idea where you are. Which I won't, of course.

I am disappointed to lose you in this way, Logan. I've always liked you."

"So that's it?" I ask, relief leaking into every tense bone in my body.

"I wouldn't look quite so pleased. You're vulnerable without my protection, and if there is a woman, she's now vulnerable too. If you love her and she's human, I would let her go if I were you."

I shake my head, about to answer him, when there is a soft knock at the door. *Silver*. I meet Ronin's steady blue gaze.

"Are you going to get that?" he asks, one brow raised.

He's never seen Silver before, I tell myself. *He won't know who she is*. My legs feel as though they are made of rubber as I cross the short distance to the door. I turn the latch with a trembling hand, praying I luck out— that it'll be Mrs. Biggins with another casserole or even Collette in her underwear.

But when I open the door, it's Silver, her beautiful, pixie face breaking into a huge smile as I appear behind the door.

I watch the smile freeze on her face as she stares over my shoulder at the man in my apartment.

The wild cry that erupts from Ronin's throat is almost feral, his voice as fractured as broken bones. "Victoria?"

Chapter 21

Silver

FOR A SECOND, THE NAME DOESN'T CLICK. WE GAWK, wide-eyed, at each other over Logan's shoulder. Me, staring into the face of a potentially dangerous stranger—him, as if he's seeing the ghost of Christmas past. I shoot a glance at Logan, who looks as though he's about to throw up on my shoes, before allowing my gaze to rest fully on the broad-shouldered, handsome man in his apartment.

Victoria.

"I'm not Victoria," I say in a wobbly voice.

Finally, the penny drops. *He thinks I'm my mother*.

The three of us continue to exchange horrified looks, and then the man with russet hair says in deep, angry tones, "What is this?"

He turns the full force of his glare on Logan, who turns to face him, hands in the air, as if facing a firing squad. "Whatever you do, leave Silver out of it."

There is a whooshing sound, like wind through a tunnel, and Logan is flung back into the wall. The whole room seems to shudder, pink plaster crumbling onto the carpet. The man pins Logan by his neck to the wall, a forearm across his throat. "You were sent to glamour her, not date her. I trusted you, Logan. I warned you what would happen if you defied me."

I launch myself onto the back of the man I've now realized is Logan's boss, raining blows down onto his shoulders and spine. It's like hitting concrete. "Stop it," I screech. "Let him go."

He releases Logan and spins around, eyes flashing like the sky in an electrical storm, and for a moment, I wonder if he's about to attack me too. Instead, he gazes at me, pupils dilating. "Good God," he says, running his hands through his reddish-brown hair, "you even have her voice."

Taking the words as a sign he's not likely to kill me right away, I drop to where Logan is collapsed in a heap. He clutches at his throat, and when he manages to speak, his voice is weak and wheezy. "Run, Silver."

I shake my head, pushing messy, dark hair from his forehead and brushing bits of plaster from his shoulders. "Never."

The sound of the front door slamming shut jolts my attention back to the man looming over us. I stand up, folding my arms across my chest to steady my trembling hands. "So I take it you're the *Godfather*." My tone is as hostile as a cupboard full of knives.

He looks startled, but then a corner of his mouth lifts into a smile. "Your mother was never afraid of me either."

I flinch as if touched by a burning-hot poker. "Would you mind explaining just how you know my mother?"

From the floor, Logan groans, "Silver, be careful."

"It doesn't matter how I know her," he says.

It's the first time I've noticed a hint of a Scottish accent. I sweep a gaze over him. He is broad and muscular but with delicate features—china-blue eyes, a refined nose, his mouth is wide and expressive. If I didn't know better, I would hazard a guess he laughed a lot. "Actually, it does matter."

"Silver, you have to go." Logan drags himself up, his voice stronger, grabbing my elbow in an iron grip.

"No," I say forcefully. "The cat is out of the bag. I want to know the truth. If he's going to murder us, I'm not going to my grave without the full story."

"I'm not going to murder you, Silver," Ronin says in smooth tones. "I've been trying to protect you."

I screw my face up. "Why would you want to do that?"

He sighs, pushing his hands into his trouser pockets. "I loved your mother."

My jaw goes slack. I dart a glance at Logan, who appears equally astonished, his brows raised. "No, you didn't."

The vampire gestures to the sofa. "You might like to take a seat."

"You take a seat," I snap.

Beside me, Logan mutters something in a low voice, but Ronin only smiles. "Let's both take a seat." He flicks a disgusted glance at Logan. "Lover boy can stand."

I step warily toward the sofa and perch on the end. The thud of my heart is beginning to slow, although my palms are still slick with sweat. I wipe them discreetly on my jeans, clasping my hands in my lap. "Spill."

Logan visibly pales at my abrupt tone, and I guess I should be more afraid too, but surely if he'd wanted to kill either of us, he would have done it by now. Besides, he doesn't look like a psycho. He looks more like he's just come from a photo shoot for *GQ*.

"I'm not sure if you know, but your mother was once involved with a vampire," he begins.

"Stephen Clegg," I cut in.

He nods. "He met her when she was very young and treated her extremely badly before moving on to his next victim."

I swallow loudly. "Then she met my dad."

"Yes. Soon after he left her, she met your father and had you. It was the happiest time of her life. She even named you Silver as a sort of good-luck gesture. After all, silver repels vampires in their transition period."

"Dad always told me they chose it because it was unusual," I say, frowning.

I twist my head to get a better look at him. He is leaning back in the seat, legs apart as if entirely comfortable in his surroundings. My eyes linger on the hands resting on his tailored trousers. Despite his muscular frame, they are not the hands of a thug. They are tapered and artistic-looking, with a sprinkling of russet hairs lit up by the watery sunlight from the window. It's as though they belong to a different man. I stare, mesmerized by the notion they once touched my mother.

"Did he kill her? This Clegg?" I ask in a weak voice, my eyes returning to his face.

"No."

I gape at him. I was so sure he was going to say yes. Logan sinks down onto a chair, his face a ghostly shade of white as he worries at his bottom lip.

"Who did?" I demand next.

He looks down at his hands. "I'm getting to that, Silver. It's not as simple as you think."

My heart begins to thud again. It's not until I taste the coppery tang of blood in my mouth that I realize I've been biting the inside of my cheek. I meet Logan's startled gaze.

Are you okay? he mouths.

I nod, forcing my eyes back to the man beside me. "So tell me."

"When you were nine years old, Clegg got back in touch and said he wanted her back. Victoria was terrified. She was afraid for her family—particularly for you—so she ran away."

"Where to?"

"London. She hoped he wouldn't be able to trace her in a big city, but he did. He threatened her loved ones if she didn't go with him. Most likely, he threw in a good bit of glamour too. She was under a glamour the night he brought her to my club in Soho."

"Wait," I say, throwing up my hands. "The police were searching for her, and she was in London all along?"

"It was only a couple of months at the most." He pauses and then, as if reading my thoughts, says, "Clegg would no doubt have glamoured her not to contact home."

I exhale slowly. "Carry on."

A crease appears between his brows, and he throws Logan a puzzled look. "Is she always this bossy?"

Logan smiles at me and blinks, as if waking from a terrible dream. "Always."

"He brought her to my club," he continues. "I hadn't met Stephen properly before, but I got the full measure of him that night. I could tell what the situation was."

He sighs, picking at an imaginary speck of lint on his sleeve. "I offered your mother a job, working the bar. I'll admit, I was attracted to her, but it went further than that—I know a tortured soul when I see one. I felt compassion, something I hadn't felt for anyone in many years. I wanted to help her." He breaks off. Swirling in the arctic depths of his eyes is regret and sorrow. "I killed Stephen Clegg. She showed up for work one night, bruised and weak, and I lost my temper. He died the same night. I should never have done it."

"Why?" I erupt. "He deserved it, surely?"

"Oh, he deserved it," he says in an acid tone. "But I still shouldn't have done it."

Logan, who has been watching us in brooding misery ever since we sat down, says, "Please tell me this doesn't have anything to do with the same vampire laws you mentioned earlier?"

"Of course it does," he growls. "You think we can just pick and choose which rules apply? We've survived this long on earth by a strict code of honor. Even murderous bitches like Anastasia abide by it. Without laws, vampires would have destroyed each other long ago."

Logan cocks an eyebrow. I know what he's thinking. They *should* have destroyed each other long ago.

"What law are you going on about?" I ask. "And what does that have to do with you killing Stephen Clegg?"

The two vampires exchange surreptitious glances.

"I'm sure Logan has told you, especially seeing how fond he is of betraying his own kind, that we live in an almost coven-like structure. There are ancient laws in place to prevent random killings. When I killed Stephen

Clegg, I opened a proverbial can of worms. Anastasia, as his ancient, was able to avenge his death."

"What? Like an eye for an eye, a tooth for a tooth?" I ask in disbelief.

"Exactly. Except in this case, a death for a death."

A chill rips through me. Surely he didn't mean... "My mother," I say.

There is a lengthy silence. "Anastasia didn't find out right away who the perpetrator was. But it didn't take her long. I tried to cover it up, of course. Particularly as I'd fallen head over heels in love by that point."

I try not to blanch at the revelation. Even though I see the obvious attraction—he's extremely good-looking—it's still weird hearing my mother spoken about in that way by a person who isn't Dad. "Did she feel the same?" I ask, pushing myself into the sofa, hoping it might swallow me whole, bracing myself for the inevitable answer.

"Yes," he says softly. "Though it was fast and foolish on both our parts. But sometimes, timing and what's right and what's wrong goes right out the window."

I look across at Logan, and our eyes lock. I momentarily lose myself within his glittering gaze.

"Yes," I mutter, still staring at Logan. "I understand completely."

"I tried to hide her, but Anastasia found out who she was. Word got back we were lovers. Anastasia decided to take your mother's life to avenge Stephen Clegg."

"And you just let her?" I ask in disgust. "You didn't offer yourself instead?"

His eyes half close, a wave of pain crossing his face. When he speaks, his voice is like splintered glass. "Of course I did. I pleaded. I went down on my knees. But it made her even more determined. Jealousy is perhaps the biggest evil in the world. Anastasia is envious of all the good in others—love, beauty"—he throws a glance at Logan—"integrity. When she found out how much I adored Victoria, Victoria instantly became a target."

"Why didn't you kill *her*?" I demand, anger leaking into my voice.

He shakes his head. "I guess that's one thing lover boy forgot to tell you. Ancients are next to impossible to destroy. I've never known one to die. We are not the same as those we create."

"Why are you telling me this? Aren't you afraid I'll tell the authorities?" As the words leave my mouth, I'm struck like a knife in the ribs by a horrifying thought. *What if he doesn't intend to let us live to tell the tale?*

As if he's picked the words right out of my head, he says, "Silver, I would never harm you." He shoots Logan a scathing look. "This is precisely what I was hoping to shield you from. Victoria would turn in her grave if she could see you dating a vampire. She didn't get in contact with you after Clegg died for the simple reason that she didn't want you involved in any of this."

"So if you had your way, I'd be happily living my life repelled by Logan and all those like him?"

"Yes. I couldn't believe it when your name was passed on to me by my contact at the Metropolitan Police. I knew it had to be Victoria's daughter. I mean, how many Silver Harrises are there in the world?"

My eyes wander back to Logan, who is sunk back into the chair, head in hands, his fingers tightly woven in his messy brown hair. "Was she in pain?" I ask, unable to look at him directly. "When she died?"

I hold my breath as the quiet stretches on for an eternity. Logan looks up, his green eyes burning with sympathy.

"She died in my arms," Ronin whispers at last. "Loved."

I look away as a tear slides down my cheek. Logan jumps up, closing the short distance between us and pulling me from the sofa into his arms. I bury my head in the warmth of his chest, forgetting the other man for a moment, forgetting that he might want to kill us, and allowing myself the luxury of tears, the comfort of Logan's strong arms around my back.

"What about her remains?" I ask, glancing over my shoulder at him.

He is staring at Logan and me with an odd expression. His head tilted to one side, blue eyes sad, as if he's not seeing us at all but remembering someone else. I wonder if he's thinking of my mother. His voice is thick with grief when he speaks. "There is a beach house in Leigh-on-Sea where we spent a lot of time together. She's buried in the little churchyard there."

"How did you bury her without permission from her next of kin?" Logan asks.

"Money talks," he replies grimly.

We lapse into an awkward silence for a minute or two. Then Logan says, "What will you do with us, Ronin?"

He rises from the sofa, and I feel Logan's arms tighten protectively around me as he turns, standing like a barrier between Ronin and me.

Ronin notices, shaking his head. "What can I do, now I've seen all this?" He motions to us with a flick of his hand. "But know this, Logan. If it wasn't for Silver, I'd be far less accommodating."

"What about Anastasia, and Gerhard's death?" he says. His hand, which has been rubbing circles into my back, stills.

"There is nothing I can do about our laws." He stares meaningfully at the huge holdall by the door. "I'm assuming you were planning on running away together?"

We nod in unison.

"Good. Go as soon as you can. Anastasia will hear nothing from me about any of this. But I warn you, she will find out, Logan. She only has to find out there was an Irish vampire at the bar right before Gerhard died to know it was you."

"How will she even know he was killed?" I pipe up.

"There is an invisible yet powerful string of connection between a vampire and the one who turned him," Ronin says, his blue eyes drilling into mine. "She will feel the loss just the same as she knew when Stephen Clegg was killed. Of course, the sensible thing to do would be to part ways. That way Silver is out of danger. But seeing how you keep moon-eyeing each other, I have the feeling that won't be happening anytime soon."

I squeeze Logan's hand tightly in mine. "No, it won't," I say quickly.

"Tried that," Logan murmurs, gazing into my eyes and making my tummy flutter. "It didn't work."

Ronin lets out a long, weary sigh. "I'll leave you to it." He turns, toying with the gold cuff links on his sleeves and looking at me with a puzzled expression. "I'm sorry about earlier," he says in his soft rumble of a

Scottish accent. "I was startled by how much you look like her."

The air turns awkward, heat rising up my neck. "That's okay," I mumble.

He nods. "If you're a tenth of the woman she was, Logan here is a lucky man."

Logan and I stare at each other like awkward teens whose love note just got read out loud in class. I poke my tongue out childishly, and he smiles, the color coming back into his cheeks.

Ronin crosses to the door.

"Wait," I say. "Before you go—thank you for telling me the truth about what happened to her."

He smiles, and it's as though someone lit him up from the inside out. I glimpse how he must have looked to my mother—a dashing hero who rescued her from the clutches of a wicked man. It's no wonder she fell for him.

"You're welcome," he says, his voice cracking with emotion.

He reaches for the door handle, but before opening it, he turns back, shoulders tightly set, and gazes at us. "Do your mother a favor, Silver," he says, eyes glassy with emotion. "Stay alive."

Logan and I exchange fretful glances, but when we look back, the door is softly clicking shut and Ronin is gone.

Chapter 22

Silver

AFTER RONIN'S DEPARTURE, WE COLLAPSE ON THE sofa, clinging to each other like apocalypse survivors as I roll the ancient vampire's words around my mind—*There is a beach house in Leigh-on-Sea where we spent a lot of time together. She's buried in the little churchyard there.*

Since Mum left all those years ago, I've often felt like there is an invisible boulder strapped to my chest—a huge, immovable rock pinning my emotions to that one point in time. But hearing the truth eases the heaviness somehow. Yes, there is heartache and grief, but I feel free, as if someday soon, I'll finally be able to love with a whole heart instead of the broken-up fragments of one.

I rub my face against Logan's rumpled gray T-shirt, now damp with my tears, and inhale his clean, soapy scent, twisting my fingers into the soft, cottony material.

His arms tighten around my back. "What are you feeling?" he whispers.

"Oddly liberated," I say, my voice muffled.

He lifts the hair from the nape of my neck and rubs my skin, his thumb kneading the tension from my muscles. "Me too."

I push myself up onto my elbows and stare into his eyes. They look very green, like grass after snow has melted, the golden flecks glittering like sun on water. I open my mouth to say the three words I've never been able to say, but he kisses me before I get the chance, guiding my lips to his and claiming my senses with the taste of his mouth on mine. Soft flicks of his tongue send tingles of pleasure shooting through my body.

"Are we still running away together?" he asks when we eventually pull apart.

"Yes. Why? You're not thinking of ditching me again, are you?"

He rakes his fingers through my hair like a comb. "No way, but we should probably leave soon, as much as I'd rather stay here and canoodle."

I swing my legs over the side of the sofa. "Ronin did say to leave as soon as we can. I'd like to say good-bye to Ollie first though. He's at home. I had a text from him saying he's home from work with a cold."

Logan sits up, tugging his T-shirt down over his satiny stomach muscles. "Friend-zoned and a cold. The poor lad doesn't have much luck."

I chuckle, holding my hands out to pull him off the sofa. "It's not like that with Ollie. There's no need to be jealous."

He grasps one of my hands and stands up, reaching for his holdall. "A man would have to be dead from the feet up not to find you attractive, Silver."

I quirk a brow. "Like you, you mean?"

He grins, throwing the massive bag over his shoulder as if it weighs no more than a sack of feathers. "You're never going to quit with the dead jibes, are you?"

"Probably not," I say, smiling. "Now, let's get out of here."

—᭱—

By the time we reach Ollie's swanky building in West
London, it's started to rain. I stand on the sidewalk for a
few moments, staring up at the glass-fronted apartment,
before taking a deep breath and pushing the button to
number thirty-seven. To say I was nervous about these
two meeting would be an understatement.

"Just make yourself scarce after the initial introduc-
tion, okay?" I say, worrying at my bottom lip.

He gives a mini salute. "Yes, ma'am."

A familiar voice crackles over the intercom. "Yo."

Only Ollie can get away with saying *yo* in the twenty-
first century.

"It's Silver."

There is a click and the door pops open. I glance over
at Logan, and we stare at each other wide-eyed.

"I'm nervous," he admits, shoving his hands deep
into his pockets.

"Me too. The last time I told him I was running away,
I was ten years old."

He pushes open the door. "Why were you running
away?"

"Dad wouldn't let me get a belly button ring."

He chuckles. "I suspect you were a force to be reckoned with even then."

I nod to the lady at the front desk and lead Logan
through the door leading to the elevators. Upstairs,
Ollie's front door is already ajar. I push it open. "Ollie?"

"In the kitchen," he yells back.

We find him bent over the toaster, trying to pull
something charred out of it with a fork. He is barefoot,

wearing a rumpled green T-shirt that looks in desperate need of laundering, with a pair of faded tracksuit bottoms. The kitchen reeks of burned toast. "It's a crumpet," he says, not turning around. "Why do they make those things so damn thick?"

I look quickly at Logan and back again. "Ollie, this is Logan."

The fork drops, clattering onto the counter. Ollie spins around, wiping hands on his sweatpants. "Oh. So that's where you've been. You didn't answer your phone all day."

They stare at each other for a few seconds, and then Logan sticks out a hand.

My God, this is awkward. I watch in morbid fascination as Ollie takes Logan's hand in his and gives it a fleeting shake. "Good to meet you," he says tightly.

"Likewise."

I make head-jerking motions at Logan to scram.

"I'll let you two catch up," he says, finally taking the hint and leaving us alone.

I close the kitchen door after him and spin around to Ollie.

He frowns, staring through the door after him. "His eyes are so green."

"I know. He's a vampire. Ollie, look, I need to tell you something. I'm leaving."

"Leaving? Where to?"

"Abroad. I'll let you know when we're settled."

"You're going with the vampire?" he asks incredulously.

"He's not just a vampire, Ollie. Don't say it like this

is some dumb obsession—it's real. Him and me, we're real and we have to leave."

"Why?"

I sigh, lowering myself into a chair at his tiny kitchen table. "You know how Mum disappeared all those years ago and they never had any leads?"

"Yeah, of course. But what does running away have to do with that?"

I tell him as much as I can, as quickly as I can—about the police asking me to inform for them and Stephen Clegg, how Logan had rescued me from the clutches of Gerhard—trying to ignore the horror etched into his freckled features.

"You need to go to the police, Silver. If you leave with him, you're putting yourself at risk. This madwoman— Arabella or whoever she is—"

"Anastasia," I cut in.

"Whatever. If she's after him, you're a target too. How long before she finds out who your mother was?"

I clench my fists, anger flaring up inside me. "I'd be in just as much danger here. At least Logan can protect me. I can't leave him, Ollie. I'm in love with him."

He snorts, running his hands through his messy red hair. "You think you love him now, but what about in ten years, when you're desperate for kids and he can't give them to you? What about in twenty years when you hit menopause and Donnie Darko is still swanning around like a male model? You'll regret this, Silver—wasting your life on a man who can't give you what you need."

I crash a fist onto the kitchen table. "How would you know what I need? It's not as if I'm the sort of woman who keeps a scrapbook of wedding dresses hidden in her bottom drawer. You said yourself I was never going to fall for someone normal."

"I said that when I thought this was some short-term fling. You're talking about giving up your whole life for him. I mean, what about your dad? He's going to need you when this stuff about your mum comes out."

"We can still talk on the phone," I say, glaring at him. "Why are you being an utter prick about this?"

He kicks a table leg, rattling the wood. "I'm not being a prick, Silver. I'm being your friend. The only reason you're getting so angry is because you know what I'm saying is true. The news about your mother will change you, make you see things differently."

I've heard enough. I stand up, the chair scraping across the tiled floor. "What I'd like to know is who died and made you Dr. *frigging* Phil?"

A heavy silence falls over us. We haven't properly argued since we were about thirteen and he wouldn't let me copy his English homework. Ollie is one of those peacemaker types who will usually do anything to avoid an argument. It's probably why we've stayed friends all these years.

"Well, if that's all you have to say, I guess I'll leave," I say icily.

Ollie stands up, scowling. "Do what you like, Silver. You always do anyway."

There is a prick of tears behind my eyes as I snatch open the kitchen door. Logan is outside on the balcony, leaning over the edge of the railing, his hair slick and black from the rain. The sliding door is shut, and I pause, wondering if he heard us arguing through the double-glazed glass. Who am I kidding? Of course he did. He's a vampire.

He turns around and slides open the wide door, stepping into the lounge without meeting my eye. From the look on his face, I know he heard everything. His expression is a mixture of fear and sadness as he stands toying with the gold medallion at his throat—a gesture he seems to make whenever he's anxious.

"I'm ready to leave," I say.

He nods, still avoiding my gaze, staring at Ollie instead. "I promise I'll look after her."

Ollie shoots him a glance, his face red with anger. "You'd better."

I don't meet his eye as I follow Logan out into the hall, holding up a hand in silent farewell.

Outside, it's still raining, the city as dull as a sepia photograph. Logan looks at the dark horizon, rain smattering onto his hair and clothes. Neither of us has spoken since leaving Ollie's place. If only I could read minds like Ronin seems to.

"I think it's dark enough to work," he mutters, gazing at me with an odd, unreadable expression, eyes blazing like green flames.

It isn't until he crouches I realize he means flight. I climb onto his back, wrapping my arms tightly around him and burying my face in the soft warmth of his neck. The crack of doubt Ollie opened closes over as I place a kiss just below his earlobe. He smells like rain and cotton sheets.

"I love you," I murmur as he leaps upward, but the

words are too late, lost in the rush of wind as we take flight, and I'm not sure if he heard them at all.

—◆◆◆—

Back in Chelsea, I haul my massive suitcase out from under the bed and begin opening and closing drawers in haste, trying to figure out what to take and what to leave behind. Logan is lying on my bed, hands behind his head, staring up at the ceiling as if all of life's answers are written there. He has barely said two words since we left Ollie's.

I grab my passport from my bedside drawer, slamming it shut as loudly as I can, and when he doesn't flinch, I realize I'll have to be the one to break the silence.

"You're angry, aren't you?" I demand. "You heard everything Ollie said and you think I might not really want this."

Still no response.

"Logan! For God's sake, say something!"

He blinks, dark eyelashes fluttering against his pale cheeks. "I'm not angry," he says finally. "I'm jealous."

I screw my face up. "Jealous? I told you that's not how it is with Ollie. I—"

Sitting up, he swings his long legs over the side of the bed. "Not jealous in that way, Silver. I know there's nothing like that between you. I'm jealous because I can't be the man who'll give you all the things you're going to want someday. It's true," he says when I immediately start shaking my head, "and that's how it should be. You deserve a guy who can live a whole life by your side. If I had any sense of honor, I'd let you go."

I could murder Ollie. "But we've been over this. I'll age well and probably won't want kids. We can have years of happiness. Just like you said last night—it doesn't matter how long something lasts. You have to seize it."

"I know, and we will seize it. But eventually, it'll end, and I'll lose you to another man. I'm so jealous of someone else being able to give you that part of your life I can't see straight."

I drop to my knees at the edge of the bed, gazing up into his eyes. "Why are you thinking like this all of a sudden?"

His hand brushes the side of my face, smoothing hair away from my cheek. "Because I can tell, deep down, you know Ollie spoke the truth. One day, you'll want things I can't give you. I'll be your first love and some other man your last. I want to be your first and last, just like you are for me."

His eyes look sad and green, like round, bottomless lakes. I take his hands in mine. "But it's like we said last night—we don't know what will happen, and right now, I want you. I want to go away with you, wake up next to you every day. Right now, you're the first and last. That's all that matters, Logan."

He squeezes my hands in his, rubbing roughened thumbs over my skin. "This is such role reversal."

I chuckle. "It's funny. I never had you pegged for the needy type."

"Needy?" he repeats, meeting my eyes, his dimples flashing. "I think I prefer *brooding and deep*."

"There's nothing brooding and deep about this conversation, Mr. Needy. It's got insecurity written all over it. It's a good thing you're a decent shag or I might jump ship."

He laughs, eyes softening. "Just a decent shag, you say? Judging by those wild animal noises you make, I'd say I was a little more than just decent."

"You do still want to run away with me, don't you?"

Leaning over, he rests his cool forehead against mine. "Of course I do."

I kiss him gently on the mouth, rubbing my face against the rough stubble on his chin like a cat. "I'm glad to hear it. Because, as it happens, you're stuck with me."

He sighs happily, brushing my lips with his. "I'll love you forever, Silver. Whatever happens."

"Good," I whisper. "Because I love you too."

~~~

After I'm packed, I stand in the tiny living room of my flat and look around at all my things with the kind of fondness you only feel when you're about to leave a place.

"I was happy here," I blurt out.

Logan, who is leaning against the kitchen counter, runs his hands along the smooth surface. "I've been very happy here too," he says, grinning. "Particularly in this spot—the place where you first molested me."

"Pffft. Don't you mean the spot where you begged me to touch you?" I adopt a bad Irish accent. "Ooh, Silver, please touch me. I'm dying for the love of a woman like you."

He laughs. "I don't think so, Miss Harris. The way I remember it, you couldn't pull my zipper down fast enough. I was almost afraid for the safety of my crown jewels."

I step across to the counter, placing my hands to either side of him on the wood, the same as he did to me all those weeks ago. His arms circle my waist and he pulls me against him, crushing me to the steely planes of his muscles before ducking to nuzzle warm lips against my neck. "I don't suppose we have time for a reenactment, do we?" he asks, trailing kisses into the collar of my blouse and liquefying me from the neck down.

"We should go," I murmur, tipping my head back to allow him better access. "Remember what Ronin said."

At the mention of his former boss, Logan's lips still mid-kiss. He groans, lifting his head up. "We'll save it for the hotel."

"Yes, the hotel. How will you ever match the luxury of the Savoy? I expect to be kept in the manner to which I've grown accustomed."

Logan smiles and opens his mouth to answer when the shrill noise of my mobile vibrating on the kitchen counter interrupts us.

"Well, look at that," I say, reaching around him and snatching up the phone. "We would have been interrupted from our shenanigans anyway."

I stare down at the display, hoping to see Ollie's name flash up, but it's an unknown caller instead.

"Aren't you going to answer?" Logan asks, watching me frown.

I hit the green button and hold it to my ear. "Hello?"

A voice bellows through the line. "Miss Harris?"

"Yes."

"Superintendent Linton Burke."

On reflex, I wrench the phone from my ear and hit the red button, staring like a startled rabbit into Logan's green eyes. "It was Linton Burke. He must have heard something about last night at the restaurant."

Logan frowns. "Or maybe they're checking in for information."

I shove the phone into the pocket of my biker jacket, my hand trembling. "I'll call them tomorrow from Kent. I was actually hoping to quit via voice mail—or text message."

"That's the way, Silver," Logan says. "Face your fears head on."

Staring at our bags by the door, I'm at once struck by the all-consuming urge to flee.

I turn to Logan. "I just need to say good-bye to Vera, and then I'm ready."

Logan nods. "Let's go."

Outside, it's stopped raining. The street is dark beneath a sky of slate gray, the houses and cars a mass of lumpy shadows. Somewhere in the distance, a car alarm begins to wail. Other than this and the faint sound of traffic from the main road, all seems eerily quiet.

"I think there's going to be a storm," I say as a whiff of the Thames hits my nostrils, salty and metallic.

He props our suitcases against the wrought-iron railings. "I think you may be right."

"It won't affect your speed, will it?" I ask, bending over to double knot the laces on my sneakers.

"Silver, we'll take a taxi," he says, shaking his head. "I won't be able to carry you and our bags all the way to Kent."

After branding him a wimp and giving his shoulder a playful shove, I dash up the steps to Vera's and pound on the door knocker. No answer. I bend over the railings at either side of the stairs to try to peer in the parlor window, but the blinds are shut. Was it this week she said she was going on a cruise with her sister? I've just taken out my mobile to call her when it starts ringing again, the same unknown number as before flashing up.

Logan is standing at the bottom of the steps, looking up at me, his dark hair tousled in the breeze. "Why not answer it? Get it over with."

Sighing in resignation, I hit the green button. "Hello, it's Silver," I say in a weak voice. "I think we must've been cut off before."

"Miss Harris?" Burke's voice is so loud I pull the phone away an inch.

"Yes?"

"Where are you?"

I frown, my gaze locked onto Logan's. "I'm at home. Listen, I have to tell you something. I—"

"Get in a taxi immediately and come straight to Scotland Yard."

"What? No, I can't. I'm on my way out."

Logan's face drops. He bounds up the steps in a single leap. "What is it?"

"Miss Harris, we have reason to believe you may be in danger and must insist you report to the nearest police station. I'm dispatching a car."

My stomach twists violently. Logan grips my shoulders. "What sort of danger?" I ask, scarcely breathing.

But I don't hear his answer. My attention is focused on Logan, who has suddenly gone as stiff as a statue, his face as white as marble.

"What is it?" I demand, my hand and the phone in it dropping limply to my side, the faint babble of Burke's urgent demands lost on the chilly wind.

His mouth opens, a muscle in his jaw throbbing like a hammer as his grip on me tightens.

At that moment, I realize we are not alone. From the corner of my eye, I notice someone standing on the street, eyes drilling into us like lasers.

Then a voice cuts through the night—a soft, feminine voice with a jagged undertone, like razor blades slicing through silk. "Hello, Logan. Aren't you going to introduce me to your friend?"

My eyes flick past Logan to the figure in the shadows at the bottom of Vera's steps and a chill hurtles up my spine. A woman, tall and slender, and with the type of fine-boned, willowy frame seen on fashion runways. She is wearing a powder-blue trench coat over an ivory satin blouse and black leather trousers, an expensive-looking pair of boots zipped high over her knees. Like the voice, her face is beautiful but sharp, high, angular cheekbones pointed like knives, and large, almond-shaped eyes that glow an odd shade of reddish-brown. With her pearly, flawless skin and thick mane of jet hair, she looks like a life-size porcelain doll—at least, one of those evil ones in movies possessed by a bad spirit.

Even before Logan says her name, I know who she is. *Anastasia*. I stare at Logan, willing him to do something, yet at the same time dreading what might come next.

At last, he blinks, loosening his almost painful hold on my arms and turning around. My phone clatters to the concrete steps at our feet.

"Anastasia." His voice is little more than a growl, loathing robbing his Irish brogue of its usual warmth. "What do you want?"

She smiles, flawless, white teeth flashing between scarlet lips. "You know what I want, sweet Logan. But first I'd like to meet your girlfriend. There's no one home, by the way," she adds, nodding toward Vera's house. "The only heartbeat I hear is *hers*."

As if answering to its name, my heart thuds louder beneath my rib cage. I lean into Logan's back as he stands wall-like between us, one hand reaching behind and gripping my hip.

"I refuse to play your games, Anastasia," Logan hisses.

But she doesn't appear to have heard him. She steps closer, peering at me through the darkness, her head tilted to one side in confusion. "Wait, have we met before?" she asks, wagging a manicured, bony finger toward me. "You look familiar. I never forget a face."

I suck in a breath, remembering Ronin when I showed up at Logan's apartment, his startled cry of my mother's name.

She remembers.

A spark of anger flares deep inside me. All these years, searching for the right person to blame for my mother not being around, and now here she is, right on my doorstep. As always, anger trumps fear.

"You fucking bitch," I spit, feeling Logan tense.

Anastasia raises her eyebrows and laughs, a sound as

melodic and cruel as a funeral march. "Victoria Harris. The little whore who turned Ronin's head all those years ago." She pauses, a frown denting the smooth, ivory skin of her forehead. "But that can't be. I remember killing her, watching the life ebb from her veins. So you're who?" Her eyes narrow. "Daughter," she says with a faint hint of surprise, as if she's reached into my head and plucked the word right out of it. "But how wonderfully poetic, isn't it, Logan? Gosh, I do love it when life throws us these curveballs. Makes me feel like a gal of five hundred years again."

Her face is a gloating mask of hatred, and in a fit of rage, I try to fling myself down the steps at her, but Logan pins me in place, clamping me to his back with a strong arm.

She laughs again. "Oh goody. I do enjoy a bit of spirit. It was always going to take something out of the ordinary to turn Logan's head after all his years of piousness. I congratulate you for that. It's such a shame one of you has to pay for what happened to poor, dear Gerhard."

As quickly as the rage reared up within me, it dies, cold fear stepping up to claim its place.

"Enough," Logan growls. "I'm the one who killed him. I'm the one who will pay the price."

Anastasia flashes me a sugar-sweet smile. "You gotta love a hero, don't you? Not bad in bed either, if I remember rightly."

Logan tenses, his muscles stiffening like steel beneath his clothes. From the corner of his mouth, he whispers, "Hang on."

I barely have a chance to register the words before he flings us both high into the air. I shriek wildly, my stomach falling from under me like a stone dropping into the sea. We land in the middle of the gardens opposite the house, Logan cushioning the impact as we roll to a stop in the damp grass.

Logan brings his face level with mine, his green eyes wild. "Silver, listen. I'm going to distract her and you have to run, fast. Go straight to the police."

"No," I hiss, grasping the collar of his jacket in a white-knuckled grip. "I won't leave you. I—"

The sentence dies in my throat as I look past his shoulder. We are not alone. Anastasia looms over us, fangs exposed, ready to strike. Her ivory skin has turned to the color of pale ash, her eyes flashing like red embers, hair fanned out around her head like Medusa.

Without wasting a millisecond, Logan dives at her. "Silver, run!" he yells before he and Anastasia become nothing more than a brawling blur of speed.

I slide backward in the grass, hot tears rolling down my cheeks. Trying to think clearly is like wading through quicksand. I can only gape in horror as the fighting continues, snarls and grunts of pain filling the air. When my back hits the trunk of a tree, I push myself up on shaky legs, but before I move another inch, a high-pitched squeal cuts through the air and a blue flash is speeding toward me across the dark garden.

A force rams into me, hard, and an arm, unyielding as iron, hooks around my neck. Something sharp prods my throat. I gasp violently, a sickly sweet odor of lilies climbing into my nostrils, as I'm dragged across the grass. It's only when we stop in the middle of the garden that I realize the object at my neck is a knife. Unable to look at the ground, I frantically scan the treetops instead. I try to call for Logan, but the knife chokes me, trapping the name in my throat.

Anastasia eases her grip and I take a gulp of air, my head sagging forward. From the new angle, I spot a dark heap lying in the grass. My heart stops beating when I recognize the familiar black jeans, a denim jacket now splattered with blood.

"Logan!" I screech, lunging forward. But her arm holds me like a vise.

His shape stirs as Anastasia cackles like a mad-woman. "Don't worry about your lover. He's going to watch you die before I finish him off—exactly how Ronin watched your mother."

"Go fuck yourself," I say, instantly regretting it as she tightens her grip, robbing me of breath.

"Get up, Logan," she croons, kicking dirt at him. "Get up and say good-bye to your sweetheart."

As he appears in my line of vision, I seize the arm across my throat, struggling to free myself from her iron grip. Anastasia snatches my hand, twisting it painfully behind my back. There is a sharp snap in my elbow and a hot, nauseating wave of pain radiates through me. Logan's battered face transforms from despair to a mask of anger as his gaze locks on my captor, his handsome features marred by hatred.

Anastasia turns the knife so the tip points directly at my throat. I feel a trickle of liquid leak into the collar of my blouse, my mouth filling with the coppery taste of fear.

"For Gerhard," she cries. But she is distracted by a movement in the trees—a flash of bright-white light at the edge of the garden. Logan leaps into action, tackling her from the side and freeing me from her grasp. The knife drops to the damp earth at my feet, and I sink to the ground after it, snatching it up with trembling hands.

My eyes seek out the shape that distracted Anastasia. Another vampire? It streaks across the grass faster than a shooting star, and I bring my knees up to my chest, bracing myself and swinging the knife blindly around in front of me.

Just when I think it will crash into me, it stops, and I find myself staring into a pair of storm-washed blue eyes. The gray turns out to be a sharply tailored suit, the flash of light the blade of a long-handled machete. It is a man, *a vampire*, with coifed blond hair, and a jawline reserved only for the pages of *Men's Health*.

He crouches, a strong hand gripping my shoulder. "I'm Inspector Ferrer, Miss Harris. Are you injured?" For some reason, I think of a period drama, a gentleman on a horse asking after the health of a swooning heroine. I must be getting delirious.

I shake my head, trying to ignore the pain in my elbow. "Logan," I croak, hearing the snarls behind me growing in intensity. The man nods, his mouth set in a grim line, and before I know what's happening, he scoops me up and speeds with me to the edge of the garden, depositing me near the shrubbery.

"My colleagues will be here soon," he says. Then, as quickly as he arrived, he is gone, whirling across the garden like a cyclone toward the brawling duo, the machete suspended above his head. I see it swing wide, moonlight glinting off the blade, and scream.

But then the ground rises up, and when a black fog threatens to engulf me, I let it, diving almost gratefully into oblivion.

Chapter 23

Logan

ANASTASIA IS WINNING. YET AS I FIGHT, DODGING razor-sharp fangs, ducking to avoid her taloned fingers, I see Silver in my mind's eye—her heart-shaped face and creamy skin, the mark of scorn jutting into her brow. For the first time in almost two hundred years, I have a future worth fighting for, a chance to take control of my life. I will not let this demon, this *thing*, rob me a second time. I will find a way to destroy her, *to walk in the light again*, as Mary Beth said all those years ago, or I will die trying.

I'm so absorbed in the battle I do not notice the stealthy advance of another vampire.

There is a *swish*, like a whip cutting through the air, and I feel something wet spray into my face, the fetid odor of poisoned blood filling my nostrils. The blows raining into my body stop, and I blink in shock, staring at the gory scene before me. Anastasia's head is severed from her neck, her vile face contorted to pure demon—bulging red eyes, her teeth like yellowed stalactites hanging from the roof of a cave. Behind her, wielding a silvery sickle, is a familiar face. Ronin's club flashes into my mind. A face as haunted by guilt as mine.

Vincent.

Our eyes lock in understanding. Whatever role he played in Ronin's plans is as over as mine is.

"Silver," I gasp, spinning around on the spot, frantically looking around the garden.

"She's fine," Vincent says, using his free hand to push blood-spattered blond hair from his eyes. "I left her by the trees."

We both stare as Anastasia's lolling head begins to slowly right itself. "Strike her again!" I yell at Vincent. "Take it off completely!"

He lifts the machete and cuts the head from her body, where it drops into the grass with a sickening thud. The body follows a second later, a deafening silence filling the air.

Vincent and I stare down at the inert body for a few seconds, and then I fly toward the trees where Silver is slumped in an unconscious heap. Gingerly, I lift her limp body into my arms, brushing soft, auburn hair from her face. I bend over, pressing my lips to hers.

"I love you," I whisper, tears dripping off my nose and splashing onto her face like raindrops. "Remember, I love you. No matter what happens, I always will."

"Logan!" Vincent shouts. "Get back over here now!"

I lay Silver back down, taking one final lingering look at her beautiful face before flying back to Vincent's side.

Anastasia's head has reattached itself, pink, puckered skin knitting back together. Her features are unrecognizable, skin gray and cracked, red, glowing eyes bulging from their sockets. Her once-immaculate blue coat is soaked with blood.

"Strike her again," I command, but Vincent shakes his head, shoulders slumped in defeat.

"There's no way of killing an ancient," he murmurs, more to himself than to me.

I take one last look over my shoulder at Silver before crossing to Vincent and grabbing him violently. "Get Silver out of here," I hiss. "By vampire law, she can only take one life to avenge Gerhard. If she kills me, it's over." My voice is steady, though inside I'm as a broken as a smashed plate.

"You love the girl," he says, eyes flickering to the place where Silver is collapsed.

"Yes. Which is why you must hurry! Keep her safe, Vincent."

He gives me a curt nod and hands me his weapon. "I'll do all I can."

I watch as he speeds across the garden like a shadow, hauling Silver into his arms and leaping over the iron railings before disappearing into the night like a phantom.

The sky is dark but for a smudge of moon glowing behind gray clouds. In the distance, I hear sirens wailing. I wonder if it's the police coming to back up Vincent. I turn to face Anastasia—my nemesis. Her ravaged features are slowly beginning to heal, fangs extending over her lips, ready to kill.

I watch the reversal in disgust—the creature who forced me into this unnatural state, never able to move on or age or live a life with the woman I love, who wanted nothing more than to turn me into a killer. When the last of the wound on her neck seals, her eyes close briefly, and when she reopens them, they are back to their usual odd shade of red brown, the same eyes from the prison hulk all those years ago. She is back on her feet in the blink of an eye.

"Where's your friend?" she asks, her bony hands clenching into fists.

"What friend?"

Her eyes flit to the machete in my hands. "Are you going to try again with that, Logan? Since the first attempt was such a huge success."

I toss the silver arc across the garden, where it buries itself in the bark of a tree. I suddenly want this over as soon as possible. Silver will be safe by now.

"It's over, Anastasia. I surrender. Destroy me and let's settle the score once and for all."

Her eerie laugh rattles through the night air. "Wow," she says, shaking her head. "How unswervingly noble." She takes a step closer. "A bit like the second movie in the *Twilight* franchise. But I'm afraid I'm still rather taken by the idea of you watching your girlfriend die."

A growl erupts from deep in my throat, and I lunge at her, my hands closing around her thin neck, nails sinking into bloodied flesh as I twist with every ounce of strength, trying to snap her in two. We tumble to the muddy, wet grass, rolling over and over in our struggle. Ordinarily, a vampire is no match for an ancient, but with hot sparks of rage coursing through my veins, I somehow manage to pin her beneath me, my hands clamped around her throat so tightly I feel the bones beneath her skin.

I squeeze harder, until my fingers knit together at the nape of her neck, my thumbs pressing down on her windpipe, but she only laughs — a bloodcurdling rumble that reminds me killing her is impossible. Her eyes pierce right through me, as if she can see into the depths of my soul, and when I loosen my grip a fraction, she reverses our positions, rolling over on top of me until I'm pinned to the ground like a butterfly in a case.

I struggle beneath her, clawing at her like a wild animal, but the super-strength has deserted me and it's suddenly as it was that night many years ago, when I was lying powerless in my bed, the sickness in my veins smothered by her poison.

She tilts her head to one side, her scraggly black hair falling into my face. I feel as if I might suffocate in the foul stench of lilies and death. Finally, she says, "Here we are again, eh?"

My eyes bulge as I brace myself for the inevitable. I say a prayer for Silver, that she will live a long and happy life.

With one hand clamped around my neck, Anastasia uses her fangs to tear into the ivory flesh of her wrist. Droplets of black blood fall onto my face, but it's only when she reaches down and tears my T-shirt open that I realize what she's about to do. Taking a sharp, red fingernail, she slits open my chest. I gasp, red-hot pain searing through my body, as she holds her wrist to the wound, my blood mingling with hers.

She grins, a glittering, evil smile. "I have a penchant for taking things full circle, Logan," she hisses, "and now you'll die mine, just as you were born again mine."

I writhe in agony as a greenish mist rises from the wound, her blood overpowering Ronin's. Somehow this is worse than any ending I could have imagined—that in death I should become hers once more.

Her bony fingers tighten around my throat. "Any last words?"

I lie very still, looking past her into the sky. There are a few stars out, twinkling behind silvery wisps of cloud. The sirens I heard earlier are growing louder, and there is a blue light beginning to pulse beyond the darkness of the trees.

Anastasia frowns. "Oh dear. Looks like your friend with the machete arranged for some reinforcements." She sighs. "Killing police officers is always rather difficult to cover up."

The sound of car doors being flung open echoes off the houses, followed by the soft click of guns being cocked. She leaps to her feet, hauling me up by my neck and dangling me in front of her like a puppet. I struggle in vain to break free, my arms and legs thrashing beneath me. My teeth are gritted so tightly my fangs have cut my bottom lip, warm blood trickling down my chin. From this angle, I notice shadowy figures crouched by the wrought-iron fencing, surrounding the whole garden. If only guns could kill her.

A voice cuts through the night, spoken through some kind of megaphone. I scan the bushes and see a middle-aged gentleman in a long, beige trench coat crouching on our side of the fence. Brave man.

"Maria Bryant," he says with a clipped British accent. "You are under arrest for crimes against humanity. Please release the hostage and put your hands in the air."

If I wasn't about to die, it might be funny.

Anastasia snorts in disgust, backing away from the

police officers, dragging me toward the other side of the garden. To my amazement, the man in the beige overcoat rises and strides fearlessly toward us. In one hand is a giant megaphone, in the other, his Metropolitan Police badge.

When we reach the trees, we stop. Anastasia grunts and from the corner of my eye I catch a spark of light glinting on metal. She is holding Vincent's machete. The one I flung earlier.

"I would rip your head off with my bare hands," she whispers in my ear, "but I had a shellac manicure today, and it would be such a waste."

"Do it," I spit. "What the hell are you waiting for?"

"As you wish."

She thrusts me forward and I fall to my knees in the mud. Gunshots whistle past my ears, but I can tell from Anastasia's delighted cackle they missed. The brave police officer shouts something I don't catch.

"Enjoy hell," she hisses.

I see a flash of light as she lifts the weapon, hear its whisper as she swings it home. I close my eyes as it hits—cold metal slamming into the flesh at the nape of my neck—but as quickly as it strikes, it stops, going no farther. I fall forward into the damp earth.

My neck is burning, and when I open my eyes, a white-hot light is glowing around my neck.

My necklace—the one my mother left me, the one I've worn since the night my family deserted me—is glowing brightly. The chain erupts into shards of white light, the medallion as orange as the brightest sunset. *What is happening?*

I roll onto my back to face Anastasia, stunned to see

that she's burning with the same orange fire of my pendant. Shards of light rip out of her body, incinerating her from the inside out. As her glowing red eyes meet mine, she lifts a ragged hand to point to the pendant at my throat.

"Witches," she says. Her voice is brittle and coarse. "Gypsy curse."

As her words drift across to me, I hear voices on the wind, a familiar chanting I haven't heard since I was young. The voice of my grandmother whispering a spell, and overlapping it, louder and desperately sad, my mother weeping, promising that although she must leave, she will always protect me, that I will always be her green-eyed boy.

I slide backward across the grass, tears pricking my eyes until I hit against something hard. I look up into the shocked face of the officer, and together we turn to stare at the burning inferno that is Anastasia.

Her face is now black and charred, an eerie banshee-like wail pouring from her throat. Then she explodes, her body obliterated as if someone lit a bomb beneath her. For one fleeting second, an image of my grandmother and mother appears in the flames, their kind faces gazing down at me with love. Then the blaze turns to smoke, and when that too fades, all that is left of the demon is a small, black crater in the ground.

The burning at my neck cools. I look down in time to see my necklace and its medallion crumble into black dust, a sudden gust of wind carrying it off on the salty air. Did my mother know this moment would come? All these years, I kept the pendant as a reminder, a good luck charm. Was it always intended to save my life?

Before I can procrastinate further, I'm struck by a spasm of pain.

The policeman bends over me. "Are you all right?"

I stare into his lined face as tiny bolts of electricity spark through me, my chest constricting, a burn flooding my body. I haven't felt real human pain for so many years, it feels foreign, as if an alien has invaded me and is hacking my internal organs with knives.

"I think I'm having a heart attack," I say, clutching my chest where my heart is pulsing hammer-like beneath my rib cage. *Beating*. I grab the collar of the man leaning over me. "I'm dying," I whisper. "There's something inside me."

Then it hits me. I'm not dying at all. I'm living. I clap a hand to my chest, feeling the thud of my heart, loud and pounding under my shirt for the first time in nearly two centuries.

"I think I'm alive," I say to the man who, from the baffled expression on his weathered face, clearly thinks I'm a lunatic. "But it's impossible." Ronin's words to Silver replay in my mind: *Ancients are next to impossible to destroy. I've never known one to die*.

Is this what happens?

I begin to shiver violently. From across the garden, a medical team is rushing toward me. "I might have cholera," I say to the tall, weary-looking man. "That's what I almost died of. Tell them to treat me for that."

My last thought before I drift into feverish unconsciousness is one of hope. Hope and Silver—a future together, hazy but as bright as a star in a pitch-black sky.

Chapter 24

Silver

I WAKE UP DISORIENTED IN A WHITE HOSPITAL BED, A strong smell of washed cotton, disinfectant, and sickness permeating my nostrils. Someone has removed my jacket and blouse, and I'm wearing a hospital gown with tiny blue diamonds. My arm is swathed in a bandage. I look down to see a ginger head of hair on the bed beside me, face buried in the starchy sheet.

"Ollie."

He sits bolt upright. From the crystal-sharp look in his eyes, I can tell he wasn't sleeping at all.

"Silver, don't try to move again. Just stay still." He rises from the seat, hands outstretched as if I'm some wild animal about to bolt for the door.

My mind is foggy. I know I'm supposed to be somewhere else—Dad's house with Logan?

Logan.

"Where's Logan?" Memories flood in—Anastasia, the garden, a blond vampire bending over me on the grass, and a hazier memory: Logan kissing me on the lips, telling me he loves me.

Ollie pushes a button by the bed. "I don't know anything. I arrived at your house to say sorry for being a judgmental jerk and the street was swarming with cars. An officer asked if I knew you, and I told them I was your brother—they never tell non-family members any-thing, do they?—then a short guy in a beige overcoat let me go with him to the hospital. Inspector Davies, he said his name was. He was all right for a copper. He asked for the score in the West Ham match."

"Ollie. Logan?"

A nurse comes in, smiling as if I'm her favorite patient. I resist the urge to drag her onto the bed by her fluorescent-pink pocket watch.

"You're a lot calmer," she says, smoothing down a corner of my bedcovers. "We had to give you a sedative when you first arrived. Screaming your head off, you were. Gave Darren our porter a cut lip."

I reach for her wrist but narrowly miss. "I need to see a police officer. A tall, blond man who looks like a movie star, a vampire. You must have seen him? He was there in the garden."

"I don't think I've seen anyone who looks like that. But I'll see if I can find out." She tucks the blanket in tight before leaving the room, and I waste no time in kicking it back off.

Ollie moves swiftly to the opposite side of the bed to block the doorway. "Silver, you need to calm down."

"You calm down, Ollie," I hiss, tears pricking the backs of my eyes. I wrench the sheets off, about to jump out of bed, when I notice the gown barely covers my butt. "Where the hell are my clothes?"

Ollie opens his mouth to answer when a shadow falls across the doorway. Sergeant Davies ducks into the room, and I pull the covers over my bare legs again. I stare at him, half expecting to find answers scrawled across his face.

"What's going on? What happened to Logan?" I demand. "If you don't give me answers, I'll rip this hospital apart."

He and Ollie exchange one of those maddening looks men give each other when a woman is screaming and they think she's crazy.

Davies slips into a chair beside the bed. "The bloke in the garden is alive. He's being treated now."

I sit bolt upright. "Treated for what? Vampires don't get sick. They're either alive or they're dead. Which is it?"

Davies sucks in a breath before saying, "He's very much alive, I assure you."

I slump back against the pillows, a hot wave of relief rolling through my veins so intensely that white dots appear in my vision. *He's alive. Logan is alive.* "What happened? Who was the other vampire? He said he was an inspector."

Davies stares pointedly at Ollie, who is about to sit down in a chair at the bottom of the bed.

"Oh," Ollie says, standing up and shoving hands into his pockets. "I'll wait outside."

After Ollie leaves, Davies turns to face me. "That was Inspector Vincent Ferrer. It's a long story, but he's recently joined our special division. We first suspected you were in danger after finding out what happened last night on your date. You see, after you gave us the name of Dolores Gericke, we were able to match a criminal ring from the Victorian era to Maria Bryant, or Anastasia as she appears to be known. Exactly the sort of information we've been looking for since we set up the operation." He smiles, leaning back in the chair and steepling his fingers as if he's some sort of mastermind genius. All that's missing is a white Persian cat sitting on his knee. When he clocks my less-than-impressed expression, he quickly continues. "Gerhard Johnson belonged to that gang for a time. When we discovered how the date ended, we realized there was a chance Maria Bryant could come after you."

I raise a hand. "Wait. Are you saying you knew all along he was a murderous villain?"

The detective fidgets in his seat. "Not until after we found out what had happened at the restaurant. If we'd known beforehand, we would have made sure you were safe."

"How thoughtful," I hiss sarcastically. "Or maybe you would have let me go anyway. You were never going to reopen my mother's case at all, were you?"

He looks away, eyes darting around the room. "It's always difficult to predict how these types of investigations will go," he mutters.

"How did you know what happened to the sleazebag anyway?"

He sinks back into his seat. "Inspector Ferrer has connections. When you dropped the phone earlier, we sent out a unit straightaway. Vincent got there faster than the rest of us."

I shiver, wanting answers but at the same time afraid of what they might be. "What happened to the woman? The ancient. Did she get away?"

Davies frowns. "She's gone," he says as though he can hardly believe it.

"Escaped?"

He scratches his balding head. "No, gone. Destroyed. Left a black hole in the ground. She burned to a cinder. We don't understand it ourselves yet."

"Is Logan burned too?"

His eyes flick away. I can tell there's something he's not telling me. "No, not burned. But he's receiving treatment. I can't say any more than that."

"Is he in intensive care?"

"I'm not sure, but I can check with Burke. He was there too when Bryant went up in smoke."

I nod. "Anastasia killed my mother—Maria Bryant as you know her."

His eyes widen. "We will, of course, need to formally question you about the events leading up to tonight."

I shake my head in disbelief. "Of course you will. Make sure you squeeze every last drop of information out of me."

Davies stands. "I'll ask Burke about the young man. I am sorry to hear about your mother."

A sob rises in my throat like bile, and I turn away from him to the dark square of window on the opposite wall, the faint outline of high-rises and skyscrapers making a shadow against the cool-blue horizon. "Just find out about Logan, please," I mutter.

By the time I turn back, he's gone.

———

Shortly after Sergeant Davies leaves, Ollie appears back in the room, Dad and Sheila trailing behind him.

"I called them," he explains sheepishly, staring at his shoes as I glare at him.

Typical Ollie—always trying to do the right thing.

"Dad, I'm fine," I say, bracing myself for a barrage of questions as he perches on the bed, hugging me tightly. When he pulls away, I notice he's still wearing his tartan slippers. Sheila, on the other hand, is fully dressed and carrying a bright-blue cooler bag. I resist the urge to roll my eyes. Whatever the situation, Sheila always finds time to make sandwiches.

She pats her hair as she gives the room a critical once-over. "I've heard the meals are terrible in these places, so I brought food from home."

Her gaze drifts to my bandaged arm and I lift it up to show them. "Just fractured apparently," I say as Dad pales.

"Ah," he says, looking relieved. "No acrobatics for a while then."

I smile for the first time in what feels like forever. "Actually," I say, eyes fixed on my father's soft-gray eyes, "I wouldn't mind talking to Dad alone."

Sheila sighs, looking across at Ollie. "Do you still like cheese-and-pickle sandwiches, Oliver? Or are you one of those gluten-free types now?"

Ollie gives her his best boy-next-door smile. "Nah, not me. I'd love a cheese-and-pickle sandwich, Sheila."

Sheila smiles, flushing pink, as they both retreat into the corridor, Ollie shutting the door behind them. I turn to Dad, who sinks onto a chair beside the bed, twisting his thin hands nervously.

"I know what happened to Mum," I start, the words sticking to the back of my throat.

His face goes slack, the light disappearing from his eyes. "What?" he asks in a voice little more than a squeak.

I pull myself up straight against the pillows, reaching to take one of his hands in mine, and tell him everything. From the V-Date setups and the police right down to what I learned from Ronin earlier today—how Stephen Clegg reappeared when I was nine years old and Mum ran away. How a powerful overlord finally killed him and ended up paying the ultimate price. I leave Logan out of it for now. There are some things he doesn't need to know yet. My being in love with a vampire is one of them.

"Don't cry, Dad," I whisper, as his face crumples, tears trickling into his wrinkles. I lean forward to wrap an arm around his shoulders. Suddenly, he feels frail and birdlike, as if he's no longer my parent but a child.

Eventually, Sheila trails back into the room and Dad tells her snatches of the things I said. Watching Sheila comfort him, arms wrapped around his shoulders, I wonder for the first time in my life if maybe I've judged her too harshly.

A tall doctor with a mop of brown hair strolls in, looking surprised to have stumbled onto such an emotional scene. He pushes black-framed glasses up the bridge of his long nose. "I'm just going to check Miss Harris's arm, and then she can be discharged."

"We'll wait outside," Dad says, steering Sheila toward the door as the doctor begins prodding my arm.

Once they're gone and he's finished poking at me, I ask, "Where are my clothes?"

The doctor opens a cupboard by my bed and brings out a pile of plastic-wrapped, grubby-looking rags. "You might want to ask your family to bring you something from home," he says, scribbling something onto a chart. He clicks his pen. "All done. I'm happy for you to leave when you're ready." He looks up through the little window out into the corridor. "I think you may have a police officer waiting to speak with you."

I let out a long, withering sigh. "Okay, send him in on your way out."

I stare at the door as the doctor leaves, expecting either the squat frame of Davies or lanky Burke to fill the gap in the frame. I jolt in surprise when a tall, handsome man in a gray suit enters. Instantly, I recognize him. Dark-blond hair swept off his forehead, storm-washed blue eyes, a jaw you could measure right angles by—it's the vampire from the garden.

I ball the sheet in my fists. "What happened? Where's Logan?" If I were fully dressed, I would fling myself across the room at him.

"Miss Harris." He nods before giving an almost imperceptible half bow, like some long-forgotten gesture of a bygone era. "I'm not sure you remember me, but I'm Inspector Vincent Ferrer. I was there earlier when you collapsed. Sergeant Davies sent me to talk to you about Logan. May I sit?" He gestures to the chair at the foot of the bed and I nod. "Logan is upstairs in the intensive care unit." He pulls the chair closer. Beneath the harsh, yellow strip light on the ceiling, I notice violet shadows under his eyes. I don't think I've ever seen a vampire look tired before.

"What's wrong with him?" I ask, heart thudding beneath my ribs. "Why was Davies being so cagey?"

His blue eyes search my face for a moment before he answers. "They are treating him for dehydration."

I screw my face up. "Dehydration? With what? Blood?"

"No, water. I'm not sure what happened yet. You see, I wasn't there when Anastasia was destroyed. Logan had made me promise to get you to safety." His eyes seem to glaze over, a trace of sadness softening the brilliant blue of his eyes. "He loves you very much," he murmurs.

I think of the hazy memory from earlier. "Did he kiss me in the garden? Was that real?"

"Yes, that was real."

I nod slowly. "Thanks for getting me out of there. I hope I didn't cut your lip open like I did Darren the porter."

He laughs, his whole face brightening. "I rather think Darren took the brunt."

"Will you take me upstairs to Logan? I have to see him."

His eyes flick to the grubby pile of clothing on the bedside cabinet. "How soon can you be ready?"

Luckily, when we leave the room, Dad and the rest are nowhere to be seen. I trail after Vincent, my stomach in knots as he leads me through a maze of corridors and stairs. Finally, we reach a small, blue-and-white waiting area outside a pair of double doors with a sign reading ICU.

"I'll wait here," Vincent says, hands thrust deep in his pockets.

I nod, stomach churning, scowling down at the dirty clothes I had to put back on—grass-stained jeans and muddy sneakers, my beloved leather biker jacket with a large gash across the back. I take a deep breath and tear my gaze from the calm blue eyes of Inspector Ferrer, raking hands through my messy hair before opening the double doors.

On the other side is a long hallway lined with closed doors. I trail up the corridor until it eventually widens out onto a spacious ward. There are rows of neatly made beds and curtained-off cubicles, the scent of disinfectant strong in the air. I'm wondering if I'm in the right place when a familiar Irish voice cuts through the air, reaching my ears like oxygen to a drowning man. My knees wobble, my heart skipping a beat.

"Are you stalking me, Miss Harris? Can't a fella even check into a hospital without being badgered by needy women?"

I turn to a bed tucked away in a corner, and there, sitting up and grinning, shirtless, with his messy, dark hair all over the place, wearing the same cocky expression as ever, is Logan.

I erupt into a flurry of pent-up tears as I hurl myself across the squeaky floor and onto the bed, his arms closing around me as I drop into the familiar folds of his body, burying my face in the stubbly warmth of his neck and sobbing so hard my head feels like it's about to crack open under the pressure.

He tightens his arms around me, fingers tangled in my hair as he rains feverish kisses onto the top of my head. "Silver," he whispers as the tears run off my face and drip onto the sheets. "I love you, Silver. Don't cry. It's more than okay now."

When the tears finally stop and my shoulders cease heaving, I lie cocooned by his warm, silky body for a few moments, reveling in the glory that he is unhurt, before propping myself up to look at him. "Your eyes look different." Though still the same beautiful shade of sea green, they are less intense, the flecks of gold around the iris softened to brown.

He smiles. "Do they?"

My eye falls onto the tube running from his arm to an intravenous drip hooked up beside the bed, and I sit up straight, legs tucked beneath me. "What's going on? What's that for?"

He grabs one of my hands and places it, palm down, over his heart.

I flinch, feeling a pulse beneath the skin—steady, like the beat of a moth's wings. "What was that? It feels like a heartbeat."

Pushing the hair away from my face, he smiles. "It *is* a heartbeat, Silver. I'm human."

I lean back. "That's not funny, Logan. I—"

But I don't get to finish my sentence. He pulls me across the bed toward him, pressing his lips to mine, and I melt into the embrace, forgetting what I was about to say as my mouth opens to the heat of his and we devour each other in a tight tangle of limbs. Pressed up against his muscled chest, I feel the odd sensation of our two heartbeats pulsing as one.

"What is that?" I gasp, breaking away and placing my palm back over his heart.

He covers my hand with his, pressing it into his satiny skin, rubbing a callused thumb in circles across my fingertips. "When Anastasia tried to kill me, it backfired. My necklace saved me."

I glance at the hollow of his throat, where his gold medallion has always rested. The skin is bare. "Your necklace?"

"My grandmother put some kind of spell on it all those years ago. She must have listened to Mary Beth's prediction and realized that one day the same creature who turned me into a vampire would also destroy me. I didn't even know magic like that was possible—but it worked. When Anastasia struck me with the machete, death bounced back at her. She exploded, and shortly after, my necklace crumbled to dust. All these years, I thought my family didn't care about me when all along I had been given the greatest gift of all."

I shut my eyes, trying to keep my breathing even. I daren't hope. Not yet. "I get how that might be possible, but human? If this is a joke, Logan, it isn't funny."

"You remember how Ronin said he'd never known an ancient to die?" he continues, toying with a strand of my hair.

"Yes." I swallow heavily, my voice little more than a squeak in my throat.

"Well, it seems that when an ancient dies, all those they turned revert back to their human selves."

"But you're Ronin's now. Like you said, an ancient's blood overpowers its vessel."

He shakes his head. "She switched me back before she killed me. She said she wanted me to die hers. If she hadn't, I would still be a vampire. It's the only good thing she ever did for me."

I gaze at him, at the rosy pallor clinging to his pale cheeks, the green eyes twinkling amid their forest of dark lashes, and a lump rises almost painfully in my throat. "Are you sure?" I mumble, tears streaking my cheeks, because how can it be true? That I get to keep him forever?

Reaching up, he brushes tears from my face, dimples flashing. "I'm quite sure. The doctors have confirmed it. They're treating me for cholera, just in case I still have it, as a precaution. I felt a little sick back in the garden, but that could have been the shock of it all. I feel fine now."

My tears stop midflow. "Cholera?" I say, gaping. "But that's bad, right?"

He laughs. "Silver. I'll be fine. Even if I did have it, it's easily treatable these days. I'm afraid you're stuck with me for the foreseeable future."

"This is too much," I say. "Am I dreaming? It feels like a dream."

"No, it's real," he says, rubbing the nape of my neck. "We can grow old together if you'll have me. We'll be two old duffers, frail and gray, hobbling along together—if you want it, that is?"

I look into the eyes of the man who I believed would never be able to share a lifetime with me, who I daren't even imagine as a long-term boyfriend, let alone a husband or a father, and smile. "Yes. I want it. I want it all with you."

"Even children?" he asks, green eyes teasing.

"Yes, even those." I beam. "Well, you know, one day."

We chuckle, and he hooks his arms around my back, drawing me into a deep, passionate kiss.

"At the very least," I murmur, running my hands over the smooth ridges of his stomach muscles, "I'm looking forward to making them."

"Oh, me too," he agrees, sliding a warm hand up under my jacket. "I think we should start practicing as soon as possible."

"Yes," I whisper, brushing my lips against his. "Shall I pull the curtain around?"

We snicker as he takes my hands in his. "Does this mean you'll hold my hand in the street now?" he asks, cocking a brow.

"Maybe," I tease. "But no pet names, agreed?"

"Marriage, kids, carnal debauchery, but no pet names—that seems completely reasonable." He cups my face in his hands. "I love you."

"I love you too," I whisper.

We kiss again, long and lingering, smiling into each other's mouths.

"I've just realized," I say when we eventually break apart. "No more biting."

"Oh, there will always be biting, Miss Harris," he says with a wicked grin. "And you needn't worry— you'll still be getting the ride of your life out of me."

He's right about that, of course.

I do get the ride of my life.

Always.

Epilogue

Three years later
Silver

"I'M A WHALE," I MOAN, STARING INTO THE FULL-length mirror at the bottom of the bed. "No, scrap that. I'm bigger than a whale. I'm the house the whale family lives in. I'm their country estate."

It's a week until my due date with our first child, and I'm growing increasingly tired of feeling like a walking, talking blob.

Logan appears in the reflection behind me, circling his arms around my waist and resting his hands on my huge pregnant belly. "You're a beautiful whale," he murmurs in my ear. "The sexiest one I've ever seen."

My jaw drops. "So you agree, then? That I'm fat?"

His eyes widen as he realizes he's dug himself into a hole. For the past few weeks, with my hormones wildly out of control, I've been trying unsuccessfully to pick a fight.

He's been quite clever up until now, stopping my rants midsentence with long, deep kisses, taking advantage of the other side effect of my pregnancy—the quadrupled sex drive. But there's no getting out of this one.

"I was playing along with the whole whale metaphor," he says. "Of course you're not fat!"

I shove his arms away. "I can't go to the party. I've

got nothing to wear." Tears replace anger. I slump down on the bed like a simpering brat.

In an ideal world, I wouldn't even have to get dressed today, let alone host a family party. But as it transpires, my husband turning two hundred years old is kind of a big deal. Drink will be taken, barbeque food consumed, and worst of all, every single member of my annoying family will be there.

Logan sinks down beside me, draping an arm around my shoulders. "I thought you were going to wear that new dress you bought."

"Oh, you mean the one with more material than a six-man tent?" I snap.

He attempts to stifle a snicker by pulling me close. "Well, I happen to think pregnancy suits you. There's nothing sexier than seeing the woman I love carrying my baby."

This isn't the first time he's pulled this line, and in spite of myself, I smile. Somehow, it always does the trick. "Sexy enough to indulge in a little fun?" I ask, squeezing his denim-clad knee.

He laughs. "Jeez, you never give up, do you?"

"Oh, come on. It's been almost a week," I whine.

"It's been three days," he exclaims. "You have back pain. I don't want to make you uncomfortable."

"Because I look like a heifer," I snipe, taking the argument full circle.

"You're beautiful. It's nothing to do with that."

I stand up and open the wardrobe. "Fine, I'll wear my tent to your two-hundredth-birthday barbecue. But I warn you, Logan: I will get you into bed today."

He grins, picking out the stretchy, pale-yellow dress and handing it to me. "Oh really?"

"Yes. Really. You'd better watch out, birthday boy."

———※———

I take my time getting ready, applying extra makeup and curling the ends of my hair in my bid to seduce Logan. After a while, the doorbell starts to ring and I hear voices and chatter drifting up the stairs.

It's a sunny July afternoon, a perfect day for a barbecue. When I finally waddle out onto the patio, our guests are already milling around and admiring our new garden. We only moved in a couple of months ago, but I love it here already. With its large rooms and quiet location, it's the perfect family home. I still pinch myself on a daily basis. Swollen feet and varicose veins aside, I feel like the luckiest girl on earth.

Dad spots me as I step out onto the patio and rushes over to help me down the steps. I'm well used to being treated like an invalid these days and accept his hand graciously. "Hello, love," he says, kissing me on the cheek. "Not long now."

Recently, that's all anyone ever seems to say to me.

I greet the rest of my family with a little wave. Sheila is parked at the buffet table, fussing over one of her famous strawberry pavlovas, and everyone else is standing or sitting, making small talk. Logan has Debra's son, Luca, my little nephew, held in the crook of his arm, chatting as he pokes at the barbecue with a pair of tongs. My heart melts as I watch them. I just know he's going to make an excellent father.

I glance around at the rest of the guests. A few of Logan's homeopathic doctor colleagues are gathered around the drink table, talking shop, and Jess is all over her latest boyfriend on the sun lounger. Then my eye snags on a tall, good-looking man chatting to my step-brother, Chris.

Surely my eyes are deceiving me.

I cross the garden as quickly as I can to the barbecue. "Logan," I hiss, jabbing a thumb over my shoulder at the handsome guy. "Is that who I think it is?"

Logan grins. "Vincent. I invited him."

"Vincent, as in *the vampire*?"

"The very one. Oh look, he's coming over to say hi. Be nice."

I cut him a look. "I'm always nice."

I turn around as Vincent strolls across the grass toward us. I haven't seen him since the night of the big showdown, when the ancient was destroyed and Logan got his mortality back, and I'd forgotten how dashing he is.

"I bet Vincent wouldn't have an issue with third-trimester sex," I mutter, watching his approach.

Logan shakes his head, chuckling as he flips a burger.

"Silver," Vincent says, leaning in to give me a kiss on the cheek. "You look—"

"Fat?" I cut in.

He laughs, blue eyes crinkling. "I was going to say radiant."

"Kind of the same thing at this stage in the game," I tease.

"Not at all. You look very happy."

"I am," I concur. "So, what's new with you? How are Burke and Davies? Still running the operation?"

He shakes his head. "No, that's all over. After what happened, we shut the division down. Back to good old-fashioned homicide these days."

"Oh," I say. "Well, at least you're keeping it simple."

He grins. "Exactly."

As the three of us stand chatting, I'm struck by just how much has changed the past few years. The idea that what we have now so easily might not have happened terrifies me. Sometimes, I dream I'm back in Chelsea in my old flat, and when I wake up, there's a few horrifying seconds where I think I'm still there, that Logan and my life since has been nothing more than a perfect dream. But then I feel the warmth of strong arms around me, the steady beat of Logan's heart against mine, and I know that everything is as it should be. That despite the odds stacked against us, life worked out.

I take Logan's hand, giving it a squeeze as he gazes down at me, his green eyes filled with love.

Vincent glances between us, an odd look of confusion and sadness lurking behind his brilliant-blue eyes. "I think I'm going to see if there's any more of that excellent pavlova on offer," he murmurs, leaving us alone.

Logan doesn't seem to notice him leave. He reaches up, tucking a stray tendril of hair behind my ear. "Are you hungry?" he asks, placing a palm on my swollen belly.

I raise a brow. "I wouldn't mind a sausage."

He laughs, wrapping an arm around my waist. "I've been thinking," he says, his tone husky. "It is my birthday, and you do look very sexy in that dress…"

My eyes widen in hope. "Meet you upstairs in ten minutes?"

He smiles and leans in, pressing his lips softly to mine. "I'll be there, Mrs. Byrne."

I resist the urge to give a fist pump of victory. Instead, I trail a finger across his stubbly jaw. "Happy two-hundredth birthday, Logan," I whisper, kissing him again before making a half-baked attempt at a sexy retreat back inside. In reality, I probably look like a melon on two toothpicks.

I've barely made it to the kitchen when I feel a sharp twinge in my pelvic area. I lean against the sink, shooting pains radiating up my side. Logan, who must have seen me stop, comes rushing through the french doors.

"Silver? Are you okay?"

Before I can answer, there is an odd sensation, like a release of pressure, and then a puddle of water splashes onto the floor at my feet.

Talk about killing the moment.

For the first time in the entire history of our relationship, I say, "I don't think we should have sex."

Logan stares between me and the wet patch on the floor in horror. "Is that…?"

I nod. "My water broke. We're about to become parents."

Here's a sneak peek at book two in Juliet Lyons's
Undead Dating Service series

ROMANCING *the* UNDEAD

Coming fall 2017

Mila

Turns out that when you date the undead, there
is a whole host of conversational faux pas you must
avoid. You can't talk about death, for example, or use the
phrase *what's at stake*, and don't get me started on the
garlic breadsticks debacle. This probably explains why
I'm on a date with a vampire and babbling about rats.

Not love rats—cheating ex-boyfriends whose names
occasionally fall into first date conversation. No, the real
kind that hang around sewers and restaurant kitchens.
Long tails, pointy noses, beady eyes. I'm prattling on
about *rats*.

"And I've heard," I say, wagging a finger like I'm
some kind of expert on rodent activity, "that they're
developing immunity to traditional poisons, which
means they'll probably take over the whole planet someday." I lift my oversize wineglass to my lips before realizing it's empty, a sticky crimson glaze clinging to the
rim along with most of my lipstick.

I shake the glass, frowning. It appears I've been gulping large mouthfuls of red wine instead of drawing breath. Being drunk would explain how this conversation got to *rise of the super rodent* in the first place. I must be way more nervous than I thought.

Setting the glass back on the table, I meet the vampire's eye. To his credit, if he's disappointed by my lack of conversational finesse, he doesn't show it. He's been eyeing me all evening with bemused fascination, as if I'm a rare and exquisite jewel he's discovered in a trash bag. There are worse ways to be looked at, let me tell you.

"So," I say, sucking in a deep breath, "what was London like in the good ole days?" I have to virtually glue my arm to my side to keep from making a Doris Day–esque fist swing.

His dark eyes flash with amusement as he signals at a passing waiter to bring more wine. "Actually, there *were* a lot of rats."

I chuckle, sitting up straight on the stool and swiping a stray lock of hair from my eyes. He made a joke. He's normal. Everything is going to be fine.

"But you're not British?" There is a definite accent to his soft voice—French or Italian maybe.

He ducks his head. "Originally, I'm from the north of Spain, the Basque region. I was born there in the eighteenth century."

My heart skips a beat, which is ridiculous because it's not like I don't know what he is. I sweep a glance around the busy London bar, at all the sleek city workers in their well-cut suits, the occasional trendy type in ripped jeans dotted amongst them. Even if they knew a vampire was sitting just feet away, no one would care. No one does anymore.

After declining his dinner offer, I figured drinks was the safest option. Of course, the *really* safe option would have been daytime coffee at Starbucks, but if you're going to date a vampire, why not go whole hog and do it under the cover of darkness?

"The world must have changed so much," I muse, meeting his steady gaze. I've been fascinated by his eyes ever since I arrived. They're dark—deep brown and ringed with violet—but they glow like burnished gold, like the early morning sun shines from their glittering depths. I watch as the pupils dilate like a cat's before looking away. Although he's handsome and looks exactly like his photo on V-Date, I'm not attracted to him in the slightest. Still, things are going a lot better than my last date—the one where my Australian boyfriend announced he was married with two kids. Compared to that, this is like an indoor Mardi Gras.

"The world has changed," he says, eyes fixed on my face. "But people are the same as ever. Greedy, materialistic, selfish." He pauses while the waiter sets down two more large glasses of wine. "Don't you ever feel disappointed with all life has to offer, Mila?"

I frown, worrying at the hem of my too-short skirt. My best friend, Laura, and I have indulged in this conversation since we were teenagers. It's a dark place to venture, and not one I care to visit when I'm supposed to be out having fun.

"Sometimes, but we're here for such a short while, it's pointless to dwell on it."

His brows shoot skyward.

"At least, some of us are only here for a short while," I mumble.

He leans back on the stool, toying with the cuffs of his crisp, white shirt. When I walked in earlier and saw him sitting here, my first thought was that he looked a little like a Spanish matador. With his olive complexion and ink-black hair, all that's missing is one of those gold brocade suits. To some women, he'd be the ultimate pinup, so I'm not quite sure why I'm so uninterested. Maybe I secretly prefer blonds.

I allow my gaze to linger on the explosion of dark hair peeking out from the front of his shirt. A pair of giggling young women sitting a couple of tables over keep whispering and checking him out, and I try hard to see him through their eyes. I'm not ready to sacrifice my sex drive as well as my faith in men just yet.

Taking a small sip of wine, I ask, "Do *you* ever feel disappointed by life? Or is living forever one big, crazy adventure?"

"Oh, there are plenty of disappointments. But I find ways to keep myself amused." The corner of his lip twitches. For the first time all evening, I feel a little like a mouse being batted between a cat's paws.

"Are you a regular on V-Date?" I ask.

He smiles, and although real vampires don't go around baring their fangs like they do in old movies, it's easy to imagine how they might look—sharp and pointed, protruding over his pink lips like spiky white pearls.

"I've only been on a couple of dates besides this one," he says. "What about you?"

"You're my first."

He arches a thick brow. "You're curious, I take it? About what we're like?"

I shrug. "I like trying new things, and I've recently come out of a relationship. So I thought, why not?"

He tips his head to one side, as if trying to figure me out. "Don't you think you might be better off on Match.com?"

"Maybe someday," I say, beginning to wish I was sitting with the giggling girls in the corner, or better still, at home with that party-size bag of Doritos I bought at Tesco's earlier. I stifle a withering sigh. If life were a movie, he'd be the soul mate I always longed for. He'd say "I've waited three hundred years to feel this way, Mila," not "Don't you think you might be better off on Match.com?"

If there's one thing I've learned in my twenty-six years on this earth it's that life is nothing like the movies. Life is waking up and finding out that the man you've spent the past two years with is a compulsive liar with an ex-lingerie model for a wife.

If I'm honest, the ex-lingerie model bit stings the most.

He leans across the table, forcing me to make eye contact. "I hope I haven't offended you, Mila."

"Nope."

Then something odd happens. When I try to look away, I can't. Not because I've suddenly realized how hot he is, or because there's some gigantic blemish on his face commanding my attention, but because I literally *can't*. I'm locked in time, the bar's chatter and music muted as I watch my own startled reflection in the depths of his bright, gold-brown eyes.

"You look flustered, Mila." His voice comes from far away, as if I'm hearing it from the other end of a tunnel. "Maybe we should step outside. Get some air."

The words should be enough to set alarm bells ringing, but to my horror I find myself nodding in agreement. It's like the real me is locked up, hidden and helpless, in a tiny part of my brain. As if I'm a puppet and he's the master.

I drop down from the stool, body and mind no longer connected, and reach to accept the smooth, olive hand he extends toward me. A gold signet ring on his middle finger catches the light from the spotlights in the ceiling. In the middle is an engraved coat of arms, a tiny dove at the tip of its crest.

"You'll feel much better once we're outside," he says in slow, honeyed tones. "I'll look after you. Don't worry."

I gaze up into his face as he leads me from the noisy bar and out onto the dark London street. *What are you doing?* I ask myself. *Stay in the bar*. But my robot feet follow his lead, my vocal cords frozen in my throat.

Outside, a misty drizzle is falling. Droplets cling to his black hair like cobwebs. The road is still busy: commuters dashing home, an endless string of buses and taxis moving slowly through the night. I shiver, goose bumps prickling my bare arms, remembering I left my jacket on the stool inside. I try to speak, but again, the words won't come. As if the connections between my thoughts and actions are severed.

He glances over his shoulder as he pulls me around a

corner onto a side street. The road here is empty, shadows hugging the edges of the pavement. There are no bars or shops, only back entrances used for deliveries. Several streetlamps cast a dull orange glow onto the shiny pavement. When we reach a gap between the buildings, his hold on my hand tightens into a viselike grip.

Just when I thought dating couldn't get any worse.

Inside, I'm petrified, but like the rest of my thoughts, the fear is contained, my heartbeat as steady as the clip of my heels on the concrete.

He stops abruptly in front of me, pulling me into a narrow brick alley lined on one side with steel Dumpsters. A whiff of kitchen waste and urine hits my nostrils.

"I'm sorry it had to be my profile you clicked on, Mila," he says.

My stomach twists with fear when I see his fangs are out, hanging over his lips in sharp, needlelike points, just like I imagined.

I watch mutely as he lets go of my hand, shoving me viciously against the wall.

"I have to say," he continues, his voice rougher than the bricks and mortar cutting into the skin on my back, "I found you to be a lot more entertaining than the other girls. It's a shame the world has to lose you."

My eyes widen as he brings his face closer, his strange eyes burning like wildfire. The scent of his strong cologne—a dark, spicy musk—crawls into my brain, overpowering my senses. But despite this hold he has over me, this *invasion*, a strangled scream rips from my throat.

"I'll make it quick," he whispers, undeterred, fangs

scraping my cheek, "and I'll wait until after you're dead to taste you."

His hands move to my head, gripping me around the temples as I close my eyes, waiting for the death blow. But as his fingers tighten around my skull, a crashing noise shatters the silence, sounding like a heavy object falling onto the steel bins. Somewhere out on the street, a siren begins to wail.

His hands fall away, and all at once, the drugged sensation leaves me. My body is mine again. The coppery tang of fear floods my mouth as my knees buckle. Before I hit the filthy, litter-strewn ground, a strong pair of arms wrap around my middle, holding me up.

I scream, thinking for a second he's returned. But when I look up into the face of my assailant, I see a pair of storm-washed blue eyes, coiffed blond hair, and a chiseled profile that could make a grown woman weep.

Perhaps I've died and gone to heaven.

"Please don't be alarmed, Miss Hart. I'm Inspector Ferrer from the Metropolitan Police. You're quite safe now."

"Wh-where is he?" I stutter, darting frantic glances around the alley. "Where did he go?"

The man grimaces. "He fled as soon as I showed up."

I stare up into his face, suddenly aware that my dress has somehow rucked up around my ass in all the drama. I must look like a hooker, and yet I feel like Marianne Dashwood in *Sense and Sensibility* when Willoughby finds her slumped on a hillside with a twisted ankle. Something about this man exudes the same gentlemanly concern.

"I couldn't scream," I say, feeling the need to explain. "I tried to, but I couldn't."

His eyes soften, and for a wild moment, I think he's going to stroke my hair. "He put a glamour on you. Vampires can—we can do that."

Oh, great. He's a vampire too. My gut reaction is to push him away, but beneath the handful of cotton shirt I grabbed on my way down, I feel the hard outline of a fine set of abs—and as every single girl worth her salt knows, good abs do not just fall from the sky. Maybe there's hope for my sex drive yet.

I'm still staring into his eyes when the alley fills with flashing lights. The sirens reach a fever pitch, forcing me to release his shirt and cover my ears.

The noise cuts out and two police officers resembling a pair of middle-aged Columbo impersonators in long beige overcoats burst into the alley. One is lanky with a thinning mop of mousy hair, and the other is short and balding, not dissimilar to the used car salesman who sold me my dilapidated VW Golf a few weeks back.

"Oh, thank God," the shorter man says as soon as he claps eyes on me. "She's alive."

His colleague barges past, a shiny police badge held aloft. "I'm Superintendent Linton Burke. Are you injured?"

I shake my head, putting the weight back into my wobbly legs. "I don't think so, psychological damage notwithstanding."

To my bitter disappointment, Inspector Abs releases me. "I think we should take you to the hospital anyway, just to be on the safe side."

"How did you all know where to find me? Did some-one at the bar call the cops?" I watch as they all stare at one another, their mouths set in the same grim line.

Burke clears his throat. "Miss Hart, I think it might be wise if we discuss this further in a more private setting."

Then it hits me. They aren't regular policemen—they're detectives.

I look between the three of them. "He said there were other girls…"

Inspector Abs nods. "There are. I mean, there were."

A violent shiver rips through me, and Inspector Ferrer removes his suit jacket, draping it around my shoulders. If it wasn't for a delicious waft of eau de hot man envel-oping me, I mightn't have noticed it at all. I pull the sur-prisingly warm blazer tight across my chest to cover my cleavage, tugging my skirt down self-consciously. "Are you saying my first vampire date was a *serial killer*?"

Their faces tell me everything I need to know.

I sway, the ground moving beneath me, as if the damp concrete has turned to water. A sound like waves rushing up a beach roars in my ears before everything turns black.

When I next open my eyes, I'm back in the hottie's arms.

"You're making a habit of this," I mutter.

"It appears so," he says quietly. "Put your weight on me. We need to get you to the car."

"You know," I say, leaning against his broad shoulder as we follow the two beige trench coats out of the alley, "I'm going to ask V-Date for a full refund after tonight."

Hearing the tiniest snort of laughter, I crane my neck

to see his face. "You can write me a note as evidence," I continue. "*Please give refund; date tried to kill her.* I think I'll treat myself to a spa day with the money."

"I can call them myself, if you'd prefer," he says dryly.

"That would be fabulous. Thank you."

The two Columbos open the car doors, and I duck into the vehicle. A marked police car is in front of us, and several regular-looking cops stand nearby. "They'll stick around," the short detective says from the front seat. "Take evidence from the crime scene."

"But I'm alive...aren't I?"

Inspector Vampire, who has climbed into the back-seat next to me, says, "Yes, but it's still a crime scene. Kidnapping and assault are very serious."

My thoughts wander back to the way I left the bar, completely under my date's control. "Wait!" I erupt. "I left my new jacket in the pub." But Superintendent Burke is already accelerating away from the curb.

"It'll still be there in the morning, Miss Hart," he says disinterestedly.

"It's Karen Millen," I say. "And I doubt it."

"I can call them," Inspector Ferrer says. "What was the name of the bar again?"

"The World's End," I say grimly, staring into his chiseled face. "Please, no smart comments."

His eyes crinkle around the edges as he smiles, and I stare openmouthed. He's so gorgeous, it burns my eyes to look at him—like watching a solar eclipse without protective glasses. He says the name of the pub into his phone and hits a button. After someone answers, he says, "There's a Karen Millen jacket left on a barstool."

"Table six," I interject.

"Table six. Can you please hold it behind the bar? Someone will collect it tomorrow. Thank you." He hangs up and puts the phone away. "Crisis averted."

Having surpassed the level of staring that is considered socially acceptable, I drag my gaze away. "Thank you."

"You're welcome."

When I dart a look back, he's still watching me, his jaw clenched. I tug my skirt down some more and he looks away. Though it's difficult to see in the low light of the vehicle, I swear a hot flush creeps up his neck.

Can vampires blush? I wonder, admiring his angular profile in the yellow light of the passing traffic. In any case, I've learned at least one thing from tonight's events.

I definitely, without a doubt, prefer blonds.

Chapter 2

Vincent

"IT STILL DOESN'T MAKE SENSE," SERGEANT LEE Davies says through a mouthful of half-chewed pizza. "Why use his real photo?"

It's shortly after midnight, and the three of us are hunched around a table in a conference room at Scotland Yard amid an explosion of crushed coffee cups and half-empty pizza boxes. Mila Hart was escorted home an hour ago by a squad car—shaken and tired, but still making quips about the sorry state of London's dating scene.

I swallow a smile, remembering her reaction after we explained the killer had been using V-Date to target victims, her pretty hazel eyes cast to the heavens as she said, "What a world, when you can't even trust the dead ones."

The room grows silent, two sets of eyes drilling into me.

"Don't you think it's a possibility, Vincent?" Linton Burke asks. From his weary tone, I can tell this isn't the first time he's asked the question.

Truth is, I was too busy thinking about Miss Hart's shapely legs. *Again*. "Sorry?"

Linton emits a heavy sigh. "That the killer put his own picture on the fake profile this time, thinking he'd throw us off the scent. After all, his other pictures were all taken from genuine profiles on the site. Maybe he hoped the confusion would buy him some time."

I loosen my tie, narrowing my eyes in thought. "It's a little farfetched, but it's a possibility. I'll get on Catherine Adair first thing in the morning and see if she's found anything of interest on her client database."

"Excellent," Burke says, his tired eyes darting to the clock above the door. Unlike me, he has a wife waiting for him at home—a wife who, judging by the number of times his phone beeped during Mila Hart's extensive witness statement, is not at all happy about being left home alone.

"The other thing I don't get," Davies says, picking at an empty polystyrene cup with a fingernail, "is why the other two women didn't react faster to a complete stranger meeting them instead of the vampire in the pictures."

"We've been over this," Burke snaps. "He would have glamoured them straightaway."

"But why didn't he glamour Mila Hart until halfway through the evening? Why take the risk? Sitting there in the middle of a busy bar, seen by dozens of people. If Miss Hart died, we'd have been in that bar the next day with his photo. There'd be plenty of witnesses to testify the man they saw her leave with was the same as the one in the picture. Which blows your throwing-us-off-the-scent theory out of the water." Lee Davies smooths a hand over his shiny bald head and leans back in the chair, looking pleased with himself. Unlike Burke, he and his wife are going through a sticky patch—he relishes late nights.

"Unless he wants to be caught," I offer, though I'm not at all surprised he didn't glamour Mila Hart until halfway through the evening. There is no denying her obvious charms. I zone out, remembering slender thighs, an ample swell of cleavage, and her mesmerizing hazel eyes—large and intelligent. In the car and all through her interview, I was horrified by my inability to stop *staring*. I just hope she didn't notice. There's nothing like being kidnapped and assaulted and then having a police officer leer at you. I cringe shamefully as my trousers tighten. The cold setting on the shower will get a thorough workout tonight.

Burke fans out the V-Date photos. "You're sure you've never met him, Vincent?"

I lean across the table, peering intently at the dark-haired man in the picture before shaking my head. "I don't think so. Though sometimes it's hard to recognize people with modern haircuts and clothing. There's always a chance Cat might know him, but even if she doesn't, someone will."

"Well, I say we break here, lads," Burke says, shuffling the pictures and copies of Mila Hart's statement back together and dropping them into a manila envelope. "Let's reconvene in the morning. What time did we ask Miss Hart to drop by tomorrow?"

"Three o'clock," I say without hesitation.

Linton raises an eyebrow, as if he knows full well why I've memorized the time. "Righto." He pushes up from his seat. "Night, lads."

As soon as the door clicks shut behind him, Davies grins, spinning around on his swivel chair so we're face-to-face. Having worked in each other's pockets these past years, I know what he's going to say before the words pass his lips.

"Blimey, that Mila Hart is a bit of all right, isn't she?"

I close my eyes briefly, and when I open them, Lee is wagging a finger in my face. "Don't pretend you didn't notice either. I clocked you checking out her rack at every given opportunity."

"Lee," I say, frowning, "don't say 'rack.' She's our witness. Have some respect."

Lee puts on a posh accent. "Oh, terribly sorry, Holy Father. I mean to say she was an absolute delight."

I shake my head, trying not to smile as I adjust the knot in my tie. Lately, I wonder if Lee's having some sort of midlife crisis. He seems to be spending an awful lot of time making inappropriate comments about the opposite sex.

"Seriously though, mate, isn't it time you had a woman in your life?"

I snort incredulously, reaching behind to pull my suit jacket from the back of the chair. At the last second, I remember Miss Hart took it home with her. The vision of her curvy frame swamped by my jacket, blond hair spilling over her shoulders like a golden waterfall, is enough to induce another dangerous wave of lust. I need that shower. Fast.

"Lee," I say, "I'm a professional. End of."

He begins swiveling his hips on the chair, twisting like he's performing a sit-down samba. "Christ, if I were in your shoes, I certainly wouldn't be going back to a cold, empty flat every night."

"I have a feeling you're going to tell me what you'd be doing," I say dryly.

"I'd be down the West End," he continues, ignoring me and staring wistfully off into space. "Wining and dining a different bird every night. I mean, what's the point in owning a Porsche and looking like you do if you don't make the most of it?"

"All that is in the past," I mutter. "Besides, none of that means anything. Not really."

"Pffft! Who cares what it means? Enjoy it. I mean, I get you have integrity by the bucketload, Vince, and I admire you for it. I do. But these days, women are usually only after one thing themselves. With vampires being *out* and all, you wouldn't even have to lie about it. Look at Mila Hart—birds like her are dying to hook up with the likes of you. Unless…" A devious glint appears in his eyes.

"Please don't ask me if I'm gay again, Lee, and stop referring to Mila Hart as a bird."

Lee snickers. "If you are gay, Vince, you should be out and proud. I'm sure Barry down in Narcotics would happily show you all the bars."

"Lee, stop." I push myself up from the table, signaling my intention to leave. "Go home to your wife. Treat her well."

He sighs, the life going out of him faster than helium from a burst balloon. "I'm pretty sure she's shagging the UPS guy."

That stops me in my tracks, one hand on the door handle. "*The UPS guy?*"

Lee sinks farther into his chair, his once-jubilant

smile reduced to a grim line. "First, she lost all that weight at Slimming World; now, she's ordering all these new clothes."

I release my grip on the door. The cold shower would have to wait. Lee may behave like a randy schoolboy when Burke isn't around to keep him in check, but he's still a good friend. "Isn't that what people do when they lose weight? Because their old clothes won't fit them?"

Lee picks at the edge of the table, his top lip quivering. "That's what I thought at first, but when I leave the house every morning, she's dolled up to the nines, even though she claims she's just popping around Rosemary's for coffee. Then when I get back, there's always another parcel. Even if I wasn't a detective, I think I'd have figured it out by now."

"So why not confront her?"

"If I do, our marriage is over. We've been together since we were fifteen. UPS guy or no UPS guy, I can't imagine life without her."

Modern marriage is obviously a lot more complicated than I thought. I always assumed things were simple these days, what with everyone being so financially independent and all. "So, is this why you don't want to go home lately?"

Lee breaks my gaze. "You noticed."

I nod, perching on the edge of the meeting table. "If you get divorced, wouldn't you be happier? 'Wining and dining a different woman every night' like you said you'd like to?"

He sputters in disbelief. "I meant I'd do that if I were *you*. Who's going to want this"—he gestures to the portly stomach, rounded beneath his tightly stretched shirt—"a middle-aged, bald bloke with a pot belly? Let's face it—I'm no Hugh Jackman. Never was either."

I suppress a smile. "Looks aren't everything, Lee."

"Easy for you to say, *Brad Pitt*."

"It's true," I say, staring out the window at the milky-blue London skyline. "If they were, matters of the heart would be simple. You can't fall in love with someone just because they're beautiful. It goes deeper than that. A lot deeper."

"Is this why you never bring a plus one to the Christmas ball?" Lee asks, putting his feet up on the table and crossing his legs. "You're still waiting for Miss Right?"

"That ship sailed long ago."

"Oh, come off it. I know they say you only get one true love, but surely if you're three hundred years old that means you get at least three, right?"

I continue to stare into the night, not speaking. It's not that I don't want anything to do with women. *Au contraire*. Though I'm not about to divulge my sexual history with the likes of Davies, I've had more than my fair share of meaningless, sexed-up encounters over the years. I've even had girlfriends—women, both vampire and human, who I've seen on a regular basis. But *love*, the real kind, takes a commitment I'm not prepared to give. I gave my heart once, hundreds of years ago, and I'm not willing to do it again. Falling in love is like leaping naked headfirst from a tall building. Life is far simpler and safer without it.

Finally, I meet Lee's probing gaze. "I'm just not interested in having that complication in my life again."

Lee nods slowly. "If I do get divorced, Vince, you and I should hit the clubs together. You can draw them in with your looks, and I'll dazzle them with my sparkling wit."

I laugh, patting my trouser pocket to make sure I have my car keys. "It's a deal. Come on, I'll give you a lift home."

After dropping Lee to the leafy suburbs of Muswell Hill, I drive back toward Chelsea, to the scene of Mila Hart's attempted murder. The streets have almost emptied out, but the odd red double-decker bus hurtles along, sending litter and dust skittering in its wake. A few pedestrians, mostly workers on their way to or from a night shift, bustle past, knapsacks flung over their shoulders, desperate to be out of the chilly night air.

I park on the street where we found Mila Hart, opposite the damp alleyway that's now cordoned off with black-and-yellow crime tape. It was a heart-stopping moment for the three of us when we found the matching profile on the V-Date website—the exact same details given by the previous two killers. Height, interests, and personal information—*verbatim*. Then enduring what felt like a hundred-year wait while Cat pulled out all the messages from her system. I can still hear her gasp of horror from the other end of the phone line when she discovered that Jeremiah Lopez, as he called himself, was meeting his date in Chelsea at that very moment.

I flew straight to the pub, leaving Scotland Yard in such haste that, stupidly, I didn't stop to pick up a copy of his picture. When I eventually tracked them down to the street around the corner, I was so relieved to see her alive, I let him slip away. If I hadn't behaved like such a pathetic Romeo by catching her midfall, I might have caught up to him. I release a slow hiss of frustration between my teeth. There's something about this case that irks me, something that goes beyond the fact that innocent women are being killed.

Innocent and *sexy*, a voice in my head reminds me.

Turning away from the silent alley, I head onto the main road to the bar where Mila met the killer. The trend these days seems to be for upmarket bars to masquerade as olde worlde pubs. This one is no different. The exterior is painted a pristine shade of royal blue, the windows buffed to a mirror shine. There are several large, carefully tended hanging baskets on the walls, overflowing with pansies, but the real giveaway we're not in Victorian England is the scent. Bars smell like cleaning fluids these days, not like tobacco and stale beer and body odors. Thank goodness.

I check my Rolex and see it's a little after one in the morning. Though the windows are dark, there are lights on behind the bar. A young man loads pint glasses onto a shelf above the optics. I push open the wooden door and step into the warm glow of the room. Inside, it's furnished with expensive distressed tables and chairs. I can tell it's one of those places fond of serving food on wooden boards and shiny slate tiles. Plates and bowls seem to be a thing of the past in London's eateries of late. The other day at lunch, Lee Davies's portion of french fries arrived in a metal flowerpot.

The lad looks over his shoulder. "Closed, mate."

"I'm not here to drink," I say, wondering if I should

take out my badge. Though I loathe being one of those types to play the police officer card, I have to admit it comes in handy at times. A bit like having a magic wand—at least where speeding tickets are concerned.

"I called earlier about a jacket that was left behind. A Karen Millen one."

The pimply youth looks me over, wiping hands on the front of his black apron. "Oh yeah, it's in the back." He grins. "No offense, but I'm not sure it's your size."

Smart-ass. "It's my girlfriend's." Using the word *girlfriend* about Mila Hart leaves me more than just a little hot under the collar. I loosen my tie while he chuckles and ducks through a door behind the bar, emerging a few seconds later with a black blazer.

"Thank you," I say, taking the soft bundle from him.

"No worries."

"I don't suppose you saw her earlier, did you? Blond hair, yea high?" I wave a downward palm level with my chest. "She was with a dark-haired gentleman?"

He shakes his head. "Nah, sorry. We were packed tonight."

I flash a smile. "Never mind. Thank you anyway."

"My ex cheated on me too," he pipes up as I turn away. "Bitches. All of them."

Deciding not to dignify that sweeping statement with a response, I beat a path to the door, stepping back out onto King's Road.

It's only when I'm back in the Porsche that a mortifying thought strikes me—tomorrow I'll have to hand it back to her in person, probably in front of my work colleagues. If she possesses an iota of common sense, she'll know collecting lost property isn't in my job description. She'll *know* I'm attracted to her. Big time.

Muttering a curse, I lift the jacket up, burying my face into the soft material. It smells like perfume and fruit shampoo, and with my heightened senses, I pick up a deeper scent. Floral, sweet, and perfectly intoxicating. *Her*.

A tingle zips through me, and I impulsively fling the coat onto the backseat of the car. I must have fallen victim to some bizarre phenomenon where a man projects displaced feelings onto the woman he saves. I sigh, turning the key in the ignition. Maybe tomorrow I'll leave her jacket with the others, make an excuse not be present at her interview. She'll think I've just been kind, picking up the lost coat for her. Perhaps Lee can say it was him. I'll never have to see her again.

With a heavy heart, I push the car into gear and make a neat U-turn on the deserted street, heading home to an empty apartment.

Chapter 3

Mila

"HE WAS A *SERIAL KILLER*?" LAURA ASKS IN DISBELIEF, crashing her coffee mug onto the table and sloshing dark-brown liquid everywhere. "Are you kidding me?"

It's the day after my would-be murder, and I'm sitting in my best friend's kitchen in Richmond. Needless to say, I didn't get an awful lot of shut-eye last night. Being targeted by London's most wanted can really mess with a sleeping pattern.

I shake my head. "I wish I were."

"And he tried to murder you in an alley?"

"Yep."

After I've told her the full story, she sits back in her seat, staring at me across the table with a curious mixture of awe and horror. "Only you, Mila," she says finally. "Only you."

"I know," I say, pulling a chocolate cookie from the tin. "If they're not cheating, they're trying to kill me. It's gone beyond a joke."

"So, what happens now?" Laura asks, eyes wide. "He won't come after you, will he? He doesn't know where you live?"

I shake my head, reaching across the table to pat her hand. "Don't worry. He didn't even have my telephone number. We arranged it all through V-Date. There's no way he can trace me."

Laura nods, some of the tension leaking out of her shoulders. "And the guy who rescued you was a vampire too?"

"Yeah." I pause, remembering his strong arms around my waist. "He was totally hot."

Laura's dour face brightens. "Really? What was his name? Did you see a wedding ring?"

This is one of the things I love most about Laura. She sits through a dramatic account of my near-death experience on a date and still believes there's a chance I might get a boyfriend out of it.

"Inspector Ferrer," I say, biting off a chunk of cookie. "I can't say I was really in the frame of mind to be looking out for a wedding ring though. He just sort of fell from the sky."

"When you say hot, how hot?"

"Super hot. You know that guy on the billboard as you drive along the M40? The one frolicking in the surf? That hot."

Laura's jaw drops. "Jesus."

We don't speak for a few seconds, silent in our worship of the billboard hottie.

"He was nice too. He loaned me his jacket. Too bad I'll never see him again."

Laura frowns. "Why won't you see him again? Don't they want to question you some more?"

I glance down at my wristwatch, vaguely aware I was supposed to be there half an hour ago. Sometime during my sleepless night, I decided wild horses wouldn't be enough to drag me to Scotland Yard today.

"I've already told them everything," I say, taking

a sip of tea. "I just want to put the whole sorry mess behind me."

"But what if they catch him?" Laura says, her blue eyes wide. "You would have to do one of those lineup things like they have on *CSI*. Then afterward, Inspector Hot Guy would ask you for coffee. He'd say something like"—she adopts a deeper voice—"'In a way, I should thank that psycho for bringing you into my life.'"

Despite my weariness, I chuckle. "Didn't we make a pact to quit pretending life is like the movies?"

"Yeah, we did," she says, a pink glow appearing in her cheeks. "Until I met Tom."

I narrow my eyes, pretending to scowl. "Yeah, thanks again for leaving me alone on Bitter Island."

Up until a few years ago, Laura had been in the exact same situation as me—building an impressive collection of douche bag ex-boyfriends and wondering if there was such a thing as happy ever after. Then the stars aligned. She met her now-husband, Tom, and experienced one of those miraculous moments when both timing and attraction come together in perfect harmony, the holy grail of dating.

Of course, I wasn't the least bit jealous.

Well, okay, maybe a tiny bit.

"I reckon something good will happen for you soon, Mila. Your days on Bitter Island are numbered," she says, gazing dreamily out the window at her gardenias. She opens her mouth to add something but then thinks better of it, pursing her lips shut instead.

I wave an accusing finger in her face. "Were you about to say what I think you were about to say?"

She shakes her head vigorously before breaking into a devious smile. "It'll happen when you least expect it."

I snatch up a tea towel dangling from the back of a chair and fling it at her. If there's one thing that drives me mental, it's hearing that phrase.

"But actually," Laura says, picking up the cloth and refolding it, "maybe it's true this time. I bet you weren't expecting to meet the gorgeous inspector in that alleyway."

"No, Laura. At that point, I was more focused on the hands about to break my neck than meeting the love of my life."

"Exactly. So, this could be it."

"With a vampire?" I ask incredulously. "Even if he swept in that door right now with a diamond engagement ring, it's completely pointless. There's no future in dating a man forever trapped in youth. I mean, it's tough enough trying to keep a regular man faithful for a lifetime. Think what life would be like with some model sort who remains eternally young. Look at Demi Moore."

She frowns. "So why were you using that site in the first place if you didn't want to seriously meet someone?"

I shrug, running a finger around the edge of my mug. "Because it interested me, that's all. I wanted to meet one. After Josh and that whole 'Oh, by the way, I'm still married to someone and we have two kids together' fiasco, I felt like dipping a toe in foreign waters. See what the other species are like. Now my curiosity is sated. The end."

Laura throws me a smug grin and raises a dark brow. "We'll see about that."

Acknowledgments

First, I would like to thank my son, James, who keeps me going with his wise words and encouragement and who is the driving force behind everything I do. Also, thank you to my good friends Maeve, Maria, Mim, Liz, Lucinda, Ellen, and Claire B. for the friendship and laughter we've shared over the years. It's thanks to our adventures—holidays, university, flat shares, living abroad, and general debauchery—that I have an endless supply of material for my stories.

Thank you to my wonderful editor, Cat Clyne, who plucked me from Wattpad in late 2015 and made all my dreams come true. And finally, to my Wattpad friends Joanne Weaver, Sally Mason, Leila Adams, RK Close, May Freighter, and CJ Laurence, who are always on hand to lift my spirits at the end of a hard day's writing and whose advice and support means so much.

About the Author

Juliet Lyons is a paranormal romance author from the UK. She holds a degree in Spanish and Latin American studies and works part-time in a local primary school, where she spends far too much time discussing Harry Potter. Since joining global storytelling site Wattpad in 2014, her work has received millions of hits online and gained a legion of fans from all over the world. When she is not writing or working, Juliet enjoys reading and spending time with her family. Visit her online at www .julietlyons.co.uk.

ROMANCING THE UNDEAD

Brooding London vampires meet
Bridget Jones-esque snark in Juliet Lyons's
second Undead Dating Service novel

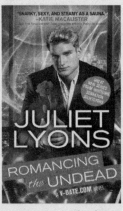

Mila Hart's first experience with the vampire dating site V-Date.com is a complete disaster—her date is wanted for murder! But things turn around when she's rescued by dashing vampire cop Vincent Ferrer. Dangerous and devastatingly attractive, he's just the undead hottie Mila was hoping for.

Haunted by his past, Vincent can't risk falling in love again—even if Mila charms him more than anyone he's ever met. But when the killer from Mila's date seeks her out, Vincent is the only one who can protect her. Protecting his heart is a different story…

"Snarky, sexy, and steamy as a sauna."

—Katie MacAlister, *New York Times* and *USA Today* bestselling author for *Dating the Undead*

For more Juliet Lyons, visit:
www.sourcebooks.com